Don't Miss the
Sweeping

THE MORTAL INSTRUMENTS

MORE THAN 3 YEARS ON THE
NEW YORK TIMES BESTSELLER LIST

THE INFERNAL DEVICES

#1 *NEW YORK TIMES* BESTSELLING SERIES

THE DARK ARTIFICES

#1 *NEW YORK TIMES* AND *USA TODAY* BESTSELLERS

A SHADOWHUNTERS NOVEL

THE INFERNAL DEVICES

Clockwork
PRINCESS

Also by Cassandra Clare

THE MORTAL INSTRUMENTS

City of Bones

City of Ashes

City of Glass

City of Fallen Angels

City of Lost Souls

City of Heavenly Fire

THE INFERNAL DEVICES

Clockwork Angel

Clockwork Prince

Clockwork Princess

THE DARK ARTIFICES

Lady Midnight

The Shadowhunter's Codex

With Joshua Lewis

The Bane Chronicles

With Sarah Rees Brennan
and Maureen Johnson

THE INFERNAL DEVICES

Clockwork PRINCESS

Book Three

CASSANDRA CLARE

Margaret K. McElderry Books
NEW YORK LONDON TORONTO SYDNEY NEW DELHI

For the Lewis family:
Melanie, Jonathan, and Helen

1 Tessa and Jem's meeting place

2 The *yin fen* house

3 The Institute

4 Mortmain's warehouses

13 The Dark Sisters' House

11 Entrance to the Council chambers

12 Cross Bones Graveyard

Cross Bones Graveyard

6

CHISWICK

13 To the Dark Sisters' House

5 The Argent Rooms

6 Lightwood House **7** Woolsey's house **8** Hatchards bookshop **9** The Devil Tavern

10 Entrance to the Faerie Courts

Foreword

For many years during the time I've been a writer, people have asked me if I get inspiration for my books from my dreams.

My response has always been that I wish that I did. It seems like such a fun way to get story ideas—dream something and wake up compelled to put the story to paper. Unfortunately, the only real dreams I ever have about my characters and stories are nonsensical: all my characters are in front of me in line at the grocery store and have too many items in their carts.

Which makes the genesis of the idea I had for the Infernal Devices pretty unusual. It wasn't a dream, but it was a daydream.

I was in London, on a trip to promote *City of Bones*, the first book of the Shadowhunters chronicles. I was crossing Blackfriars Bridge, which is a lovely old bridge in the City of London over the river Thames. It was a gray cloudy day, and mist was drifting along the bridge. I leaned against the parapet and looked down at the water.

I thought about how the bridge had stood for so many years, and of all that it must have witnessed. Slowly the image of a girl with brown hair and a boy dressed in Victorian clothing came into my mind, and as I pictured them there on the bridge, I imagined a strange army of clockwork monsters hidden in the shadows, waiting to pounce.

I went home feeling unsettled and inspired. Slowly the story of Tessa, Jem, and Will began to take shape in my mind—I chose the location of the London Institute for its proximity to Blackfriars Bridge, for I always knew the bridge would be central to the tale.

After much wandering around London (using a map dated 1879, which led to a lot of getting lost) I decided the Institute would be Saint Bride's Church off Fleet Street, a gorgeous church gutted by firebombs during the Blitz.

I chose 1878 because it was a time of transition from an old England to a new England: there was regular train service, there was gas light, there were sewers, and yet the time period retained the graciousness and beauty of the past. It seemed like a wonderful era in which to set a story about three young people learning who they are and all they are capable of, especially when it came to the story of a young girl learning she is destined for more than an arranged marriage—that she is destined for an extraordinary love.

I believe that historical fiction is the closest thing we have to time travel. I wanted to feel as much as I could that I was living and breathing the time period of the Infernal Devices, so I set myself a project: for six months I read nothing but books set in the mid and late Victorian era.

It was research by immersion. Soon I started to imagine that I was seeing horse-drawn carriages instead of cars, that I could smell the Thames River and hear the Bow Bells. I wanted my readers to feel that the past was accessible, so the characters of a bygone time's pain and joy would seem real and true. It was a time obsessed with death, in which diseases which are now cured easily were rife, and sicknesses we now understand seemed as mysterious as the corrupting touch of a demon. The real world as it was then slotted neatly into my already-imagined world of the Shadowhunters, demon-hunters, and magic users and gave it new depth and richness: creating a hero who could see and talk to imploring ghosts and another who was condemned to die young of a fatal demonic illness, no matter how desperate the efforts to save him, just as in reality victims of consumption sickened and died without penicillin. The Brontë family, who produced *Wuthering Heights* and *Jane Eyre*, were decimated by consumption, and to mark my respect for and debt to their work I named the head of the London Institute—Charlotte Branwell—after two of the Brontë siblings. It was a difficult time for a woman to have authority in the Shadowhunter world and the mundane world, but Charlotte manages it. Tessa, Charlotte, Sophie, and Jessamine are all heroines who I adore, coping with the prejudice of a time more difficult for women than our own in a way that I hoped would also resonate with the oppression women still face today.

I immersed myself in books to write this series, and in this series two of the characters also find inspiration and comfort in books. Tessa and Will bond over Charles Dickens's *A Tale of Two Cities*, in which one of the heroes considers himself a soul doomed to wickedness. Will thinks he too is doomed to be corrupt and unloved; over the course of the books he learns how wrong he was. His best friend, James Carstairs, who is dying, believes that he is fated to die without love, like the poet Keats, whom his character is partially based on. Both Will and Jem love each other—they are blood brothers—but despite that love, they have no hope. In Tessa they both find their salvation, because Tessa believes in hope—not just because she is stalwart and a heroine, but also because she has discovered hope in books.

Tessa is a bookworm: she doesn't only love classics by the Brontës and Dickens, but the many novels of her time that I read during my months-long reading project. She reads voraciously, in the same way I did, books considered both high- and lowbrow, and she gains enjoyment from both kinds. She learns she has the power to shapeshift, reflecting our real-life ability to slip inside the skin of fictional characters when we read.

I wanted to write a heroine who was invested in books as much as I was and as I knew my readers were: a girl who learned that adventure was possible from books, that romance was potentially as wonderful as it was painful, that courage and kindness would carry her through, and that she could be marvelously transformed. I wanted every girl reading the Infernal Devices to feel that she could be the heroine of a novel—maybe even this one.

I held it truth, with him who sings
To one clear harp in divers tones,
That men may rise on stepping-stones
Of their dead selves to higher things.
—Alfred, Lord Tennyson, "In Memoriam A.H.H."

PROLOGUE

York, 1847.

"I'm afraid," said the little girl sitting on the bed. "Grandfather, can you stay with me?"

Aloysius Starkweather made an impatient noise in the back of his throat as he drew a chair closer to the bedside and seated himself. The impatient noise was only part in earnest. It pleased him that his granddaughter was so trusting of him, that often he was the only one who could calm her. His gruff demeanor had never bothered her, despite her delicate nature.

"There's nothing to be afraid of, Adele," he said. "You'll see."

She looked at him with large eyes. Normally the ceremony of first runing would have been held in one of the grander spaces of the York Institute, but because of Adele's fragile nerves and health, it had been agreed that it could occur in the safety of her bedroom. She was sitting at the edge of her bed, her back very straight. Her ceremonial dress was red, with a red ribbon holding back her fine, fair hair. Her eyes were huge in her thin face, her arms narrow. Everything about her was as fragile as a china cup.

"The Silent Brothers," she said. "What will they do to me?"

"Give me your arm," he said, and she held out her right arm trustingly. He turned it over, seeing the pale blue tracery of veins below the skin. "They will use their steles—you know what a stele is—to draw a Mark upon you. Usually they start with the Voyance rune, which you will know from your studies, but in your case they will begin with Strength."

"Because I am not very strong."

"To build your constitution."

"Like beef broth." Adele wrinkled her nose.

He laughed. "Hopefully not so unpleasant. You will feel a little sting, so you must be brave and not cry out, because Shadowhunters do not cry out in pain. Then the sting will be gone, and you will feel so much stronger and better. And that will be the end of the ceremony, and we will go downstairs and there will be iced cakes to celebrate."

Adele kicked her heels. "And a party!"

"Yes, a party. And presents." He tapped his pocket, where a small box was hidden away—a small box wrapped in fine blue paper, that held an even smaller family ring. "I have one for you right here. You'll get it as soon as the Marking ceremony is over."

"I've never had a party for me before."

"It's because you're becoming a Shadowhunter," said Aloysius. "You know why that's important, don't you? Your first Marks mean you are Nephilim, like me, like your mother and father. They mean you are part of the Clave. Part of our warrior family. Something different and better than everyone else."

"Better than everyone else," she repeated slowly as her bedroom door opened and two Silent Brothers came in. Aloysius saw the flicker of fear in Adele's eyes. She drew her arm back from his grasp. He frowned—he did not like to see fear in his progeny, though he could not deny that the Brothers were eerie in their silence and their peculiar, gliding motions. They moved around to Adele's side of the bed as the door opened again and Adele's mother and father entered: her father, Aloysius's son, in scarlet gear; his wife in a red dress that belled out at the waist, and a golden necklace from which hung an *enkeli* rune. They smiled at their daughter, who gave a tremulous smile back, even as the Silent Brothers surrounded her.

Adele Lucinda Starkweather. It was the voice of the first Silent Brother, Brother Cimon. *You are now of age. It is time for the first of the Angel's Marks to be bestowed on you. Are you aware of the honor being done you, and will you do all in your power to be worthy of it?*

Adele nodded obediently. "Yes."

And do you accept these Marks of the Angel, which will be upon your body forever, a reminder of all that you owe to the Angel, and of your sacred duty to the world?

She nodded again, obediently. Aloysius's heart swelled with pride. "I do accept them," she said.

Then we begin. A stele flashed forth, held in the Silent Brother's long white hand. He took Adele's trembling arm and set the tip of the stele to her skin, and began to draw.

Black lines swirled out from the stele's tip, and Adele stared in wonderment as the symbol for Strength took shape on the pale skin of her inner arm, a delicate design of lines intersecting with each other, crossing her veins, wrapping her arm. Her body was tense, her small teeth sunk into her upper lip. Her eyes flashed upward at Aloysius, and he started at what he saw in them.

Pain. It was normal to feel some pain at the bestowing of a Mark, but what he saw in Adele's eyes—was agony.

Aloysius jerked upright, sending the chair he had been sitting on skittering away behind him. "Stop!" he cried, but it was too late. The rune was complete. The Silent Brother drew back, staring. There was blood on the stele. Adele was whimpering, mindful of her grandfather's admonition that she not cry out—but then her bloody, lacerated skin began to peel back from the bones, blackening and burning under the rune as if it were fire, and she could not help but throw her head back, and scream, and scream . . .

London, 1873.

"Will?" Charlotte Fairchild eased the door of the Institute's training room open. "Will, are you in there?"

A muffled grunt was the only response. The door swung all the way open, revealing the wide, high-ceilinged room on the other side. Charlotte herself had grown up training here, and she knew every warp of the floorboards, the ancient target painted on the north wall, the square-paned windows, so old that they were thicker at the base than the top. In the center of the room stood Will Herondale, a knife held in his right hand.

He turned his head to look at Charlotte, and she thought again what an odd child he was—although at twelve he was barely still a child. He was a very pretty boy, with thick dark hair that waved slightly where it touched his collar—wet now with sweat, and pasted to his forehead. His skin had been tanned by country air and sun when he had first come to the Institute, though six months of city life had drained its color, causing the red flush across his cheekbones to stand out. His eyes were an unusually luminous blue. He would be a handsome man one day, if he could do something about the scowl that perpetually twisted his features.

"What is it, Charlotte?" he snapped.

He still spoke with a slight Welsh accent, a roll to his vowels that would have been charming if his tone hadn't been so sour. He drew his sleeve across his forehead as she came partway through the door, then paused. "I've been looking for you for hours," she said with some asperity, though asperity had little effect on Will. Not much had an effect on Will when he was in a mood, and he was nearly always in a mood. "Didn't you recall what I told you yesterday, that we were welcoming a new arrival to the Institute today?"

"Oh, I remembered." Will threw the knife. It stuck just outside the circle of the target, deepening his scowl. "I just don't care."

The boy behind Charlotte made a stifled noise. A laugh, she would have thought, but certainly he couldn't be laughing? She had been warned the boy coming to the Institute from Shanghai was not well, but she had still been startled when he had stepped from the carriage, pale and swaying like a reed in the wind, his curling dark hair streaked with silver as if he were a man in his eighties, not a boy of twelve. His eyes were wide and silvery-black, strangely beautiful but haunting in such a delicate face. "Will, you *shall* be polite," she said now, and drew the boy out from behind her, ushering him ahead into the room. "Don't mind Will; he's only moody. Will Herondale, may I introduce you to James Carstairs, of the Shanghai Institute."

"Jem," said the boy. "Everyone calls me Jem." He took another step forward into the room, his gaze taking in Will with a friendly curiosity. He spoke without the trace of an accent, to Charlotte's surprise, but then his father was—had been—British. "You can too."

"Well, if everyone calls you that, it's hardly any special favor to me, is it?" Will's tone was acid; for someone so young, he was amazingly capable of unpleasantness. "I think you will find, James Carstairs, that if you keep to yourself and let me alone, it will be the best outcome for both of us."

Charlotte sighed inwardly. She had so hoped that this boy, the same age as Will, would prove a tool to disarm Will of his anger and his viciousness, but it seemed clear that Will had been speaking the truth when he had told her he did not care if another Shadowhunter boy was coming to the Institute. He did not want friends, or want for them. She glanced at Jem, expecting to see him blinking in surprise or hurt, but he was only smiling a little, as if Will were a kitten that had tried to bite him. "I haven't trained since I left Shanghai," he said. "I could use a partner—someone to spar with."

"So could I," said Will. "But I need someone who can keep up with me, not some sickly creature that looks as if he's doddering off to the grave. Although I suppose you might be useful for target practice."

Charlotte, knowing what she did about James Carstairs—a fact she had not shared with Will—felt a sickly horror come over her. *Doddering off to the grave, oh dear Lord. What was it her father had said? That Jem was dependent on a drug to live, some kind of medicine that would extend his life but not save it. Oh, Will.*

She made as if to move in between the two boys, as if she could protect Jem from Will's cruelty, more awfully accurate in this instance that even he knew—but then she paused.

Jem had not even changed expression. "If by 'doddering off to the grave' you mean dying, then I am," he said. "I have about two years more to live, three if I am lucky, or so they tell me."

Even Will could not hide his shock; his cheeks flushed red. "I . . ."

But Jem had set his steps toward the target painted on the wall; when he reached it, he yanked the knife free from the wood. Then he turned and walked directly up to Will. Delicate as he was, they were of the same height, and only inches from each other their eyes met and held. "You may use me for target practice if you wish," said Jem, as casually as if he were talking about the weather. "It seems to me I have little to fear from such an exercise, as you are not a very good shot." He turned, took aim, and let the knife fly. It stuck directly into the heart of the target, quivering slightly. "Or," Jem went on, turning back to Will, "you could allow *me* to teach *you*. For I am a *very* good shot."

Charlotte stared. For half a year she had watched Will push away everyone who'd tried to get near him—tutors; her father; her fiancé, Henry; both the Lightwood brothers—with a combination of hatefulness and precisely accurate cruelty. If it were not that she herself was the only person who had ever seen him cry, she imagined she would have given up hope as well, long ago, that he would ever be any good to anybody. And yet here he was, looking at Jem Carstairs, a boy so fragile-looking that he appeared to be made out of glass, with the hardness of his expression slowly dissolving into a tentative uncertainty. "You are not *really* dying," he said, the oddest tone to his voice, "are you?"

Jem nodded. "So they tell me."

"I am sorry," Will said.

"No," Jem said softly. He drew his jacket aside and took a knife from the belt at his waist. "Don't be ordinary like that. Don't say you're sorry. Say you'll train with me."

He held out the knife to Will, hilt first. Charlotte held her breath, afraid to move. She felt as if she were watching something very important happen, though she could not have said what.

Will reached out and took the knife, his eyes never leaving Jem's face. His fingers brushed the other boy's as he took the weapon from him. It was the first time, Charlotte thought, that she had ever seen him touch any other person willingly.

"I'll train with you," he said.

1

A Dreadful Row

Marry on Monday for health,
Tuesday for wealth,
Wednesday the best day of all,
Thursday for crosses,
Friday for losses, and
Saturday for no luck at all.
—Folk rhyme

"December is a fortuitous time for a marriage," said the seamstress, speaking around her mouthful of pins with the ease of years of practice. "As they say, 'When December snows fall fast, marry, and true love will last.'" She placed a final pin in the gown and took a step back. "There. What do you think? It is modeled after one of Worth's own designs."

Tessa looked at her reflection in the pier glass in her

bedroom. The dress was a deep gold silk, as was the custom for Shadowhunters, who believed white to be the color of mourning, and would not marry in it, despite Queen Victoria herself having set the fashion for doing just that. Duchesse lace edged the tightly fitted bodice and dripped from the sleeves.

"It's lovely!" Charlotte clapped her hands together and leaned forward. Her brown eyes shone with delight. "Tessa, the color looks so fine on you."

Tessa turned and twisted in front of the mirror. The gold put some much-needed color into her cheeks. The hourglass corset shaped and curved her everywhere it was supposed to, and the clockwork angel around her throat comforted her with its ticking. Below it dangled the jade pendant that Jem had given her. She had lengthened the chain so she could wear them both at once, not being willing to part with either. "You don't think, perhaps, that the lace is a trifle too much adornment?"

"Not at all!" Charlotte sat back, one hand resting protectively, unconsciously, over her belly. She had always been too slim—skinny, in truth—to really need a corset, and now that she was going to have a child, she had taken to wearing tea gowns, in which she looked like a little bird. "It is your wedding day, Tessa. If there is ever an excuse for excessive adornment, it is that. Just imagine it."

Tessa had spent many nights doing just that. She was not yet sure where she and Jem would be married, for the Council was still deliberating their situation. But when she imagined the wedding, it was always in a church, with her being marched down the aisle, perhaps on Henry's arm, looking neither to the left or right but straight ahead at her betrothed, as a proper bride should. Jem would be wearing gear—not the sort one fought in, but specially designed, in the manner of a military uniform, for the occasion: black with bands of gold at the wrists, and gold runes picked out along the collar and placket.

He would look so young. They were *both* so young. Tessa knew it was unusual to marry at seventeen and eighteen, but they were racing a clock.

The clock of Jem's life, before it wound down.

She put her hand to her throat, and felt the familiar vibration of her clockwork angel, its wings scratching her palm. The seamstress looked up at her anxiously. She was mundane, not Nephilim, but had the Sight, as all who served the Shadowhunters did. "Would you like the lace removed, miss?"

Before Tessa could answer, there was a knock at the door, and a familiar voice. "It's Jem. Tessa, are you there?"

Charlotte sat bolt upright. "Oh! He mustn't see you in your dress!"

Tessa stood dumbfounded. "Whyever not?"

"It's a Shadowhunter custom—bad luck!" Charlotte rose to her feet. "Quickly! Hide behind the wardrobe!"

"The wardrobe? But—" Tessa broke off with a yelp as Charlotte seized her about the waist and frog-marched her behind the wardrobe like a policeman with a particularly resistant criminal. Released, Tessa dusted off her dress and made a face at Charlotte, and they both peeked around the side of the furniture as the seamstress, after a bewildered look, opened the door.

Jem's silvery head appeared in the gap. He looked a bit disheveled, his jacket askew. He glanced around in puzzlement before his gaze lighted on Charlotte and Tessa, half-concealed behind the wardrobe. "Thank goodness," he said. "I'd no idea where any of you had gone. Gabriel Lightwood's downstairs, and he's making the most dreadful row."

"Write to them, Will," said Cecily Herondale. "Please. Just one letter."

Will tossed his sweat-soaked dark hair back and glared at her. "Get your feet into position," was all he said. He pointed, with the tip of his dagger. "There, and there."

Cecily sighed, and moved her feet. She had known she was out of position; she'd been doing it intentionally, to needle Will. It was easy to needle her brother. That much she remembered about him from when he was twelve years old. Even then daring him to do something, like climb the steeply pitched roof of their manor house, had resulted in the same thing: an angry blue flame in his eyes, a set jaw, and sometimes Will with a broken leg or arm at the end of it.

Of course this brother, the nearly adult Will, was not the brother she remembered from her childhood. He had grown both more explosive and more withdrawn. He had all their mother's beauty, and all their father's stubbornness—and, she feared, their father's propensity for vices, though she had guessed that only from whispers among the occupants of the Institute.

"Raise your blade," Will said. His voice was as cool and professional as her governess's.

Cecily raised it. It had taken her some time to get used to

the feel of gear against her skin: the loose tunic and trousers, the belt around her waist. Now she moved in it as comfortably as she had ever moved in the loosest nightgown. "I don't understand why you won't consider writing a letter. A single letter."

"I don't understand why you won't consider going home," Will said. "If you would just agree to return to Yorkshire yourself, you could stop worrying about our parents and I could arrange—"

Cecily interrupted him, having heard this speech a thousand times. "Would you consider a wager, Will?"

Cecily was both pleased and a little disappointed to see Will's eyes spark, just the way her father's always did when a gentleman's bet was suggested. Men were so easy to predict.

"What sort of a wager?" Will took a step forward. He was wearing gear; Cecily could see the Marks that twined his wrists, the *mnemosyne* rune on his throat. It had taken her some time to see the Marks as something other than disfiguring, but she was used to them now—as she had grown used to the gear, to the great echoing halls of the Institute, and to its peculiar denizens.

She pointed at the wall in front of them. An ancient target had been painted on the wall in black: a bull's-eye inside a larger circle. "If I hit the center of that three times, you have to write a letter to Dad and Mam and tell them how you are. You must tell them of the curse and why you left."

Will's face closed like a door, the way it always did when she made this request. But, "You'll never hit it three times without missing, Cecy."

"Well, then it should be no great concern to you to make the bet, William." She used his full name purposefully. She knew it bothered him, coming from her, though when his best friend—no, his *parabatai*; she had learned since coming to the Institute that these were quite different things—Jem did it, Will seemed to take it as a term of affection. Possibly it was because he still had memories of her toddling after him on chubby legs, calling *Will, Will*, after him in breathless Welsh. She had never called him "William," only ever "Will" or his Welsh name, *Gwilym*.

His eyes narrowed, those dark blue eyes the same color as her own. When their mother had said affectionately that Will would be a breaker of hearts when he was grown, Cecily had always looked at her dubiously. Will had been all arms and legs then, skinny and disheveled and always dirty. She could see it now, though, had seen it when she had first walked into the dining room of the Institute and he had stood up in astonishment, and she had thought: *That can't be Will.*

He had turned those eyes on her, her mother's eyes, and she had seen the anger in them. He had not been pleased to see her, not at all. And where in her memories there had been a skinny boy with a wild tangle of black hair like a Gypsy's and leaves in his clothes, there was now this tall, frightening *man* instead. The words she had wanted to say had dissolved on her tongue, and she had matched him, glare for glare. And so it had been since, Will barely enduring her presence as if she were a stone in his shoe, a constant but minor annoyance.

Cecily took a deep breath, raised her chin, and prepared to throw the first knife. Will did not know, would never know, of the hours she had spent in this room, alone, practicing, learning to balance the weight of the knife in her hand, discovering that a good knife throw began from behind the body. She held both arms straight down and drew her right arm back, behind her head, before bringing it, and the weight of her body, forward. The tip of the knife was in line with the target. She released it and snapped her hand back, sucking in a gasp.

The knife stuck, point-down in the wall, exactly in the center of the target.

"One," Cecily said, giving Will a superior smile.

He looked at her stonily, yanked the knife from the wall, and handed it to her again.

Cecily threw it. The second throw, like the first, flew directly to its target and stuck there, vibrating like a mocking finger.

"Two," Cecily said in a sepulchral tone.

Will's jaw set as he took the knife again and presented it to her. She took it with a smile. Confidence was flowing through her veins like new blood. She knew she could do this. She had always been able to climb as high as Will, run as fast, hold her breath as long. . . .

She threw the knife. It struck its target, and she leaped into the air, clapping her hands, forgetting herself for a moment in the thrill of victory. Her hair came down from its pins and spilled into her face; she pushed it back and grinned at Will. "You *shall* write that letter. You agreed to the bet!"

To her surprise he smiled at her. "Oh, I will write it," he said. "I will write it, and then I will throw it into the fire." He held up a hand against her outburst of indignation. "I said I would write it. I never said I would *send* it."

Cecily's breath went out of her in a gasp. "How *dare* you trick me like that!"

"I told you that you were not made of Shadowhunter stuff, or you would not be so easily fooled. I am not going to write a letter, Cecy. It's against the Law, and that's the end of it."

"As if *you* care about the Law!" Cecily stamped her foot, and was immediately more annoyed than ever; she detested girls who stamped their feet.

Will's eyes narrowed. "And *you* don't care about being a Shadowhunter. How is this? I shall write a letter and give it to you if you promise to deliver it home yourself—and not to return."

Cecily recoiled. She had many memories of shouting matches with Will, of the china dolls she had owned that he had broken by dropping them out an attic window, but there was also kindness in her memories—the brother who had bandaged up a cut knee, or retied her hair ribbons when they had come loose. That kindness was absent from the Will who stood before her now. Mam used to cry for the first year or two after Will went; she had said, holding Cecily to her, that the Shadowhunters would "take all the love out of him." A cold people, she had told Cecily, a people who had forbidden her marriage to her husband. What could he want with them, her Will, her little one?

"I will *not* go," Cecily said, staring her brother down. "And if you insist that I must, I will—I will—"

The door of the attic slid open, and Jem stood silhouetted

in the doorway. "Ah," he said, "threatening each other, I see. Has this been going on all afternoon, or did it just begin?"

"He began it," Cecily said, jerking her chin at Will, though she knew it was pointless. Jem, Will's *parabatai*, treated her with the distant sweet kindness reserved for the little sisters of one's friends, but he would always side with Will. Kindly, but firmly, he put Will above everything else in the world.

Well, nearly everything. She had been most struck by Jem when she first came to the Institute—he had an unearthly, unusual beauty, with his silvery hair and eyes and delicate features. He looked like a prince in a fairy-tale book, and she might have considered developing an attachment to him, were it not so absolutely clear that he was entirely in love with Tessa Gray. His eyes followed her where she went, and his voice changed when he spoke to her. Cecily had once heard her mother say in amusement that one of their neighbors' boys looked at a girl as if she were "the only star in the sky" and that was the way Jem looked at Tessa.

Cecily didn't resent it: Tessa was pleasant and kind to her, if a little shy, and with her face always stuck in a book, like Will. If that was the sort of girl Jem wanted, she and he never would have suited—and the longer she remained at the Institute, the more she realized how awkward it would have made things with Will. He was ferociously protective of Jem, and he would have watched her constantly in case she ever distressed or hurt him in any way. No—she was far better out of the whole thing.

"I was just thinking of bundling up Cecily and feeding her to the ducks in Hyde Park," said Will, pushing his wet hair back and favoring Jem with a rare smile. "I could use your assistance."

"Unfortunately, you may have to delay your plans for sororicide a bit longer. Gabriel Lightwood is downstairs, and I have two words for you. Two of your *favorite* words, at least when you put them together."

"'Utter simpleton'?" inquired Will. "'Worthless upstart'?"

Jem grinned. "'*Demon pox,*'" he said.

Sophie balanced the salver on one hand with the ease of long practice while she rapped on Gideon Lightwood's door with the other.

She heard the sound of a hurried shuffle, and the door swung open. Gideon stood before her in trousers, braces, and a white shirt rolled up to the elbows. His hands were wet, as if he had just run quick fingers through his hair, which was also damp. Her heart took a little leap inside her chest before settling. She forced herself to frown at him.

"Mr. Lightwood," she said. "I've brought the scones you rang for, and Bridget's made you up a plate of sandwiches as well."

Gideon took a step back to allow her into the room. It was like all the other rooms in the Institute: heavy dark furniture, a great four-poster bed, a wide fireplace, and high windows, which in this case looked down upon the courtyard below. Sophie could feel his gaze on her as she moved across the room to place the salver on the table before the fire. She straightened up and turned to him, her hands folded in front of her apron.

"Sophie—," he began.

"Mr. Lightwood," she interrupted. "Is there anything else you require?"

He looked at her half-mutinously, half-sadly. "I wish you would call me Gideon."

"I have told you, I cannot call you by your Christian name."

"I am a Shadowhunter; I do not have a Christian name. Sophie, please." He took a step toward her. "Before I took up residence in the Institute, I had thought we were well on our way to a friendship. Yet since the day I arrived, you have been cold to me."

Sophie's hand went involuntarily to her face. She remembered Master Teddy, the son of her old employer, and the horrible way he would catch her in dark corners and press her up against the wall, hands creeping under her bodice, murmuring in her ear that she had better be friendlier to him, if she knew what was good for her. The thought filled her with sickness, even now.

"Sophie." Gideon's eyes crinkled worriedly at the corners. "What is it? If there is some wrong I have done you, some slight, please tell me what it is that I may remedy it—"

"There is no wrong, no slight. You are a gentleman and I am a servant; anything more would be a familiarity. Please do not make me uncomfortable, Mr. Lightwood."

Gideon, who had half-raised his hand, let it drop to his side. He looked so woebegone that Sophie's heart softened. *I have everything to lose, and he has nothing to lose*, she reminded herself. It was what she told herself late at night, lying in her narrow bed, with the memory of a pair of storm-colored eyes hovering in her mind. "I had thought we were friends," he said.

"I cannot be your friend."

He took a step forward. "What if I were to ask you—"

"Gideon!" It was Henry, at the open door, breathless, wearing one of his terrible green-and-orange-striped waistcoats. "Your brother's here. Downstairs—"

Gideon's eyes widened. "Gabriel's here?"

"Yes. Shouting something about your father, but he won't tell us anything more unless you're there. He swears it. Come along."

Gideon hesitated, his eyes moving from Henry to Sophie, who tried to look invisible. "I . . ."

"Come *now*, Gideon." Henry rarely spoke sharply, and when he did, the effect was startling. "He's covered in blood."

Gideon paled, and he reached for the sword that hung on a set of double pegs by his door. "I'm on my way."

Gabriel Lightwood leaned against the wall inside the Institute doors, his jacket gone, his shirt and trousers drenched in scarlet. Outside, through the open doors, Tessa could see the Lightwood carriage, with its flame blazon on the side, drawn up at the foot of the steps. Gabriel must have driven it here himself.

"Gabriel," Charlotte said soothingly, as if she were trying to gentle a wild horse. "Gabriel, tell us what happened, please."

Gabriel—tall and slender, brown hair sticky with blood—scrubbed at his face, wild-eyed. His hands were bloody too. "Where's my brother? I have to talk to my brother."

"He's coming down. I sent Henry to fetch him, and Cyril to ready the Institute's carriage. Gabriel, are you injured? Do you need an *iratze?*" Charlotte sounded as motherly as if this boy had never faced her down from behind Benedict Lightwood's chair, had never conspired with his father to take the Institute away from her.

"That is a great deal of blood," said Tessa, pushing forward. "Gabriel, it is not all yours, is it?"

Gabriel looked at her. It was the first time, Tessa thought, that she had seen him behave with no posturing at all. There was only stunned fear in his eyes, fear and—confusion. "No. . . . It's *theirs*—"

"Theirs? Who are *they?*" It was Gideon, hurrying down the stairs, a sword in his right hand. Along with him came Henry, and Jem, and behind him, Will and Cecily. Jem paused on the steps in startlement, and Tessa realized that he had caught sight of her in her wedding dress. His eyes widened, but the others were already pushing by, and he was carried down the steps like a leaf in a current.

"Is Father hurt?" Gideon went on, coming to a stop before his brother. "Are you?" He put his hand up and took his brother's face, his hand cupping Gabriel's chin and turning it toward him. Though Gabriel was taller, the look of a younger sibling was clear in his face—relief that his brother was there, and a flicker of resentment at his peremptory tone.

"Father . . . ," Gabriel began. "Father is a worm."

Will gave a short laugh. He was in gear as if he had just come from the practice room, and his hair curled damply against his temples. He was not looking at Tessa, but she had grown used to that. Will hardly ever looked at her unless he had to. "It's good to see you've come round to our view of things, Gabriel, but this is an unusual way of announcing it."

Gideon shot Will a reproachful look before turning back to his brother. "What do you mean, Gabriel? What did Father do?"

Gabriel shook his head. "He's a worm," he said again, tonelessly.

"I know. He has brought shame on the name of Lightwood, and lied to both of us. He shamed and destroyed our mother. But we need not be like him."

Gabriel pulled away from his brother's grip, his teeth suddenly flashing in an angry scowl. "You're not listening to me," he said. "He's a worm. *A worm.* A bloody great serpent-like thing. Since Mortmain stopped sending the medicine, he's been getting worse. Changing. Those sores upon his arms, they started to cover him. His hands, his neck, h-his *face* . . ." Gabriel's green eyes sought Will. "It was the pox, wasn't it? You know all about it, don't you? Aren't you some sort of expert?"

"Well, you needn't act as if I invented it," said Will. "Just because I believed it existed. There are accounts of it—old stories in the library—"

"Demon pox?" said Cecily, her face screwed up in confusion. "Will, what is he talking about?"

Will opened his mouth, and flushed faintly across his cheekbones. Tessa hid a smile. It had been weeks since Cecily had come to the Institute, and still her presence bothered and upset Will. He did not seem to know how to behave around this younger sister, who was not the child he remembered, and whose presence he insisted was unwelcome. And yet

Tessa had seen him follow Cecily around a room with his eyes, with the same protective love in his gaze that he sometimes bent on Jem. Certainly the existence of demon pox, and how one acquired it, was the last thing he would want to explain to Cecily. "Nothing you need know about," he muttered.

Gabriel's eyes went to Cecily, and his lips parted in surprise. Tessa could see him taking Cecily in. Will's parents must both have been very beautiful, Tessa thought, for Cecily was as pretty as Will was handsome, and with the same gleaming black hair and startling dark blue eyes. Cecily gazed boldly back at him, her expression curious; she must have been wondering who this boy was, who seemed to so dislike her brother.

"Is Father dead?" Gideon demanded, his voice rising. "Has the demon pox killed him?"

"Not killed," said Gabriel. "Changed. It has changed him. Some weeks ago he moved our household to Chiswick. He would not say why. Then a few days ago he locked himself in his study. He wouldn't come out, not even to eat. This morning I went to the study to try to rouse him. The door had been torn off its hinges. There was a . . . a *trail* of some slimy stuff leading down the hall. I followed it downstairs and into the gardens." He looked around the now silent entryway. "He has become a worm. That is what I am telling you."

"I don't suppose it would be possible," said Henry into the silence, "to, er, step on him?"

Gabriel looked at him in disgust. "I searched around the gardens. I found some of the servants. And when I say

'I found' some of them, I mean exactly what I say. They had been torn into—into pieces." He swallowed and looked down at his bloody clothes. "I heard a sound—a high-pitched howling noise. I turned and saw it coming toward me. A great blind worm like a dragon out of a legend. Its mouth was open wide, lined with dagger teeth. I turned and ran for the stables. It slithered after me, but I leaped upon the carriage and drove it out through the gates. The creature—Father—did not follow. I think it fears to be seen by the general populace."

"Ah," said Henry. "Too big to be stepped on, then."

"I shouldn't have run," said Gabriel, looking at his brother. "I should have stood and fought the creature. Maybe it could be reasoned with. Maybe Father is in there somewhere."

"And maybe it would have bitten you in half," said Will. "What you are describing, the transformation into a demon, is the last stage of the pox."

"Will!" Charlotte threw up her hands. "Why didn't you *say* so?"

"You know, the books on demon pox are in the library," Will said with an injured tone. "I wasn't preventing anyone from reading them."

"Yes, but if Benedict was going to turn into an enormous *serpent*, you'd think you could at least have mentioned it," said Charlotte. "As a matter of general interest."

"First," said Will, "I didn't know he was going to turn into a gigantic worm. The end stage of demon pox is turning into a demon. It could have been any sort. Second, it takes weeks for the transformation process to occur. I would have thought even a certified idiot like Gabriel here would have taken account of it and notified someone."

"Notified who?" asked Jem, not unreasonably. He had moved closer to Tessa as the conversation had continued. As they stood side by side, the backs of their hands brushed.

"The Clave. The postman. Us. *Anyone*," said Will, shooting an irritated look at Gabriel, who was starting to get some color back and looked furious.

"I am not a certified idiot—"

"Lack of certification hardly proves intelligence," Will muttered.

"And as I told you, Father locked himself in his study for the past week—"

"And you didn't think to take any special notice of that?" said Will.

"You don't know our father," said Gideon in the flat tone of voice he used sometimes when conversation about his family was inescapable. He turned back to his brother and put his hands on Gabriel's shoulders, speaking quietly, in measured tones none of them could hear.

Jem, beside Tessa, hooked his smallest finger through hers. It was a habitual affectionate gesture, one that Tessa had grown used to over the past months, enough that she sometimes put out her hand without thinking when he was standing by her. "Is that your wedding dress?" he asked under his breath.

Tessa was saved answering by the appearance of Bridget, carrying gear, and Gideon suddenly turning to the rest of them and saying, "Chiswick. We must go. Gabriel and I, if no one else."

"Go alone?" Tessa said, startled enough to speak out of

turn. "But why would you not call upon others to come with you—"

"The Clave," said Will, his blue eyes keen. "He doesn't want the Clave to know about his father."

"Would you?" said Gabriel hotly. "If it were *your* family?" His lip curled. "Never mind. It's not as if you know the meaning of loyalty—"

"Gabriel." Gideon's voice was a reprimand. "Do not speak to Will in that manner."

Gabriel looked surprised, and Tessa could hardly blame him. Gideon knew of Will's curse, of the belief that had caused his hostility and his abrupt manners, as all in the Institute did, but the story was private to them, and none outside had been told of it.

"We will come with you. Of course we will come with you," said Jem, releasing Tessa's hand and stepping forward. "Gideon did us a service. We have not forgotten, have we, Charlotte?"

"Of course not," said Charlotte, turning. "Bridget, the gear—"

"I am conveniently already in gear," said Will as Henry shucked off his coat and traded it for a gear jacket and a weapons belt; Jem did the same, and suddenly the entryway was full of motion—Charlotte speaking quietly to Henry, her hand hovering just above her stomach. Tessa looked away from the private moment and saw a dark head bent with a fair one. Jem was at Will's side with his stele drawn, tracing a rune on the side of Will's throat. Cecily looked at her brother and scowled.

"I, too, am conveniently already in gear," she announced.

Will jerked his head up, causing Jem to make a sound of annoyed protest. "Cecily, absolutely not."

"You have no right to tell me yes or no." Her eyes flashed. "I am going."

Will jerked his head toward Henry, who shrugged apologetically. "She does have the right. She has trained for nearly two months—"

"She's a little girl!"

"You were doing the same at fifteen," said Jem quietly, and Will spun back toward him. For a moment everyone seemed to hold their breath, even Gabriel. Jem's gaze held Will's, steadily, and not for the first time Tessa had the sense of unspoken words passing between them.

Will sighed and half-closed his eyes. "Tessa will be wanting to come next."

"Of course I am coming," Tessa said. "I may not be a Shadowhunter, but I too have trained. Jem is not going without me."

"You are in your *wedding dress*," Will protested.

"Well, now that you've all seen it, I can't possibly wear it to be married in," said Tessa. "Bad luck, you know."

Will groaned something in Welsh—unintelligible, but clearly the tone of a man defeated. Across the room Jem cast Tessa a slight, worried smile. The Institute door swung open then, letting a blaze of autumn sunlight into the entryway. Cyril stood on the threshold, breathless.

"The second carriage is now ready," he said. "Who'll be coming, then?"

To: Consul Josiah Wayland
From: The Council

Dear Sir,

As you are doubtless aware, your term of service as Consul, after ten years, is coming to an end. The time has come to appoint a successor.

As for ourselves, we are giving serious consideration to the appointment of Charlotte Branwell, née Fairchild. She has done good work as the head of the London Institute, and we believe her to have your stamp of approval, as she was appointed by you after the death of her father.

As your opinion and esteem are to us of the highest value, we would appreciate any thoughts that you might have on the matter.

Yours with the highest regards,
Victor Whitelaw, Inquisitor, on behalf of the Council

2

THE CONQUEROR WORM

And much of Madness, and more of Sin,
And Horror the soul of the plot.
—Edgar Allan Poe, "The Conqueror Worm"

As the Institute's carriage rolled through the gates of Lightwood House in Chiswick, Tessa was able to appreciate the place as she had not the first time she had been there, in the dead of night. A long gravel road flanked by trees led up to an immense white house with a circular drive in front of it. The house bore a strong resemblance to sketches she had seen of the classical temples of Greece and Rome with its strong, symmetrical lines and clean columns. There was a carriage drawn up before the steps, and gravel paths spread out through a network of gardens.

And lovely gardens they were. Even in October they were

a riot of blooms—late-flowering red roses and chrysanthemums in bronze-orange, yellow, and dark gold bordered neat paths that wandered through the trees. As Henry drew their carriage to a stop, Tessa stepped out of the carriage, helped by Jem, and heard the sound of water: a stream, she suspected, diverted to run through the gardens. It was such a lovely place, she could hardly associate it in her mind with the same location where Benedict had held his devilish ball, though she could see the path that wound around the side of the house that she had taken that night. It led to a wing of the house that looked as if it had been recently added. . . .

The Lightwood carriage rolled up behind them, driven by Gideon. Gabriel, Will, and Cecily spilled out. The Herondale siblings were still arguing with each other as Gideon climbed down, Will illustrating his points with bold sweeps of his arms. Cecily was scowling at him, the furious expression on her face making her look so much like her brother that it would, under other circumstances, have been amusing.

Gideon, even paler than before, turned in a circle, his blade unsheathed in his hand.

"Tatiana's carriage," he said shortly as Jem and Tessa reached him. He pointed toward the vehicle drawn up by the steps. Its doors were both open. "She must have decided to pay a call."

"Of all the times . . ." Gabriel sounded furious, but his green eyes were sick with fear. Tatiana was their sister, recently married. The coat of arms on the carriage, a wreath of thorns, must have been the symbol of her husband's family, Tessa thought. The group stood frozen, watching, as

Gabriel moved to the carriage, slipping a long sabre from his belt. He leaned in the door, and cursed aloud.

He pulled back, his eyes meeting Gideon's. "There's blood on the seats," he said. "And . . . this stuff." He prodded at a wheel with the tip of the sabre; when he drew it away, a long thread of stinking slime trailed from it.

Will whipped a seraph blade from his coat and called aloud, *"Eremiel!"* As it began to blaze, a pale white star in the autumn light, he pointed first north, then south. "The gardens run all round the house, down to the river," he said. "I ought to know—I chased the demon Marbas all up through here one night. Wherever Benedict is, I doubt he'll leave these grounds. Too much of a chance of being seen."

"We'll take the west side of the house. You take the east," said Gabriel. "Shout if you see anything and we'll converge."

Gabriel cleaned his blade on the gravel of the drive, stood, and followed his brother around the side of the house. Will headed the other way, followed by Jem, with Cecily and Tessa just behind them. Will paused at the corner of the house, scanning the gardens with his gaze, alert for any unusual sight or sound. A moment later, he beckoned for the others to follow.

As they moved forward, the heel of Tessa's shoe caught on one of the loose bits of gravel beneath the hedges. She stumbled, and immediately righted herself, but Will glanced back, and scowled. "Tessa," he said. There had been a time when he had called her Tess, but no longer. "You shouldn't be with us. You're not prepared. At least wait in the carriage."

"I shan't," said Tessa mutinously.

Will turned back to Jem, who appeared to be hiding a smile. "Tessa's *your* fiancée. You make her see sense."

Jem, holding his sword-cane in one hand, moved across the gravel to her. "Tessa, do it as a favor to me, could you?"

"You don't think I can fight," Tessa said, drawing back and matching his silvery gaze with her own. "Because I'm a girl."

"I don't think you can fight because you're wearing a wedding dress," said Jem. "For what it's worth, I don't think Will could fight in that dress either."

"Perhaps not," said Will, who had ears like a bat's. "But I would make a radiant bride."

Cecily raised her hand to point into the distance. "What's that?"

All four of them whirled to see a figure racing toward them. The sunlight was directly ahead, and for a moment, as Tessa's eyes adjusted, all she saw was a blur. The blur quickly resolved itself into the figure of a running girl. Her hat was gone; her light brown hair flew on the wind. She was tall and bony, dressed in a bright fuchsia dress that had probably once been elegant but was now torn and bloodstained. She continued shrieking as she barreled toward them and threw herself into Will's arms.

He staggered backward, nearly dropping Eremiel. "Tatiana—"

Tessa couldn't quite tell if Will pushed her away or she drew back on her own, but either way Tatiana moved an inch or so away from Will, and Tessa could see her face for the first time. She was a narrow, angular girl. Her hair was sandy like Gideon's, her eyes green like Gabriel's, and she might have

been pretty had her face not borne the lines of pinched disap-
proval. Even though she was tearstained and gasping, there
was something theatrical about it, as if she were aware of all
eyes on her—especially Will's.

"A great monster," she wept. "A creature—it seized darling
Rupert from the carriage and made off with him!"

Will pushed her a bit farther away. "What do you mean
'made off with him'?"

She pointed. "Th-there," she sobbed. "It dragged him to
the Italian gardens. He managed to elude its maw at first,
but it harried him through the paths. No matter how much I
screamed, it would not put him d-down!" She burst into a fresh
wave of tears.

"You screamed," Will said. "Is that all you did?"

"I screamed a great deal." Tatiana sounded injured. She
drew fully away from Will and fixed him with a green gaze. "I
see you are as ungenerous as you ever were." Her eyes skated
to Tessa, Cecily, and Jem. "Mr. Carstairs," she said stiffly, as if
they were at a garden party. Her eyes narrowed as they fell on
Cecily. "And you—"

"Oh, in the name of the Angel!" Will pushed past her; Jem,
with a smile at Tessa, followed.

"You *cannot* be other than Will's sister," said Tatiana to
Cecily as the boys vanished into the distance. Tessa she pointedly ignored.

Cecily looked at her incredulously. "I am, though I cannot imagine what difference it makes. Tessa—are you coming?"

"I am," Tessa said, and joined her; whether Will wanted
her there or not—or Jem either—she could not watch the

two of them walk into danger and not want to be where they were. After a moment she heard Tatiana's reluctant footsteps on the gravel behind her.

They were moving away from the house, toward the formal gardens half-hidden behind their high hedges. In the distance sunlight sparked off a wood-and-glass greenhouse with a cupola on the roof. It was a fine autumn day: There was a brisk wind, the smell of leaves in the air. Tessa heard a rustle and glanced at the house behind her. Its smooth white facade rose high, broken only by the arches of balconies.

"Will," she whispered as he reached up and unlocked her hands from around his neck. He drew her gloves off, and they joined her mask and Jessie's pins on the stone floor of the balcony. He pulled off his own mask next and cast it aside, running his hands through his damp black hair, pushing it back from his forehead. The lower edge of the mask had left marks across his high cheekbones, like light scars, but when she reached to touch them, he gently caught at her hands and pressed them down.

"No," he said. "Let me touch you first. I have wanted ..."

Blushing furiously, Tessa pulled her gaze away from the house and the memories it contained. The group had reached a gap in the hedges on their right. Through it what was clearly "the Italian garden" was visible, ringed round by foliage. Within the circle the garden was lined with rows of statuary depicting classical heroes and figures of myth. Venus poured water from an urn in a central fountain, while statues of great historians and statesmen—Caesar, Herodotus, Thucydides— regarded each other with blank eyes across the walkways that radiated out from the central point. There were also poets and playwrights. Tessa, hurrying along, passed Aristotle,

Ovid, Homer—his eyes bound with a stone mask to indicate his blindness—Virgil and Sophocles, before an earsplitting scream rent the air.

She whirled around. Several feet behind her Tatiana was standing stock-still, her eyes bulging out of her head. Tessa dashed back toward her, the others on her heels; she reached the girl first, and Tatiana caught at her blindly, as if forgetting for the moment who Tessa was. "Rupert," Tatiana moaned, staring ahead of her, and Tessa, following her gaze, saw a man's boot protruding from behind a hedge. She thought for a moment that he must have been lying stunned upon the ground, the rest of his body hidden by foliage, but as she leaned forward, she realized that the boot—and the several inches of gnawed-upon, bloody flesh that protruded from the boot's opening—were all there was to see.

"A forty-foot worm?" Will muttered to Jem as they moved through the Italian garden, their boots—thanks to a pair of Soundless runes—making no noise on the gravel. "Think of the size of the fish we could catch."

Jem's lips twitched. "It's not funny, you know."

"It is a bit."

"You cannot reduce the situation to worm jokes, Will. This is Gabriel and Gideon's father we're discussing."

"We're not just discussing him; we're chasing him through an ornamental sculpture garden because he's turned into a *worm*."

"A demonic worm," said Jem, pausing to peer cautiously around a hedgerow. "A great serpent. Would that help your inappropriate humor?"

"There was a time when my inappropriate humor brought you a certain amusement," sighed Will. "How the worm has turned."

"*Will*—"

Jem was interrupted by an earsplitting scream. Both boys spun, in time to see Tatiana Blackthorn reel backward into Tessa's arms. Tessa caught the other girl, supporting her, as Cecily moved toward a gap in the hedges, whipping a seraph blade from her belt with the ease of a practiced Shadowhunter. Will did not hear her speak, but the blade sprang up in her hand, lighting her face and setting a sick blaze of dread alight in Will's stomach.

He began to run, Jem at his heels. Tatiana was sagging limply in Tessa's arms, her face starkly twisted into a wail. "Rupert! *Rupert!*" Tessa was struggling with the other girl's weight, and Will wanted to pause to help her—but Jem already had, his hand on Tessa's arm, and it was reasonable. It was his place, as her fiancé.

Will savagely yanked his attention away, back to his sister, who was moving between the gap in the hedges, her blade held high as she edged around the grisly remains of Rupert Blackthorn.

"*Cecily!*" Will called in exasperation. She began to turn—

And the world exploded. A fountain of dirt and mud sprayed up before them, geysering into the sky. Clods of earth and mud clattered down on them like hail. In the center of the geyser—an enormous, blind serpent, a pale grayish-white color. The color of dead flesh, Will thought. A stench came off it like the stench of a grave. Tatiana gave a wail and went limp, pulling Tessa to the ground with her.

The worm began to fling itself to and fro, trying to pull free of the earth. Its mouth opened—it was less of a mouth and more of an enormous slash bisecting its head, lined with shark-like teeth. A great keening hiss came from its throat.

"Halt!" Cecily cried. She held her blazing seraph blade out in front of her; she looked absolutely fearless. "Get back, damned creature!"

The worm lashed down toward her. She stood fast, her blade in hand, as its great jaws descended—and Will leaped at her, knocking her out of the way. They both rolled into a hedge as the worm's head struck the ground where she had been standing, leaving a sizeable dent.

"Will!" Cecily pulled herself away from him, but not quite in time. Her seraph blade slashed across his forearm, leaving a red burn behind. Her eyes were blue fire. "That was unneces-sary!"

"You're not trained!" Will shouted, half out of his mind with fury and terror. "You'll get yourself killed! Stay where you are!" He reached for her blade, but she twisted away from him and onto her feet. A moment later the worm was surging down again, its mouth open. Will had dropped his own blade diving for his sister; it was several feet away. He leaped to the side, avoiding the creature's jaws by inches, and then Jem was there, sword-cane in hand. He drove the blade up, hard, into the side of the worm's body. A hellish scream burst from its throat, and it whipped backward, spraying black blood. With a hiss it dis-appeared behind a hedgerow.

Will spun around. He could barely see Cecily; Jem had thrown himself between her and Benedict, and he was spat-tered in black blood and mud. Behind Jem, Tessa had dragged

Tatiana into her lap; their skirts belled out together, Tatiana's gaudy pink mixing with the ruined gold of Tessa's wedding dress. Tessa had bent over her as if to protect her from the sight of her father, and much of the demon blood had splashed upon Tessa's hair and clothes. She looked up, her face pale, and her eyes met Will's.

For a moment the garden, the noise, the stench of blood and demon, vanished away, and he was alone in a soundless place with only Tessa. He wanted to run to her, wrap her in his arms. Protect her.

But it was Jem's place to do those things, not his. *Not his.*

The moment passed, and Tessa was on her feet, pulling Tatiana up by main force, looping the other girl's arm about her own shoulders even as Tatiana lolled against her, half-conscious.

"You must move her from here. She'll be killed," Will said, sweeping his gaze over the garden. "She has no training."

Tessa's mouth began to set in its familiar, stubborn line. "I don't wish to leave you."

Cecily looked horrified. "You don't think . . . Wouldn't the creature hold off? She's his daughter. If it—if he—has any family feeling left—"

"He *consumed* his son-in-law, Cecy," Will snapped. "Tessa, go with Tatiana if you want to save her life. And stay with her by the house. It would be a disaster if she came rushing back here."

"Thank you, Will," Jem murmured as Tessa drew the stumbling girl away as quickly as she could, and Will felt the words as three needle pricks inside his heart. Always when Will did something to protect Tessa, Jem thought it was for his sake, not for Will's. Always Will wished Jem could be entirely right. Each needle prick had its own name. *Guilt. Shame. Love.*

Cecily screamed. A shadow blotted out the sun, and the hedgerow in front of Will burst apart. He found himself staring down the dark red gullet of the massive worm. Ropes of spittle hung between its enormous teeth. Will snatched for the sword at his belt, but the worm was already rearing back, a dagger protruding from the side of its neck. Will recognized it without turning. It was Jem's. He heard his *parabatai* cry out a warning, and then the worm was hurtling toward Will again and he slammed his sword upward, through the underside of its jaw. Blood spurted through its teeth, splattering Will's gear with a hissing noise. Something struck the back of his knees and, unprepared, he went over hard, his shoulders slamming into the turf.

He choked as the wind was knocked out of him. The worm's thin, annulated tail was wrapped around his knees. He kicked out, seeing stars, Jem's anxious face, blue sky above him—

Thunk. An arrow embedded itself in the worm's tail, just below Will's knee. Benedict's grip loosened, and Will rolled away across the dirt and struggled to his knees, just in time to see Gideon and Gabriel Lightwood pounding toward them across the dirt path. Gabriel held a bow. He was notching it again as he ran, and Will realized with a distant surprise that Gabriel Lightwood had just shot his father to save Will's life.

The worm caromed backward, and there were hands under Will's arms, hauling him to his feet. *Jem.* He released Will, who turned to see that his *parabatai* already had his sword-cane out and was glaring ahead. The demon worm appeared to be writhing in agony, undulating as it swept its great, blind head from side to side, uprooting shrubbery with its thrashings. Leaves filled the air, and the small group of Shadowhunters choked on dust. Will could hear Cecily coughing and longed to tell her to run back to the house, but he knew she wouldn't do it.

Somehow the worm, by thrashing its jaws, had worked the sword free; the weapon clattered to the ground among the rosebushes, smeared with black ichor. The worm began to slide backward, leaving a trail of slime and blood. Gideon grimaced and dashed forward to seize up the fallen sword with a gloved hand.

Suddenly Benedict reared up like a cobra, his jaws apart and dripping. Gideon raised the sword, looking impossibly small against the creature's vast bulk.

"*Gideon!*" It was Gabriel, white-faced, raising his bow; Will spun aside as an arrow flew past him and buried itself in the worm's body. The worm yelped and spun, humping its body away from them with incredible speed. As it slithered away, a flick of its tail caught the edge of a statue, and squeezed it tightly—the statue exploded into dust, showering into the dry ornamental pool.

"By the Angel, it just crushed Sophocles," noted Will as the worm vanished behind a large structure shaped like a Greek temple. "Has no one respect for the classics these days?"

Gabriel, breathing hard, lowered his bow. "You *fool*," he said savagely to his brother. "What were you thinking, rushing up to him like that?"

Gideon whirled, pointing his bloody sword at Gabriel. "Not 'him.' *It.* That is not our father any longer, Gabriel. If you cannot countenance that fact—"

"I shot him with an arrow!" Gabriel shouted. "What more do you want of me, Gideon?"

Gideon shook his head as if disgusted with his brother; even Will, who did not like Gabriel, felt a twinge of sympathy for him. He *had* shot the beast.

"We must pursue it," said Gideon. "It has gone behind the folly—"

"The *what*?" said Will.

"A folly, Will," said Jem. "It is a decorative structure. I assume there is no real interior."

Gideon shook his head. "It is merely plaster. If we two were to go around one side of it, and you and James the other—"

"Cecily, *what* are you doing?" Will demanded, interrupting Gideon; he knew he sounded like a distracted parent, but he didn't care. Cecily had slid her blade into her belt and appeared to be trying to climb one of the small yew trees inside the first row of hedges. "Now is not the time for climbing trees!"

She looked toward him angrily, her black hair blowing across her face. She opened her mouth to answer, but before she could speak, there was a sound like an earthquake, and the folly burst apart in shards of plaster. The worm hurtled forth, heading straight toward them with the terrifying speed of an out-of-control train.

By the time they reached the front courtyard of Lightwood House, Tessa's neck and back were aching. She was tightly laced into her corset beneath the heavy wedding dress, and the weight of the sobbing Tatiana dragged down her left shoulder painfully.

She was relieved to see the carriages come into view—relieved, and also startled. The scene in the courtyard was so peaceful—the carriages where they had left them, the horses cropping grass, the facade of the house undisturbed. After half-carrying, half-dragging Tatiana to the first carriage, Tessa wrenched the door open and helped her in, wincing when the other girl's sharp nails dug into her shoulders as she heaved herself and her skirts into the space inside.

"Oh, God," Tatiana moaned. "The shame of it, the terrible shame. That the Clave might know of what has befallen my father. For pity's sake, could he not have thought of me, even for a moment?"

Tessa blinked. "That *thing*," she said. "I do not think it was capable of thinking of anyone, Mrs. Blackthorn."

Tatiana looked at her dizzily, and for a moment Tessa was ashamed of the resentment she had felt toward the other girl. She had not liked being sent away from the gardens, where she might perhaps have helped—but Tatiana had just seen her husband torn to pieces before her eyes by her own father. She was deserving of more sympathy than Tessa had been feeling.

Tessa made her voice more gentle. "I know you have had a bad shock. If you would lie down—"

"You are *very* tall," Tatiana said. "Do gentlemen complain of it?"

Tessa stared.

"And you are dressed as a bride," said Tatiana. "Is that not *very* odd? Would not gear suit the task better? I understand it is unflattering, and needs must as the devil drives, but—"

There was a sudden loud crash. Tessa detached herself

from the carriage and glanced about; the sound had come from inside the house. *Henry*, Tessa thought. Henry had gone into the house, alone. Of course, the creature was out in the gardens, but nevertheless—it was Benedict's house. She thought of the ballroom, full of demons the last time Tessa had been there, and she gathered up her skirts in both hands. "Remain here, Mrs. Blackthorn," she said. "I must discover the cause of that noise."

"No!" Tatiana sat bolt upright. "Do not leave me!"

"I am sorry." Tessa backed away, shaking her head. "I must. Please stay inside the carriage!"

Tatiana cried something after her, but Tessa had already turned to dash up the steps. She pushed her way through the front doors and emerged in a grand entryway floored with alternating squares of black and white marble, like a checkerboard. A massive chandelier hung from the ceiling, though none of its tapers were lit; the only light in the place came from the daylight flooding in through the high windows. A curving staircase of great grandeur wound its way upward. "Henry!" Tessa cried. "Henry, where are you?"

An answering cry and another crash came from the floor above. Tessa dashed up the stairs, stumbling as her foot caught on the hem of her dress and ripped a seam wide open. She switched the skirt out of the way impatiently and continued running, down a long corridor whose walls were painted powder blue and were hung with dozens of gilt-framed etchings, through a pair of doors, and into another room.

It was most assuredly a man's room, a library or an office: the curtains a heavy dark fabric, oil paintings of great ships of war hung on the walls. Rich green wallpaper covered the walls, though it appeared to be mottled with odd dark stains. There was a strange smell to the place—a smell like the one down by the banks of the Thames, where odd things rotted in the weak daylight. And laid over that, the coppery tang of blood. A bookcase had tipped over, a welter of smashed glass and broken wood, and on the Persian rug beside it was Henry, locked in a wrestling match with a *thing* with gray skin and an unnerving number of arms. Henry was yelling and kicking out with his long legs, and the thing—a demon, no doubt—was tearing at his gear with claws, it's wolflike snout snapping at his face.

Tessa looked around wildly, seized up the poker that lay by the dormant fireplace, and charged. She tried to keep her training in mind—all those hours of Gideon's careful talk of calibration and speed and grip—but in the end it seemed pure instinct to drive the long steel rod into the creature's torso, where there would have been a rib cage if it had been a real, earthly animal.

She heard *something* crunch as the weapon went in. The demon gave a howl like a baying dog and rolled off Henry, and the poker clattered to the floor. Black ichor sprayed, filling the room with the stench of smoke and rot. Tessa stumbled back, her heel catching on the torn edge of her gown. She fell to the ground just as Henry heaved himself over and, with a muttered curse, slashed the demon across the throat with a daggerlike blade that glowed with runes. The demon gave a gurgling cry and folded up like paper.

Henry lurched to his feet, his gingery hair matted with blood and ichor. His gear was torn at the shoulder, scarlet fluid leaking from the wound. "Tessa," he exclaimed, and then he was beside her, helping her to her feet. "By the Angel, we're a pair," he said in his rueful Henry way, looking at her worriedly. "You're not hurt, are you?"

She glanced down at herself and saw what he meant: Her dress was soaked with a spray of ichor, and there was an ugly cut on her forearm where she had fallen on the broken glass. It didn't hurt much, yet, but there was blood. "I am quite all right," she said. "What happened, Henry? What was that thing and why was it in here?"

"A guardian demon. I was searching Benedict's desk, and I must have moved or touched something that awoke it. A black smoke poured from the drawer, and became *that*. It lunged at me—"

"And clawed you," Tessa said in concern. "You're bleeding—"

"No, I did that myself. Fell on my dagger," Henry said sheepishly, drawing a stele from his belt. "Don't tell Charlotte."

Tessa almost smiled; then, remembering, she dashed across the room and tugged open the curtains across one of the tall windows. She could see out across the gardens, but not, frustratingly, the Italian garden; they were on the wrong side of the house for that. Green box hedges and flat grass, beginning to brown with winter, stretched out before her. "I must go," she said. "Will and Jem and Cecily—they were battling the creature. It has killed Tatiana Blackthorn's husband. I had to convey her back to the carriage as she was near fainting."

There was a silence. Then: "Tessa," Henry said in an odd voice, and she turned to see him, arrested in the act of applying an *iratze* to his inner arm. He was staring at the wall across from him—the wall Tessa had thought earlier was oddly mottled and splotched with stains. She saw now that they were no accidental mess. Letters a foot tall each stretched across the wallpaper, written in what looked like dried black blood.

THE INFERNAL DEVICES ARE WITHOUT PITY.
THE INFERNAL DEVICES ARE WITHOUT REGRET.
THE INFERNAL DEVICES ARE WITHOUT NUMBER.
THE INFERNAL DEVICES WILL NEVER STOP COMING.

And there, beneath the scrawls, a last sentence, barely readable, as if whoever had written it had been losing the use of his hands. She pictured Benedict locked in this room, going slowly mad as he transformed, smearing the words on the wall with his own ichor-ridden blood.

MAY GOD HAVE MERCY ON OUR SOULS.

The worm lunged—and Will dived forward into a roll, narrowly missing its snapping jaws. He came up into a crouch, then to his feet, and raced along the length of the creature until he reached its thrashing tail. He whirled around and saw the demon looming like a cobra over Gideon and Gabriel—though, to his surprise, it seemed to have frozen, hissing but not attacking. Did it recognize its children? Feel anything for them? It was impossible to tell.

Cecily was halfway up the yew tree, clinging to a branch.

Hoping that she would see sense and stay there, Will spun toward Jem and held up a hand so his *parabatai* could see him. They had long ago worked out a series of gestures they used to communicate what they needed in the midst of battle, in case they could not hear each other's voices. Jem's eyes lit with understanding, and he tossed his cane toward Will. In a perfect throw it sailed end over end till Will caught it in one hand and clicked the handle. The blade shot out, and Will brought it down swift and hard, cleaving straight through the creature's thick skin. The worm jerked back and howled as Will struck again, parting its tail from its body. Benedict thrashed at both ends, and ichor gushed forth in a sticky blast, coating Will. He ducked away with a shout, his skin burning.

"*Will!*" Jem darted toward him. Gideon and Gabriel were slashing at the worm's head, doing their best to keep its attention focused on them. As Will wiped burning ichor from his eyes with his free hand, Cecily dropped from the yew tree and landed squarely on the worm's back.

Will dropped the sword-cane in shock. He had never done that before, never dropped a weapon in the middle of a battle, but there was his little sister, clinging with grim determination to the back of a massive demon worm, like a tiny flea clinging to the fur of a dog. As he stared in horror, Cecily yanked a dagger from her belt and drove it viciously into the demon's flesh.

What does she think she's doing? As if that tiny dagger could kill a thing that size! "Will, Will," Jem was saying in his ear, his voice urgent, and Will realized he had spoken aloud, and, name of the Angel, the worm's head was swinging around toward Cecily, its mouth open and vast and lined with teeth—

Cecily let go of the dagger's handle and rolled sideways, off the body of the worm. Its jaws missed her by a hairsbreadth and snapped viciously shut on its own body. Black ichor gushed and the worm jerked its head back, a howl like the wail of a banshee erupting from its throat. A massive wound gaped in its side, and gobbets of its own flesh hung from its jaws. As Will stared, Gabriel raised his bow and let an arrow fly.

It sang home to its target and buried itself in one of the worm's lidless black eyes. The creature reared back—and then its head sagged forward and it crumpled in on itself, folding up, disappearing as demons did when the life left them.

Gabriel's bow fell to the ground with a clatter that Will barely heard. The trampled ground was soaked with blood from the worm's savaged body. In the midst of it all, Cecy was rising slowly to her feet, wincing, her right wrist twisted at an odd angle.

Will did not even feel himself begin to run toward her—he realized it only when he was brought up short by Jem's restraining hand. He turned on his *parabatai* wildly. "My *sister*—"

"Your *face*," replied Jem, with remarkable calm, considering the situation. "You are covered in demon blood, William, and it is burning you. I must give you an *iratze* before the damage cannot be undone."

"Let me go," Will insisted, and tried to pull away, but Jem's cool hand was cupping the back of his neck, and then there was the burn of a stele on his wrist, and the pain he had not even known he was feeling began to ebb. Jem let go of him with a small hiss of pain of his own; he had gotten some of the ichor on his fingers. Will paused, irresolute—but Jem waved him away, already applying his own stele to his hand.

It was only a moment's delay, but by the time Will reached his sister's side, Gabriel had gotten there first. Gabriel had his hand under her chin, his green eyes flicking over her face. She was looking up at him with astonishment, when Will arrived and caught her by the shoulder.

"Get *away* from my sister," he barked, and Gabriel stepped back, his mouth thinning into a hard line. Gideon was hard on his heels, and they swarmed around Cecily as Will held her fast with one hand, drawing his stele with the other. She looked at him with flashing blue eyes as he carved a black *iratze* against one side of her throat, and a *mendelin* on the other. Her black hair had escaped from its braid, and she looked like the wild girl he remembered, fierce and unafraid of anything.

"Are you hurt, *cariad?*" The word slipped out before he could stop it—a childhood endearment he had almost forgotten.

"*Cariad?*" she echoed, her eyes flashing disbelief. "I am quite unhurt."

"Not quite," Will said, indicating her injured wrist and gashes on her face and hands, which had begun to close up as the *iratze* did its work. Anger swirled up inside him, so much that he did not hear Jem, behind him, begin to cough—usually a sound that would have lit him to action like a spark thrown into dry tinder. "Cecily, what could you possibly have been—"

"That was one of the bravest things I've seen a Shadowhunter do," interrupted Gabriel. He was not looking at Will but at Cecily, with a mixture of surprise and something else in his expression. There was mud and blood in his hair, as there was on all of them, but his green eyes were very bright.

Cecily flushed. "I was only—"

She broke off, her eyes widening as she looked past Will. Jem coughed again, and this time Will heard it; he turned just in time to see his *parabatai* slump to his knees on the ground.

3

To the Last Hour

Not, I'll not, carrion comfort, Despair, not feast on thee;
Not untwist—slack they may be—these last strands of man
In me or, most weary, cry I can no more. I can;
Can something, hope, wish day come, not choose not to be.
—Gerard Manley Hopkins, "Carrion Comfort"

Jem was leaning against the side of the Institute's carriage, his eyes closed, his face as pale as paper. Will stood beside him, his hand tightly gripping Jem's shoulder. Tessa knew as she hurried toward them that it was not just a brotherly gesture. His grip would be much of what was keeping Jem upright.

She and Henry had heard the dying scream of the worm. Gabriel had found them, what felt like moments later, racing down the front steps. He had told them breathlessly of the death of the creature, and then of what had happened to Jem, and everything for Tessa had gone white, as if she had been struck suddenly and hard across the face.

They were words she had not heard in a long time, but half-expected always, and dreamed of sometimes in nightmares that left her bolting upright, fighting for air—"Jem," "collapse," "breathing," "blood," "Will," "Will is with him," "Will—"

Of course Will was with him.

The others were swarming about, the Lightwood brothers with their sister, and even Tatiana was quiet, or perhaps Tessa simply could not hear her hysterics. Tessa was aware of Cecily nearby as well, and Henry standing awkwardly beside her, as if he wished to comfort her but did not know how to begin.

Will's eyes met Tessa's as she came closer, almost tripping again over her torn gown. For a moment they were in perfect understanding. Jem was what they could still look each other straight in the eye about. On the topic of Jem they were both fierce and unyielding. Tessa saw Will's hand tighten on Jem's sleeve. "She's here," he said.

Jem's eyes opened slowly. Tessa fought to keep the look of shock from her face. His pupils were blown out, his irises a thin ring of silver around the black. *"Ni shou shang le ma, quin ai de?"* he whispered.

Jem had been teaching Tessa Mandarin, at her insistence. She understood *"quin ai de,"* at least, if not the rest. *My dear, my darling.* She reached for his hand, squeezed it. "Jem . . ."

"Are you hurt, my love?" Will said. His voice was as level as his eyes, and for a moment the blood came up in Tessa's cheeks and she glanced down at her hand where it held Jem's; his fingers were paler than hers, like a doll's hands, made of porcelain. How had she not seen he was so ill?

"Thank you for the translation, Will," she answered, not looking away from her fiancé. Jem and Will were both splattered with black ichor, but Jem's chin and throat were also stained with flecks of red blood. His own blood.

"I am not hurt," Tessa whispered, and then she thought, *No, this will not do, not at all. Be strong for him.* She straightened her shoulders, keeping her grip on Jem's hand. "Where is his medicine?" she demanded of Will. "Did he not take it before we left the Institute?"

"Do not talk about me as if I am not here," Jem said, but there was no anger in it. He turned his head to the side and said something, softly, under his breath to Will, who nodded and let go of his shoulder. Tessa could sense the tension in Will's posture; he was poised, catlike, to seize Jem again if the other boy should slip or fall, but Jem remained standing. "I am stronger when Tessa is here, you see. I told it to you," said Jem, still in the same soft voice.

At that, Will did duck his head so that Tessa could not see his eyes. "I see it," he said. "Tessa, there is none of his medicine here. I believe he left the Institute without taking enough of it, though he will not admit it. Ride back to the Institute with him in the carriage, and watch over him—someone must."

Jem took a rough breath. "The others—"

"I will drive for you. It will be little trouble; Balios and Xanthos know the way. Henry can drive the Lightwoods." Will was brisk and efficient, too brisk and efficient to even be thanked; he did not seem as if he wanted it. He helped Tessa get Jem into the carriage, very careful not to brush her shoulder or touch her hand as he did. He moved to tell the others what was happening. She caught a bit of Henry explaining that he needed to remove Benedict's record books from the house, before she reached to swing the carriage door closed, shutting herself and Jem into a welcome silence.

"What was inside the house?" Jem asked as they rattled through the open gate bordering the Lightwoods' property. He still looked ghastly, his head back against the cushions of the carriage, his eyes at half-mast, his cheekbones shining with fever. "I heard Henry speaking of Benedict's study . . ."

"He had gone mad in there," she said, chafing his cold hands between hers. "In the days before he transformed, when Gabriel said he would not leave the room, his mind must have gone. He had scrawled on the wall in what looked like blood, sentences about 'the Infernal Devices.' That they had no pity, that they would never stop coming—"

"He must have meant the automaton army."

"He must have." Tessa shivered slightly, and moved closer to Jem. "I suppose it was foolish of me—but it has been so peaceful for these past two months—"

"You had forgotten about Mortmain?"

"No. Never forgotten." She glanced toward the window, though she could not see out; she had drawn the curtains when the light had seemed to be hurting Jem's eyes. "Hoped, perhaps, that he might have turned his mind elsewhere."

"We do not know that he hasn't." Jem's fingers wrapped around hers. "Benedict's death is a tragedy perhaps, but those wheels were set in motion long ago. This has nothing to do with you."

"There were other items in the library. Notes and books of Benedict's. Journals. Henry is bringing them back to the

Institute to study. My name was in them." Tessa stopped herself; how could she trouble Jem with these things when he was so unwell?

As if Jem were reading her mind, his finger moved over her wrist, resting lightly on her pulse point. "Tessa, it is only a passing attack. It will not last. I would rather you told me the truth, all the truth, whether it is bitter or frightening, that I might share it with you. I would never let harm come to you, nor would any in the Institute." He smiled. "Your pulse is quickening."

The truth, all the truth, whether it is bitter or frightening. "I love you," she said.

He looked at her with a light in his thin face that made it more beautiful. *"Wo xi wang ni ming tian ke yi jia gei wo."*

"You . . ." She drew her brows together. "You want to get married? But we are already engaged. I do not think one can get engaged twice."

He laughed, which turned into a cough; Tessa's whole body tightened, but the cough was slight, and there was no blood. "I said I would marry you tomorrow if I could."

Tessa pretended to toss her head. "Tomorrow is not convenient for me, sir."

"But you are already appropriately attired," he said with a smile.

Tessa looked down at the ruined gold of her wedding dress. "If I were getting married in a slaughterhouse," she allowed. "Ah, well. I did not like this one very much as it was. Much too gaudy."

"I thought you looked beautiful." His voice was soft.

Tessa laid her head against his shoulder. "There will be

another time," she said. "Another day, another dress. A time when you are well and everything is perfect."

His voice was still gentle, but it held a terrible weariness. "There is no such thing as perfect, Tessa."

Sophie was standing at the window of her small bedroom, the curtain drawn back, her eyes fixed on the courtyard. It had been hours since the carriages had gone rattling away, and she was meant to be sweeping out the grates, but the brush and bucket were motionless at her feet.

She could hear Bridget's voice drifting softly up from the kitchen below:

> *"Earl Richard had a daughter;*
> *A comely maid was she.*
> *And she laid her love on Sweet William,*
> *Though not of his degree."*

Sometimes, when Bridget was in a particularly melodious mood, Sophie thought about stalking downstairs and pushing her into the oven like the witch in "Hansel and Gretel." But Charlotte would certainly not approve. Even if Bridget *were* singing about forbidden love between the social classes just at the same moment that Sophie was cursing herself for clutching the curtain fabric tightly in her hand, seeing gray-green eyes in her mind as she wondered and worried—Would Gideon be all right? Was he hurt? Could he fight his father? And how dreadful if he had to—

The gates of the Institute creaked open, and a carriage rattled inside; Will was driving. Sophie recognized him, hatless, his black hair wild in the wind. He leaped down from the driver's seat and came around to help Tessa out of the carriage—even at this distance Sophie could see that a bleak wreck had been made of her golden gown—and then Jem, leaning heavily on his *parabatai*'s shoulder.

Sophie sucked in her breath. Though she no longer fancied herself in love with Jem, she still cared for him a great deal. It was hard not to, considering his openheartedness, his sweetness and graciousness. He had never been anything but exquisitely kind to her. She had been relieved over the past months that he had not had one of his "bad spells," as Charlotte called them—that though happiness had not healed him, he had seemed to be stronger, better. . . .

The threesome had disappeared inside the Institute. Cyril had come from the stables and was dealing with the whickering Balios and Xanthos. Sophie took a deep breath and let the curtain fall away from her hand. Charlotte might need her, want her, to assist with Jem. If there was anything she could do . . . She pulled herself away from the window and hurried out into the corridor and down the narrow servants' stairs.

In the hall downstairs she met Tessa, ashen and pinched-looking, hesitating just outside Jem's bedroom. Through the partly open door Sophie could see Charlotte bending over Jem, who was sitting on the bed; Will leaned by the fireplace, his arms crossed, tension clear in every line of his body. Tessa raised her head as she saw Sophie, a little of the color coming back into her face. "Sophie," she cried softly. "Sophie, Jem isn't well. He's had another . . . another bout of illness."

"It will be all right, Miss Tessa. I've seen him very ill before, and he always comes through it, right as rain."

Tessa closed her eyes. The shadows beneath them were gray. She did not need to say what they were both thinking, that one day there would be a time when he would have an attack and he would not come through it.

"I ought to be fetching hot water," Sophie added, "and cloths—"

"I should be fetching those things," said Tessa. "And I would, but Charlotte says that I must change out of this dress, that demon blood can be dangerous if it too greatly encounters the skin. She sent Bridget for cloths and poultices, and Brother Enoch will arrive at any moment. And Jem will not hear otherwise, but—"

"That is enough," Sophie said firmly. "You will do him no good at all if you let yourself become ill as well. I will help you with the dress. Come, let us manage it, and quickly."

Tessa's eyes fluttered open. "Dear sensible Sophie. Of course you are right." She began to move across the corridor, toward her room. At the door she paused, and turned to look at Sophie. Her wide gray eyes searched the other girl's face, and she seemed to nod to herself, as if she had been proved right in a guess. "*He* is all right, you know. Not hurt at all."

"Master Jem?"

Tessa shook her head. "Gideon Lightwood."

Sophie blushed.

Gabriel wasn't sure quite why he was in the Institute's drawing room, except that his brother had told him to come here and wait, and even after everything that had happened, he was still used to doing what Gideon said. He was surprised at how plain the room was, nothing like the grand drawing rooms in either the Lightwoods' Pimlico house or the one in Chiswick. The walls were papered with a faded print of cabbage roses, the surface of the desk stained with ink and scarred with the marks of letter openers and pen nibs, and the grate was sooty. Over the fireplace hung a water-blotched mirror, framed in gilt.

Gabriel glanced at his own reflection. His gear was torn at the neck, and there was a red mark on his jaw where a long graze was in the process of healing. There was blood all over his gear—*Your own blood, or your father's blood?*

He pushed the thought away quickly. It was odd, he thought, how he was the one who looked like their mother, Barbara. She had been tall and inclined toward slenderness, with curling brown hair and eyes he remembered as the purest green, like the grass that sloped down toward the river behind the house. Gideon looked like their father: broad and stocky, with eyes more gray than green. Which was ironic, because Gabriel was the one who had inherited their father's temperament: headstrong and quick to anger, slow to forgive. Gideon and Barbara were more peacemakers, quiet and steady, faithful in their beliefs. They were both much more like—

Charlotte Branwell came in through the open door of the drawing room in a loose dress, her eyes as bright as a small bird's. Whenever Gabriel saw her, he was struck by how small she was, how he towered over her. What had Consul Wayland been thinking, giving this tiny creature power over the Institute and all the Shadowhunters of London?

"Gabriel." She inclined her head. "Your brother says you were not hurt."

"I'm quite all right," he said shortly, and immediately

knew he had sounded rude. He had not meant to, precisely. His father had drilled into his head for years now what a fool Charlotte was, how useless and easily influenced, and though he knew his brother disagreed—disagreed enough to come and live in this place and leave his family behind—it was a hard lesson to put aside. "I thought you would be with Carstairs."

"Brother Enoch has arrived, with another of the Silent Brothers. They have banned us all from Jem's room. Will is pacing outside in the corridor like a caged panther. Poor boy." Charlotte looked at Gabriel briefly before walking to the fireplace. In her glance was a look of keen intelligence, quickly masked by the lowering of her eyelashes. "But enough of that. I understand that your sister has already been delivered to the Blackthorns' residence in Kensington," she said. "Is there someone you would like me to send a message to for you?"

"A—message?"

She paused before the fireplace, clasping her hands behind her back. "You need to go somewhere, Gabriel, unless you want me to turn you out of doors with only the key of the streets to your name."

Turn me out of doors? Was this horrible woman actually throwing him out of the Institute? He thought of what his father had always told him: *The Fairchilds don't care about anyone but themselves and the Law.* "I—the house in Pimlico—"

"The Consul will shortly be informed of all that transpired at Lightwood House," said Charlotte. "Both of your family's London residences will be confiscated in the name of the Clave, at least until they can be searched and it can be determined that your father left nothing behind that could provide the Council with clues."

"Clues to *what?*"

"To your father's plans," she said, unfazed. "To his connection to Mortmain, his knowledge of Mortmain's plans. To the Infernal Devices."

"I've never even heard of the bloody Infernal Devices," Gabriel protested, and then blushed. He had sworn, and in front of a lady. Not that Charlotte was quite like any other lady.

"I believe you," she said. "I don't know if Consul Wayland will, but that is your lookout. If you will give me an address—"

"I haven't *got* one," Gabriel said, in desperation. "Where do you think I could go?"

She just looked at him, one eyebrow raised.

"I want to stay with my brother," he said finally, aware that he sounded petulant and angry, but not quite sure what to do about it.

"But your brother lives here," she said. "And you have made your feelings about the Institute and about my claim to it very clear. Jem told me what you believe. That my father drove your uncle to suicide. It isn't true, you know, but I don't expect you to believe me. It does leave me wondering, however, why you would wish to remain here."

"The Institute is a refuge."

"Was your father planning on running it as a refuge?"

"I don't know! I don't know what his plans are—what they were!"

"Then why did you go along with them?" Her voice was soft but merciless.

"Because he was my *father!*" Gabriel shouted. He spun away from Charlotte, his breath becoming ragged in his throat. Only barely aware of what he was doing, he wrapped his arms around himself, hugging his own body tight, as if he could keep himself from coming undone.

Memories of the past few weeks, memories that Gabriel had been doing his best to press back into the very recesses of his mind, threatened to burst out into the light: weeks in the house after the servants had been sent away, hearing the noises coming from the upstairs rooms, screams in the night, blood on the stairs in the morning, Father shouting gibberish from behind the locked library door, as if he could no longer form words in English . . .

"If you are going to throw me out on the street," Gabriel said, with a sort of terrible desperation, "then do it now. I do not want to think I have got a home when I have not. I do not want to think I am going to see my brother again if I am not going to."

"You think he would not go after you? Find you wherever you were?"

"I think he has proved who he cares for most," said Gabriel, "and it is not me." He slowly straightened, loosing his grip on himself. "Send me away or let me stay. I will not beg you."

Charlotte sighed. "You will not have to," she said. "Never before have I sent away anyone who told me they had nowhere else to go, and I will not start now. I will ask of you only one thing. To allow someone to live in the Institute, in the very heart of the Enclave, is to place my trust in their good intentions. Do not make me regret that I have trusted you, Gabriel Lightwood."

The shadows had lengthened in the library. Tessa sat in a pool of light by one of the windows, beside a shaded blue lamp. A book had been open on her lap for several hours, but she had not been able to concentrate on it. Her eyes skidded over the words on the pages without absorbing them, and she would often find that she was pausing to try to remember who a character was, or why they were doing what they were doing.

She was in the middle of beginning chapter five yet again when the creak of a floorboard alerted her, and she looked up to find Will standing before her, damp-haired, his gloves in his hands.

"Will." Tessa set the book down on the windowsill beside her. "You startled me."

"I didn't mean to interrupt," he said in a low voice. "If you are reading . . ." He began to turn away.

"I am not," she said, and he stopped, looking back at her over his shoulder. "I cannot lose myself in words now. I cannot calm the distraction of my mind."

"Nor I," he said, turning fully now. He was no longer spattered in blood. His clothes were clean, and his skin mostly unmarked, though she could see the pinkish-white lines of grazes on his neck, disappearing down into the collar of his shirt, healing as the *iratzes* did their work.

"Is there news of my—is there news of Jem?"

"There is no change," he said, though she had guessed as much. If there had been a change, Will would not have been here. "The Brothers will still not let anyone into the room, not even Charlotte.

"And why are you here?" he went on. "Sitting in the dark?"

"Benedict wrote on the wall of his study," she said in a low voice. "Before he turned into that creature, I imagine, or while it was happening. I don't know. 'The Infernal Devices are without pity. The Infernal Devices are without regret. The Infernal Devices are without number. The Infernal Devices will never stop coming.'"

"The infernal devices? I assume he means Mortmain's clockwork creatures. Not that we have seen any of them for months."

"That does not mean they will not come back," Tessa said. She looked down at the library table, its scratched veneer. How often Will and Jem must have sat here together, studying, carving their initials, as bored schoolboys did, into the table's surface. "I am a danger to you here."

"Tessa, we have talked about this before. You are not the danger. You are the thing Mortmain wants, yes, but if you were not here and protected, he could get you easily, and to what destruction would he turn your powers? We don't know—only that he wants you for something, and that it is to our advantage to keep you from him. It is not selflessness. We Shadowhunters are not selfless."

She looked up at that. "I think you are very selfless." At his noise of disagreement she said: "Surely you must know that what you do is exemplary. There is a coldness to the Clave, it is true. *We are dust and shadows.* But you are like the heroes of ancient times, like Achilles and Jason."

"Achilles was murdered with a poisoned arrow, and Jason died alone, killed by his own rotting ship. Such is the fate of heroes; the Angel knows why anyone would want to be one."

Tessa looked at him. There were shadows under his blue eyes, she saw, and his fingers were worrying at the material of his cuffs, thoughtlessly, as if he were not aware he was doing it. Months, she thought. Months since they had been alone together for more than a moment. They'd had only accidental encounters in hallways, in the courtyard, awkwardly exchanged pleasantries. She had missed his jokes, the books he had lent her, the flashes of laughter in his gaze. Caught in the memory of the easier Will of an earlier time, she spoke without thinking:

"I cannot stop recollecting something you told me once," she said.

He looked at her in surprise. "Yes? And what is that?"

"That sometimes when you cannot decide what to do, you pretend you are a character in a book, because it is easier to decide what they would do."

"I am," Will said, "perhaps, not someone to take advice from if you are seeking happiness."

"Not happiness. Not exactly. I want to help—to do good—" She broke off and sighed. "And I have turned to many books, but if there is guidance in them, I have not found it. You said you were Sydney Carton—"

Will made a sound, and sank down onto a chair on the opposite side of the table from her. His lashes were lowered, veiling his eyes.

"And I suppose I know what that makes the rest of us," she said. "But I do not want to be Lucie Manette, for she did nothing to save Charles; she let Sydney do it all. And she was cruel to him."

"To Charles?" Will said.

"To Sydney," Tessa said. "He wanted to be a better man, but she would not help him."

"She could not. She was engaged to Charles Darney."

"Still, it was not kind," Tessa said.

Will threw himself out of his chair as quickly as he had thrown himself into it. He leaned forward, his hands on the table. His eyes were very blue in the blue light of the lamp. "Sometimes one must choose whether to be kind or honorable," he said. "Sometimes one cannot be both."

"Which is better?" Tessa whispered.

Will's mouth twisted with bitter humor. "I suppose it depends on the book."

Tessa craned her head back to look at him. "You know that feeling," she said, "when you are reading a book, and you know that it is going to be a tragedy; you can feel the cold and darkness coming, see the net drawing close around the characters who live and breathe on the pages. But you are tied to the story as if being dragged behind a carriage, and you cannot let go or turn the course aside." His blue eyes were dark with understanding—of course Will would understand—and she hurried on. "I feel now as if the same is happening, only not to characters on a page but to my own beloved friends and companions. I do not want to sit by while tragedy comes for us. I would turn it aside, only I struggle to discover how that might be done."

"You fear for Jem," Will said.

"Yes," she said. "And I fear for you, too."

"No," Will said hoarsely. "Don't waste that on me, Tess."

Before she could reply, the library door opened. It was Charlotte, looking drained and exhausted. Will turned toward her quickly.

"How is Jem?" he said.

"He is awake and talking," said Charlotte. "He has had some of the *yin fen*, and the Silent Brothers have been able to make his condition stable, and to stop the internal bleeding."

At the mention of internal bleeding, Will looked as if he were going to throw up; Tessa imagined she looked much the same.

"He can have a visitor," Charlotte went on. "In fact, he has requested it."

Will and Tessa exchanged a quick glance. Tessa knew what both were thinking: Which of them should the visitor be? Tessa was Jem's fiancée, but Will was his *parabatai*, which was sacred in and of itself. Will had begun to step back, when Charlotte spoke again, sounding tired down to her bones:

"He has asked for you, Will."

Will looked startled. He darted a glance at Tessa. "I—"

Tessa could not deny the little burst of surprise and almost-jealousy she had felt behind her rib cage at Charlotte's words, but she pushed it down ruthlessly. She loved Jem enough to want whatever he wanted for himself, and he always had his reasons. "You go," she said gently. "Of course he would want to see you."

Will began to move toward the door to join Charlotte. Halfway there he turned back and crossed the room to Tessa. "Tessa," he said, "while I am with Jem, would you do something for me?"

Tessa looked up and swallowed. He was too close, too close: All the lines, shapes, angles of Will filled her field of vision as the sound of his voice filled her ears. "Yes, certainly," she said. "What is it?"

* * *

To: Edmund and Branwen Herondale
Ravenscar Manor
West Riding, Yorkshire

Dear Dad and Mam,

I know it was cowardly of me to have left as I did, in the early morning before you woke, with only a note to explain my absence. I could not bear to face you, knowing what I had decided to do, and that I was the worst of disobedient daughters.

How can I explain the decision I made, how I arrived at it? It seems, even now, like madness. Each day in fact is madder than the one before it. You did not lie, Dad, when you said the life of a Shadowhunter was like a feverish dream—

Cecily drew the nib of the pen viciously through the lines she had written, then crumpled up the paper in one hand and rested her head on the desk.

She had started this letter so many times, and had yet to arrive at any satisfactory version. Perhaps she should not be attempting it now, she thought, not when she had been trying to calm her nerves since they had returned to the Institute. Everyone had been swarming about Jem, and Will, after roughly checking her for injuries in the garden, had barely spoken to her again. Henry had gone running for Charlotte, Gideon had drawn Gabriel aside, and Cecily had found herself climbing the Institute stairs alone.

She had slipped into her bedroom, not bothering to divest herself of her gear, and curled up on the soft four-poster bed. As she'd lain among the shadows, hearing the faint sounds of London passing by outside, her heart had clenched with sudden, painful homesickness. She'd thought of the green hills of Wales, and of her mother and father, and had bolted out of the bed as if she had been pushed, stumbling to the desk and taking up pen and paper, the ink staining her fingers in her haste. And yet the right words would not come. She felt as if she bled her regret and her loneliness from her very pores, and yet she could not shape those feelings into any sentiment she could imagine her parents could bear reading.

At that moment there was a knock on the door. Cecily reached for a book she had left resting on the desk, propped it up as if she had been reading, and called: "Come in."

The door swung open; it was Tessa, standing hesitantly in the doorway. She was no longer wearing her destroyed wedding dress but a simple gown of blue muslin with her two necklaces glittering at her throat: the clockwork angel and the jade pendant that had been her bridal gift from Jem. Cecily looked at Tessa curiously. Though the two girls were friendly, they were not close. Tessa had a certain wariness around her that Cecily suspected the source of without ever being able to prove it; on top of that there was something fey and strange about her. Cecily knew she could shape-shift, could transform herself into the likeness of any person, and Cecily could not rid herself of the sense that it was unnatural. How could you know someone's true face if they could change it as easily as someone else might change a gown?

"Yes?" Cecily said. "Miss Gray?"

"Please call me Tessa," said the other girl, shutting the door behind her. It was not the first time she had asked Cecily to call her by her given name, but habit and perversity kept Cecily from doing it. "I came to see if you were all right and if you needed anything."

"Ah." Cecily felt a slight pang of disappointment. "I am quite all right."

Tessa moved forward slightly. "Is that *Great Expectations*?"

"Yes." Cecily did not say that she had seen Will reading it, and had picked it up to try to gain insight into what he was thinking. So far she was woefully lost. Pip was morbid, and Estella so awful that Cecily wanted to shake her.

"'Estella,'" Tessa said softly. "'To the last hour of my life, you cannot choose but remain part of my character, part of the little good in me, part of the evil.'"

"So you memorize passages of books, just like Will? Or is this a favorite?"

"I don't have Will's memory," said Tessa, coming forward slightly. "Or his *mnemosyne* rune. But I do love that book." Her gray eyes searched Cecily's face. "Why are you still in your gear?"

"I was thinking of going up to the training room," Cecily said. "I find I can think well there, and it isn't as if anyone minds one way or the other what I do."

"More training? Cecily, you've just been in a battle!" Tessa protested. "I know it can sometimes take more than one application of runes to entirely heal— Before you start training again, I should call someone to you: Charlotte, or—"

"Or Will?" Cecily snapped. "If either of them cared, they would have come already."

Tessa paused by the bedside. "You cannot think Will doesn't care about you."

"He isn't here, is he?"

"He sent me," Tessa said, "because he is with Jem," as if that explained everything. Cecily supposed that in a way it did. She knew that Will and Jem were close friends, but also that it was more than that. She had read of *parabatai* in the *Codex*, and knew that the bond was one that did not exist among mundanes, something closer than brothers and better than blood. "Jem is his *parabatai*. He has made a vow to be there in times like this."

"He would be there, vow or not. He would be there for *any* of you. But he has not so much as come by to see if I needed another *iratze*."

"Cecy . . . ," Tessa began. "Will's curse—"

"It wasn't a real curse!"

"You know," Tessa said thoughtfully, "in its way, it was. He believed no one could love him, and that if he allowed them to, it would result in their death. That is why he left you all. He left you to keep you safe, and here you are now—the very definition, to him, of *not* safe. He cannot bear to come and look at your injuries, because to him it is as if he had put them there himself."

"I chose this. Shadowhunting. And not only because I wanted to be with Will."

"I know that," Tessa said. "But I also sat with Will while he was delirious from exposure to vampire blood, choking on holy water, and I know the name he called out. It was yours."

Cecily looked up in surprise. "Will called out for me?"

"Oh, yes." A small smile touched the edge of Tessa's mouth. "He wouldn't tell me who you were, of course, when

I asked him, and it drove me half-mad—" She broke off, and looked away.

"Why?"

"Curiosity," said Tessa with a shrug, though there was a flush on her cheekbones. "It's my besetting sin. In any event, he loves you. I know that with Will everything is backward and upside down, but the fact that he *isn't* here is only further proof to me of how precious you are to him. He is used to pushing away everyone he loves, and the more he loves you, the more he will violently try not to show it."

"But there is no curse—"

"The habits of years are not unlearned so quickly," Tessa said, and her eyes were sad. "Do not make the mistake of believing that he does not love you because he plays at not caring, Cecily. Confront him if you must and demand the truth, but do not make the mistake of turning away because you believe that he is a lost cause. Do not cast him from your heart. For if you do, you will regret it."

To: Members of the Council
From: Consul Josiah Wayland

Forgive the delay in my reply, gentlemen. I wished to be sure that I was not giving you my opinions in any spirit of precipitate haste, but rather that my words were the sound and well-reasoned results of patient thought.

I am afraid I cannot second your recommendation of Charlotte Branwell as my successor. Though possessed of a good heart, she is altogether too flighty, emotional, passionate, and disobedient to have the mak-

ing of a Consul. As we know, the fair sex has its weak-nesses that men are not heir to, and sadly she is prey to all of them. No, I cannot recommend her. I urge you to consider another—my own nephew, George Penhallow, who will be twenty-five this November and is a fine Shadowhunter and an upstanding young man. I believe he has the moral certainty and strength of character to lead the Shadowhunters into a new decade.

In Raziel's name,
Consul Josiah Wayland

4

TO BE WISE AND LOVE

For to be wise and love
Exceeds man's might.
—Shakespeare, *Troilus and Cressida*

"I thought you'd at least make a song out of it," said Jem.

Will looked at his *parabatai* curiously. Jem, though he had asked for Will, did not seem in a forthcoming mood. He was sitting quietly on the edge of his bed in a clean shirt and trousers, though the shirt was loose and made him look thinner than ever. There were still flecks of dried blood around his collarbones, a sort of brutal necklace. "Make a song out of what?"

Jem's mouth quirked. "Our defeat of the worm?" he said. "After all those jokes you made . . ."

"I have not been in a joking mood, these past few hours,"

Will said, his eyes flicking to the bloody rags that covered the nightstand by the bed, the bowl half-full of pinkish fluid.

"Don't fuss, Will," Jem said. "Everyone's been fussing over me and I can't abide it; I wanted you because—because you wouldn't. You make me laugh."

Will threw his arms up. "Oh, all right," he said. "How's this?

> *"Forsooth, I no longer toil in vain,*
> *To prove that demon pox warps the brain.*
> *So though 'tis pity, it's not in vain*
> *That the pox-ridden worm was slain:*
> *For to believe in me, you all must deign."*

Jem burst out laughing. "Well, that was awful."

"It was impromptu!"

"Will, there is such a thing as *scansion*—" Between one moment and the next Jem's laughter turned into a fit of coughing. Will darted forward as Jem doubled up, his thin shoulders heaving. Blood splattered the bed's white coverlet.

"Jem —"

With a hand, Jem gestured toward the box on his nightstand. Will reached for it; the delicately drawn woman on the lid, pouring water from a jug, was intimately familiar to him. He hated the sight of her.

He snapped the box open—and froze. What looked like a light dusting of silvery powdered sugar barely covered the wooden bottom. Perhaps there had been a greater quantity before the Silent Brothers had treated Jem; Will did not know. What he did know was that there should have remained much,

much more. "Jem," he said in a strangled voice, "how is this all there is?"

Jem had stopped coughing. There was blood on his lips, and as Will watched, too shocked to move, Jem raised his arm and scrubbed the blood from his face with his sleeve. The linen was instantly scarlet. He looked feverish, his pale skin glowing, though he showed no other outward sign of agitation.

"Will," he said softly.

"Two months ago," Will began, realized his voice was rising, and forced it down again with an effort. "Two months ago I purchased enough *yin fen* that it should have lasted a year."

There was a mixture of challenge and sadness in Jem's glance. "I have accelerated the process of taking it."

"Accelerated it? By how much?"

Now Jem did not meet his gaze. "I have been taking twice, perhaps three times, as much."

"But the rate at which you take the drug is tied to the deterioration of your health," Will said, and when Jem said nothing back, his voice rose and cracked on a single word: "*Why?*"

"I do not want to live half a life—"

"At this rate you won't even live a fifth of one!" shouted Will, and he sucked in his breath. Jem's expression had changed, and Will had to slam the box he was holding back onto the nightstand to keep himself from punching the wall.

Jem was sitting up straight, his eyes blazing. "There is more to living than *not dying*," he said. "Look at the way you live, Will. You burn as bright as a star. I had been taking only enough of the drug to keep me alive but not enough to keep me *well*. A little extra of the drug before battles, perhaps, to give me energy, but otherwise, a half life, a gray twilight of a life—"

"But you have changed your dosage now? Has this been since the engagement?" Will demanded. "Is this because of Tessa?"

"You cannot blame her for this. This was my decision. She has no knowledge of it."

"She would want you to live, James—"

"*I am not going to live!*" And Jem was on his feet, his cheeks flushed; it was the angriest, Will thought, that he had ever seen him. "I am not going to live, and I can choose to be as much for her as I can be, to burn as brightly for her as I wish, and for a shorter time, than to burden her with someone only half-alive for a longer time. It is my choice, William, and you cannot make it for me."

"Maybe I can. I have always been the one to buy your *yin fen* for you—"

The color went in Jem's face. "If you refuse to do it, I will buy it on my own. I have always been willing. You said you wished to be the one who bought it. And as to that—" He pulled the Carstairs family ring from his finger and held it out to Will. "Take it."

Will let his eyes drift down toward it, and then up to Jem's face. A dozen awful things he could say, or do, went through his mind. One did not slough off a persona so quickly, he had found. He had pretended to be cruel for so many years that the pretense was still what he reached for first, as a man might absently turn his carriage toward the home he had lived in for all his life, despite the fact that he had recently moved. "You wish to marry *me* now?" he said, at last.

"Sell the ring," Jem said. "For the money. I told you, you should not have to pay for my drugs; I paid for yours, once, you know, and I recall the feeling. It was unpleasant."

Will winced, then looked down at the Carstairs family symbol glittering in Jem's pale, scarred palm. He reached out and took his friend's hand gently, closing his fingers over the ring. "When did you become reckless and I cautious? Since when have I had to guard you from yourself? It is always you who has guarded me." His eyes searched Jem's face. "Help me to understand you."

Jem stood very still. Then he said, "In the beginning, when I first realized I loved Tessa, I did think that perhaps love was making me well. I had not had an attack in so long. And when I asked her to marry me, I told her that. That love was healing me. So the first time I was—the first time it happened again, after that, I could not bear to tell her, lest she think it meant a lessening of my love for her. I took more of the drug, to fend off another illness. Soon it was taking more of the drug to simply keep me on my feet than it used to take to keep me going for a week. I don't have years, Will. I might not even have months. And I don't want Tessa to know. Please don't tell her. Not just for her sake but for mine."

Against his own will, almost, Will felt himself understanding; he would have done anything, he thought, told any lie, taken any risk, to make Tessa love him. He would have done—

Almost anything. He would not betray Jem for it. That was the one thing he would not do. And here Jem stood, his hand in Will's, his eyes asking for Will's sympathy, his understanding. And how could Will not understand? He recalled himself in Magnus's drawing room, begging to be sent to the demon realms rather than live another hour, another moment, of a life he could no longer bear.

"So you are dying for love, then," Will said finally, his voice sounding constricted to his own ears.

"Dying a little faster for love. And there are worse things to die for."

Will released Jem's hand; Jem looked from the ring to him, his eyes questioning. "Will—"

"I'll go to Whitechapel," said Will. "Tonight. I will get you all the *yin fen* there is, everything you could need."

Jem shook his head. "I cannot ask you to do something that goes against your conscience."

"My conscience," Will whispered. "You are my conscience. You have ever been, James Carstairs. I will do this for you, but I will extract one promise first."

"What sort of promise?"

"You asked me years ago to cease looking for a cure for you," Will said. "I want you to release me from that promise. Free me to look, at least. Free me to search."

Jem looked at him with some wonder. "Just when I think I know you perfectly, you surprise me again. Yes, I will free you. Search. Do what you must. I cannot fetter your best intentions; it would only be cruel, and I would do the same for you, were I in your place. You know that, don't you?"

"I know it." Will took a step forward. He put his hands on Jem's shoulders, feeling how sharp they were beneath his grip, the bones like the wings of a bird. "This is not some empty promise, James. Believe me, there is no one who knows more than I do the pain of false hope. I will look. If there is anything to be found, I will find it. But until then—your life is yours to live as you choose."

Incredibly, Jem smiled. "I know that," he said, "but it is gracious of you to remind me."

"I am nothing if not gracious," Will said. His eyes searched Jem's face, that face as familiar to him as his own. "And determined. *You will not leave me.* Not while I live."

Jem's eyes widened, but he said nothing. There was no more to be said. Will dropped his hands from his *parabatai*'s shoulders and turned toward the door.

Cecily stood where she had stood earlier that day, the knife in her right hand. She sighted along her eye line, then drew the knife back and let it fly. It stuck in the wall, just outside the drawn circle.

Her conversation with Tessa had not relieved her nerves; it had only made them worse. There had been an air of trapped, resigned sadness about Tessa that had made Cecily feel prickly and anxious. As angry as she was at Will, she could not help but feel that Tessa held some fear for him, some dread she would not speak of, in her heart, and Cecily longed to know what it was. How could she protect her brother if she didn't know what he needed protecting from?

After retrieving the knife, she raised it to shoulder level again and let fly. It stuck even farther outside the circle this time, prompting an angry exhale of breath. *"Uffern nef!"* she muttered in Welsh. Her mother would have been horrified, but then, her mother was not there.

"Five," said a drawling voice from the corridor outside.

Cecily started and turned. There was a shadow in the

doorway, a shadow that as it moved forward became Gabriel Lightwood, all tousled brown hair and green eyes as sharp as glass. He was as tall as Will, perhaps taller, and more lanky than his brother. "I don't take your meaning, Mr. Lightwood."

"Your throw," he said with an elegantly outflung arm. "I rate it at five points. Your skill and technique may, perhaps, require work, but the native talent is certainly there. What you require is *practice*."

"Will has been training me," she said as he drew closer.

The corner of his mouth turned up slightly. "As I said."

"I suppose you could do better."

He paused, and jerked the knife from the wall. It sparked as he twirled it between his fingers. "I could," he said. "I was trained by the best, and I had been training Miss Collins and Miss Gray—"

"I heard. Until you grew bored. Not the commitment one might perhaps look for in a tutor." Cecily kept her voice cool; she remembered Gabriel's touch as he had lifted her to her feet at Lightwood House, but she knew Will disliked him, and the smug distance in his voice grated.

Gabriel touched the tip of his finger to the point of the knife. Blood sprang up in a red bead. He had callused fingers, with a spray of freckles across the backs of his hands. "You changed your gear."

"It was covered in blood and ichor." She glanced at him, her gaze raking him up and down. "I see you have not."

For a moment an odd look flashed across his face. Then it was gone, but she had seen her brother hide emotion enough times to recognize the signs. "None of my clothes are here," he said, "and I do not know where I will be living. I could return to one of the family residences, but—"

"You are considering remaining at the Institute?" Cecily said in surprise, reading it on his face. "What does Charlotte say?"

"She will allow it." Gabriel's face changed briefly, a sudden vulnerability showing where only hardness had shown before. "My brother is here."

"Yes," said Cecily. "So is mine."

Gabriel paused for a moment, almost as if that had not occurred to him. "Will," he said. "You do look very much like him. It is . . . unnerving." He shook his head then, as if clearing it of cobwebs. "I just saw your brother," he said. "Pounding down the front steps of the Institute as if the Four Horsemen were chasing him. I don't suppose you'd know what that's about?"

Purpose. Cecily's heart leaped. She seized the knife out of Gabriel's hand, ignoring his startled exclamation. "Not at all," she said, "but I intend to find out."

Just as the City of London seemed to shutter itself as the workday ended, the East End was bursting into life. Will moved through streets lined with stalls selling secondhand clothes and shoes. Rag-and-bone men and knife sharpeners pushed their carts through the byways, shouting their wares in hoarse voices. Butchers lounged in open doorways, their aprons spattered with blood, carcasses hanging in their windows. Women putting out washing called to each other across the streets in voices so tinged with the accent of everyone born within the sound of Bow Bells that they might as well have been speaking Russian, for all that Will could understand them.

A faint drizzle had begun to fall, dampening Will's hair as he crossed in front of a wholesale tobacconist's, closed now, and turned a corner onto a narrower street. He could see the spire of Whitechapel Church in the distance. The shadows gathered in here, the fog thick and soft and smelling of iron and rubbish. A narrow gutter ran down the center of the street, filled with stinking water. Up ahead was a doorway, a gas carriage lamp hanging to either side. As Will was passing, he ducked into it suddenly and thrust out his hand.

There was a cry, and then he was hauling a slim, black-clad figure toward him—Cecily, a velvet cloak thrown on hastily over her gear. Dark hair spilled from the edges of her hood, and his own blue eyes gazed back at him, snapping with fury. "Let go of me!"

"What are you doing following me about the back streets of London, you little idiot?" Will gave her arm a light shake.

Her eyes narrowed. "This morning it was *cariad*, now it's *idiot*?"

"These streets are dangerous," Will said. "And you know nothing of them. You are not even using a glamour rune. It is one thing to declare you are not afraid of anything when you live in the country, but this is London."

"I am not afraid of London," Cecily said defiantly.

Will leaned close, almost hissing into her ear. *"Fyddai'n wneud unrhyw dda yn ddweud wrthych i fynd adref?"*

She laughed. "No, it would not do you any good to tell me to go home. *Rwyt ti fy mrawd ac rwy eisiau mynd efo chi.*"

Will blinked at her words. *You are my brother and I want to go with you.* It was the sort of thing he was used to hearing Jem say, and though Cecily was unlike Jem in every other conceivable way, she did share one quality with him: an absolute stubbornness. When Cecily said she wanted something, it did not express an idle desire but an iron determination.

"Don't you even care where I'm going?" he said. "What if I were going to Hell?"

"I've always wanted to see Hell," Cecily said calmly. "Doesn't everyone?"

"Most of us spend our time struggling to stay out of it," said Will. "I am going to an ifrit den, if you must know, to purchase drugs from violent, dissolute reprobates. They may clap eyes on you and decide to sell you."

"Wouldn't you stop them?"

"I suppose it would depend on how much they would give me."

She shook her head. "Jem is your *parabatai*," she said. "He is your brother, given to you by the Clave. But I am your sister by blood. Why will you do anything in the world for him but you only want me to go home?"

"How do you know the drugs are for Jem?"

"I am not a fool, Will."

"No, more's the pity," Will muttered. "Jem—Jem is all the better part of myself. I would not expect you to understand. I owe him this."

"Then what am I?" Cecily asked.

Will exhaled, too exasperated to check himself. "You are my weakness."

"And Tessa is your heart," she said, not angrily but thoughtfully. "Not a fool, as I told you," she added at his startled expression. "I know that you love her."

Will put his hand to his head, as if her words had caused a splitting pain there. "Have you told anyone? You mustn't, Cecily. No one knows, and it must remain that way."

"I would hardly tell anyone."

"No, I suppose you wouldn't, would you?" His voice had gone hard. "You must be ashamed of your brother—harboring illicit feelings for his *parabatai*'s fiancée—"

"I am not ashamed of you, Will. Whatever you feel, you have not acted on it, and I suppose we all want things we cannot have."

"Oh?" Will said. "And what do you want that you cannot have?"

"For you to come home." A strand of black hair was stuck to her cheek by the dampness, making her look as if she had been crying, though Will knew she had not.

"The Institute is my home." Will sighed and leaned his head back against the stone archway. "I cannot stand out here arguing with you all evening, Cecy. If you are determined to follow me into Hell, I cannot stop you."

"Finally, you have seen sense. I knew you would; you are related to me, after all."

Will fought the urge to shake her, again. "Are you ready?"

She nodded, and Will raised his hand to knock on the door.

The door flew open, and Gideon stood on the threshold of his bedroom, blinking as if he had been in a dark place and had just come out into the light. His trousers and shirt were wrinkled, and one of his braces had slid halfway down his arm.

"Mr. Lightwood?" Sophie said, hesitating on the threshold. She was carrying a tray in her hands, loaded with scones and tea, just heavy enough to be uncomfortable. "Bridget told me you had rung for a tray—"

"Yes. Of course, yes. Do come in." As if snapped into full wakefulness, Gideon straightened and ushered her over the threshold. His boots were off, kicked into a corner. The whole room lacked its usual neatness. Gear was strewn over a high-backed chair—Sophie winced inside to think what that would do to the upholstery—a half-eaten apple was on the nightstand, and sprawled in the middle of the bed was Gabriel Lightwood, fast asleep.

He was clearly wearing his brother's clothes, for they were far too short at his wrists and ankles. Asleep he looked younger, the usual tension smoothed from his face. One of his hands clutched a pillow as if for reassurance.

"I couldn't wake him," Gideon said, unconsciously hugging his elbows. "I ought to have brought him back to his own room, but . . ." He sighed. "I couldn't bring myself."

"Is he staying?" Sophie asked, setting the tray down on the nightstand. "At the Institute, I mean."

"I—I don't know. I think so. Charlotte told him he was welcome. I think she terrified him." Gideon's mouth quirked slightly.

"Mrs. Branwell?" Sophie bristled, as she always did when she thought her mistress was being criticized. "But she is the gentlest of people!"

"Yes—that is *why* I think she terrified him. She embraced him and told him that if he remained here, the incident with my father would be put into the past. I am not sure *which* incident with my father she was referring to," Gideon added dryly. "Most likely the one where Gabriel supported his bid to take over the Institute."

"You don't think she meant the most recent?" Sophie pushed a lock of hair that had come free back under her cap. "With the . . ."

"Enormous worm? No, oddly, I don't. It is not in my brother's nature, though, to expect to be forgiven. For anything. He understands only the strictest discipline. He may think Charlotte is trying to play a trick on him, or that she is mad. She showed him to a room he could have, but I think the entire business frightened him. He came to speak to me about it, and fell asleep." Gideon sighed, looking at his brother with a mixture of fondness, exasperation, and sorrow that made Sophie's heart beat in sympathy.

"Your sister . . . ," she began.

"Oh, Tatiana wouldn't even consider staying here for a moment," Gideon said. "She has fled to the Blackthorns', her in-laws, and good riddance. She is not a stupid girl—in fact, she considers her intelligence to be quite superior—but she is a self-important and vain one, and there is no love lost between her and my brother. And he had been awake for days, mind you. Waiting in that great blasted house, locked out of the library, pounding on the door when no answer came from my father . . ."

"You feel protective of him," Sophie observed.

"Of course I do; he is my little brother." He moved toward the bed and brushed a hand over Gabriel's tousled brown hair; the other boy moved and made a restless sound but did not wake.

"I thought he would not forgive you for going against your father," Sophie said. "You had said—that you were frightened of it. That he would consider your actions a betrayal of the Lightwood name."

"I think he has begun to question the Lightwood name. Just as I did, in Madrid." Gideon stepped away from the bed.

Sophie ducked her head. "I am sorry," she said. "Sorry about your father. Whatever anyone said about him, or whatever he might have done, he was your father."

He turned toward her. "But, Sophie—"

She did not correct him for the use of her Christian name. "I know that he did deplorable things," she said. "But you should be allowed to mourn him nonetheless. No one can take your grief from you; it belongs to you, and you alone."

He touched her cheek lightly with the tips of his fingers. "Did you know your name means 'wisdom'? It was very well-given."

Sophie swallowed. "Mr. Lightwood—"

But his fingers had spread out to cup her cheek, and he was bending to kiss her. "*Sophie,*" he breathed, and then their lips found each other, a light touch giving way to a greater pressure as he leaned in. Lightly and delicately she curved her hands—*so rough, worn down with washing and carrying, with scraping the grates and dusting and polishing,* she fretted, but he didn't seem to be bothered or notice—around his shoulders.

Then she moved closer to him, and the heel of her shoe caught on the carpet, and she was slipping to the floor, Gideon catching at her. They tumbled to the ground together, Sophie's face flaming in embarrassment—dear God, he would think she had pulled him down on purpose, that she was some sort of wanton madwoman intent on passion. Her cap had fallen off, and her dark curls fell over her face. The rug was soft beneath her, and Gideon, above her, was whispering her name with concern. She turned her head aside, her cheeks still burning, and found herself gazing beneath his four-poster bed.

"Mr. Lightwood," she said, raising herself up on her elbows. "Are those *scones* under your bed?"

Gideon froze, blinking, a rabbit cornered by hounds. "What?"

"There." She pointed to the mounded dark shapes piled beneath the four-poster. "There is a veritable *mountain* of scones beneath your bed. What on earth?"

Gideon sat up, raking his hands through his tumbled hair as Sophie scrambled back away from him, her skirts rustling around her. "I . . ."

"You called for those scones. Nearly every day. You *asked* for them, Mr. Lightwood. Why would you do that if you didn't want them?"

His cheeks darkened. "It was the only way I could think of to see you. You wouldn't speak to me, wouldn't listen when I tried to talk to you—"

"So you lied?" Seizing up her fallen cap, Sophie rose to her feet. "Do you have any idea how much work I have to do, Mr. Lightwood? Carrying coal and hot water, dusting, polishing, cleaning up after *you* and the others—and I don't mind or complain, but how dare you make extra work for me, make me drag heavy trays up and down the stairs, just to bring you something you didn't even *want*?"

Gideon scrambled to his feet, his clothes even more wrinkled now. "Forgive me," he said. "I did not think."

"No," Sophie said, furiously tucking her hair up under her cap. "You lot never do, do you?"

And with that, she stalked from the room, leaving Gideon staring hopelessly after her.

"Nicely done, brother," said Gabriel from the bed, blinking sleepy green eyes at Gideon.

Gideon threw a scone at him.

"Henry." Charlotte moved across the floor of the crypt. The witchlight torches were burning so brightly it looked almost as if it were day, though she knew it was closer to midnight. Henry was hunched over the largest of the great wooden tables scattered about the center of the room. Something or other odious was burning in a beaker on another table, giving off great puffs of lavender smoke. A massive piece of paper, the sort butchers used to wrap their wares in, was spread across Henry's table, and he was covering it with all sorts of mysterious ciphers and calculations, muttering to himself under his breath as he scribbled. "Henry, darling, aren't you exhausted? You've been down here for hours."

Henry started and looked up, pushing the spectacles he wore when he worked up into his gingery hair. "Charlotte!" He seemed astonished, if thrilled, to see her; only Henry, Charlotte thought dryly, would be astonished to see his own wife in their own home. "My angel. What are you doing down here? It's freezing cold. It can't be good for the baby."

Charlotte laughed, but she didn't object when Henry hurried over to her and gave her a gentle hug. Ever since he had found out they were going to have a child, he had been treating her like fine china. He pressed a kiss into the top of her hair now and drew back to study her face. "In fact, you look a little peaked. Perhaps rather than supper you should have Sophie bring you some strengthening beef tea in your room? I shall go and—"

"Henry. We decided not to have supper hours ago—everyone was brought sandwiches in their rooms. Jem is still too ill to eat, and the Lightwood boys too shaken up. And you know how Will is when Jem is unwell. And Tessa, too, of course. Really, the whole house is going all to pieces."

"Sandwiches?" said Henry, who seemed to have seized on this as the substantive part of Charlotte's speech, and was looking wistful.

Charlotte smiled. "There are some for you upstairs, Henry, if you can tear yourself away. I suppose I shouldn't scold you—I've been going through Benedict's journals, and quite fascinating they are—but what *are* you working on?"

"A portal," said Henry eagerly. "A form of transport. Something that might conceivably whisk a Shadowhunter from one point of the globe to another in a matter of seconds. It was Mortmain's rings that gave me the idea."

Charlotte's eyes were wide. "But Mortmain's rings are assuredly dark magic. . . ."

"But this is not. Oh, and there is something else. Come. It is for Buford."

Charlotte allowed her husband to take her wrist and draw her across the room. "I have told you a hundred times, Henry, no son of mine will ever be named Buford— By the Angel, is that a *cradle?*"

Henry beamed. "It is better than a cradle!" he announced,

flinging his arm out to indicate the sturdy-looking wooden baby's bed, hung between two poles that it might rock from side to side. Charlotte had to admit to herself it was quite a nice-looking piece of furniture. "It is a self-rocking cradle!"

"A what?" Charlotte asked faintly.

"Watch." Proudly Henry stepped forward and pressed some sort of invisible button. The cradle began to rock gently from side to side.

Charlotte expelled a breath. "That's lovely, darling."

"Don't you like it?" Henry beamed. "There, it's rocking a bit faster now." It was, with a slight jerkiness to the motion that gave Charlotte the feeling that she had been cast adrift on a choppy sea.

"Hm," she said. "Henry, I do have something I wish to speak to you about. Something important."

"More important than our child being rocked gently to sleep each night?"

"The Clave has decided to release Jessamine," Charlotte said. "She is returning to the Institute. In two days."

Henry turned to her with an incredulous look. Behind him the cradle was rocking even faster, like a carriage hurtling ahead at full tilt. "She is coming back *here*?"

"Henry, she has nowhere else to go."

Henry opened his mouth to reply, but before a word could emerge, there was a terrible ripping sound, and the cradle tore free of its mooring and flew across the room to crash against the farthest wall, where it exploded into splinters.

Charlotte gave a little gasp, her hand rising to cover her mouth. Henry's brow furrowed. "Perhaps with some refinements to the design . . ."

"No, Henry," Charlotte said firmly.

"But—"

"Under no circumstances." There were daggers in Charlotte's voice.

Henry sighed. "Very well, dear."

The Infernal Devices are without pity. The Infernal Devices are without regret. The Infernal Devices are without number. The Infernal Devices will never stop coming.

The words written on the wall of Benedict's study echoed in Tessa's head as she sat by Jem's bed, watching him sleep. She was not sure what time it was exactly; certainly it was "in the wee smalls," as Bridget would have said, no doubt past midnight. Jem had been awake when she had come in, just after Will had gone, awake and sitting up and well enough to take some tea and toast, though he'd been more breathless than she would have liked, and paler.

Sophie had come later to clear away the food, and had smiled at Tessa. "Fluff his pillows up," she had suggested in a whisper, and Tessa had done it, though Jem had looked amused at her fussing. Tessa had never had much experience with sickrooms. Taking care of her brother when he'd been drunk was the closest she had come to playing nursemaid. She did not mind it now that it was Jem, did not mind sitting holding his hand while he breathed softly, his eyes half-closed, his eyelashes fluttering against his cheekbones.

"Not very heroic," he said suddenly without opening his eyes, though his voice was steady.

Tessa started, and leaned forward. She had slid her fingers into his earlier, and their linked hands lay beside him on the bed. His fingers were cool in hers, his pulse slow. "What do you mean?"

"Today," he said in a low voice, and coughed. "Collapsing and coughing up blood all over Lightwood House—"

"It only improved the look of the place," said Tessa.

"Now you sound like Will." Jem gave a sleepy smile. "And you're changing the subject, just like he would."

"Of course I am. As if I would ever think any less of you for being ill; you know that I don't. And you were quite heroic today. Though Will was saying earlier," she added, "that heroes all come to bad ends, and he could not imagine why anyone would want to be one anyway."

"Ah." Jem's hand squeezed hers briefly, and then let it go. "Well, Will is looking at it from the hero's viewpoint, isn't he? But as for the rest of us, it's an easy answer."

"Is it?"

"Of course. Heroes endure because we need them. Not for their own sakes."

"You speak of them as though you were not one." She reached to brush the hair from his forehead. He leaned into her touch, his eyes closing. "Jem—have you ever—" She hesitated. "Have you ever thought of ways to prolong your life that are not a cure for the drug?"

At that his eyelids flew open. "What do you mean?"

She thought of Will, on the floor of the attic, choking on holy water. "Becoming a vampire. You would live forever—"

He scrambled upright against the pillows. "Tessa, *no*. Don't—you can't think that way."

She darted her eyes away from him. "Is the thought of becoming a Downworlder truly so horrible to you?"

"Tessa . . ." He exhaled. "I am a Shadowhunter. Nephilim. Like my parents before me. It is the heritage I claim, just as I claim my mother's heritage as part of myself. It does not mean I hate my father. But I honor the gift they gave me, the blood of the Angel, the trust placed in me, the vows I have taken. Nor, I think, would I make a very good vampire. Vampires by and large despise us. Sometimes they Turn a Nephilim, as a joke, but that vampire is scorned by the others. We carry day and the fire of angels in our veins, everything they hate. They would shun me, and the Nephilim would shun me. I would no longer be Will's *parabatai*, no longer be welcome in the Institute. No, Tessa. I would rather die and be reborn and see the sun again, than live to the end of the world without day-light."

"A Silent Brother, then," she said. "The *Codex* says that the runes they put upon themselves are powerful enough to arrest their mortality."

"Silent Brothers cannot marry, Tessa." He had lifted his chin. Tessa had known for a long time that beneath Jem's gentleness lay a stubbornness as strong as Will's. She could see it now, steel under silk.

"You know I would rather have you alive and not married to me than—" Her throat closed on the word.

His eyes softened slightly. "The path of Silent Brotherhood is not open to me. With the *yin fen* in my blood, contaminating it, I cannot survive the runes they must put upon themselves. I would have to cease the drug until it was purged from my system, and that would most likely kill me." He must have seen something in her expression, for he gentled his voice. "And it is not much of a life they have, Silent Brothers, shadows and darkness, silence and—no music." He swallowed. "And besides, I do not wish to live forever."

"I may live forever," Tessa said. The enormity of it was something she could still not quite comprehend. It was as hard to comprehend that your life would never end as it was to comprehend that it would.

"I know," Jem said. "And I am sorry for it, for I think it is a burden no one should have to bear. You know I believe we live again, Tessa. I will return, if not in this body. Souls that love each other are drawn to each other in their next lives. I will see Will, my parents, my uncles, Charlotte and Henry . . ."

"But you will not see me." It was not the first time she had thought it, though she often pushed the thought down when it rose. *If I am immortal, then I have only this, this one life. I will not turn and change as you do, James. I will not see you in Heaven, or on the banks of the great river, or in whatever life lies beyond this one.*

"I see you now." He reached out and put his hand on her cheek, his clear silver-gray eyes searching hers.

"And I see you," she whispered, and he smiled tiredly, closing his eyes. She put her hand over his, her cheek resting in the hollow of his palm. She sat, wordless, his fingers cool against her skin, until his breathing slowed and his fingers went boneless in hers; he had fallen asleep. With a rueful smile she lowered his hand gently so that it rested on the coverlet, by his side.

The bedroom door opened; Tessa turned round in her chair and saw Will standing on the threshold, still in his coat and gloves. One look at his stark, distraught face had her rising to her feet and following Will out into the corridor.

Will was already striding down the corridor with the haste

of a man with the devil at his heels. Tessa closed the bedroom door carefully behind her and hurried after him. "What is it, Will? What's happened?"

"I just came back from the East End," Will said. There was pain in his voice, pain she had not heard the likes of since that day in the drawing room when she had told him she was engaged to Jem. "I had gone to look for more *yin fen*. But there is no more."

Tessa nearly stumbled as they reached the steps. "What do you mean, there's no more? Jem has a supply, does he not?"

Will turned to face her, walking backward down the stairs. "It's gone," he said curtly. "He did not want you to know, but there is no way to hide it. It is gone, and I cannot find more. I have always been the one to buy it. I had suppliers—but they have either vanished or come up empty-handed. I went first to that place—that place where you came and found me, you and Jem, together. They had no *yin fen*."

"Then another place—"

"I went *everywhere*," Will said, spinning back around. They emerged into the corridor on the second level of the Institute; the library and the drawing room were here. Both their doors were open, spilling yellow light into the hall. "Everywhere. In the last place I went, someone told me that it had all been deliberately bought up in the last few weeks. There is nothing."

"But Jem," Tessa said, shock buzzing through her like fire. "Without the *yin fen* . . ."

"He'll die." Will paused for a moment in front of the library door; his eyes met hers. "Just this afternoon he gave me permission to seek a cure for him. To search. And now he will die because I cannot keep him alive long enough to find it."

"No," Tessa said. "He will not die; we will not let him."

Will moved into the library, Tessa beside him, his gaze roaming over the familiar room, the lamplit tables, the shelves of old volumes. "There were books," he said, as if she hadn't spoken. "Books I was consulting, volumes about rare poisons." He moved away from her, toward a nearby shelf, his gloved hands running feverishly over the tomes that rested there. "It was years ago, before Jem forbade any more research. I have forgotten—"

Tessa moved to join him, her skirts swishing about her ankles. "Will, stop."

"But I have to *remember*." He moved to another shelf, and then another, his long, slender body casting an angled shadow across the floor. "I have to find—"

"Will, you can't read every book in the library in time. Stop." She had moved behind him, close enough to see where the collar of his jacket was damp from the rain. "This will not help Jem."

"Then what will? *What will?*" He reached for another book, stared at it, and threw it to the floor; Tessa jumped.

"Stop," she said again, and caught at his sleeve, turning him to face her. He was flushed, breathless, his arm as tense as iron beneath her grip. "When you searched for the cure before, you did not know what you know now. You did not have the allies you have now. We will go and we will ask Magnus Bane. He has eyes and ears in Downworld; he knows of all kinds of magic. He helped you with your curse; he can help us with this as well."

"There was no curse," said Will, as if he were reciting the lines of a play; his eyes were glassy.

"Will—listen to me. Please. Let us go to Magnus. He can help."

He closed his eyes and drew a deep breath. Tessa stared. She could not help watching him when she knew he could not see her—the fine spidering dark lashes against his cheekbones, the faint blue tint to his eyelids. "Yes," he said finally. "Yes. Of course. Tessa—thank you. I did not think."

"You were grieved," she said, suddenly aware that she was still holding his arm, and that they were close enough that she could have pressed a kiss to his cheek, or wrapped her arms about his neck to comfort him. She stepped back, releasing him. His eyes opened. "And you had thought he would always forbid you from searching for a cure. You know I have never been at peace with that. I had thought of Magnus before."

His eyes searched her face. "But you have never asked him?"

She shook her head. "Jem did not wish it. But now— All is changed now."

"Yes." He drew back from her, his eyes lingering on her face. "I will go down and call Cyril to fetch the carriage. Meet me in the courtyard."

To: Consul Josiah Wayland
From: Members of the Council

Dear Sir,

We can but express our great distress at receiving your letter. It was our impression that Charlotte Branwell was a choice you wholeheartedly embraced, and that she had proven herself a fit leader of the London Institute. Our own Inquisitor Whitelaw speaks highly of her and the manner in which she managed the challenge laid against her authority by Benedict Lightwood.

It is our opinion as a body that George Penhallow is not a fit successor to the place of Consul. Unlike Mrs. Branwell, he has not proven himself as a leader of others. It is true Mrs. Branwell is young and passionate, but the role of Consul is one that requires passion. We urge you to put aside thoughts of Mr. Penhallow, who is too young and green for the position, and take time to consider again the possibility of Mrs. Branwell.

Yours in Raziel's name,

Members of the Council

5

A HEART DIVIDED

Yea, though God search it warily enough,
There is not one sound thing in all thereof;
Though he search all my veins through, searching them
He shall find nothing whole therein but love.
—Algernon Charles Swinburne, "Laus Veneris"

To: Members of the Council
From: Josiah Wayland, Consul

It is with a weighted heart that I take up my pen to write to you, gentlemen. Many of you have known me for a good number of years, and for many of those I have led you in the position of Consul. I believe I have led you well, and have served the Angel as best I could. It is, however, human to err, and I believe I have done such in appointing

Charlotte Branwell head of the London Institute.

When I granted her the position, I believed that she would follow in the footsteps of her father and prove a faithful leader, obedient to the rule of the Clave. I also believed that her husband would stem her natural feminine tendencies toward impulsivity and thoughtlessness. Unfortunately, this has not proved to be the case. Henry Branwell lacks the strength of character to restrain his wife, and, unfettered by womanly duty, she has left the virtues of obedience far behind. Only the other day I discovered that Charlotte had given orders to have the spy Jessamine Lovelace recalled to the Institute upon her release from the Silent City, despite my express wishes that she be sent to Idris. I also suspect she lends an ear to those who are not friendly to the cause of the Nephilim and may in fact even be in league with Mortmain, such as the werewolf Woolsey Scott.

The Council does not serve the Consul; it has always been the other way around. I am a symbol of the power of the Council and the Clave. When my authority is undermined by disobedience, it undermines the authority of us all. Better a dutiful boy like my nephew, whose worth is untested, than one whose worth has been tested and found wanting.

In the Angel's name,

Consul Josiah Wayland

Will remembered.

Another day, months ago, in Jem's bedroom. Rain pounding against the windows of the Institute, streaking the glass with clear lines.

"And that is all?" Jem had asked. "That is the whole of it?

The truth?" He'd been sitting at his desk, one of his legs bent up on the chair beneath him; he'd looked very young. His violin had been propped against the side of the chair. He had been playing it when Will had come in and, without preamble, announced that it was the end of pretense—he had a confession to make, and he meant to make it now.

That had ended the Bach. Jem had put the violin away, his eyes on Will's face the whole time, anxiety blooming behind his silver eyes as Will had paced and spoken, paced and spoken, until he had run out of words.

"That is all of it," Will had said finally when he was done. "And I do not blame you if you hate me. I could understand it."

There'd been a long pause. Jem's gaze had been steady on his face, steady and silver in the wavering light of the fire. "I could never hate you, William."

Will's guts contracted now as he saw another face, a pair of steady blue-gray eyes looking up at his. "I tried to hate you, Will, but I could never manage it," she had said. In that moment Will had been painfully aware that what he had told Jem was not "the whole of it." There was more truth. There was his love for Tessa. But it was his burden to bear, not Jem's. It was something that must be hidden for Jem to be happy. "I deserve your hatred," Will had said to Jem, his voice cracking. "I put you in danger. I believed I was cursed and that all who cared for me would die; I let myself care for you, and let you be a brother to me, risking the danger to you—"

"There was no danger."

"But I believed there was. If I held a revolver to your head, James, and pulled the trigger, would it really matter if I did not know that there were no bullets in the chambers?"

Jem's eyes had widened, and then he'd laughed, a soft laugh. "Did you think I did not know you had a secret?" he'd said. "Did you think I walked into my friendship with you with my eyes shut? I did not know the nature of the burden you carried. But I knew there was a burden." He'd stood up. "I knew you thought yourself poison to all those around you," he'd added. "I knew you thought there to be some corruptive force about you that would break me. I meant to show you that I would not break, that love was not so fragile. Did I do that?"

Will had shrugged once, helplessly. He had almost wished Jem would be angry with him. It would have been easier. He'd never felt so small within himself as he did when he faced Jem's expansive kindness. He thought of Milton's Satan. *Abashed the Devil stood, / And felt how awful goodness is.* "You saved my life," Will had said.

A smile had spread across Jem's face, as brilliant as the sunrise breaking over the Thames. "That is all I ever wanted."

"Will?" A soft voice broke him from his reverie. Tessa, sitting across from him inside the carriage, her gray eyes the color of rain in the dim light. "What are you thinking of?"

With an effort he pulled himself out of memory, his eyes fixing on her face. Tessa's face. She wore no hat, and the hood of her brocade cloak had fallen back. Her face was pale—wider across the cheekbones, slightly pointed at the chin. He thought he had never seen a face that had such a power of expression: Her every smile divided his heart as lightning might split a blackened tree, as did her every look of sorrow. At the moment she was gazing at him with a wistful concern that caught his heart. "Jem," he said, with perfect honesty. "I was thinking of his reaction when I told him of Marbas's curse."

"He felt only sorrow for you," she said immediately. "I know he did; he told me as much."

"Sorrow but not pity," said Will. "Jem has always given me exactly what I needed in the way that I needed it, even when I did not know myself what I required. All *parabatai* are devoted. We must be, to give so much of ourselves to each other, even if we gain in strength by doing so. But with Jem it is different. For so many years I needed him to live, and he kept me alive. I thought he did not know that he was doing it, but maybe he did."

"Perhaps," Tessa said. "He would never have counted a moment of such effort as wasted."

"He has never said anything to you of it?"

She shook her head. Her small hands, in their white gloves, were in fists in her lap. "He speaks of you only with the greatest pride, Will," she said. "He admires you more than you could ever know. When he learned of the curse, he was heartbroken for you, but there was also, almost, a sort of . . ."

"Vindication?"

She nodded. "He had always believed you were good," she said. "And then it was proven."

"Oh, I don't know," he said bitterly. "To be good and to be cursed, it is not the same thing."

She leaned forward and caught at his hand, pressing it between her own. The touch was like white fire through his veins. He could not feel her skin, only the cloth of the gloves, and yet it did not matter. *You kindled me, heap of ashes that I am, into fire.* He had wondered once why love was always phrased in terms of burning. The conflagration in his own veins, now, gave the answer. "You *are* good, Will," she said. "There is no one better placed than I am to be able to say with perfect confidence how good you really are."

He said slowly, not wanting her to move her hands away, "You know, when we were fifteen years old, Yanluo, the demon who murdered Jem's parents, was finally slain. Jem's uncle determined to relocate himself from China to Idris and invited Jem to come and live with him there. Jem refused—for me. He said you do not leave your *parabatai*. That it was part of the words of the oath. 'Thy people shall be my people.' I wonder, if I had had the chance to return to my family, would I have done the same for him?"

"You are doing it," Tessa said. "Do not think I do not know that Cecily wants you to return home with her. And do not think I do not know that you remain for Jem's sake."

"And yours," he said before he could stop himself. She withdrew her hands from his, and he cursed himself silently and savagely: *How could you have been so foolish? How could you, after two months? You've been so careful. Your love for her is only a burden she endures out of politeness. Remember that.*

But Tessa was only pulling aside the curtain as the carriage came to a stop. They were rolling into a mews, from whose entry hung a sign: ALL DRIVERS OF VEHICLES ARE DIRECTED TO WALK THEIR HORSES WHILE PASSING UNDER THIS ARCHWAY. "We are here," she said, as if he had not said a word. Perhaps he had not, Will thought. Perhaps he had not spoken aloud. Perhaps he was only losing his mind. Certainly it was not unimaginable, under the circumstances.

When the carriage door opened, it brought with it a blast of cool Chelsea air. He saw Tessa raise her head as Cyril helped her down. He joined Tessa on the cobblestones. The place smelled of the Thames. Before the Embankment had been built, the river had come much closer to these rows of houses, their edges softened by gaslight in the darkness. Now the river was separated by a greater distance, but one could still smell the salt-dirt-iron tang of water.

The front of No. 16 was Georgian, made of plain red brick-work, with a bay window that jutted out over the front door. There was a small paved court and a garden behind an elegant fence with a great deal of delicate scrolling ironwork. The gate was already open. Tessa pushed through and marched up the front steps to knock upon the door, Will only a few steps behind her.

The door was opened by Woolsey Scott, wearing a canary-yellow brocaded silk dressing gown over trousers and a shirt. He had a gold monocle perched in one eye socket, and regarded them both through it with some distaste. "Bother," he said. "I would have had the footman answer and send you away, but I thought you were somebody else."

"Who?" Tessa inquired, which did not seem to Will to be germane to the issue, but it was Tessa's way—she was forever asking questions; leave her alone in a room, and she'd begin asking questions of the furniture and plants.

"Someone with absinthe."

"Swallow enough of that stuff and you'll think *you're* somebody else," said Will. "We're seeking Magnus Bane; if he isn't here, just tell us and we'll not take up more of your time."

Woolsey sighed as if greatly prevailed upon. "Magnus," he called. "It's your blue-eyed boy."

There were footsteps in the corridor behind Woolsey, and

Magnus appeared in full evening dress, as if he had just come from a ball. Starched white shirtfront and cuffs, swallowtail black coat, and hair like a ragged fringe of dark silk. His eyes flicked from Will to Tessa. "And to what do I owe the honor, at such a late hour?"

"A favor," Will said, and amended himself when Magnus's eyebrows went up. "A question."

Woolsey sighed and stepped back from the door. "Very well. Come into the drawing room."

No one offered to take their hats or coats, and once they reached the drawing room, Tessa stripped off her gloves and stood with her hands close to the fire, shivering slightly. Her hair was a damp mass of curls at the back of her neck, and Will looked away from her before he could remember what it felt like to put his hands through that hair and feel the strands wind about his fingers. It was easier at the Institute, with Jem and the others to distract him, to remember that Tessa was not his to recall that way. Here, feeling as if he were facing the world with her by his side—feeling that she was here for him instead of, quite sensibly, for the health of her own fiancé—it was nearly impossible.

Woolsey threw himself into a flower-patterned armchair. He had plucked the monocle from his eye and was swinging it around his fingers on its long gold chain. "I simply cannot wait to hear what this is about."

Magnus moved toward the fireplace and leaned against the mantel, the very picture of a young gentleman at leisure. The room was painted a pale blue, and decorated with paintings that featured vast fields of granite, gleaming blue seas, and men and women in classical dress. Will thought he recognized a reproduction of an Alma-Tadema—or at least it *must* have been a reproduction, mustn't it?

"Don't gape at the walls, Will," said Magnus. "You have been all but absent for months. What brings you here now?"

"I did not want to trouble you," Will muttered. It was only partly the truth. Once the curse Will had believed he was under had been proved, by Magnus, to be false, he had avoided Magnus—not because he was angry with the warlock, or had no more need of him, but because the sight of Magnus caused him pain. He had written him a short letter, telling him what had happened and that his secret was a secret no more. He had spoken of Jem's engagement to Tessa. He had asked that Magnus not reply. "But this—this is a crisis."

Magnus's cat eyes widened. "What sort of crisis?"

"It is about *yin fen*," said Will.

"Gracious," Woolsey said. "Don't tell me my pack is taking the stuff again?"

"No," Will said. "There is none of it to take." He saw dawning comprehension on Magnus's face and went on to explain the situation, as best he could. Magnus didn't change expression as Will spoke, any more than Church did when someone spoke to him. Magnus only watched out of his gold-green eyes until Will was done.

"And without the *yin fen*?" Magnus said at last.

"He will die," said Tessa, turning from the fireplace. Her cheeks were flushed carnation pink, whether from the heat of the fire or from the stress of the situation, Will could not tell. "Not immediately, but—within the week. His body cannot sustain itself without the powder."

"How does he take it?" Woolsey inquired.

"Dissolved in water, or inhaled— What has that got to do with anything?" Will demanded.

"Nothing," Woolsey said. "I was only wondering. Demon drugs are a curious thing."

"For us, who love him, it is a sight more than curious," Tessa said. Her chin was up, and Will remembered what he had said to her once, about being like Boadicea. She *was* brave, and he adored her for it, even as it was employed in the defense of her love for someone else.

"Why have you come to me with this?" Magnus's voice was quiet.

"You helped us before," Tessa said. "We thought perhaps you could help again. You helped with de Quincey—and Will, with his curse—"

"I am not at your beck and call," Magnus said. "I helped with de Quincey because Camille requested it of me, and Will, once, because he offered me a favor in return. I am a warlock. And I do not serve Shadowhunters for free."

"And I am not a Shadowhunter," said Tessa.

There was a silence. Then: "Hmm," Magnus said, and turned away from the fire. "I understand, Tessa, that you are to be congratulated?"

"I . . ."

"On your engagement to James Carstairs."

"Oh." She flushed, and her hand went to her throat, where she always wore Jem's mother's necklace, his gift to her. "Yes. Thank you."

Will *felt* rather than saw Woolsey's eyes on all three of them—Magnus, Tessa, and himself—sliding from one to the other, the mind behind the eyes examining, deducing, *enjoying*.

Will's shoulders tightened. "I would be happy to offer anything," he said. "This time. Another favor, or whatever you wanted, for the *yin fen*. If it's payment, I could arrange—that is, I could try—"

"I may have helped you before," Magnus said. "But this—" He sighed. "*Think*, the pair of you. If someone is buying up all the *yin fen* in the country, then it is someone who has a reason. And who has a reason to do that?"

"Mortmain," Tessa whispered before Will could say it. He could still remember his own voice:

"Mortmain's minions have been buying up the yin fen *supply in the East End. I confirmed it. If you had run out and he was the only one with a supply . . ."*

"*We would have been put in his power,*" said Jem. "*Unless you were willing to let me die, of course, which would be the sensible course of action.*"

But with enough *yin fen* to last them twelve months, Will had thought there was no danger. Had thought that Mortmain would find some other way to harry and torment them, for surely he would see this plan could not work. Will had not expected a year's worth of the drug to be gone in eight weeks.

"You do not want to help us," Will said. "You do not want to position yourself as an enemy of Mortmain's."

"Well, can you blame him?" Woolsey rose in a whirl of yellow silk. "What could *you* possibly have to offer that would make the risk worth it to him?"

"I will give you anything," said Tessa in a low voice that Will felt in his bones. "Anything at all, if you can help us help Jem."

Magnus gripped a handful of his black hair. "God, the two of you. I can make inquiries. Track down some of the more unusual shipping routes. Old Molly—"

"I've been to her," Will said. "Something's frightened her so badly, she won't even crawl out of her grave."

Woolsey snorted. "And that doesn't tell you anything, little Shadowhunter? Is it really worth all this, just to stretch your friend's life out another few months, another year? He will die anyway. And the sooner he dies, the sooner you can have his fiancée, the one you're in love with." He cut his amused gaze toward Tessa. "Really you ought to be counting with great eagerness the days till he expires."

Will did not know what happened after that; everything went suddenly white, and Woolsey's monocle was flying across the room. Will's head hit something painfully, and the werewolf was under him, kicking and swearing, and they were rolling across the rug, and there was a sharp pain in his wrist, where Woolsey had clawed him. The pain cleared his head, and he was aware that Woolsey was pinning him to the ground, his eyes gone yellow and his teeth bared and as sharp as daggers, ready to bite.

"Stop it. Stop it!" Tessa, by the fire, had seized up a poker; Will choked and put his hand against Woolsey's face, pushing him away. Woolsey yelled, and suddenly the weight was off Will's chest; Magnus had lifted the werewolf and shoved him away. Then Magnus's hands were fisted in the back of Will's jacket, and Will found himself being dragged from the room, Woolsey staring after him, one hand to his face where Will's silver ring had burned his cheekbone.

"Let me go. Let me go!" Will struggled, but Magnus's grip was like iron. He marched Will down the corridor and into a half-lit library. Will pulled free just as Magnus let go of him, resulting in an inelegant stumble that fetched him up against the back of a red velvet sofa. "I cannot leave Tessa alone with Woolsey—"

"Her virtue is hardly in danger from him," Magnus said dryly. "Woolsey will behave himself, which is more than I can say for you."

Will turned around slowly, wiping blood from his face. "You're glaring at me," he said to Magnus. "You look like Church before he bites someone."

"Picking a fight with the head of the Praetor Lupus," Magnus said bitterly. "You know what his pack would do to you if they had an excuse. You *want* to die, don't you?"

"I don't," Will said, surprising even himself a little.

"I don't know why I ever helped you."

"You like broken things."

Magnus took two strides across the room and seized Will's face in his long fingers, forcing his chin up. "You are *not* Sydney Carton," he said. "What good will it do you to die for James Carstairs, when he is dying anyway?"

"Because if I save him, then it is worth it—"

"God!" Magnus's eyes narrowed. "*What* is worth it? What could possibly be worth it?"

"Everything I have lost!" Will shouted. "*Tessa!*"

Magnus dropped his hand from Will's face. He took several paces backward and breathed in and out slowly, as if mentally counting to ten. "I'm sorry," he said finally. "About what Woolsey said."

"If Jem dies, I cannot be with Tessa," said Will. "Because it will be as if I were waiting for him to die, or took some joy in his death, if it let me have her. And I will not be that person. I will not profit from his death. So he must live." He lowered his arm, his sleeve bloody. "It is the only way any of this can ever mean anything. Otherwise it is only—"

"Pointless, needless suffering and pain? I don't suppose it would help if I told you that is the way life is. The good suffer, the evil flourish, and all that is mortal passes away."

"I want more than that," said Will. "*You* made me want more than that. You showed me I was only ever cursed because I had chosen to believe myself so. You told me there was possibility, meaning. And now you would turn your back on what you created."

Magnus laughed shortly. "You are incorrigible."

"I've heard that." Will pulled himself away from the sofa, wincing. "You'll help me, then?"

"I'll help you." Magnus reached down his shirtfront and drew out something that dangled on a chain, something that glowed with a soft red light. A square red stone. "Take this."

He folded it into Will's hand.

Will looked at him in confusion. "This was Camille's."

"I gave it to her as a gift," said Magnus, a bitter quirk to the side of his mouth. "She returned all my gifts to me last month. You might as well take it. It warns when demons are close. It might work on those clockwork creations of Mortmain's."

"'True love cannot die,'" Will said, translating the inscription on the back in the light from the corridor. "I can't wear this, Magnus. It's too pretty for a man."

"So are you. Go home and clean yourself up. I will call upon you as soon as I have information." He looked at Will keenly. "In the meantime do your best to be worthy of my assistance."

"If you come near me, I shall bash in your head with this poker," Tessa said, brandishing the fireplace instrument between herself and Woolsey Scott as if it were a sword.

"I've no doubt you would too," he said, looking at her with a grudging sort of respect as he mopped the blood from his chin with a monogrammed handkerchief. Will had been bloody too, his own blood and Woolsey's; he was doubtless in another room with Magnus now, getting more blood smeared everywhere. Will was never overconcerned with neatness, and even less so when he was emotional. "I see you've begun to be like them, the Shadowhunters you seem to adore so much. Whatever possessed you to engage yourself to one of them? And a dying one at that."

Rage flared up in Tessa, and she considered smacking Woolsey with the poker whether he came near her or not. He had moved awfully quickly while fighting Will, though, and she didn't fancy her chances. "You don't know James Carstairs. Don't speak about him."

"Love him, do you?" Woolsey managed to make it sound unpleasant. "But you love Will, too."

Tessa froze inside. She had known that Magnus knew of Will's affection for her, but the idea that what she felt for him in return was written across her face was too terrifying to contemplate. "That's not true."

"Liar," said Woolsey. "Really, what is the difference if one of them dies? You always have a fine secondary option."

Tessa thought of Jem, of the shape of his face, his eyes shut in concentration as he played the violin, the curve of his mouth when he smiled, his fingers careful in hers—every line of him inexpressibly dear to her. "If you had two children," she said, "would you say that it was all right if one of them died, because then you'd still have another?"

"One can love two children. But your heart can be given in romantic love to only a single other," said Woolsey. "That is the nature of Eros, is it not? So novels would tell us, though I have no experience of it myself."

"I have come to understand something about novels," Tessa said.

"And what is that?"

"That they are not true."

Woolsey quirked an eyebrow. "You are a funny thing," he said. "I would say I could see what those boys see in you, but . . ." He shrugged. His yellow dressing gown had a long, bloody tear in it now. "Women are not something I have ever understood."

"What about them do you find mysterious, sir?"

"The point of them, mainly."

"Well, you must have had a mother," said Tessa.

"Someone whelped me, yes," said Woolsey without much enthusiasm. "I remember her little."

"Perhaps, but you would not exist without a woman, would you? However little use you may find us, we are cleverer and more determined and more patient than men. Men may be stronger, but it is women who endure."

"Is that what you are doing? Enduring? Surely an engaged woman should be happier." His light eyes raked her. "A heart divided against itself cannot stand, as they say. You love them both, and it tears you apart."

"House," said Tessa.

He raised an eyebrow. "What was that?"

"A house divided against itself cannot stand. Not a heart. Perhaps you should not attempt quotations if you cannot get them correct."

"And maybe you should stop pitying yourself," he said. "Most people are lucky to have even one great love in their life. You have found two."

"Says the man who has none."

"Oh!" Woolsey staggered back with his hand against his heart, mock swooning. "The dove has teeth. Very well, if you don't wish to discuss personal matters, then perhaps something more general? Your own nature? Magnus seems convinced you are a warlock, but I am not so sure. I think there may be some of the blood of faeries about you, for what is the magic of shape-changing if it is not a magic of illusion? And who are the masters of magic and illusion if not the Fair Folk?"

Tessa thought of the blue-haired faerie woman at Benedict's party who had claimed to know her mother, and her breath hitched in her throat. Before she could say another word to Woolsey, though, Magnus and Will came back in through the door—Will, as predicted, just as bloody as before, and scowling. He looked from Tessa to Woolsey and laughed a short laugh. "I suppose you were right, Magnus," he said. "Tessa is in no danger from him. One cannot say the same in reverse."

"Tessa, darling, put the poker down," Magnus said, holding out his hand. "Woolsey can be dreadful, but there are better ways of handling his moods."

With a last glare at Woolsey, Tessa handed the poker to Magnus. She went to retrieve her gloves, and Will his coat, and there was a blur of movement and voices, and she heard

Woolsey laugh. She was barely paying attention; she was too focused on Will. She could tell already from the look on his face that whatever he and Magnus had said to each other in private, it had not solved the problem of Jem's drugs. He looked haunted, and a little deadly, the blood freckling his high cheekbones only making the blue of his eyes more startling.

Magnus led them from the drawing room and out to the front door, where the cool air hit Tessa like a wave. She tugged her gloves on and nodded a good-bye to Magnus, who shut the door, closing the two of them out in the night.

The Thames glittered past the trees, the roadway, and the Embankment, and the gas lamps on Battersea Bridge shone down into the water, a nocturne in blue and gold. The shadow of the carriage was visible beneath the trees by the gate. Above them the moon appeared and disappeared between moving banks of gray cloud.

Will was utterly still. "Tessa," he said.

His voice sounded peculiar, odd and choked. Tessa stepped quickly down to stand beside him, looking up into his face. Will's face was so often changeable as moonlight itself; she had never seen his expression so still.

"Did he say he would help?" she whispered. "Magnus?"

"He will try, but—the way he looked at me—he felt *sorry* for me, Tess. That means there's no hope, doesn't it? If even Magnus thinks the endeavor is doomed, there is nothing more I can do, is there?"

She laid her hand upon his arm. He did not move. It was so peculiar, being this close to him, the familiar feel and presence of him, when for months they had avoided each other, had barely spoken. He had not even wanted to meet her eyes.

And now he was here, smelling of soap and rain and blood and Will. . . . "You have done so much," she whispered. "Magnus will try to help, and we will keep searching, and something may yet come to light. You cannot abandon hope."

"I know. I know it. And yet I feel such dread in my heart, as if it were the last hour of my life. I have felt hopelessness before, Tess, but never such fear. And yet I have known—I have always *known* . . ."

That Jem would die. She did not say it. It was between them, unspoken.

"Who am I?" he whispered. "For years I pretended I was other than I was, and then I gloried that I might return to the truth of myself, only to find there is no truth to return to. I was an ordinary child, and then I was a not very good man, and now I do not know how to be either of those things any longer. I do not know what I am, and when Jem is gone, there will be no one to show me."

"I know just who you are. You're Will Herondale," was all she said, and then suddenly his arms were around her, his head on her shoulder. She froze at first out of pure astonishment, and then carefully she returned the embrace, holding him as he shuddered. He was not crying; this was something else, a sort of paroxysm, as if he were choking. She knew she should not touch him, yet she could not imagine Jem wanting her to push Will away at such a moment. She could not be Jem for him, she thought, could not be his compass that always pointed north, but if nothing else she could make his a slighter burden to carry.

"Would you like this rather dreadful snuffbox someone gave me? It's silver, so I can't touch it," Woolsey said.

Magnus, standing at the bay window of the drawing room, the curtain pulled aside just enough so that he could see Will and Tessa on his front steps, clinging to each other as if their lives depended on it, hummed noncommittally in response.

Woolsey rolled his eyes. "Still out there, are they?"

"Quite."

"Messy, all that romantic love business," said Woolsey. "Much better to go on as we do. Only the physical matters."

"Indeed." Will and Tessa had broken apart at last, though their hands were still joined. Tessa appeared to be coaxing Will down the steps. "Do you think you would have married, if you hadn't had nephews to carry on the family name?"

"I suppose I would have had to. Cry God for England, Harry, Saint George, and the Praetor Lupus!" Woolsey laughed; he had poured himself a glass of red wine from the decanter on the sideboard, and he swirled it now, gazing down into its changeable depths. "You gave Will Camille's necklace," he observed.

"How did you know?" Magnus's mind was only half on the conversation; the other half was watching Will and Tessa walk toward their carriage. Somehow, despite the difference in their height and build, she appeared to be the one who was being leaned upon.

"You were wearing it when you left the room with him, but not when you returned. I don't suppose you told him what it's worth? That he's wearing a ruby that would cost more than the Institute?"

"I didn't want it," Magnus said.

"Tragic reminder of lost love?"

"Didn't suit my complexion." Will and Tessa were in the

carriage now, and their driver was snapping the reins. "Do you think there's a chance for him?"

"A chance for who?"

"Will Herondale. To be happy."

Woolsey sighed gustily and put down his glass. "Is there a chance for you to be happy if he *isn't*?"

Magnus said nothing.

"Are you in love with him?" Woolsey asked—all curiosity, no jealousy. Magnus wondered what it was like to have a heart like that, or rather to have no heart at all.

"No," Magnus said. "I have wondered that, but no. It is something else. I feel that I owe him. I have heard it said that when you save a life, you are responsible for that life. I feel I am responsible for that boy. If he never finds happiness, I will feel I have failed him. If he cannot have that girl he loves, I will feel I have failed him. If I cannot keep his *parabatai* by him, I will feel I failed him."

"Then you will fail him," Woolsey said. "In the meantime, while you are moping and seeking *yin fen*, I think I may take myself traveling. See the countryside. The city depresses me in the winter."

"Do as you like." Magnus let the curtain fall back, blocking the view of Will and Tessa's carriage as it passed out of sight.

To: Consul Josiah Wayland
From: Inquisitor Victor Whitelaw

Josiah,
    I was deeply concerned to hear of your letter to the Council on the topic of Charlotte Branwell. As old

acquaintances, I had hoped you could perhaps speak more freely to me than you have to them. Is there some issue regarding her that concerns you? Her father was a dear friend of ours both, and I have not known her to do a dishonorable thing.

Yours in concern,
Victor Whitelaw

6

LET DARKNESS

Let Love clasp Grief lest both be drown'd,
Let darkness keep her raven gloss:
Ah, sweeter to be drunk with loss,
To dance with death, to beat the ground.
—Alfred, Lord Tennyson, "In Memoriam A.H.H."

To: Inquisitor Victor Whitelaw
From: Consul Josiah Wayland

It is with some trepidation that I pen this letter to you, Victor, for all that we have known each other for some years now. I feel a bit like the prophetess Cassandra, doomed to know the truth and to have no one believe her. Perhaps it is my sin of hubris, which put Charlotte Branwell in the place she now occupies and from which she devils me.

Her undermining of my authority is constant, the ~~instability which I fear it will cause in the Clave severe.~~ ~~What should have been a disaster for her—the revelation~~ ~~that she harbored spies under her roof, the Lovelace girl's~~ ~~complicity in the Magister's schemes—has been recast as a~~ ~~triumph. The Enclave hails the inhabitants of the Institute~~ ~~as those who uncovered the Magister and have harried him~~ ~~from London. That he has not been seen or heard from in the~~ ~~past months has been put down to Charlotte's good judg-~~ ~~ment and is not seen, as I suspect it is, as a tactical retreat~~ ~~and regrouping on his part. Though I am the Consul and~~ ~~lead the Clave, it seems very much to me that this will go~~ ~~down as the time of Charlotte Branwell, and that my legacy~~ ~~will be lost—~~

To: Inquisitor Victor Whitelaw
From: Consul Josiah Wayland

Victor,

While your concern is much appreciated, I have no anxiety regarding Charlotte Branwell that I did not touch on in my letter to the Council.

May you take heart in the strength of the Angel in these troubled times,

Josiah Wayland

Breakfast was at first a quiet affair. Gideon and Gabriel came down together, both subdued, Gabriel barely saying a word, aside from asking Henry to pass the butter. Cecily had placed herself at the far end of the table and was reading a book as she ate; Tessa longed to see the title, but Cecily had placed the book at such an angle that it was not visible. Will, across from Tessa, had the dark shadows of sleeplessness below his eyes, a memory of their eventful night; Tessa herself poked unenthusiastically at her kedgeree, silent until the door opened and Jem came in.

She looked up with surprise and a lurch of delight. He did not look unusually ill, only tired and pale. He slid gracefully into the seat beside her. "Good morning."

"You look much better, Jemmy," Charlotte observed with delight.

Jemmy? Tessa looked at Jem with amusement; he shrugged and gave her a self-deprecating grin.

She looked across the table and found Will watching them. Her gaze brushed his, just for a moment, a question in her eyes. Was there any chance that somehow Will had found some replacement *yin fen* in the time between returning home and this morning? But no, he looked as surprised as she felt.

"I am, quite," Jem said. "The Silent Brothers were of great assistance." He reached to pour himself a cup of tea, and Tessa watched the bones and tendons move in his thin wrist, distressingly visible. When he set the pot down, she reached for his hand beneath the table, and he clasped it. His slim fingers wound about hers reassuringly.

Bridget's voice floated out from the kitchen.

> "Cold blows the wind tonight, sweetheart,
> Cold are the drops of rain;
> The very first love that ever I had
> In greenwood he was slain.

I'll do as much for my sweetheart
As any young woman may;
I'll sit and mourn at his graveside
A twelve-month and a day."

"By the Angel, she's depressing," said Henry, setting down his newspaper directly on his plate and causing the edge to soak through with egg yolk. Charlotte opened her mouth as if to object, and closed it again. "It's all heartbreak, death, and unrequited love."

"Well, that is what most songs are about," said Will. "Requited love is ideal but doesn't make much of a ballad."

Jem looked up, but before he could say anything, a great reverberation sounded through the Institute. Tessa was familiar enough with her London home now to know it as the sound of the doorbell. They all looked down the table at the same time at Charlotte, as if their heads were mounted on springs.

Charlotte, looking startled, put down her fork. "Oh, dear," she said. "There is something I had meant to tell you all, but—"

"Ma'am?" It was Sophie, drifting into the room with a salver in one hand. Tessa could not help but notice that though Gideon was staring at her, she seemed to be deliberately avoiding his gaze, her cheeks pinking slightly. "Consul Wayland is downstairs requesting to speak with you."

Charlotte took the folded paper off the salver, gazed at it, sighed, and said, "Very well. Send him up."

Sophie vanished in a swirl of skirts.

"Charlotte?" Henry sounded puzzled. "What is going on?"

"Indeed." Will let his cutlery clatter onto his plate. "The Consul? Breaking up our breakfast time? Whatever next? The

Inquisitor over for tea? Picnics with the Silent Brothers?"

"Duck pies in the park," said Jem under his breath, and he and Will smiled at each other, just a flash, before the door opened and the Consul swept it.

Consul Wayland was a big man, broad-chested and thick-armed, and the robes of the Consul's status always seemed to hang a bit awkwardly from his wide shoulders. He was blond bearded like a Viking, and at the moment his expression was stormy. "Charlotte," he said without preamble. "I am here to talk to you about Benedict Lightwood."

There was a faint rustling; Gabriel's fingers had clenched on the tablecloth. Gideon put a hand lightly over his brother's wrist, stilling him, but the Consul was already looking at them. "Gabriel," he said. "I had rather thought you might go to the Blackthorns' with your sister."

Gabriel's fingers tightened on the handle of his teacup. "They are quite overset in their grief for Rupert," he said. "I did not think now was the time to intrude."

"Well, you are grieving your father, are you not?" said the Consul. "Grief shared is grief lessened, they say."

"Consul—," Gideon began, shooting a worried look at his brother.

"Though perhaps it might be rather awkward to lodge with your sister, considering that she has brought a complaint against you for murder."

Gabriel made a noise as if someone had spilled boiling water over him. Gideon threw his napkin down and stood up.

"Tatiana did *what*?" he demanded.

"You heard me," the Consul said.

"It was not murder," said Jem.

"As you say," said the Consul. "I was informed that it was."

"Were you also *informed* that Benedict had turned into a gigantic worm?" Will inquired, and Gabriel looked at him in surprise, as if he had not expected to be defended by Will.

"Will, please," Charlotte said. "Consul, I notified you yesterday that Benedict Lightwood had been discovered to be in the last stages of *astriola*—"

"You told me there was a battle, and he was killed," the Consul replied. "But what I am hearing reported is that he was ill with the pox, and that as a result he was hunted down and killed despite offering no resistance."

Will, his eyes suspiciously bright, opened his mouth. Jem reached out and clapped a hand over it. "I cannot understand," Jem said, talking over Will's muffled protests, "how you could know that Benedict Lightwood is dead but not the manner of his death. If there was no body to find, it was because he had become more demon than human, and had vanished when slain, as demons do. But the missing servants—the death of Tatiana's *own husband*—"

The Consul looked weary. "Tatiana Blackthorn says that a group of Shadowhunters from the Institute murdered her father and that Rupert was killed in the brawl."

"Did she mention that her father had eaten her husband?" Henry inquired, finally looking up from his newspaper. "Oh, yes. Ate him. Left his bloody boot in the garden for us to find. There were teeth marks. Love to know how that could have been an accident."

"I would think that counted as offering resistance," Will said. "Eating one's son-in-law, that is. Though I suppose everyone has their family altercations."

"You are not seriously suggesting," Charlotte said, "that the worm—that Benedict should have been subdued and restrained, are you, Josiah? He was in the last stages of the pox! He had gone mad and become a worm!"

"He could have become a worm and *then* gone mad," Will said diplomatically. "We cannot be entirely sure."

"Tatiana is greatly upset," the Consul said. "She is considering demanding reparations—"

"Then I will pay them." It was Gabriel, having pushed his chair back from the table and risen to his feet. "I will give my ridiculous sister my salary for the rest of my life if she desires it, but I will *not* admit to wrongdoing—not for myself, not for any of us. Yes, I put an arrow through his eye. *Its* eye. And I would do it again. Whatever that thing was, it was not my father anymore."

There was a silence. Even the Consul did not seem to have a ready word to hand. Cecily had put her book down and was looking intently from Gabriel to the Consul and back again.

"I beg your pardon, Consul, but whatever Tatiana is telling you, she does not know the truth of the situation," said Gabriel. "Only I was there in the house with my father as he sickened. I was alone with him as he was going mad for the past fortnight. Finally I came here; I begged for my brother's help," Gabriel said. "Charlotte kindly lent me the assistance of her Shadowhunters. By the time we had arrived back at the house, the thing that had been my father had torn my sister's husband apart. I assure you, Consul, there was no manner in which my father could have been saved. We were in a fight for our lives."

"Then why would Tatiana—"

"Because she is humiliated," Tessa said. It was the first

words she had spoken since the Consul had entered the room. "She said as much to me. She believed it would be a blight on the family name if the demon pox was known of; I assume she is trying to present some kind of alternate narrative in the hopes you will repeat it to the Council. But she is not telling the truth."

"Really, Consul," said Gideon. "What makes more sense? That we all ran mad and killed my father, and his sons are covering it up, or that Tatiana is lying? She never thinks things through; you know that."

Gabriel stood with his hand on the back of his brother's chair. "If you believe I would have so lightly committed patricide, feel free to bring me to the Silent City to be questioned."

"That would probably be the most sensible course of action," the Consul said.

Cecily set her teacup down with a sharp bang that made everyone at the table jump. "That is not fair," she said. "He is telling the truth. We all are. You must know that."

The Consul gave her a long, measuring look, then turned back to Charlotte. "You expect my trust?" he said. "And yet you conceal your actions from me. Actions have consequences, Charlotte."

"Josiah, I informed you about what happened at Lightwood House the moment everyone returned and I was assured they were all right—"

"You should have told me before," the Consul said flatly. "The moment Gabriel arrived. This was no routine mission. As it is, you have left yourself in a position in which I must defend you, despite the fact that you disobeyed protocol and set out upon this mission without Council approval."

"There wasn't time—"

"Enough," said the Consul, in a voice that implied it was anything but enough. "Gideon and Gabriel, you will come with me to the Silent City to be questioned." Charlotte began to protest, but the Consul held up a hand. "To have Gabriel and Gideon cleared by the Brothers is expedient; it will avoid any mess and allow me to have Tatiana's request for reparations dismissed swiftly. The two of you." Consul Wayland turned to the Lightwood brothers. "Go downstairs to my carriage and wait for me. We will all *three* adjourn to the Silent City; when the Brothers are done with you, if they find nothing of interest, we will return you here."

"*If* they find nothing," Gideon said in a disgusted tone. He took his brother by the shoulders and guided him out of the room. As Gideon closed the door behind them, Tessa noticed something spark on his hand. He was wearing his Lightwood ring again.

"All right," said the Consul, rounding on Charlotte. "Why did you not tell me the very moment your Shadowhunters returned and told you Benedict was dead?"

Charlotte fixed her eyes on her tea. Her mouth was pressed into a firm line. "I wanted to protect the boys," she said. "I wanted them to have some moments of peace and quiet. Some respite, after seeing their father die before their eyes, before you started asking questions, Josiah!"

"That is hardly all," the Consul went on, ignoring her expression. "Benedict's books and papers. Tatiana told us of them. We searched his house, but his journals are gone, his desk is empty. This is not your investigation, Charlotte; those papers belong to the Clave."

"What are you searching for in them?" Henry asked, moving his newspaper off his plate. He sounded deceptively uninterested in the answer, but there was a hard glint in his eyes that belied his apparent disinterest.

"Information about his connection to Mortmain. Information about any other Clave members that might have had a connection to Mortmain. Clues as to Mortmain's whereabouts—"

"And his devices?" Henry said.

The Consul paused midsentence. "His devices?"

"The Infernal Devices. His army of automatons. It is an army created for the purpose of destroying Shadowhunters, and he means to bend it against us," Charlotte, seemingly recovered, said as she set her napkin down. "In fact, if Benedict's increasingly incomprehensible notes are believed, that time will come sooner rather than later."

"So you *did* take his notes and journals. The Inquisitor was convinced of it." The Consul rubbed the back of his hand across his eyes.

"Of course I took them. And of course I will give them to you. I always planned to do so." Eminently composed, Charlotte picked up the small silver bell by her plate and rang it; when Sophie appeared, she whispered to the girl for a moment, and Sophie, with a curtsy to the Consul, slipped out of the room.

"You should have left the papers where they were, Charlotte. It is procedure," said the Consul.

"There was no reason for me not to look at them—"

"You must trust my judgment, and the Law's. Protecting the Lightwood boys is not a higher priority than discovering Mortmain's whereabouts, Charlotte. You are not running the

Clave. You are part of the Enclave, and you *will* report to me. Is that clear?"

"Yes, Consul," Charlotte said as Sophie reentered the room with a packet of papers, which she silently offered to the Consul. "The next time one of our esteemed members turns into a worm and eats another esteemed member, we will inform you immediately."

The Consul's jaw set. "Your father was my friend," he said. "I trusted him, and because of that I have trusted you. Do not make me sorry I appointed you, or supported you against Benedict Lightwood when he challenged your position."

"You went along with Benedict!" Charlotte cried. "When he suggested I be given a fortnight only to complete an impossible task, you agreed to it! You spoke not a word in my defense! If I were not a woman, you would not have behaved in such a way."

"If you were not a woman," said the Consul, "I would not have had to."

And with that, he was gone, in a swirl of dark robes and dully sparking runes. No sooner had the door closed behind him than Will hissed: "How could you give him those papers? We need those—"

Charlotte, who had sagged back in her chair, her eyes half-closed, said, "Will, I have already been up all night copying down the relevant parts. Much of it was—"

"Gibberish?" Jem suggested.

"Pornographic?" said Will at the same time.

"Could be both," said Will. "Haven't you ever heard of pornographic gibberish before?"

Jem grinned, and Charlotte put her face in her hands. "It was more the former than the latter, if you must know," she said. "I copied down all I could, with Sophie's invaluable assistance." She looked up then. "Will—you need to remember. This is no longer our charge. Mortmain is the Clave's problem, or at least that is how they see it. There was a time when we were singularly responsible for Mortmain, but—"

"We are responsible for protecting Tessa!" Will said with a sharpness that startled even Tessa. Will paled slightly when he realized everyone had looked at him with surprise, but he went on anyway: "Mortmain wants Tessa, still. We cannot imagine he has given up. He may come with automatons, he may come with witchcraft and fire and betrayal, but *he will come*."

"Of course we will protect her," Charlotte said. "We need no reminders, Will. She is one of our own. And speaking of our own . . ." She glanced down at her plate. "Jessamine returns to us tomorrow."

"What?" Will upset his teacup, soaking the tablecloth with the dregs. There was a buzz around the table, though Cecily only stared in puzzlement, and Tessa, after a sharp intake of breath, stayed silent. She was remembering the last time she had seen Jessamine, in the Silent City, pale and red-eyed, weeping and terrified. . . . "She tried to betray us, Charlotte. And you are simply allowing her back?"

"She has no other family, her wealth has been confiscated by the Clave, and she is besides in no fit state to live on her own. Two months of questioning in the Bone City has left her nearly mad. I do not think she will be a danger to any of us."

"Neither did we think she would be a danger before," said Jem, in a harder voice than Tessa would have expected of him, "and yet the course of action she took nearly placed Tessa in Mortmain's hands, and the rest of us in disgrace."

Charlotte shook her head. "There is a need here for mercy and pity. Jessamine is not what she once was—as any of you would know if you had visited her in the Silent City."

"I have no wish to visit with traitors," said Will coldly. "Was she still gibbering about Mortmain being in Idris?"

"Yes—that is why the Silent Brothers finally gave up; they could get no sense out of her. She has no secrets, nothing of worth that she knows. And she understands that. She *feels* worthless. If you could but put yourself in her shoes—"

"Oh, I don't doubt she's putting on a show for you, Charlotte, weeping and rending her garments—"

"Well, if she's rending her *garments*," said Jem, with a flick of a smile toward his *parabatai*. "You know how much Jessamine likes her garments."

Will's smile back was grudging but real. Charlotte saw her opening and pressed the advantage. "You will not even know her when you see her, I promise you that," she said. "Give it a week, a week only, and if none of you can bear to have her here, I will arrange for her transport to Idris." She pushed her plate away. "And now to go through my copies of Benedict's papers. Who will assist me?"

To: Consul Josiah Wayland
From: The Council

Dear Sir,

Until our receipt of your last letter, we had thought our difference in thought on the topic of Charlotte Branwell to be a matter of simple opinion. Though you may not have given express permission for the removal of Jessamine

Lovelace to the Institute, the approval was granted by the Brotherhood, who are in charge of such things. It seemed to us the action of a generous heart to allow the girl back into the only home she has known, despite her wrongdoing. As for Woolsey Scott, he leads the Praetor Lupus, an organization we have long considered allies.

Your suggestion that Mrs. Branwell may have given her ear to those who do not have the Clave's best interests at heart is deeply troubling. Without proof, however, we are reluctant to move forward with this as a basis of information.

In Raziel's name,
The Members of the Nephilim Council

The Consul's carriage was a shining red five-glass landau with the four Cs of the Clave on the side, drawn by a pair of impeccable gray stallions. It was a wet day, drizzling faintly; his driver sat slumped in the seat up front, almost entirely hidden by an oilskin hat and cloak. With a frown the Consul, who had said not a word since they had left the breakfast room of the Institute, ushered Gideon and Gabriel into the carriage, climbed up after, and latched the door behind them.

As the carriage lurched away from the church, Gabriel turned to stare out the window. There was a faint burning pressure behind his eyes and in his stomach. It had come and gone since the previous day, sometimes rolling over him so strongly that he thought he might be sick.

A gigantic worm . . . the last stages of astriola . . . the demon pox.

When Charlotte and the rest of them had first made their accusations against his father, he hadn't wanted to believe it. Gideon's defection had seemed like madness, a betrayal so monstrous it could be explained only by insanity. His father had promised that Gideon would rethink his actions, that he would return to help with the running of the house and the business of being a Lightwood. But he had not come back, and as the days had grown shorter and darker, and Gabriel had seen less and less of his father, he had first begun to wonder and then to be afraid.

Benedict was hunted down and killed.

Hunted and killed. Gabriel rolled the words around in his mind, but they made no sense. He had killed a monster, as he had grown up being trained to do, but that monster had not been his father. His father was still alive somewhere, and any moment Gabriel would look out the window of the house and see him striding up the walk, his long gray coat flapping in the wind, the clean sharp lines of his profile outlined against the sky.

"Gabriel." It was his brother's voice, cutting through the fog of memory and daydream. "Gabriel, the Consul asked you a question."

Gabriel looked up. The Consul was regarding him, his dark eyes expectant. The carriage was rolling through Fleet Street, journalists and barristers and costermongers all hurrying to and fro in the traffic.

"I asked you," the Consul said, "how you were enjoying the hospitality of the Institute."

Gabriel blinked at him. Little stood out for him among the fog of the past few days. Charlotte, putting her arms around him. Gideon, washing the blood off his hands. Cecily's face, like a bright, angry flower. "It is all right, I suppose," he said in a rusty voice. "It is not my home."

"Well, Lightwood House is magnificent," said the Consul. "Built on blood and spoils, of course."

Gabriel stared at him, uncomprehending. Gideon was looking out the window, his expression faintly sick. "I thought you wished to speak to us about Tatiana," he said.

"I know Tatiana," said the Consul. "None of your father's sense and none of your mother's kindness. Rather a bad bargain for her, I'm afraid. Her request for reparations will be dismissed, of course."

Gideon twisted about in his seat and looked at the Consul incredulously. "If you credit her account so little, why are we here?"

"So I could speak with you alone," the Consul said. "You understand, when I first turned over the Institute to Charlotte, I had some thought that a woman's touch would be good for the place. Granville Fairchild was one of the strictest men I've known, and though he ran the Institute according to the Law, it was a cold, unwelcoming place. Here, in London, the greatest city in the world, and a Shadowhunter could not feel at home." He shrugged fluidly. "I thought giving over administration of the place to Charlotte might help."

"Charlotte *and* Henry," Gideon corrected.

"Henry was a cipher," said the Consul. "We all know, as the saying goes, that the gray mare is the better horse in that marriage. Henry was never meant to interfere, and indeed he does not. But neither was Charlotte. She was meant to be docile and obey my wishes. In that she has disappointed me deeply."

"You backed her against our father," Gabriel blurted, and was immediately sorry he had. Gideon shot him a quelling glare, and Gabriel folded his gloved hands tightly in his lap, pressing his lips together.

The Consul's eyebrows went up. "Because your father would have been docile?" he said. "There were two bad ends, and I chose the best of them. I still had hopes of controlling her. But now . . ."

"Sir," Gideon cut in, in his best polite voice. "Why are you telling us this?"

"Ah," said the Consul, glancing out the rain-streaked window. "Here we are." He rapped on the carriage window. "Richard! Stop the carriage at the Argent Rooms."

Gabriel flicked his eyes toward his brother, who shrugged in bafflement. The Argent Rooms were a notorious music hall and gentleman's club in Piccadilly Circus. Ladies of ill repute frequented the place, and there were rumors that the business was owned by Downworlders, and that on some evenings the "magic shows" featured real magic.

"I used to come here with your father," said the Consul, once all three of them were on the pavement. Gideon and Gabriel were staring up through the drizzle at the rather tasteless Italianate theater front that had clearly been grafted onto the more modest buildings that had stood there before. It featured a triple loggia and some rather loud blue paint. "Once the police revoked the Alhambra's license because the management had allowed the cancan to be danced upon their premises. But then, the Alhambra is run by mundanes. This is much more satisfactory. Shall we go in?"

His tone left no room for disagreement. Gabriel followed the Consul through the arcaded entrance, where money changed hands and a ticket was purchased for each of them.

Gabriel looked at his ticket with some puzzlement. It was in the form of an advertisement, promising THE BEST ENTERTAINMENT IN LONDON!

"*Feats of strength,*" he read off to Gideon as they made their way down a long corridor. "*Trained animals, strongwomen, acrobats, circus acts, and comic singers.*"

Gideon was muttering under his breath.

"And contortionists," Gabriel added brightly. "It looks like there's a woman here who can put her foot on top of her—"

"By the Angel, this place is barely better than a penny gaff," Gideon said. "Gabriel, don't look at anything unless I tell you it's all right."

Gabriel rolled his eyes as his brother took firm hold of his elbow and propelled him into what was clearly the grand salon—a massive room whose ceiling was painted with reproductions of the Italian Great Masters, including Botticelli's *Birth of Venus*, now rather smoke-stained and the worse for wear. Gasoliers hung from gilded mounds of plaster, filling the room with a yellowish light.

The walls were lined with velvet benches, on which dark figures huddled—gentlemen, surrounded by ladies whose dresses were too bright and whose laughter was too loud. Music poured from the stage at the front of the room. The Consul moved toward it, grinning. A woman in a top hat and tails was slinking up and down the stage, singing a song entitled "It's Naughty, but It's Nice." As she turned, her eyes flashed out green beneath the light of the gasolier.

Werewolf, Gabriel thought.

"Wait here for me a moment, boys," said the Consul, and he disappeared into the crowd.

"Lovely," Gideon muttered, and pulled Gabriel closer toward him as a woman in a tight-bodiced satin dress swayed by them. She smelled of gin and something else beneath it, something dark and sweet, a bit like James Carstairs's scent of burned sugar.

"Who knew the Consul was such a ramper?" Gabriel said. "Couldn't this have waited until after he took us to the Silent City?"

"He's not taking us to the Silent City." Gideon's mouth was tight.

"He's not?"

"Don't be a half-wit, Gabriel. Of course not. He wants something else from us. I don't know what yet. He took us here to unsettle us—and he wouldn't have done it if he weren't fairly sure he has something over us that will prevent us from telling Charlotte or anyone else where we've been."

"Maybe he did used to come here with Father."

"Maybe, but that's not why we're here now," Gideon said with finality. He tightened his grip on his brother's arm as the Consul reappeared, carrying with him a small bottle of what looked like soda water but what Gabriel guessed likely had at least a tuppence worth of spirit in it.

"What, nothing for us?" Gabriel inquired, and was met with a glare from his brother and a sour smile from the Consul. Gabriel realized he had no idea if the Consul himself had a family, or children. He was just the Consul. "Do you boys have any idea," he said, "what kind of peril you're in?"

"Peril? From who, Charlotte?" Gideon sounded incredulous.

"Not from Charlotte." The Consul returned his gaze to them.

"Your father did not just break the Law; he blasphemed it. He did not just deal with demons; he lay down among them. You are the Lightwoods—you are *all* that is left of the Lightwoods. You have no cousins, no aunts and uncles. I could have your whole family stricken off the registers of the Nephilim and turn you and your sister out into the street to starve or beg a living amid the mundanes, and I would be within the rights of Clave and Council to do it. And who do you think would stand up for you? Who would speak in your defense?"

Gideon had gone very pale, and his knuckles, where he gripped Gabriel's arm, were white. "That is not fair," he said. "We did not know. My brother trusted my father. He cannot be held responsible—"

"Trusted him? He delivered the deathblow, didn't he?" said the Consul. "Oh, you all contributed, but his was the coup de grâce that slew your father—which rather indicates that he knew exactly what your father was."

Gabriel was aware of Gideon looking at him with concern. The air in the Argent Rooms was hot and close, stealing his breath. The woman onstage was now singing a song called "All Through Obliging a Lady" and striding up and down, hitting the stage over and over with the end of a walking stick, which made the floor shudder.

"The sins of the fathers, children. You can and will be punished for his crimes if I desire it. What will you do, Gideon, while your brother and Tatiana have their runes burned off? Will you stand and watch?"

Gabriel's right hand twitched; he felt sure he would have reached out and seized the Consul by the throat if Gideon hadn't caught hold of him first and held his wrist. "What do you want from us?" Gideon asked, his voice controlled. "You didn't bring us here just to threaten us, not unless you want something in return. And if it was something you could ask easily or legally, you would have done it in the Silent City."

"Clever boy," the Consul said. "I want you to do something for me. Do it, and I will see to it that, though Lightwood House may be confiscated, you retain your honor and your name, your lands in Idris, and your place as Shadowhunters."

"What do you want us to do?"

"I wish you to observe Charlotte. Most specifically her correspondence. Tell me what letters she receives and sends, especially to and from Idris."

"You want us to spy on her." Gideon's voice was flat.

"I don't want any more surprises like the one about your father," said Consul. "She should never have kept his disease a secret from me."

"She had to," Gideon said. "It was a condition of the agreement they made—"

The Consul's lips tightened. "Charlotte Branwell has no right to make agreements of such scope without consulting me. I am her superior. She should not and cannot go over my head in that manner. She and that group in the Institute behave as if they are their own country that exists under its own laws. Look what happened with Jessamine Lovelace. She betrayed us all, nearly to our destruction. James Carstairs is a dying drug addict. That Gray girl is a changeling or a warlock and has no place in an Institute, ridiculous engagement be damned. And Will Herondale—Will Herondale is a liar and a spoiled brat who will grow up to be a criminal, if he grows up at all." The Consul paused, breathing hard.

"Charlotte may run that place like a fiefdom, but it is not. It is an Institute and reports to the Consul. And so will you."

"Charlotte has done nothing to deserve such a betrayal from me," Gideon said.

The Consul jabbed a finger toward him. "That is exactly what I speak of. Your loyalty is not to her; it cannot be to her. It is to me. It must be to me. Do you understand that?"

"And if I say no?"

"Then you lose everything. House, lands, name, lineage, purpose."

"We'll do it," said Gabriel, before Gideon could speak again. "We will watch her for you."

"Gabriel—," Gideon began.

Gabriel turned on his brother. "No," he said. "It's too much. You don't want to be a liar, I understand that. But our first loyalty is to family. The Blackthorns would throw Tati out on the streets, and she wouldn't last a moment there, her and the child—"

Gideon whitened. "Tatiana is going to have a child?"

Despite the horror of the situation, Gabriel felt a flash of satisfaction at knowing something his brother hadn't known. "Yes," he said. "You would have known it, if you were still part of our family."

Gideon glanced around the room as if searching for a familiar face, then looked helplessly back at his brother and the Consul. "I . . ."

Consul Wayland smiled coldly at Gabriel, and then his brother. "Have we an agreement, gentlemen?"

After a long moment Gideon nodded. "We will do it."

Gabriel would not soon forget the look that spread over the

Consul's face at that. There was satisfaction in it, but there was little surprise. It was clear he had expected nothing else, and nothing better, from the Lightwood boys.

"Scones?" Tessa said incredulously.

Sophie's mouth twitched into a smile. She was down on her knees before the grate with a rag and a bucket of soapy water. "You could have knocked me into a cocked hat, I was that startled," she confirmed. "Dozens of scones. Under his bed, all gone hard as rocks."

"My goodness," Tessa said, sliding to the edge of the bed and leaning back on her hands. Whenever Sophie was in her room cleaning, Tessa always had to hold herself back from rushing over to help the other girl with the tinderbox or the dusting. She had tried it on a few occasions, but after Sophie had set Tessa down gently but firmly for the fourth time, she had given it up.

"And you were angry?" Tessa said.

"Of course I was! Making all that extra work for me, carrying the scones up and down stairs, and then hiding them like that—I shouldn't be surprised if we end the autumn with mice."

Tessa nodded, gravely acknowledging the potential rodent issue. "But isn't it a bit flattering that he went to such lengths just to see you?"

Sophie sat up straight. "It's not flattering. He is not thinking. He is a Shadowhunter, and I am a mundane. I can expect nothing from him. In the best of all possible worlds, he might offer to take me as a mistress while he marries a Shadowhunter girl."

Tessa's throat tightened, remembering Will on the roof, offering her just that, offering her shame and disgrace, and how small she had felt, how worthless. It had been a lie, but the memory still held pain.

"No," Sophie said, looking back down at her red, work-roughened hands. "It is better that I never entertain the idea. That way there will be no disappointment."

"I think the Lightwoods are better men than that," Tessa offered.

Sophie brushed her hair back from her face, her fingers lightly touching the scar that bisected her cheek. "Sometimes I think there are no better men than that."

Neither Gideon nor Gabriel spoke as their carriage rattled back through the streets of the West End to the Institute. The rain was pouring down now, rattling the carriage so noisily that Gabriel doubted anyone would have heard him if he had spoken.

Gideon was studying his shoes, and did not look up as they rolled back to the Institute. As it loomed up out of the rain, the Consul reached across Gabriel and opened the door for them to exit.

"I trust you boys," he said. "Now go make Charlotte trust you too. And tell no one of our discussion. As far as this afternoon is concerned, you spent it with the Brothers."

Gideon climbed down out of the carriage without another word, and Gabriel followed him. The landau swung around and rattled off into the gray London afternoon. The sky was black and yellow, the drizzle as heavy as lead pellets, the fog so thick that Gabriel could barely see the Institute gates as they swung shut behind the carriage. He certainly didn't see his brother's hands as they darted forward, seized him by the collar of his jacket, and dragged him halfway around the side of the Institute.

He nearly fell as Gideon pushed him up against the stone wall of the old church. They were near the stables, half-hidden from view by one of the buttresses, but not protected from the rain. Cold drops assaulted Gabriel's head and neck and slid into his shirt. "Gideon—," he protested, slipping on the muddy flagstones.

"Be quiet." Gideon's eyes were huge and gray in the dull light, barely tinged with green.

"You're right." Gabriel dropped his voice. "We should organize our story. When they ask us what we did this afternoon, we must be in perfect accord in our answer, or it will not be believable—"

"I said be *quiet*." Gideon slammed his brother's shoulders back against the wall, hard enough for Gabriel to let out a gasp of pain. "We are not going to tell Charlotte of our conversation with the Consul. But neither are we going to *spy* on her. Gabriel, you are my brother, and I love you. I would do anything to protect you. But I will not sell out your soul and mine."

Gabriel looked at his brother. Rain soaked Gideon's hair and dripped into the collar of his coat. "We could die on the street if we refuse to do what the Consul says."

"I am not going to lie to Charlotte," said Gideon.

"Gideon—"

"Did you see the look on the Consul's face?" Gideon interrupted. "When we agreed to spy for him, to betray the generosity of the house that hosts us? He was not in the least surprised.

He never had a moment's doubt about us. He expects nothing but treachery from Lightwoods. That is our birthright." His hands tightened on Gabriel's arms. "There is more to life than surviving," he said. "We have honor, we are Nephilim. If he takes that, we truly have nothing."

"Why?" Gabriel asked. "Why are you so sure that Charlotte's side is the right one?"

"Because our father's was not," said Gideon. "Because I know Charlotte. Because I have lived among these people for months and they are good people. Because Charlotte Branwell has been nothing but kind to me. And Sophie loves her."

"And you love Sophie."

Gideon's mouth tensed.

"She's a mundane and a servant," said Gabriel. "I don't know what you expect to come of it, Gideon."

"Nothing," Gideon said roughly. "I expect nothing. But the fact that you believe I should shows that our father brought us up to believe that we should do right only if some reward was the result. I will not betray the word I have given Charlotte; that is the situation, Gabriel. If you do not want a part of it, I will send you to live with Tatiana and the Blackthorns. I am sure they will take you in. But I will not lie to Charlotte."

"Yes, you will," said Gabriel. "We are both going to lie to Charlotte. But we are going to lie to the Consul, too."

Gideon narrowed his eyes. Rainwater dripped off his eyelashes. "What do you mean?"

"We will do as the Consul says and read Charlotte's correspondence. Then we will report to him, but the reports will be false."

"If we are going to give him false reports anyway, why read her correspondence?"

"To know what *not* to say," Gabriel said, tasting dampness in his mouth. It tasted as if it had dripped from the Institute roof, bitter and dirty. "To avoid accidentally telling him the truth."

"If we are discovered, we could face consequences of the utmost severity."

Gabriel spit rainwater. "Then you tell me. Would you risk severe consequences for the inhabitants of the Institute, or not? Because I—I am doing this for *you*, and because . . ."

"Because?"

"Because I made a mistake. I was wrong about our father. I believed in him, and I should not have." Gabriel took a deep breath. "I was wrong, and I seek to undo that, and if there is a price to be paid, then I will pay it."

Gideon looked at him for a long time. "Was this your plan all along? When you agreed to the Consul's demands, in the Argent Rooms, was this your plan?"

Gabriel looked away from his brother, toward the rain-wet courtyard. In his mind he could see the two of them, much younger, standing where the Thames cut through the edge of the house's property, and Gideon showing him the safe paths through the swampy ground. His brother had always been the one to show him the safe paths. There had been a time when they had trusted each other implicitly, and he did not know when it had ended, but his heart ached for it more than it ached at the loss of his father.

"Would you believe me," he said bitterly, "if I told you it was? Because it is the truth."

Gideon was still for a long moment. Then Gabriel found himself hauled forward, his face mashed into the wet wool of Gideon's overcoat while his brother held him tightly, murmuring, "All right, little brother. It's going to be all right," as he rocked them both back and forth in the rain.

To: *Members of the Council*
From: *Consul Josiah Wayland*

Very well, gentlemen. In that case I ask only for your patience and that you not act in haste. If it is proof you want, I will furnish proof.
I shall write again on this subject soon.
In Raziel's name and in defense of his honor,
Consul Josiah Wayland

7

DARE TO WISH

If the past year were offered me again,
And choice of good and ill before me set
Would I accept the pleasure with the pain
Or dare to wish that we had never met?
—Augusta, Lady Gregory,
"If the Past Year Were Offered Me Again"

To: Consul Wayland
From: Gabriel and Gideon Lightwood

Dear Sir,

    We are most thankful that you have assigned us the task of monitoring Mrs. Branwell's behavior. Women, as we know, need to be closely watched so they do not go astray. We are grieved to announce that we have shocking tidings to report.

A woman's management of her household is her most important duty, and one of the most important womanly virtues is frugality. Mrs. Branwell, however, seems addicted to expenditure and cares for nothing save vulgar display.

Though she may be dressed plainly when you pay a visit, we are saddened to report that in her leisure hours she bedecks herself with the finest silks and the most costly jewels imaginable. You asked us to, and loath though we were to invade a lady's privacy, we did so. We would report the exact details of her letter to her modiste, but we fear you would be overcome. Suffice it to say, the money outlaid upon hats rivals the annual income of a large estate or a small country. We fail to see why one small woman needs so many hats. She is unlikely to be concealing additional heads upon her person.

We would be too gentlemanly to comment upon a lady's attire, except for the deleterious effect it has on our duties. She skimps on household necessities to the most horrifying degree. Every night we sit down to a dinner of gruel as she sits at table dripping with gems and gewgaws. This is, you may conceive, hardly fighting fare for your valiant Shadowhunters. We are so weak that we were almost vanquished by a Behemoth demon last Tuesday, and of course those creatures are chiefly composed of a viscous substance. At our peak, and sustained with good victuals, either of us would be capable of crushing beneath our boot heels a dozen Behemoth demons at a time.

We very much hope that you will be able to render us

assistance in this matter, and that Mrs. Branwell's outlay
upon hats—and other feminine articles of clothing that we
hesitate in delicacy to name—will be checked.
  Yours truly,
  Gideon and Gabriel Lightwood

"What's a gewgaw?" Gabriel asked, blinking owlishly down
at the epistle he had just helped compose. Actually, Gideon
had dictated most of it; Gabriel had merely moved the pen
across the page. He was beginning to suspect that behind his
brother's dour facade lay an unsung comic genius.

Gideon waved a dismissive hand. "It doesn't matter. Seal
the envelope and let us give it to Cyril that it may go out with
the morning post."

It had been several days since the battle with the great worm,
and Cecily was in the training room again. She was beginning
to wonder if she should simply move her bed and other furnish-
ing into this space, as she seemed to spend most of her time
here. The bedroom Charlotte had given her was nearly bare of
decoration or anything that might remind her of home. She
had brought almost nothing personal with her from Wales, not
expecting that she would be staying for a lengthy time.

Here at least in the weapons room she felt secure. Perhaps
because there was no room like it where she had grown up;
it was purely a Shadowhunter place. Nothing about it could
possibly make her homesick. The walls were hung with dozens of weapons. Her first lesson with Will, when he had still
been blazing with rage that she was there at all, had involved
memorizing all their names and what they did. *Katana* blades

from Japan, double-handed broadswords, thin-bladed miseri-
cords, morning stars and maces, curved Turkish blades,
crossbows and slingshots and tiny pipes that blew poisoned
needles. She remembered him spitting the words out as if
they were poison.

Be as angry as you want, big brother, she had thought. *I may
pretend I wish to be a Shadowhunter now, because it gives you no
choice but to keep me here. But I will show you that these people are
not your family. I will bring you home.*

She lifted a sword down from the wall now and balanced it
carefully in her hands. Will had explained to her that the way
to hold a two-handed sword was just below the rib cage, pointing straight out. Legs should be balanced with equal weight on
them, and the sword should be swung from the shoulders, not
the arms, to get the most force into a killing blow.

A killing blow. For so many years she had been angry at
her brother for leaving them all to join the Shadowhunters in
London, for giving himself up to what her mother had termed
a life of mindless murder, of weapons and blood and death.
What was so poor to him about the green mountains of Wales?
What did their family lack? Why turn your back on the bluest
of blue seas, for something as empty as all that?

And yet here she was, choosing to spend her time alone in
the training room with the silent collection of weaponry. The
weight of the sword in her hand was comforting, almost as if it
served as a barrier between herself and her feelings.

She and Will had wandered all over the city a few nights
before, from opium dens to gambling hells to ifrit haunts,
a blur of color and scents and light. He had not been exactly
friendly, but she knew that, for Will, allowing her to accom-

pany him on such a sensitive errand had been a gesture indeed.

She had enjoyed their companionship that night. It had been like having her brother back. But as the evening had worn on, Will had become progressively more silent, and when they'd returned to the Institute, he had stalked away, clearly wishing to be alone, leaving Cecily with nothing to do but return to her room and lie awake staring at the ceiling until dawn came.

She had thought, somehow, when she had planned to come here, that the bonds that held him here could not be that strong. His attachment to these people could not be like his attachment to family. But as the night had gone on and she had seen his hope, and then his disappointment, at each new establishment when he'd asked after *yin fen* and there was none to be had, she had understood—oh, she had been told it before, had known it before, but that was not the same as *understanding*—that the ties that bound him here were as strong as any ties of blood.

She was tired now, and though she gripped the sword as Will had taught her—right hand below the guard, left hand on the pommel—it slipped from her grasp and tipped forward, burying itself point-down in the floor.

"Oh, dear," said a voice from the doorway. "I'm afraid I could only give *that* effort a three. Four perhaps, if I were inclined to give you an extra point for practicing swordplay in an afternoon dress."

Cecily, who indeed had not bothered to change into gear, flung her head back and glared at Gabriel Lightwood, who had appeared in the doorway like some sort of imp of the perverse. "Perhaps I am not interested in your opinion, sir."

"Perhaps." He took a step forward into the room. "The Angel knows your brother never has been."

"In that we are united," Cecily remarked, pulling the sword free of the floor.

"But not in much else." Gabriel moved to stand behind her. They were both reflected in one of the training mirrors; Gabriel was a good head taller than her, and she could see his face clearly over her shoulder. He had one of those odd sharp-boned faces: handsome from some angles, and peculiarly interesting-looking from others. There was a small white scar on his chin, as if he had been nicked there by a thin blade. "Would you like me to show you how to properly hold the sword?"

"If you must."

He did not reply but reached around her, adjusting her grip on the pommel. "You never want to hold your sword point-down," he said. "Hold it like this—point out—so that if your opponent charges you, they will skewer themselves on your blade."

Cecily adjusted her grip accordingly. Her mind was racing. She had thought of Shadowhunters as monsters for such a long time. Monsters who had kidnapped her brother, and she a heroine, riding up to rescue him even if he didn't realize he needed rescuing. It had been strange and gradual, realizing how human they were. She could feel the warmth rising from Gabriel's body, his breath stirring her hair, and oh, it was odd, to be conscious of so many things about someone else: the way they felt, the brush of their skin, the way they *smelled*—

"I saw the way you fought at Lightwood House," Gabriel Lightwood murmured. His callused hand brushed down over her fingers, and Cecily fought back a small shiver.

"Badly?" she said, attempting a teasing tone.

"With passion. There are those who fight because it is their duty and those who fight because they love it. You love it."

"I don't—," Cecily began, but she was interrupted as the training room door flew open with a loud bang.

It was Will, filling the doorway with his lanky, broad-shouldered frame. His blue eyes were thunderous. "What are you doing here?" he demanded.

So much for the brief peace they had achieved the night before. "I am practicing," Cecily said. "You told me I would get no better without practice."

"Not you. Gabriel Lightworm over here." Will jerked his chin toward the other boy. "Sorry. Light*wood*."

Gabriel slowly unhitched his arms from around Cecily. "Whoever has been tutoring your sister in swordplay has imparted many bad habits. I was merely endeavoring to help."

"I told him it was all right," Cecily said, having no idea why she was defending Gabriel, except that she suspected it would annoy Will.

It did. His eyes narrowed. "And did *he* tell *you* he has been looking for years for a way to get back at me for what he per-ceives as an insult to *his* sister? And what better way to do it than through you?"

Cecily whipped her head around to stare at Gabriel, who wore an expression of mixed annoyance and defiance. "Is that true?"

He did not reply to her but to Will. "If we are going to live in the same house, Herondale, then we shall have to learn to treat each other cordially. Don't you agree?"

"As long as I can still break your arm as easily as look at you,

I agree to no such thing." Will reached up and plucked a rapier off the wall. "Now get out of here, Gabriel. And leave my sister alone."

With a single scornful look, Gabriel pushed his way past Will and out of the room. "Was that absolutely necessary, Will?" Cecily demanded as soon as the door had shut behind him.

"I know Gabriel Lightwood and you do not. I suggest you leave it to me to be the best judge of his character. He wishes to use you to hurt me—"

"Really, you cannot imagine a motivation he might have that is not yourself?"

"I know him," Will said again. "He has shown himself to be a liar and a traitor—"

"People change."

"Not that much."

"You have," Cecily said, striding across the room and dropping her sword onto a bench with a clatter.

"So have you," Will said, surprising her. She turned on him.

"I have changed? How have *I* changed?"

"When you came here," he said, "you spoke over and over of getting me to come home with you. You disliked your training. You pretended otherwise, but I could tell. Then it ceased to be 'Will, you must go home,' and became 'Write a letter, Will.' And you began to enjoy your training. Gabriel Lightwood is a bounder, but he was right about one thing: You did enjoy fighting the great worm at Lightwood House. Shadowhunter blood is like gunpowder in your veins, Cecy. Once it is lit, it is not so easily extinguished. Remain much longer here, and there is every likelihood you will be like me—too entwined to leave."

Cecily squinted at her brother. His shirt was open at the collar, showing something scarlet winking in the hollow of his throat. "Are you wearing a woman's necklace, Will?"

Will put a hand to his neck with a startled look, but before he could respond, the door to the training room opened once more and Sophie stood there, an anxious expression upon her scarred face.

"Master Will, Miss Herondale," she said. "I have been looking for you. Charlotte has requested that everyone come to the drawing room right away; it is a matter of some urgency."

Cecily had always been something of a lonely child. It was difficult not to be when your elder siblings were dead or missing and there were no young people your age nearby whom your parents considered suitable companions. She had learned early to amuse herself with her own observations of people, unshared with others but kept close that she might take them out later and examine them when she was in solitude.

The habits of a lifetime were not broken quickly, and though Cecily was no longer lonely, since she had come to the Institute eight weeks ago, she had made its inhabitants the subject of her close study. They were Shadowhunters, after all—the enemy at first, and then, as that had become less and less her view, simply the subject of fascination.

She examined them now as she walked into the drawing room beside Will. First was Charlotte, seated behind her desk. Cecily had not known Charlotte long, and yet she knew that Charlotte was the sort of woman who kept her calm even under pressure. She was tiny but strong, a bit like Cecily's own mother, although with less of a penchant for muttering in Welsh.

Then there was Henry. He might have been the first of them all to convince Cecily that though Shadowhunters were different, they were not dangerously alien. There was nothing frightening about Henry, all lanky legs and angles as he leaned against Charlotte's desk.

Her eyes slid over Gideon Lightwood next, shorter and stockier than his brother—Gideon, whose green-gray eyes usually followed Sophie about the Institute like a hopeful puppy's. She wondered if the others in the Institute had noticed his attachment to their maid, and what Sophie thought about it herself.

And then there was Gabriel. Cecily's thoughts where he was concerned were jumbled and confused. His eyes were bright, his body tense as a coiled spring as he leaned against his brother's armchair. On the dark velvet sofa just across from the Lightwoods sat Jem, with Tessa beside him. He had looked up as the door had opened and, as he always did, had seemed to glow a little brighter when he saw Will. It was a quality peculiar to both of them, and Cecily wondered if it was that way for all *parabatai*, or if they were a unique case. In either eventuality, it must be terrifying to be so intertwined with another person, especially when one of them was as fragile as Jem.

As she watched, Tessa laid her hand over Jem's and said something quiet to him that made him smile. Tessa looked quickly to Will, but he only crossed the room as he always did to lean against the fireplace mantel. Cecily had never been able to decide if he did this because he was perpetually cold or because he thought he looked dashing standing before the leaping flames.

You must be ashamed of your brother—harboring illicit feel-

ings for his parabatai*'s fiancée,* Will had said to her. If he had been anyone else, she would have told him there was no point keeping secrets. The truth would out, eventually. But in Will's case, she was not sure. He had the skill of years of hiding and pretending on his side. He was a master actor. If it were not that she was his sister, if it were not that she saw his face at the moments when Jem was not looking, she did not think she would have guessed it either.

And then there was the awful truth that he would not need to hide his secret forever. He needed to hide it only as long as Jem lived. If James Carstairs were not so unrelentingly kind and well intentioned, Cecily thought, she might have hated him on her brother's behalf. Not only was he marrying the girl Will loved, but when he himself died, she feared, Will would never recover. But you could not blame someone for dying. For leaving on purpose, perhaps, as her brother had left her and her parents, but not for dying, the power over which was surely beyond the grasp of any mortal human.

"I'm glad you're all here," Charlotte said in a strained voice that snapped Cecily out of her brown study. Charlotte was looking gravely down at a polished salver on her desk, on which was an opened letter and a small packet wrapped in waxed paper. "I have received a disturbing piece of correspondence. From the Magister."

"From *Mortmain?*" Tessa leaned forward, and the clockwork angel she always wore around her neck swung free, glittering in the light from the fire. "He *wrote* to you?"

"Not to inquire about your health, one presumes," said Will. "What does he want?"

Charlotte took a deep breath. "I will read you the letter."

My Dear Mrs. Branwell,

Forgive me for troubling you at what must be a distressing time for your household. I was grieved, though I must confess not shocked, to hear of Mr. Carstairs's grave indisposition.

I believe you are aware that I am the happy possessor of a large—I might say exclusively large—portion of the medicine that Mr. Carstairs requires for his continued well-being. Thus we find ourselves in a most interesting situation, which I am eager to resolve to the satisfaction of us both. I would be very glad to make an exchange: If you are willing to confide Miss Gray to my keeping, I will place a large portion of yin fen in yours.

I send a token of my goodwill. Pray let me know your decision by writing to me. If the correct sequence of numbers that are printed at the bottom of this letter, are spoken to my automaton, I am sure to receive it.

Yours sincerely,

Axel Mortmain

"That is all," Charlotte said, folding the letter in half and placing it back on the salver. "There are instructions on how to summon the automaton to which he wishes us to give our answer, and there are the number he speaks of, but they give no clue as to his location."

There was a shocked silence. Cecily, who had seated herself in a small flowered armchair, glanced at Will and saw him look away quickly as if to hide his expression. Jem paled, his face turning the color of old ash, and Tessa—Tessa sat very still, the light from the fire chasing shadows across her face.

"Mortmain wants *me*," she said finally, breaking the silence. "In exchange for Jem's *yin fen*."

"It is ridiculous," Jem said. "Untenable. The letter should be given to the Clave to see if they can discern anything about his location from it, but that is all."

"They will not be able to discern anything about his location from it," said Will quietly. "The Magister has proved himself over and over too clever for that."

"This is not clever," said Jem. "This is the crudest form of blackmail—"

"I do not disagree," said Will. "I say we take the packet as a blessing, a handful more of *yin fen* that will help you, and we ignore the rest."

"Mortmain wrote the letter about me," Tessa said, interrupting them both. "The decision should be mine." She angled her body toward Charlotte. "I will go."

There was another dead silence. Charlotte looked ashen; Cecily could feel her own hands slippery with sweat where they twisted in her lap. The Lightwood brothers seemed desperately uncomfortable. Gabriel looked as if he wished he were anywhere else but there. Cecily could hardly blame them. The tension between Will, Jem, and Tessa felt like a powder keg that needed only a match to blow it to kingdom come.

"No," Jem said finally, rising to his feet. "Tessa, you cannot."

She followed his motion, rising as well. "I can. You are my fiancé. I cannot allow you to die when I might help you, and Mortmain does not mean me physical harm—"

"We do not know what he means! He cannot be trusted!" Will said suddenly, and then he put his head down, his hand gripping the mantel so hard that his fingers were white. Cecily could tell he was forcing himself to be silent.

"If it were you Mortmain wanted, Will, you would go," said Tessa, looking at Cecily's brother with a meaning in her eyes that brooked no contradiction. Will flinched at her words.

"No," said Jem. "I would forbid him as well."

Tessa turned to Jem with the first expression of anger toward him Cecily had ever seen on her face. "You cannot forbid me—any more than you could Will—"

"I can," Jem said. "For a very simple reason. The drug is not a *cure*, Tessa. It only extends my living. I will not allow you to throw away your own life for a remnant of mine. If you go to Mortmain, it will be for nothing. I still won't take the drug."

Will lifted his head. "James—"

But Tessa and Jem were staring at each other, eyes locked. "You would not," Tessa breathed. "You would not insult me by hurling a sacrifice I made for you back in my face like that."

Jem strode across the room and seized the packet—and the letter—off Charlotte's desk. "I would rather insult you than lose you," he said, and before any of them could make a move to stop him, he cast both items into the fire.

The room erupted in shouts. Henry dashed forward, but Will had already dropped to his knees before the grate and thrust both his hands into the flames.

Cecily bolted out of her chair. *"Will!"* she shouted, and darted over to her brother. She seized him by the shoulders of his jacket and pulled him away from the fire. He tumbled backward, the still-burning packet falling from his hands. Gideon was there a moment later, stamping out the small flames with his feet, leaving a mess of burned paper and silvery powder on the rug.

Cecily stared into the grate. The letter with the instructions telling how to summon Mortmain's automaton was gone, burned into ashes.

"Will," Jem said. He looked sick. He fell to his knees next to Cecily, still holding her brother's shoulders, and drew a stele from his jacket. Will's hands were scarlet, livid white where blisters were already forming on the skin, and patched black with soot. His breath was hitching and harsh in Cecily's ear— gasps of pain, the way he had sounded when he'd fallen off the roof of their house when he was nine and had shattered the bones in his left arm. "*Byddwch yn iawn, Will,*" she said as Jem put the stele to her brother's forearm and drew quickly. "You'll be all right."

"Will," Jem said, half under his breath. "Will, I'm so sorry, I'm so sorry. Will—"

Will's hitching breaths were slowing as the *iratze* took effect, his skin paling back to its normal color. "There's still some *yin fen* that can be preserved," Will said, slumping back against Cecily. He smelled like smoke and iron. She could feel his heart pounding through his back. "It had better be gathered up before anything else—"

"Here." It was Tessa, kneeling down; Cecily was dimly aware that all the others were standing, Charlotte with one hand over her mouth in shock. In Tessa's right hand was a handkerchief, in which was perhaps half a handful of *yin fen*, all that Will had saved from the fire. "Take this," she said, and put it in Jem's free hand, the one that did not hold the stele. He looked as if he were about to speak to her, but she had already straightened up. Looking utterly shattered, Jem watched as she walked from the room.

"Oh, Will. Whatever are we going to do with you?"

Will sat, feeling rather incongruous in the flowered armchair in the drawing room, letting Charlotte, perched on a small stool before him, smear salve on his hands. They no longer hurt much, after three *iratzes*, and they had returned to their normal color, but Charlotte insisted on treating them anyway.

The others had gone, save for Cecily and Jem; Cecily sat beside him, perched on the arm of his chair, and Jem knelt on the burned rug, his stele still in his hands, not touching Will but close. They had refused to leave, even after the others had drifted away and Charlotte had sent Henry back to the cellar to work. There was nothing more to be done, after all. The instructions on how to contact Mortmain were gone, burned to ash, and there was no more decision to be made.

Charlotte had insisted that Will stay and have his hands salved, and Cecily and Jem had refused to leave him. And Will had to admit he liked it, liked having his sister there on the arm of his chair, liked the fiercely protective glares she shot at anyone who came near him, even Charlotte, sweet and harmless with her salve and her motherly clucking. And Jem, at his feet, leaning a bit against his chair, as he had so many times when Will was being bandaged up from fights or *iratzed* because of wounds he'd gotten in battle.

"Do you remember the time Meliorn tried to knock your teeth out for calling him a pointy-eared layabout?" Jem said. He had taken some of the *yin fen* Mortmain had sent, and there was color in his cheeks again.

Will smiled, despite everything; he couldn't help it. It had been the one thing in the past few years that had made him feel fortunate: that he had someone in his life who knew him, knew what he was thinking before he said it out loud. "I would have knocked his teeth out in return," he said, "but when I went to find him again, he had emigrated to America. To avoid my wrath, no doubt."

"Hmph," said Charlotte, the way she always did when she thought Will was getting above himself. "He had many enemies in London, to my understanding."

"Dydw I ddim yn gwybod pwy yw unrhyw un o'r bobl yr ydych yn siarad amdano," said Cecily plaintively.

"You may not know who we are talking about, but no one else knows what you are *saying*," said Will, though his tone held no real reproof. He could hear the exhaustion in his own voice. The lack of sleep of the night before was taking its toll. "Speak English, Cecy."

Charlotte rose, returned to her desk, and set the jar of salve down. Cecily tugged on a lock of Will's hair. "Let me see your hands."

He held them up. He remembered the fire, the white-hot agony of it, and more than anything else Tessa's shocked face. He knew she would understand why he had done what he had done, why he had not thought twice about it, but the look in her eyes—as if her heart had broken for him.

He only wished that she were still here. It was good to be here with Jem and Cecily and Charlotte, to be surrounded by their affection, but without her there would always be something missing, a Tessa-shaped part chiseled out of his heart that he would never get back.

Cecily touched his fingers, which looked quite normal now, aside from the soot under his fingernails. "It is quite astonishing," she said, then patted his hands lightly, careful not to smear the salve. "Will has always been prone to damaging himself," she added, with fondness in her tone. "I cannot count the broken limbs he sustained when we were children—the scratches, the scars."

Jem leaned closer against the chair, staring into the fire. "Better it were my hands," he said.

Will shook his head. Exhaustion was muting the edges of everything in the room, blurring the flocked wallpaper into a single mass of dark color. "No. Not your hands. You need your hands for the violin. What do I need mine for?"

"I should have known what you would do," Jem said in a low voice. "I always know what you will do. I should have known you would put your hands into the fire."

"And I should have known you would throw that packet away," said Will, without rancor. "It was—it was a madly noble thing to do. I understand why you did it."

"I was thinking of Tessa." Jem drew his knees up and rested his chin on them, then laughed softly. "Madly noble. Isn't that meant to be your area of expertise? Suddenly I am the one who does ridiculous things and you tell me to stop?"

"God," said Will. "When did we change places?"

The firelight played over Jem's face and hair as he shook his head. "It is a very strange thing, to be in love," he said. "It changes you."

Will looked down at Jem, and what he felt, more than jealousy, more than anything else, was a wistful desire to commiserate with his best friend, to speak of the feelings he held in his heart. For were they not the same feelings? Did they not love the same way, the same person? But, "I wish you wouldn't risk yourself," was all he said.

Jem stood up. "I have always wished that about you."

Will raised his eyes, so drowsy with sleep and the tiredness that came with healing runes that he could see Jem only as a haloed figure of light. "Are you going?"

"Yes, to sleep." Jem touched his fingers lightly to Will's healing hands. "Let yourself rest, Will."

Will's eyes were already drifting closed, even as Jem turned to go. He did not hear the door close behind Jem. Somewhere down the corridor Bridget was singing, her voice rising above the crackle of the fire. Will did not find it as annoying as he usually did, but rather more like a lullaby that his mother would once have sung him, to guide him to sleep.

"Oh, what is brighter than the light?
What is darker than the night?
What is keener than an axe?
What is softer than melting wax?

Truth is brighter than the light,
Falsehood darker than the night.
Revenge is keener than an axe,
And love is softer than melting wax."

"A riddle song," Cecily said, her voice drowsy and half-awake. "I've always liked those. Do you remember when Mam used to sing to us?"

"A little," Will admitted. If he were not so tired, he might not have admitted it at all. His mother had always been singing, music filling the corners of the manor house, singing while she walked beside the waters in the Mawddach estuary, or among the daffodils in the gardens. *Llawn yw'r coed o ddail a blode, llawn o goriad merch wyf inne.*

"Do you remember the sea?" he said, exhaustion making his voice heavy. "The lake at Tal-y-Llyn? There is nothing so blue here in London as either of those things."

He heard Cecily take a sharp breath. "Of course I remember. I thought you did not."

Images from dreams painted themselves on the inside of Will's eyelids, sleep reaching for him like a current, pulling him away from the lighted shore. "I don't think I can get up out of this chair, Cecy," he murmured. "I shall rest here tonight."

Her hand came up, felt for his, and circled it in a loose clasp. "Then I will stay with you," she said, and her voice became part of the current of dreams and sleep that caught him finally and drew him down and over and under.

> *To: Gabriel and Gideon Lightwood*
> *From: Consul Josiah Wayland*
>
> *I was most surprised to receive your missive. I fail to perceive how I could possibly have made myself more clear. I wish for you to relay the details of Mrs. Branwell's correspondence with her relatives and well-wishers in Idris. I did not request any persiflage about the woman's milliner. I care neither about her manner of dress nor about your daily menu.*

Pray write back to me a letter containing relevant information. I devoutly hope such a letter will also be one more befitting Shadowhunters and less Bedlamites.

In Raziel's name,

Consul Wayland

8

THAT FIRE OF FIRE

You call it hope—that fire of fire!
It is but agony of desire.
—Edgar Allan Poe, "Tamerlane"

Tessa sat at her vanity table methodically brushing out her hair. The air outside was cool but humid, seeming to trap the water of the Thames, scented with iron and city dirt. It was the sort of weather that made her normally thick, wavy hair tangle at the ends. Not that her mind was on her hair; it was simply a repetitive motion, the brushing, that allowed her to keep a sort of forcible calm.

Over and over in her mind she saw Jem's shock as Charlotte read out Mortmain's letter, and Will's burned hands, and the tiny bit of *yin fen* she had managed to gather up off the floor.

She saw Cecily's arms about Will, and Jem's anguish as he apologized to Will, *I'm so sorry, I'm so sorry.*

She hadn't been able to bear it. They had been in agony, both of them, and she loved them both. Their pain had been because of her—*she* was what Mortmain wanted. She was the cause of Jem's *yin fen* being gone, and Will's misery. When she had whirled and run out of the room, it had been because she could not stand it any longer. How could three people who cared for one another so much cause one another so much pain?

She set the hairbrush down and looked at herself in the mirror. She looked tired, with shadowed eyes, as Will had looked all day as he'd sat with her in the library and helped Charlotte with Benedict's papers, translating some of the passages that were in Greek or Latin or Purgatic, his quill pen moving swiftly over paper, his dark head bent. It was odd to look at Will in the daylight and remember the boy who had held her as if she were a life raft in a storm on the steps of Woolsey's house. Will's daylight face was not untroubled, but it was not open or giving either. He had not been unfriendly or cold, but neither had he looked up, or smiled over the library table at her, or acknowledged in any way the events of the previous night.

She had wanted to pull him aside and ask him if he had heard from Magnus, to say to him: *No one understands what you feel but me, and no one understands what I feel but you, so can we not feel together?* But if Magnus had contacted him, Will would have told her; he was honorable. They were all honorable. If they had not been, she thought, looking down at her hands, perhaps everything would not be so awful.

It had been foolish to offer to go to Mortmain—she knew that now—but the thought had seized her as fiercely as a passion. She could *not* be the cause of all this unhappiness and not do something to alleviate it. If she gave herself up to Mortmain, Jem would live longer, and Jem and Will would have each other, and it would be as if she had never come to the Institute.

But now, in the cold hours of the evening, she knew that nothing she could do would turn back the clock, or unmake the feelings that existed between them all. She felt hollow inside, as if a piece of her were missing, and yet she was paralyzed. Part of her wanted to run to Will, to see if his hands were healed and to tell him she understood. The rest of her wanted to flee across the hall to Jem's room and beg him to forgive her. They had never been angry with each other before, and she did not know how to navigate a Jem who was furious. Would he want to end their engagement? Would he be disappointed in her? Somehow that thought was as hard to bear, that Jem might be disappointed in her.

Skritch. She looked up and around the room—a faint noise. Perhaps she had imagined it? She was tired; perhaps it was time to call for Sophie to help her with her dress, and then to retire to bed with a book. She was partway through *The Castle of Otranto* and finding it an excellent distraction.

She had risen from her chair and gone to ring the servants' bell when the noise came again, more determined. A *skritch, skritch*, against the door of her bedroom. With slight trepidation she crossed the room and flung the door open.

Church crouched on the other side, his blue-gray fur

ruffled, his expression furious. Around his neck was tied a bow of silver lace, and attached to the bow was a small piece of rolled paper, like a tiny scroll. Tessa dropped to her knees, reached for the bow, and untied it. The bow fell away, and the cat immediately bolted down the hall.

The paper came free of the lace, and Tessa picked up the paper and unrolled it. Familiar looping script traced its way across the page.

Meet me in the music room.
—J

"There's nothing here," Gabriel said.

He and Gideon were in the drawing room. It was quite dark, with the curtains drawn; if they had not had their witchlights, it would have been as black as pitch. Gabriel was going hastily through the correspondence on Charlotte's desk, for the second time.

"What do you mean, nothing?" said Gideon, standing by the door. "I see a pile of letters there. Certainly one of them must be—"

"Nothing scandalous," Gabriel said, slamming a desk drawer shut. "Or even interesting. Some correspondence with an uncle in Idris. He appears to have gout."

"Fascinating," Gideon muttered.

"One cannot help but wonder exactly what it is that the Consul believes Charlotte to be involved in. Some sort of betrayal of the Council?" Gabriel picked up her sheaf of letters and made a face. "We could reassure him of her innocence if only we knew what it was that he suspected."

"And if I believed he wanted to be reassured of her innocence," Gideon said. "It seems to me more likely that he is hoping to catch her out." He reached out a hand. "Give me that letter."

"The one to her uncle?" Gabriel was dubious, but did as directed. He held the witchlight up, shining its rays over the desk as Gideon bent over and, having appropriated one of Charlotte's pens, began to scratch out a missive to the Consul.

Gideon was blowing on the ink to dry it when the door of the drawing room flew open. Gideon jerked upright. A yellow glow poured into the room, far brighter than the dim witchlight; Gabriel put up a hand to cover his eyes, blinking. He ought to have put on a Night Vision rune, he thought, but they took time to fade, and he had been concerned it would have raised questions. In the moments that it took his vision to adjust, he heard his brother exclaim, aghast:

"*Sophie?*"

"I have told you not to call me that, Mr. Lightwood." Her tone was cold. Gabriel's vision resolved, and he saw the maid standing in the doorway, a lit lamp in one hand. She was squinting. Her eyes narrowed further as they lit on Gabriel, Charlotte's letters still in his hand. "Are you— Is that Mrs. Branwell's correspondence?"

Gabriel dropped the letters hastily onto the desk. "I . . . We . . ."

"Have you been *reading her letters?*" Sophie looked furious, like some sort of avenging angel, lamp in hand. Gabriel glanced quickly at his brother, but Gideon appeared to be struck speechless.

In all Gabriel's life he could not remember his brother giving even the prettiest of Shadowhunter girls a second glance. Yet he looked at this scarred mundane servant as if she were the sun rising. It was inexplicable, but it was also undeniable. He could see the horror on his brother's face as Sophie's good opinion of him shattered before his eyes.

"Yes," Gabriel said. "Yes, we are indeed going through her correspondence."

Sophie took a step back. "I shall fetch Mrs. Branwell immediately—"

"No—" Gabriel held out a hand. "It isn't what you think. Wait." Quickly he outlined what had happened: the Consul's threats, his request that they spy on Charlotte, and their solution to the problem. "We never intended to reveal a word she had actually written," he finished. "Our intention was to protect her."

Sophie's suspicious expression did not change. "And why should I believe a word of that, Mr. Lightwood?"

Gideon finally spoke. "Ms. Collins," he said. "Please. I know that since the—unfortunate business—with the scones you have not held me in esteem, but please do believe I would not betray the trust Charlotte has placed in me, nor reward her kindness to me with betrayal."

Sophie wavered for a moment, then dropped her gaze. "I am sorry, Mr. Lightwood. I *wish* to believe you, but it is with Mrs. Branwell that my first loyalty must lie."

Gabriel snatched up from the desk the letter his brother had just written. "Miss Collins," he said. "Please read this missive. It was what we had intended to send the Consul. If, after reading it, you are still determined in your heart to seek out Mrs. Branwell, then we will not try to stop you."

Sophie looked from him to Gideon. Then, with a quick inclination of her head, she came forward and set the lamp down on the desk. Taking the letter from Gideon, she unfolded it and read out loud:

> "*To: Consul Josiah Wayland*
> *From: Gideon and Gabriel Lightwood*
>
> *Dear Sir,*
> *You have displayed your usual great wisdom in asking us to read Mrs. Branwell's missives to Idris. We obtained a private glance into said correspondence and observed that she is in almost daily communication with her great-uncle Roderick Fairchild.*
> *The contents of these letters, sir, would shock and disappoint you. It has robbed us of much of our belief in the fairer sex.*
> *Mrs. Branwell displays a most callous, inhumane, and unfeminine attitude toward his many grievous ills. She recommends the application of less liquor to cure his gout, shows unmistakable signs of being amused by his dire ailment of dropsy, and entirely ignores his mention of a suspicious substance building up within his ears and other orifices.*
> *Signs of the tender feminine care one would expect from a woman to her male relatives, and the respect any relatively young woman should give her elder as his due—there are none! Mrs. Branwell, we fear, has run mad with power. She must be stopped before it is too late and many*

*brave Shadowhunters have fallen by the wayside for lack
of feminine care.*

    Yours faithfully,
    Gideon and Gabriel Lightwood"

There was silence when she had finished. Sophie stood for
what felt like an eternity, staring wide-eyed at the paper. At last
she said, "Which one of you wrote this?"

Gideon cleared his throat. "I did."

She looked up. She had pressed her lips together, but they
were trembling. For a horrible moment Gabriel thought she
was about to cry. "Oh, my gracious," she said. "And is this the
first?"

"No, there has been one other," Gabriel admitted. "It was
about Charlotte's hats."

"Her hats?" A peal of laughter escaped Sophie's lips, and
Gideon looked at her as if he had never seen anything so marvelous. Gabriel had to admit she did look quite pretty when she
laughed, scar or not. "And was the Consul furious?"

"Murderously so," said Gideon.

"Are you going to tell Mrs. Branwell?" demanded Gabriel,
who could not stand the suspense another moment.

Sophie had stopped laughing. "I will not," she said, "for I do
not wish to compromise you in the eyes of the Consul, and also,
I think such news would hurt her, and to no good end. Spying
on her like that, that awful man!" Her gaze sparked. "If you
would like aid in your plan to frustrate the Consul's schemes,
I am happy to give it. Let me keep the letter, and I shall ensure
that it is posted tomorrow."

* * *

The music room was not as dusty as Tessa remembered it—it looked as if it had received a good cleaning recently; the mellow wood of the windowsills and floors shone, as did the grand piano in the corner. A fire was leaping in the grate, outlining Jem in fire as he turned away from it and, seeing her, smiled a nervous smile.

Everything in the room seemed soft, as muted as watercolor—the light of the fire bringing the white-sheeted instruments to life like ghosts, the dark gleam of the piano, the flames a dim reflected gold in the windowpanes. She could see her and Jem too, facing each other: a girl in a dark blue evening dress, and a thin rake of a boy with a mop of silvery hair, his black jacket hanging just slightly too loose on his slender frame.

His face in the shadows was all vulnerability, anxiety in the soft curve of his mouth. "I was not sure that you would come."

At that, she took a step forward, wanting to fling her arms about him, but she stopped herself. She had to speak first. "Of course I came," she said. "Jem, I am so sorry. So very sorry. I cannot explain—it was a sort of madness. I could not bear the thought that harm would come to you because of me, because in some way I am connected to Mortmain, and he to me."

"That is not your fault. It was never your choice—"

"I was not seeing sense. Will was right; Mortmain cannot be trusted. Even if I went to him, there is no guarantee that he would honor his end of the bargain. And I would be placing a weapon in the hands of your enemy. I do not know what he wants to use me for, but it is not for the good of Shadowhunters; of that we can be sure. I could even in the end yet be what hurts you all." Tears stung her eyes, but she held them back by force. "Forgive me, Jem. We cannot waste the time we have together in anger. I understand why you did what you did—I would have done it for you."

His eyes went soft and silver as she spoke. "*Zhe shi jie shang, wo shi zui ai ne de,*" he whispered.

She understood it. *In all the world, you are what I love the most.*

"Jem—"

"You know that; you must know that. I could never let you go away from me, not into danger, not while I have breath." He held his hand up, before she could take a step toward him. "Wait." He bent down, and when he rose, he was holding his square violin case and bow. "I— There was something I wished to give you. A bridal gift, when we were married. But I would like to give it to you now, if you will let me."

"A gift?" she said, wonderingly. "After— But we quarreled!"

He smiled at that, the lovely smile that lit his face and made you forget how thin and drawn he looked. "An integral part of married life, I have been informed. It will have been good practice."

"But—"

"Tessa, did you imagine that there exists any quarrel, large or small, that could make me stop loving you?" He sounded amazed, and she thought suddenly of Will, of the years that Will had tested Jem's loyalty, driven him mad with lies and evasion and self-harm, and through all of it Jem's love for his blood brother had never frayed, much less broken.

"I was afraid," she said softly. "And I—I have no gift for you."

"Yes, you do." He said it quietly but firmly. "Sit down, Tessa, please. Do you remember how we met?"

Tessa sat down on a low chair with gilded arms, her skirts crinkling around her. "I barged into your room in the middle of the night like a madwoman."

Jem grinned. "You glided *gracefully* into my bedroom and found me playing the violin." He was tightening the screw on the bow; he finished, set it down, and lovingly took his violin out of its case. "Would you mind if I play for you now?"

"You know I love to hear you play." It was true. She even loved to hear him talk about the violin, though she understood little of it. She could listen to him rattle on passionately for hours about rosin, pegs, scrolls, bowing, finger positions, and the tendency of A strings to break—without getting bored.

"*Wo wei ni xie de,*" he said as he raised the violin to his left shoulder and tucked it under his chin. He had told her that many violinists used a shoulder rest, but he did not. There was a slight mark on the side of his throat, like a permanent bruise, where the violin rested.

"You—made something for me?"

"I *wrote* something for you," he corrected with a smile, and began to play.

She watched in amazement. He began simply, softly, his grip light on the bow, producing a soft, harmonic sound. The melody rolled over her, as cool and sweet as water, as hopeful and lovely as sunrise. She watched his fingers in fascination as they moved and an exquisite note rose from the violin. The sound deepened as the bow moved faster, Jem's forearm sawing back and forth, his slim body seeming to blur into motion from the shoulder. His fingers slid up and down slightly, and the pitch of the music deepened, thunderclouds gathering on a bright horizon, a river that had become a torrent. The notes crashed at her feet, rose to surround her; Jem's whole body seemed to be moving in tune with the sounds he wrung from the instrument, though she knew his feet were firmly planted on the floor.

Her heart raced to keep pace with the music; Jem's eyes were shut, the corners of his mouth downturned as if in pain. Part of her wanted to rush to her feet, to put her arms about him; the other part of her wanted to do nothing to stop the music, the lovely sound of it. It was as if he had taken his bow and used it as a paintbrush, creating a canvas upon which his soul was clearly displayed. As the last soaring notes reached higher and higher, climbing toward Heaven, Tessa was aware that her face was wet, but only when the last of the music had faded away and he had lowered the violin did she realize she had been crying.

Slowly Jem put the violin back into its case and laid the bow beside it. He straightened and turned to her. His expression was shy, though his white shirt was soaked through with sweat and the pulse in his neck was pounding.

Tessa was speechless.

"Did you like it?" he said. "I could have given you . . . jewelry, but I wanted it to be something that was wholly *yours*. That no one else would hear or own. And I am not good with words, so I wrote how I felt about you in music." He paused. "Did you like it?" he said again, and the soft dropping-off of his voice at the end of the question indicated that he expected to receive an answer in the negative.

Tessa raised her face so that he could see the tears on it. "Jem."

He dropped to his knees before her, his face all contrition. *"Ni jue de tong man, qin ai de?"*

"No—no," she said, half-crying, half-laughing. "I am not hurt. Not unhappy. Not at all."

A smile broke across his face, lighting his eyes with delight. "Then you did like it."

"It was like I saw your soul in the notes of the music. And it was beautiful." She leaned forward and touched his face lightly, the smooth skin over his hard cheekbone, his hair like feathers against the back of her hand. "I saw rivers, boats like flowers, all the colors of the night sky."

Jem exhaled, sinking down onto the floor by her chair as if the strength had gone out of him. "That is a rare magic," he said. He leaned his head against her, his temple against her knee, and she kept up the stroking of his hair, carding her fingers through its softness. "Both my parents loved music," he said abruptly. "My father played the violin, my mother the *qin*. I chose the violin, though I could have learned either. I regretted it sometimes, for there are melodies of China I cannot play on the violin, that my mother would have liked me to know. She used to tell me the story of Yu Boya, who was a great player of the *qin*. He had a best friend, a woodcutter named Zhong Ziqi, and he would play for him. They say that when Yu Boya played a song of water, his friend would know immediately that he was describing rushing rivers, and when he played of mountains, Ziqi would see their peaks. And Yu Boya would say, 'It is because you understand my music.'" Jem looked down at his own hand, curled loosely on his knee. "People still use the expression 'zhi yin' to mean 'close friends' or 'soul mates,' but what it really means is 'understanding music.'" He reached up and took her hand. "When I played, you saw what I saw. You understand my music."

"I don't know anything about music, Jem. I cannot tell a sonata from a partita—"

"No." He turned, rising up onto his knees, bracing himself on the arms of her chair. They were close enough now that she could see where his hair was damp with sweat at his temples and nape, smell his scent of rosin and burned sugar. "That is not the kind of music I mean. I mean—" He made a sound of frustration, caught at her hand, brought it to his chest, and pressed it flat over his heart. The steady beat hammered against her palm. "Every heart has its own melody," he said. "You know mine."

"What happened to them?" Tessa whispered. "The woodcutter and the musician?"

Jem's smile was sad. "Zhong Ziqi died, and Yu Boya played his last song over his friend's grave. Then he broke his qin and never played again."

Tessa felt the hot press of tears under her lashes, trying to force its way through. "What a terrible story."

"Is it?" Jem's heart skipped and stuttered under her fingers. "While he lived and they were friends, Yu Boya wrote some of the greatest music that we know. Would he have been able to do that alone? Our hearts, they need a mirror, Tessa. We see our better selves in the eyes of those who love us. And there is a beauty that brevity alone provides." He dropped his gaze, then raised it to hers. "I would give you everything of myself," he said. "I would give you more in two weeks than most men would give you in a lifetime."

"There is nothing you haven't given me, nothing I am dissatisfied with. . . ."

"I am," he said. "I want to be married to you. I would wait for you forever, but . . ."

But we do not have forever. "I have no family," Tessa said slowly, her eyes on his. "No guardian. No one who might be . . . offended . . . by a more immediate marriage."

Jem's eyes widened slightly. "I— Do you mean that? I would not want you to not have all the time you require to prepare."

"What kind of preparation do you imagine I might require?" Tessa said, and for just that moment her thoughts ghosted back to Will, to the way he had put his hands in the fire to save Jem's drugs, and watching him, she could not help but remember that day in the drawing room when he had told her he loved her, and when he had left, she had closed her hand around a poker, that the burning pain of it against her skin might shut out, even for a moment, the pain in her heart.

Will. She had lied to him then—if not in exact words, then in implication. She had let him think she did not love him. The thought still gave her pain, but she did not regret it. There had been no other way. She knew Will well enough to know that even had she broken things off with Jem, he would not have been with her. He could not have stood a love bought at the price of his *parabatai*'s happiness. And if there was some part of her heart that belonged to Will and Will alone, and always would, then it served no one to reveal it. She loved

Jem, too—loved him even more now than she had when she had agreed to marry him.

Sometimes one must choose whether to be kind or honorable, Will had said to her. *Sometimes one cannot be both.*

Perhaps it did depend on the book, she thought. But in this, the book of her life, the way of dishonor was only unkindness. Even if she had hurt Will in the drawing room, over time as his feelings for her faded, he would someday thank her for keeping him free. She believed that. He could not love her forever.

She had set her feet on this path long ago. If she intended to see it through next month, then she could see it through the next day. She knew that she loved Jem, and though there was a part of her that loved Will as well, it was the best gift she could give both of them that neither Will nor Jem should ever know it.

"I don't know," Jem said, gazing up at her from the floor, his expression a mixture of hope and disbelief. "The Council has not yet approved our request . . . and you do not have a dress . . ."

"I do not care about the Council. And I do not care what I wear, if you do not. If you mean it, Jem, I will marry you whenever you like."

"Tessa," he breathed. He reached for her as if he were drowning, and she ducked her head down to brush her lips against his. Jem raised himself up on his knees. His mouth ghosted across hers, once, twice, until her lips opened and she could taste his burned-sugar sweetness. "You are too far away," he whispered, and then his arms were around her, and there was no space between them, and he was drawing her down off the chair, and they were kneeling together on the floor, their arms around each other.

He held her to him, and her hands traced the shape of his face, his sharp cheekbones. *So sharp, too sharp, the bones of his face, the pulse of his blood too close to the surface of the skin, collarbones as hard as a metal necklace.*

His hands slid from her waist to her shoulders; his lips skimmed across her collarbone, the hollow of her throat, as her fingers twisted in his shirt, drawing it up so that her palms were against his bare skin. He was so thin, his spine sharp under her touch. Against the firelight she could see him painted in shadow and fire, the moving golden path of the flames turning his white hair to gilt.

I love you, he had said. *In all the world, you are what I love the most.*

She felt the hot press of his mouth again at the hollow of her throat, then lower. His kisses ended where her dress began. She felt her heart beating beneath his mouth, as if trying to reach him, trying to beat for him. She felt his shy hand slip around her body, to where the lacings fastened her dress closed. . . .

The door opened with a creak, and they sprang apart, both gasping as if they had been running a race. Tessa heard her own blood thunder loudly in her ears as she stared at the empty doorway. Beside her Jem's gasp turned into a hitch of laughter.

"What—," she began.

"Church," he said, and Tessa dropped her gaze down to see the cat sauntering across the floor of the music room, having nudged the door open, and looking very pleased with himself.

"I've never seen a cat look so self-satisfied," she said as

Church—ignoring her, as always—padded up to Jem and nudged at him with his head.

"When I said we might need a chaperon, this wasn't what I had in mind," said Jem, but he stroked the cat's head anyway, and smiled at her out of the corner of his mouth. "Tessa," he said. "Did you mean what you said? That you would marry me tomorrow?"

She raised her chin and looked directly into his eyes. She could not bear the thought of waiting, and wasting another instant of his life. She wanted suddenly and fiercely to be tied to him—in sickness, in health, for better, for worse—tied to him with a promise and able to give him her word and her love without holding back.

"I meant it," she said.

The dining room was not quite full, not everyone having yet arrived for breakfast, when Jem made his announcement.

"Tessa and I are going to get married," he said, very calmly, draping his napkin over his lap.

"Is this meant to be a surprise?" asked Gabriel, who was dressed in gear as if he intended to train after breakfast. He had already taken all the bacon from the serving platter, and Henry was looking at him mournfully. "Aren't you engaged already?"

"The wedding date was set for December," said Jem, reaching beneath the table to give Tessa's hand a reassuring squeeze. "But we have changed our minds. We intend to marry tomorrow."

The effect was galvanic. Henry choked on his tea and had to be pounded on the back by Charlotte, who appeared to have been stricken speechless. Gideon dropped his cup into his saucer with a clatter, and even Gabriel paused with his fork halfway to his mouth. Sophie, who had just come in from the kitchen carrying a rack of toast, gave a gasp. "But you can't!" she said. "Miss Gray's dress was ruined, and the new one isn't even started yet!"

"She can wear any dress," Jem said. "She does not have to wear Shadowhunter gold, for she is not a Shadowhunter. She has several pretty gowns; she can choose her favorite." He ducked his head shyly toward Tessa. "That is, if that is all right with you."

Tessa did not answer, for at that moment Will and Cecily had crowded in through the doorway. "I have *such* a crick in my neck," Cecily was saying with a smile. "I can hardly believe I managed to fall asleep in such a position—"

She broke off as both of them seemed to sense the mood of the room and paused, glancing around. Will did seem better rested than he had the day before, and pleased to have Cecily by him, though that cautious good mood was clearly evaporating as he glanced around at the expressions of the others in the room. "What's going on?" he said. "Has something happened?"

"Tessa and I have decided to move up our wedding ceremony," Jem said. "It will be in the next few days."

Will said nothing, and his expression did not change, but he went very white. He did not look at Tessa.

"Jem, the Clave," Charlotte said, ceasing to pound Henry's back and standing up with a look of agitation on her face. "They have not approved your marriage yet. You cannot go against them—"

"We cannot wait for them either," Jem said. "It could be months, a year—you know how they prefer to delay than give an answer they fear you will not like."

"And it is not as if our marriage can be their focus at the moment," Tessa said. "Benedict Lightwood's papers, searching for Mortmain—all must take priority. But this is a personal matter."

"There are no personal matters to the Clave," Will said. His voice sounded hollow and odd, as if he were a great distance away. There was a pulse pounding at his throat. Tessa thought of the delicate rapport they had begun to build between them over the past few days and wondered if this would destroy it, dashing it into pieces like a fragile craft against rocks. "My mother and father—"

"There are Laws about marriage to mundanes. There are no Laws about marriage between a Nephilim and what Tessa is. And if I must, like your father, I will give up being a Shadowhunter for this."

"James—"

"I would have thought you of all people would understand that," said Jem, the look he bent on Will both puzzled and hurt.

"I am not saying I don't understand. I'm only urging you to *think*—"

"I have thought." Jem sat back. "I have a mundane marriage license, legally procured and signed. We could walk into any church and marry today. I would much prefer you all be there, but if you cannot be, we will do it regardless."

"To marry a girl just to make her a widow," said Gabriel Lightwood. "Many would say that was not a kindness."

Jem went rigid beside Tessa, his hand stiff in hers. Will

started forward, but Tessa was already on her feet, burning holes in Gabriel Lightwood with her eyes.

"Do not *dare* speak about it as if Jem has all the choice about it and I have none," she said, never moving her eyes from his face. "This engagement was not forced on me, nor do I have any illusions about Jem's health. I choose to be with him for however many days or minutes we are granted, and to count myself blessed to have them."

Gabriel's eyes were as cold as the sea off the Newfoundland coast. "I was only concerned for your welfare, Miss Gray."

"Better to look out for your own," Tessa snapped.

And now those green eyes narrowed. "Meaning?"

"I believe the lady means," Will drawled, "that *she* is not the one who killed her father. Or have you so quickly recovered from it that we have no need for concern for your sensibilities, Gabriel?"

Cecily gave a gasp. Gabriel rose to his feet, and in his expression Tessa saw again the boy who had challenged Will to single combat the first time she had met him—all arrogance, stiffness, and hate. "If you ever dare—," he began.

"*Stop*," Charlotte said—and then she broke off, as through the windows came the sound of the rusty gates of the Institute grinding open and the clop of horse hooves on pavement. "Oh, by the Angel. *Jessamine*." Charlotte scrambled to her feet, discarding her napkin on her plate. "Come—we must go down to greet her."

It proved, if an ill-timed arrival in other respects, at least an excellent distraction. There was a slight hubbub, and a deal of puzzlement on the part of Gabriel and Cecily, neither of whom really understood precisely who Jessamine was or the part she had played in the life of the Institute. They proceeded down the corridor in a disorderly fashion, Tessa hanging back slightly; she felt breathless, as if her corset had been laced too tightly. She thought of the night before, holding Jem in the music room as they kissed and whispered to each other for hours of the wedding they would have, the marriage that would follow—as if they had all the time in the world. As if getting married would grant him immortality, though she knew it would not.

As she started down the stairs toward the entryway, she stumbled, distracted. A hand on her arm steadied her. She looked up, and saw Will.

They stood there for a moment, frozen together like a statue. The others were already on their way down the stairs, their voices rising up like smoke. Will's hand was gentle on Tessa's arm, though his face was almost expressionless, seeming carved out of granite. "You do not agree with the rest of them, do you?" she said, with more of a sharp edge than she meant. "That I should not marry Jem today. You asked me if I loved him enough to marry him and make him happy, and I told you I did. I don't know if I can make him happy entirely, but I can try."

"If anyone can, you can," he said, his eyes locking with hers.

"The others think I have illusions about his health."

"Hope is not illusion."

The words were encouraging, but there was something in his voice, something dead that frightened her.

"Will." She caught at his wrist. "You would not abandon me now—not leave me the only one who still searches for a cure? I cannot do it without you."

He took a deep breath, half-closing his shadowed blue eyes. "Of course not. I would not give up on him, on you. I will help. I will continue. It is only—"

He broke off, turning his face away. The light that came down through the window high above illuminated cheek and chin and the curve of his jaw.

"Only what?"

"You remember what else I said to you that day in the drawing room," he said. "I want you to be happy, and him to be happy. And yet when you walk that aisle to meet him and join yourselves forever you will walk an invisible path of the shards of my heart, Tessa. I would give over my own life for either of yours. I would give over my own life for your happiness. I thought perhaps that when you told me you did not love me that my own feelings would fall away and atrophy, but they have not. They have grown every day. I love you now more desperately, this moment, than I have ever loved you before, and in an hour I will love you more than that. It is unfair to tell you this, I know, when you can do nothing about it." He took a shuddering breath. "How you must despise me."

Tessa felt as if the ground had dropped out from beneath her. She remembered what she had told herself the night before: that surely Will's feelings for her had faded. That over the term of years, his pain would be less than hers. She had believed it. But now— "I do not despise you, Will. You have been nothing but honorable—more honorable than ever I could have asked you to be—"

"No," he said bitterly. "You expected nothing of me, I think."

"I have expected *everything* of you, Will," she whispered.

"More than you ever expected of yourself. But you have given even more than that." Her voice faltered. "They say you cannot divide your heart, and yet—"

"Will! Tessa!" It was Charlotte's voice, calling up to them from the entryway. "Do stop dawdling! And can one of you fetch Cyril? We may need help with the carriage if the Silent Brothers intend to stay at all."

Tessa looked helplessly at Will, but the moment between them had snapped; his expression had closed; the desperation that had fueled him a moment before was gone. He was shut away as if a thousand locked doors stood between them. "You go on down. I will be there shortly." He said it without inflection, turned, and sprinted up the steps.

Tessa put a hand against the wall as she made her way numbly down the stairs. What had she almost done? What had she nearly told Will?

And yet I love you.

But God in Heaven, what good would that do, what benefit would it be to anyone to say those words? Only the most awful burden on him, for he would know what she felt but not be able to act on it. And it would tie him to her, would not free him to seek out someone else to love—someone who was *not* engaged to his best friend.

Someone else to love. She stepped out onto the front stairs of the Institute, feeling the wind cut through her dress like a knife. The others were there, gathered on the steps a bit awkwardly, especially Gabriel and Cecily, who looked as if they were wondering what on earth they were doing there. Tessa barely noticed them. She felt sick at the heart and knew it was not the cold. It was the idea of Will in love with someone else.

But that was pure selfishness. If Will found someone else to love, she would suffer through it, biting her lips in silence, as he had suffered her engagement to Jem. She owed him that much, she thought, as a dark carriage driven by a man in the parchment robes of the Silent Brothers rattled through the open gates. She owed Will behavior that was as honorable as his own.

The carriage clattered up to the foot of the stairs and paused. Tessa felt Charlotte move uneasily behind her. "Another carriage?" she said, and Tessa followed her gaze to see that there was indeed a second carriage, all black with no crest, rolling silently in behind the first.

"An escort," said Gabriel. "Perhaps the Silent Brothers are worried she will try to escape."

"No," said Charlotte, bewilderment shading her voice. "She wouldn't—"

The Silent Brother driving the first carriage put away his reins and dismounted, moving to the carriage door. At that moment the second carriage pulled up behind him, and he turned. Tessa could not see his expression, as his face was hidden by his hood, but something in the cast of his body betokened surprise. She narrowed her eyes—there was something strange about the horses drawing the second carriage: their bodies gleamed not like the pelts of animals but like metal, and their movements were unnaturally swift.

The driver of the second carriage leaped down from his seat, landing with a jarring thud, and Tessa saw the gleam of metal as his hand went to the neck of his parchment robes— and pulled the robes away.

Beneath was a shimmering metal body with an ovoid head,

eyeless, copper rivets holding together the joints of elbows, knees, and shoulders. Its right arm, if you could call it that, ended it a crude bronze crossbow. It raised that arm now and flexed it. A steel arrow, fletched with black metal, flew through the air and punched into the chest of the first Silent Brother, lifting him off his feet and sending him flying several feet across the courtyard, before he struck the earth, blood soaking the chest of the familiar robes.

9

GRAVEN IN METAL

The liquid ore he drained
Into fit moulds prepared; from which he formed
First his own tools; then, what might else be wrought
Fusil or graven in metal.
—John Milton, *Paradise Lost*

Silent Brothers, Tessa saw with a frozen shock, bled as red as any mortal man did.

She heard Charlotte shout out orders, and then Henry was tearing down the stairs, racing for the first carriage. He yanked the door open, and Jessamine tumbled out into his arms. Her body was limp, her eyes half-closed. She wore the ragged white dress Tessa had seen her in when she had visited her in the Silent City, and her lovely blond hair was shorn close to her skull like a fever patient's. "Henry," she sobbed audibly, clutching at his lapels. "Help me, Henry. Get me inside the Institute, *please—*"

Henry rose, turning, with Jessamine in his arms, just as the doors of the second carriage burst open and automatons poured out, joining the first one. They seemed to be unfolding themselves as they stepped out, like children's paper toys—one, two, three, and then Tessa lost count as the Shadowhunters around her seized weapons from their belts. She saw the flash of the metal that shot from the tip of Jem's sword-cane, heard the murmur of Latin as seraph blades blazed up around her like a circle of holy fire.

And the automatons charged. One of them raced toward Henry and Jessamine, while the others darted for the steps. She heard Jem call her name, and realized she had no weapon. She had not planned to train today. She looked around wildly, for anything, for a heavy rock, or even a stick. Inside the entryway there were weapons hung on the walls— as adornment, but a weapon was a weapon. She dashed inside and seized a sword from its peg on the wall before spinning about and racing back outside.

The scene that met her eyes was chaos. Jessamine was on the ground, crouched against a wheel of her carriage, her arms up over her face. Henry stood before her, a seraph blade slashing back and forth in his hands as he fended off the automaton trying to get by him, its spiked hands reaching for Jessamine. The rest of the clockwork creatures had spread out across the steps and were locked in combat with individual Shadowhunters.

As Tessa lifted the sword in her hands, her eyes darted about the courtyard. These automatons were different from those she had seen before. They moved more swiftly, with less jerking to their steps, their copper joints folding and unfolding smoothly.

On the lowest step both Gideon and Gabriel were battling furiously with a ten-foot mechanical monster, its spiked hands swinging down at them like maces. Gabriel already had a wide slash across his shoulder that was pouring blood, but he and his brother were harrying the creature, one from the front, one from the back. Jem rose from a crouch to drive his sword-cane through the head of another automaton. Its arms spasmed and it tried to jerk back, but the sword was buried in its metal skull. Jem tugged his blade free, and when the automaton came at him again, he sliced at its legs, taking one out from under the creature. It lurched to the side, toppling to the cobblestones.

Closer to Tessa, Charlotte's whip flashed through the air like lightning, slicing the crossbow arm from the first automaton. It did not even slow the creature down. As it reached for her with its second, spatulate and taloned arm, Tessa darted between them and swung her sword the way Gideon had taught her to, using her whole body to drive the force and striking from above to add the power of gravity to her strike.

The blade fell, shearing away the creature's second arm. This time blackish fluid jetted from the wound. The automaton kept its course, bending to butt at Charlotte with the crown of its head, from which a short, sharp blade protruded. She cried out as it struck her upper arm. Then she flashed forth with her whip, the silver-gold electrum winding about the creature's throat and pulling tight. Charlotte yanked her wrist back, and the head, sheared away, fell to the side; finally the creature toppled, dark fluid pulsing sluggishly from the gashes in its metal chassis.

Tessa gasped and tossed her head back; sweat was sticking her hair to her forehead and temples, but she needed both hands for the heavy sword and couldn't push it away. Through stinging eyes she saw that Gabriel and Gideon had their automaton on the ground and were hacking at it; behind them Henry ducked just in time to miss a swing from the creature that had him cornered against the carriage. Its clublike hand punched through the carriage window, and glass rained down on Jessamine, who screamed and covered her head. Henry drove his seraph blade up, burying it in the automaton's torso. Tessa was used to seeing seraph blades burn through demons, reducing them to nothing, but the automaton only staggered back and then came on again, the blade buried in its chest burning like a torch.

With a cry Charlotte began to dart down the stairs toward her husband. Tessa glanced around—and did not see Jem. Her heart lurched. She took a step forward—

And a dark figure rose up in front of her, robed all in black. Black gloves covered its hands and black boots its feet. Tessa could see nothing but a snow-white face surrounded by the folds of a black hood, as familiar and horrible as a recurring nightmare.

"Hello, Miss Gray," said Mrs. Black.

Despite ducking his head into every room he could think of, Will had not been able to find Cyril. He was irritable about it, and his irritable mood had not been helped by his encounter with Tessa on the stairs. After two months of being so careful around her that it had felt like walking a knife's edge, he had spilled what he was feeling like blood from an open wound, and only Charlotte's call had prevented his foolishness from turning into disaster.

And still, her response nagged at him as he made his way down the corridor and past the kitchen. *They say you cannot divide your heart, and yet—*

And yet what? What had she been about to say?

Bridget's voice trilled out from the dining room, where she and Sophie were doing the cleaning up.

> *"'Oh, Mother, Mother, make my bed*
> *Make it soft and narrow.*
> *My William died for love of me,*
> *And I shall die of sorrow.'*

> *"They buried her in the old churchyard.*
> *Sweet William's grave was nigh hers*
> *And from his grave grew a red, red rose*
> *And from her grave a briar.*

> *"They grew and grew up the old church spire*
> *Until they could grow no higher*
> *And there they twined, in a true love knot,*
> *The red, red rose and the briar."*

Will was wondering idly how Sophie refrained from hitting Bridget over the head with a plate, when a shock went through him as if he had been struck in the chest. He stumbled back against the wall with a short gasp, his hand going to his throat. He could feel something beating there, like a second heart against his own. The chain of the pendant Magnus had given him was cold to the touch, and he drew it hastily from his shirt and stared as the pendant that dangled there was revealed—deep red and pulsing with a scarlet light like the center of a flame.

Dimly he was aware that Bridget had stopped singing, and that both girls had crowded into the doorway of the dining room, staring at him in owlish astonishment. He released the pendant, letting it fall against his chest.

"What is it, Master Will?" Sophie said. She had stopped calling him Mr. Herondale since the truth of his curse had come out, though he still wondered sometimes if she liked him very much. "Are you well?"

"It is not I," he said. "We must go downstairs, quickly. Something has gone terribly wrong."

"But you're dead," Tessa gasped, backing up a step. "I saw you die—"

She broke off with a shriek as long metal arms snaked around from behind her like bands, jerking her off her feet. Her sword clattered to the ground as an automaton's grip tightened about her, and Mrs. Black smiled her terrible cold smile.

"Now, now, Miss Gray. Aren't you at least a little glad to see me? After all, I was the first to welcome you to England. Though you've made yourself quite at home since, I dare-say."

"Let me go!" Tessa kicked out hard, but the automaton

only slammed its head into hers, making her bite down hard on her lip. She choked and spit: saliva and blood spattered Mrs. Black's still white face. "I'd rather die than go with you—"

The Dark Sister wiped away the fluid with a glove and a scowl of distaste. "Unfortunately, that cannot be arranged. Mortmain wants you alive." She snapped her fingers at the automaton. "Take her to the carriage."

The automaton took a step forward, Tessa in its arms—and collapsed forward. Tessa barely had time to throw her arms out to break her fall as they hit the ground, the clockwork creature on top of her. Agony shot through her right wrist, but she pushed against it anyway, a scream ripping free of her throat as she tore herself sideways and slid down several steps, Mrs. Black's shriek of frustration echoing in her ears.

She looked up dizzily. Mrs. Black was gone. The automaton that had been holding Tessa listed sideways on the steps, part of its metal body sheared away. Tessa caught a quick glimpse of what was inside it as it turned: gears and mechanisms and clear tubes pumping brackish fluid. Jem stood behind and above it, breathing hard, splattered with the automaton's oily black blood. His face was white and set. He glanced at her quickly, a swift check to assess that she was all right, and sprang down the stairs, slicing again at the automaton, severing one of its legs from its torso. It spasmed like a dying snake, and its remaining arm shot out and seized Jem by the ankle and yanked hard.

Jem's feet went out from under him, and he clattered to the ground, rolling over and over down the steps, clutched in an awful embrace with the metal monster. The noise as the automaton skidded down, of metal being dragged along stone, was awful. As they hit the ground together, the force of the fall knocked them apart. Tessa stared in horror as Jem staggered dizzily to his feet, his own red blood mixing with the black fluid staining his clothes. His sword-cane was gone—lying on one of the stone steps where he had dropped it as he'd fallen.

"*Jem*," she whispered, and hauled herself to her knees. She tried to crawl forward, but her wrist gave way; she dropped to her elbows and reached for the cane—

Just as arms came around her, jerking her upright, and she heard Mrs. Black's hissing voice in her ear. "Don't struggle, Miss Gray, or it'll go very badly for you, very badly indeed." Tessa tried to twist away, but something soft came down over her mouth and nose. She smelled a sickly sweet stench, and then blackness came down over her vision and carried her away into unconsciousness.

Seraph blade in hand, Will bolted out of the open door of the Institute and into a scene of chaos.

He looked automatically for Tessa first, but she was nowhere to be seen—thank God. She must have had the sense to hide herself away. A black carriage was drawn up at the foot of the steps. Slumped against one of the wheels, amid a pile of broken glass, was Jessamine. On either side of her were Henry and Charlotte: Henry with his sword and Charlotte with her whip, fending off three long-legged metal automatons with bladed arms and smooth, blank heads. Jem's sword-cane lay on the steps, which were everywhere slippery with oily black fluid. Near the doors Gabriel and Gideon Lightwood were fighting another two automatons with the practiced competence of two warriors who had trained together for years. Cecily was kneeling by the body of a Silent Brother, his robes stained scarlet with blood.

The Institute gates were open, and through them was pounding a second black carriage, hurtling away from the Institute at top speed. But Will barely spared it a thought, for at the foot of the stairs was Jem. As pale as paper but upright, he was backing away as another automaton advanced on him. It was staggering, almost drunkenly, half its side and an arm sheared away, but Jem was unarmed.

The cold sharpness of battle came over Will, and everything seemed to slow down around him. He was aware that Sophie and Bridget, both armed, had fanned out on either side of him—that Sophie had run to Cecily's side, and that Bridget, a whirl of red hair and slashing blades, was busy reducing a surprisingly enormous automaton to scrap metal with a ferocity that would in other cases have astonished him. But his world had narrowed, narrowed to the automatons and to Jem, who, looking up, saw him and reached out a hand.

Leaping down four steps and skidding sideways, Will seized up Jem's sword-cane and threw it. Jem caught it out of the air just as the automaton lunged for him, and Jem carved it cleanly in two. The top half fell away, though the legs and lower torso, now pumping an excess of disgusting black and greenish fluids, continued lurching toward him. Jem whirled to the side and swung his sword again, cutting the thing off at the knees. It fell finally, its disparate bits still twitching.

Jem turned his head and looked up at Will. Their eyes met for a moment, and Will offered a smile—but Jem did not smile back; he was as white as salt, and Will could not read his eyes. Was he injured? He was covered in so much oil and fluid that Will could not tell if he was bleeding. Anxiety spearing through him, Will began to move down the stairs toward Jem—but before he could go more than a few steps, Jem had whirled around and run for the gates. As Will stared, Jem disappeared through them, vanishing into the streets of London beyond.

Will broke into a run—and was brought up short at the foot of the steps when an automaton slid in front of him, moving as quickly and gracefully as water, to block his pathway. Its arms ended in long scissors; Will ducked as one slashed at his face, and Will drove his seraph blade into its chest.

There was the spitting noise of melting metal, but the creature only staggered back a foot and then lunged again. Will ducked under its bladed arms, seizing a dagger from his belt. He whirled back, slashing out with the blade—only to see the automaton suddenly come apart in ribbons before him, great slices of metal peeling back like the skin of an orange. Black fluid boiled up and splashed across his face as the thing went down in crumpled pieces.

He stared. Bridget looked at him serenely across its ruined body. Her hair was standing out around her head in a frizz of red curls, and her white apron was covered in black blood, but she was expressionless. "You ought to be more careful," she said. "Don't you think?"

Will was speechless; fortunately, Bridget did not seem

to be waiting for an answer. She tossed her hair and walked away toward Henry, who was battling a particularly fearsome-looking automaton, at least fourteen feet high. Henry had deprived it of one of its arms, but the other, a long, multi-jointed monstrosity ending in a curved blade like a *kindjal*, was still stabbing at him. Bridget walked up behind it calmly and stuck it through the jointure of the torso with her blade. Sparks flew, and the creature began to totter forward. Jessamine, still crouched against the wheel of the carriage, gave a scream and began to crawl out of its way on her hands and knees, toward Will.

Will watched her in stunned surprise for a moment as she bloodied her hands and knees on the glass shards of the broken carriage window but kept crawling. Then, as if slapped into action, he moved forward, darting around Bridget until he reached Jessie, and slid his arms under her, deadlifting her from the ground. She gave a little gasp—his name, he thought—and then went limp against him, only her hands tautly gripping his lapels.

He carried her away from the brougham, his eyes on what was happening in the courtyard. Charlotte had dispatched her automaton, and Bridget and Henry were in the middle of slicing another into bits. Sophie, Gideon, Gabriel, and Cecily had two automatons on the ground among them, and were carving them up like a Christmas roast. Jem had not returned.

"Will," Jessie said, her voice a weak thread. "Will, please set me down."

"I need to get you inside, Jessamine."

"No." She coughed, and Will saw to his horror that blood

was running from the corners of her mouth. "I won't survive that long. Will—if ever you cared about me at all, even a bit, put me down."

Will sank to the foot of the stairs with Jessie in his arms, trying his best to cradle her head against his shoulder. Blood freely stained her throat and the front of her white dress, pasting the material to her body. She was terribly thin, her collarbone sticking out like the wings of a bird, her cheeks sunk into hollows. She resembled a patient staggering out of Bedlam more than the pretty girl who had left them only eight weeks ago.

"Jess," he said softly. "Jessie. Where are you hurt?"

She gave a ghastly sort of smile. Red rimmed the edges of her teeth. "One of the creature's talons went through my back," she whispered, and indeed, as Will looked down, he saw that the back of her dress was soaked through with blood. Blood stained his hands, his trousers, his shirt, filling his throat with its choking coppery smell. "It pierced my heart. I can feel it."

"An *iratze*—" Will began to fumble at his belt for his stele.

"No *iratze* will help me now." Her voice was sure.

"Then the Silent Brothers—"

"Even their power cannot save me. Besides, I cannot bear to have them touch me again. I would rather die. I *am* dying, and I am glad of it."

Will looked down at her, stunned. He could remember when Jessie had come to the Institute, fourteen years old and as wicked as an angry cat with all her claws out. He had never been kind to her, nor she to him—he had never been kind to anyone save Jem—but Jessie had saved him the trouble of regretting it.

Still, he had admired her in an odd way, admired the strength of her hatred and the force of her will.

"Jessie." He put his hand on her cheek, awkwardly smearing the blood.

"You needn't." She coughed again. "Be kind to me, that is. I know you hate me."

"I don't hate you."

"You never visited me in the Silent City. The others all came. Tessa and Jem, Henry and Charlotte. But not you. You are not forgiving, Will."

"No." He said it because it was true, and because part of the reason he had never liked Jessamine was that in some ways she reminded him of himself. "Jem is the forgiving one."

"And yet I always liked you better." Her eyes darted over his face thoughtfully. "Oh, no, not like that. Don't think it. But the way you hated yourself . . . I understood that. Jem always wanted to give me a chance, as Charlotte did. But I do not want the gifts of generous hearts. I want to be seen as I am. And because you do not pity me, I know if I ask you to do something, you will do it."

She gave a gasping breath. The blood had formed bubbles about her mouth. Will knew what that meant: Her lungs were punctured or dissolving, and she was drowning in her own blood. "What is it?" he said urgently. "What is it you want me to do?"

"Take care of them," she whispered. "Baby Jessie and the others."

It took Will a moment before he realized that she meant her dolls. Good God. "I will not let them destroy any of your things, Jessamine."

She gave the ghost of a smile. "I thought they might—not want anything to remember me by."

"You are not hated, Jessamine. Whatever world lies beyond this one, do not go to it thinking that."

"Oh, no?" Her eyes were fluttering shut. "Though surely you would all have liked me a bit better if I had told you where Mortmain was. I might not have lost your love then."

"Tell me now," Will urged. "Tell me, if you can, and earn that love back—"

"Idris," she whispered.

"Jessamine, we *know* that's not true—"

Jessamine's eyes flew open. The whites were tinted scarlet now, like blood in water. "You," she said. "You of all people should have understood." Her fingers tightened suddenly, spasmodically, on his lapel. "You are a terrible Welshman," she said thickly, and then her chest hitched, and did not hitch again. She was dead.

Her eyes were open, fixed on his face. He touched them lightly, closing her eyelids, leaving the bloody prints of his thumb and forefinger behind. "*Ave atque vale*, Jessamine Lovelace."

"*No!*" It was Charlotte. Will looked up through a mist of shock to see others gathered about him—Charlotte, slumped in Henry's arms; Cecily with her eyes wide; and Bridget, holding two oil-spattered blades, quite expressionless. Behind them Gideon was sitting on the steps of the Institute with his brother and Sophie on either side of him. He was leaning back, very pale, his jacket off; a torn strip of cloth was tied about one of his legs, and Gabriel was applying what was likely a healing rune to his arm.

Henry nuzzled his face into Charlotte's neck and murmured

soothing things as tears ran down his wife's face. Will looked at them, and then at his sister.

"Jem," he said, and the name was a question.

"He went off after Tessa," said Cecily. She was staring down at Jessamine, her expression a mixture of pity and horror.

A white light seemed to flash in front of Will's eyes. "*Went off after Tessa?* What do you mean?"

"One—one of the automatons seized her and threw her into a carriage." Cecily faltered at the fierceness in his tone. "None of us could follow. The creatures were blocking us. Then Jem ran through the gates. I assumed—"

Will found that his hands had tightened, quite unconsciously, on Jessamine's arms, leaving livid marks in the skin. "Someone take Jessamine from me," he said raggedly. "I must go after them."

"Will, no—," Charlotte began.

"*Charlotte.*" The word tore out of his throat. "I must go—"

There was a clang—the sound of the Institute gates slamming shut. Will's head jerked up, and he saw Jem.

The gates had just closed behind him, and he was walking toward them. He was moving slowly, as if drunk or injured, and as he drew closer, Will saw that he was covered in blood. The coal-black blood of the automatons, but a great deal of red blood as well—on his shirt, streaking his face and hands, and in his hair.

He neared them, and stopped dead. He looked the way Thomas had looked when Will had found him on the steps of the Institute, bleeding out and nearly dead.

"James?" Will said.

There was a world of questions in that one word.

"She's gone," Jem said in a flat, uninflected voice. "I ran after the carriage—but it was gaining speed and I could not run fast enough. I lost them near Temple Bar." His eyes flicked toward Jessamine, but he did not even seem to see her body, or Will holding her, or anything at all. "If I could have run faster—," he said, and then he doubled up as if he had been struck, a cough ripping through him. He hit the ground on his knees and elbows, blood spattering the ground at his feet. His fingers clawed at the stone. Then he rolled onto his back and was still.

10

Like Water upon Sand

*For I wondered that others, subject to death, did live, since he
whom I loved, as if he should never die, was dead; and I wondered
yet more that myself, who was to him a second self, could
live, he being dead. Well said one of his friends, "Thou half of
my soul"; for I felt that my soul and his soul were "one soul in
two bodies": and therefore was my life a horror to me, because
I would not live halved. And therefore perchance I feared to die,
lest he whom I had much loved should die wholly.*
—Saint Augustine, *Confessions, Book IV*

Cecily pushed open the door of Jem's bedroom with the tips of
her fingers, and stared inside.

The room was quiet but aflutter with movement. Two
Silent Brothers stood by the side of Jem's bed, with Charlotte
between them. Her face was grave and tearstained. Will knelt

by the side of the bed, still in his bloodstained clothes from the courtyard fight. His head was down on his crossed arms, and he looked as if he was praying. He seemed young and vulnerable and despairing, and despite her conflicted feelings, some part of Cecily longed to go into the room and comfort him.

The rest of her saw the still, white figure lying in the bed, and quailed. She had been here such a short time; she could feel nothing but that she was intruding on the inhabitants of the Institute—their grief, their sorrow.

But she *must* talk to Will. She had to. She moved forward—

And felt a hand on her shoulder, pulling her away. Her back hit the wall of the corridor, and Gabriel Lightwood immediately released her.

She looked up at him in surprise. He looked exhausted, his green eyes shadowed, flecks of blood in his hair and on the cuffs of his shirt. His collar was damp. He had clearly come from his brother's room. Gideon had been wounded badly in the leg by an automaton's blade, and though the *iratzes* had helped, it seemed there was a limit to what they could cure. Both Sophie and Gabriel had assisted him to his room, though he had protested the whole way that all available attention should go to Jem.

"Do not go in there," Gabriel said in a low voice. "They are trying to save Jem. Your brother needs to be there for him."

"Be there for him? What can he do? Will is not a doctor."

"Even unconscious, James will draw strength from his *parabatai*."

"I need to talk to Will for only a moment."

Gabriel ran his hands through his mop of tousled hair. "You have not been with the Shadowhunters very long," he said. "You may not understand. To lose your *parabatai*—it is no small thing. We take it as seriously as losing a husband or wife, or a brother or sister. It is as if it were you lying in that bed."

"Will would not care so much if I were lying in that bed."

Gabriel snorted. "Your brother would not have taken so much trouble to warn me off you if he did not care about you, Miss Herondale."

"No, he does not like you much. Why is that? And why are you giving me advice about him now? You do not like him, either."

"No," Gabriel said. "It is not quite like that. I do not *like* Will Herondale. We have disliked each other for years. In fact, he broke my arm once."

"Did he?" Cecily's eyebrows shot up despite herself.

"And yet I am beginning to come to see that many things that I had always thought were certain, are not certain. And Will is one of those things. I was certain he was a scoundrel, but Gideon has told me more about him, and I begin to understand he has a very peculiar sense of honor."

"And you respect that."

"I wish to respect it. I wish to understand it. And James Carstairs is one of the best of us; even if I hated Will, I would want him spared now, for Jem's sake."

"The thing I must tell my brother," Cecily said. "Jem would want me to tell him. It is important enough. And it will take but a moment."

Gabriel rubbed the skin at his temples. He was so very tall—

he seemed to tower above Cecily, for all that he was very slender. He had a sharply planed face, not quite pretty, but elegant, his lower lip shaped nearly exactly like a bow. "All right," he said. "I will go in and send him out."

"Why you? And not me?"

"If he is angry, if he is grief-stricken, it is better I see it, and that he be furious with me than with you," Gabriel said matter-of-factly. "I am trusting you, Miss Herondale, that this is important. I hope you won't disappoint me."

Cecily said nothing, just watched as Gabriel pushed the door of the sickroom open and went in. She leaned against a wall, her heart pounding, as a murmur of voices came from within. She could hear Charlotte say something about blood replacement runes, which were apparently dangerous—and then the door opened and Gabriel came out.

She stood up straight. "Is Will—"

Gabriel's eyes flashed at her, and a moment later Will appeared, on Gabriel's heels, reaching around to shut the door firmly behind him. Gabriel nodded at Cecily and set off down the hall, leaving her alone with her brother.

She had always wondered how you could be alone with someone else, really. If you were with them, weren't you by definition *not* alone? But she felt entirely alone now, for Will seemed to be somewhere else completely. He did not even seem to be angry. He leaned against the wall by the door, beside her, and yet he seemed as insubstantial as a ghost.

"Will," she said.

He did not seem to hear her. He was trembling, his hands shaking with strain and tension.

"Gwilym Owain," she said again, more softly.

He turned his head to look at her at least, though his eyes were as blue and cold as the water of Llyn Mwyngil in the lee of the mountains. "I first came here when I was twelve," he said.

"I know," Cecily said, bewildered. Did he think she could have forgotten? Losing Ella, and then her Will, her beloved older brother, in only a matter of days? But Will did not even seem to hear her.

"It was, to be precise, the tenth of November of that year. And every year after, on the anniversary of that day, I would fall into a black mood of despair. That was the day—that and my birthday—when I was most strongly reminded of Mam and Dad, and of you. I knew you were alive, that you were out there, that you wanted me back, and I could not go, could not even send you a letter. I wrote dozens, of course, and burned them. You had to hate me and blame me for Ella's death."

"We never blamed you—"

"After the first year, even though I still dreaded the day's approach, I began to find that there was something Jem simply *had* to do every November tenth, some training exercise or some search that would take us to the far end of the city in the cold, wet winter weather. And I would abuse him bitterly for it, of course. Sometimes the damp chill made him ill, or he would forget his drugs and become ill on the day, coughing blood and confined to bed, and that would be a distraction too. And only after it had happened three times—for I am very stupid, Cecy, and think only of myself—did I realize that of course he was doing it *for* me. He had noticed the date and was doing all he could to draw me from my melancholy."

Cecily stood stock-still, staring at him. Despite the words that pounded in her head to be spoken, she could say nothing, for it was as if the veil of years had fallen away and she was seeing her brother at last, as he had been as a child, petting her clumsily when she was hurt, falling asleep on the rug in front of the fire with a book open on his chest, climbing out of the pond laughing and shaking water out of his black hair. Will, with no wall between himself and the world outside.

He put his arms about himself as if he were cold. "I do not know who to be without him," he said. "Tessa is gone, and every moment she is gone is a knife ripping me apart from the inside. She is gone, and they cannot track her, and I have no idea where to go or what to do next, and the only person I can imagine speaking my agony to is the one person who cannot know. Even if he were not dying."

"Will. *Will*." She put her hand on his arm. "Please listen to me. This is about finding Tessa. I believe I know where Mortmain is."

His eyes snapped wide at that. "How could *you* know?"

"I was close enough to you to hear what Jessamine said when she was dying," Cecily said, feeling the blood pounding in him under his skin. His heart was hammering. "She said you were a terrible Welshman."

"Jessamine?" He sounded bewildered, but she saw the slight narrowing of his eyes. Perhaps, unconsciously, he was beginning to follow the same line of thought that she had.

"She kept saying Mortmain was in Idris. But the Clave knows he is not," said Cecily rapidly. "You did not know Mortmain when he lived in Wales, but I did. He knows it well.

And once you did too. We grew up in the shadow of the mountain, Will. *Think.*"

He stared at her. "You don't imagine—Cadair Idris?"

"He knows those mountains, Will," she said. "And he would find it all funny, a great joke on you and all the Nephilim. He has taken her exactly where you fled from. He has taken her to our home."

"A posset?" said Gideon, taking the steaming mug from Sophie. "I feel like a child again."

"It has spice and wine in it. It will do you good. Build up your blood." Sophie fussed about, not looking at Gideon directly as she set the tray she had been carrying down on the nightstand beside his bed. He was sitting up, one of the legs of his trousers cut away below the knee and the leg itself wrapped in bandages. His hair was still disarrayed from the fight, and though he had been given clean clothes to wear, he still smelled slightly of blood and sweat.

"*These* build up my blood," he said, holding out an arm on which two blood-replacement runes, *sangliers*, had been inked.

"Is that supposed to mean that you don't like possets, either?" she demanded, her hands on her hips. She could still recall how annoyed she'd been with him about the scones, but she had forgiven him completely the night before, while reading his letter to the Consul (which she had not had a chance to post yet—it was still in the pocket of her bloodstained apron). And today, when the automaton had sliced at his leg on the Institute steps and he'd fallen, blood pouring from the open wound, her heart had seized up with a terror that had surprised her.

"No one likes possets," he said with a faint but charming smile.

"Do I have to stay and make sure you drink it, or are you going to throw it under the bed? Because then we'll have mice."

He had the grace to look sheepish; Sophie rather wished she had been there when Bridget had swept into his room and announced that she was there to clean the scones out from under the bed. "Sophie," he said, and when she gave him a stern look, he took a hasty swig of the posset. "Miss Collins. I have not yet had a chance to properly apologize to you, so let me take it now. Please forgive me for the trick I played on you with the scones. I did not mean to show you disrespect. I hope you do not imagine I think any less of you for your position in the household, for you are one of the finest and bravest ladies I have ever had the pleasure of knowing."

Sophie took her hands off her hips. "Well," she said. It was not many gentlemen who would apologize to a servant. "That is a very pretty apology."

"And I am sure the scones are very good," he added hastily. "I just don't like scones. I never have liked scones. It's not *your* scones."

"Do please stop saying the word 'scone,' Mr. Lightwood."

"All right."

"And they are not my scones; Bridget made them."

"All right."

"And you are not drinking your posset."

He opened his mouth, then shut it hastily and lifted the mug. When he was looking at her over the rim, she relented, and smiled. His eyes lit up.

"Very well," she said. "You do not like scones. How do you feel about sponge cake?"

It was midafternoon and the sun was high and weak in the sky. A dozen or so of the Enclave Shadowhunters, and several Silent Brothers, were spread out across the property of the Institute. They had taken away Jessamine earlier, and the body of the dead Silent Brother, whose name Cecily had not known. She could hear voices from the courtyard, and the clank of metal, as the Enclave sifted through remnants of the automaton attack.

In the drawing room, however, the loudest noise was the ticking of the grandfather clock in the corner. The curtains were drawn back, and in the pale sunlight the Consul stood scowling, his thick arms crossed over his chest. "This is madness, Charlotte," he said. "Utter madness, and based on the fancy of a child."

"I am not a child," Cecily snapped. She was seated in a chair by the fireplace, the same one Will had fallen asleep in the night before—had it been such a short time ago? Will stood beside her, glowering. He had not changed his clothes. Henry was in Jem's room with the Silent Brothers; Jem had still not regained consciousness, and only the arrival of the Consul had dragged Charlotte and Will from his side. "And my parents knew Mortmain, as you well know. He befriended my family, my father. He gave us Ravenscar Manor when my father had—when we lost our house near Dolgellau."

"It is true," said Charlotte, who stood behind her desk, papers spread out before her on the surface. "I spoke to you of it this summer, of what Ragnor Fell had reported to me about the Herondales."

Will pulled his fists from his trouser pockets and faced the Consul angrily. "It was a joke to Mortmain, giving my family that house! He toyed with us. Why would he not extend the joke in this manner?"

"Here, Josiah," said Charlotte, indicating one of the papers on the desk in front of her. A map of Wales. "There is a Lake Lyn in Idris—and here, Tal-y-Llyn lake, at the foot of Cadair Idris—"

"'Llyn' *means* 'lake,'" said Cecily in an exasperated tone. "And we call it Llyn Mwyngil, though some call it Tal-y-Llyn—"

"And there are probably other locations in the world with the name of Idris," snapped the Consul, before he seemed to realize that he was arguing with a fifteen-year-old girl, and subsided.

"But this one *means something*," Will said. "They say the lakes around the mountain are bottomless—that the mountain itself is hollow, and inside it sleep the Cŵn Annwn, the Hounds of the Underworld."

"The Wild Hunt," said Charlotte.

"Yes." Will raked his dark hair back. "We are Nephilim. We believe in legends, in myths. *All the stories are true.* Where better than a hollow mountain already associated with dark magic and portents of death to hide himself and his contraptions? No one would find it odd if strange noises came from the mountain, and no locals would investigate. Why else would he even be in the area? I always wondered why he took a particular interest in my family. Maybe it was simple proximity—the opportunity to devil a Nephilim family. He would have been unable to resist it."

The Consul was leaning against the desk, his eyes on the map beneath Charlotte's hands. "It is not enough."

"Not enough? Not enough for what?" Cecily cried.

"To convince the Clave." The Consul stood. "Charlotte, *you* will understand. To launch a force against Mortmain on the assumption that he is in Wales, we will have to convene a Council meeting. We cannot take a small force and risk being outnumbered, especially by those creatures—how many of them were here this morning when you were attacked?"

"Six or seven, not counting the creature that seized Tessa," said Charlotte. "We believe they can fold in upon themselves and were therefore able to fit within the small confines of a brougham."

"And I believe that Mortmain did not realize that Gabriel and Gideon Lightwood would be with you, and thus underestimated the numbers he would need. Otherwise I suspect you might all be dead."

"Hang the Lightwoods," muttered Will. "I believe he underestimated Bridget. She carved those creatures up like a Christmas turkey."

The Consul threw his hands up. "We have read Benedict Lightwood's papers. In them he states that Mortmain's stronghold is just outside London, and that Mortmain intends to send a force against the London Enclave—"

"Benedict Lightwood was going rapidly insane when he wrote that," Charlotte interrupted. "Does it seem likely Mortmain would have shared with him his true plans?"

"What next and next?" The Consul's voice was snappish, but also deadly cold. "Benedict had no reason to lie in his own journals, Charlotte, which *you* should not have read. If you were not so convinced that you should know more than the Council, you would have given them over immediately. Such displays of disobedience do not incline me to trust you. If you must, you can bring this issue of Wales up with the Council when we meet in a fortnight—"

"A fortnight?" Will's voice rose; he was pale, with splotches of red standing out on his cheekbones. "Tessa was taken *today*. She does not have a fortnight."

"The Magister wanted her unharmed. You know that, Will," said Charlotte in a soft voice.

"He also wants to marry her! Do you not think she would hate becoming his plaything more than she would hate death? She could be married by tomorrow—"

"And to the devil with it if she is!" said the Consul. "One girl, who is not Nephilim, is not, *cannot*, be our priority!"

"She is *my* priority!" Will shouted.

There was a silence. Cecily could hear the sound of the damp wood popping in the grate. The fog that smeared the windows was dark yellow, and the Consul's face was cast in shadow. Finally: "I thought she was your *parabatai*'s fiancée," he said tightly. "Not yours."

Will raised his chin. "If she is Jem's fiancée, then I am duty bound to guard her as if she were my own. That is what it means to be *parabatai*."

"Oh, yes." The Consul's voice dripped sarcasm. "Such loyalty is commendable." He shook his head. "Herondales. As stubborn as rocks. I remember when your father wanted to marry your mother. Nothing would dissuade him, though she was no candidate for Ascension. I had hoped for more amenability in his children."

"You'll forgive my sister and myself if we do not agree," said Will, "considering that if my father had been more amenable, as you say, we would not exist."

The Consul shook his head. "This is a war," he said. "Not a rescue."

"And she is not just a girl," said Charlotte. "She is a weapon in the hands of the enemy. I am telling you, Mortmain intends to use her against us."

"Enough." The Consul lifted his overcoat from the back of a chair and shrugged himself into it. "This is a profitless conversation. Charlotte, see to your Shadowhunters." His gaze swept over Will and Cecily. "They seem . . . overexcited."

"I see that we cannot force your cooperation, Consul." Charlotte's face was like thunder. "But remember that I will put it on record that we warned you of this situation. If in the end we were correct and disaster comes from this delay, all that results will be on your head."

Cecily expected the Consul to look angry, but he only flipped up his hood, hiding his features. "That is what it means to be Consul, Charlotte."

Blood. Blood on the flagstones of the courtyard. Blood staining the stairs of the house. Blood on the leaves of the garden, the remains of what had once been Gabriel's brother-in-law lying in thick pools of drying blood, hot jets of blood splattering Gabriel's gear as the arrow he had released drove into his father's eye—

"Regretting your decision to remain at the Institute, Gabriel?" The cool, familiar voice cut through Gabriel's feverish thoughts, and he looked up with a gasp.

The Consul stood over him, outlined by weak sunlight. He

wore a heavy overcoat, gloves, and an expression as if Gabriel had done something to amuse him.

"I—" Gabriel caught his breath, forced the words to come out evenly. "No. Of course not."

The Consul quirked an eyebrow. "That must be why you are crouching here around the side of the church, in bloodstained clothes, looking as if you're terrified someone might find you."

Gabriel scrambled to his feet, grateful for the hard stone wall behind him, bearing him up. He glared at the Consul. "Are you suggesting that I did not fight? That I ran away?"

"I am not suggesting any such thing," said the Consul mildly. "I know that you stayed. I know that your brother was injured—"

Gabriel took a sharp rattling breath, and the Consul's eyes narrowed.

"Ah," he said. "So that is it, isn't it? You saw your father die, and you thought you were going to see your brother die as well?"

Gabriel wanted to scrabble at the wall behind him. He wanted to hit the Consul in his unctuous, falsely sympathetic face. He wanted to run upstairs and throw himself down by his brother's bed, refuse to leave, as Will had refused to leave Jem until Gabriel had forced him away. Will was a better brother to Jem than he himself was to Gideon, he had thought bitterly, and there was no blood shared between them. It was that in part that had driven him back out of the Institute, to this hiding space behind the stables. Surely no one would look for him here, he had told himself.

He had been wrong. But he was wrong so often, what was one more time?

"You saw your brother bleed," said the Consul, still in the same mild voice. "And you remembered—"

"I killed my father," Gabriel said. "I put an arrow through his eye—I spilled his blood. Do you think I don't know what that means? His blood will cry to me from the ground, as Abel's blood called to Cain. Everyone says he wasn't my father anymore, but he was still all that remained of him. He was a Lightwood once. And Gideon could have been killed today. To lose him as well—"

"You see what I meant," said the Consul. "When I spoke of Charlotte and her refusal to obey the Law. The cost of life it engenders. It could have been your brother's life sacrificed to her overweening pride."

"She does not seem proud."

"Is that why you wrote this?" The Consul drew from his coat pocket the first letter Gabriel and Gideon had sent him. He looked at it in contempt and let it flutter to the ground. "This ridiculous missive, calculated to annoy me?"

"Did it work?"

For a moment Gabriel thought the Consul was going to hit him. But the look of anger passed quickly from the older man's eyes; when he spoke again, it was calmly. "I suppose I should not have expected a Lightwood to react well to being blackmailed. Your father would not have. I confess I thought you of weaker stuff."

"If you intend to try another avenue to persuade me, do not bother," Gabriel said. "There is no point in it."

"Really? You're that loyal to Charlotte Branwell, after all her family did to yours? Gideon I might have expected this from—he takes after your mother. Too trusting in nature.

But not you, Gabriel. From you I expected more pride in your blood."

Gabriel let his head fall back against the wall. "There was nothing," he said. "You understand? There was nothing in Charlotte's correspondence to interest you, to interest *anyone*. You told us you would destroy us utterly if we did not report on her activities, but there was nothing to report on. You gave us no choice."

"You could have told me the truth."

"You did not want to hear it," said Gabriel. "I am not stupid, and neither is my brother. You want Charlotte removed as head of the Institute, but you do not want it to be too clear that it was your hand that removed her. You wished to discover her engaged in some sort of illegal dealing. But the truth is that there is nothing to be discovered."

"Truth is malleable. Truth can be uncovered, certainly, but it can also be created."

Gabriel's gaze snapped to the Consul's face. "You would rather I lied to you?"

"Oh, no," said the Consul. "Not to *me*." He put a hand on Gabriel's shoulder. "The Lightwoods have always had honor. Your father made mistakes. You should not pay for them. Let me give you back what you have lost. Let me return to you Lightwood House, the good name of your family. You could live in the house with your brother and sister. You need no longer be dependent on the charity of the Enclave."

Charity. The word was bitter. Gabriel thought of his brother's blood on the flagstones of the Institute. Had Charlotte not been so foolish, so determined to take the shape-changer girl into the bosom of the Institute against the objections of Clave and

Consul, the Magister would not have sent his forces against the Institute. Gideon's blood would not have been spilled.

In fact, whispered a small voice at the back of his mind, *had it not been for Charlotte, my father's secret would have remained a secret.* Benedict would not have been forced to betray the Magister. He would not have lost the source of the drug that held off the *astriola.* He might never have transformed. His sons might never have learned of his sins. The Lightwoods could have continued in blissful ignorance.

"Gabriel," said the Consul. "This offer is for you only. It must be kept a secret from your brother. He is like your mother, too loyal. Loyal to Charlotte. His mistaken loyalty may do him credit, but it will not help us here. Tell him that I grew tired of your antics; tell him that I no longer desire any action from you. You are a good liar"—here he smiled sourly—"and I feel sure you can convince him. What do you say?"

Gabriel set his jaw. "What do you wish me to do?"

Will shifted in the armchair by the side of Jem's bed. He had been here for hours now, and his back was growing stiff, but he refused to move. There was always the chance that Jem might wake, and expect him there.

At least it was not cold. Bridget had built up the fire in the grate; the damp wood popped and crackled, sending up the occasional blaze of sparks. The night outside the windows was dark without a hint of blue or clouds, only a flat black as if it had been painted on the glass.

Jem's violin leaned against the foot of his bed, and his cane, still slicked with blood from the fight in the courtyard, lay beside it. Jem himself lay still, propped up on pillows, no color at all in his pale face. Will felt as if he were seeing him for the first time after a long absence, for that brief moment when you were apt to notice changes in familiar faces before they became part of the scenery of one's life once again. Jem looked so thin—how had Will not noticed?—all extra flesh stripped away from the bones of cheek and jaw and forehead, so he was all hollows and angles. There was a faint bluish sheen to his closed eyelids, and to his mouth. His collarbones curved like the prow of a ship.

Will upbraided himself. How had he not realized all these months that Jem was dying—so quickly, so soon? How had he not seen the scythe and the shadow?

"Will." It was a whisper at the door. He looked up dully and saw Charlotte there, her head around the doorway. "There is . . . someone here to see you."

Will blinked as Charlotte moved out of the way and Magnus Bane stepped around her and into the room. For a moment Will could think of nothing to say.

"He says you summoned him," Charlotte said, sounding a little dubious. Magnus stood, looking indifferent, in a charcoal-gray suit. He was slowly rolling his gloves, dark gray kid, off his thin brown hands.

"I *did* summon him," Will said, feeling as if he were waking up. "Thank you, Charlotte."

Charlotte gave him a look that mixed sympathy with the unspoken message *Be it on your head, Will Herondale*, and went out of the room, closing the door conspicuously behind her.

"You came," Will said, aware that he sounded stupid. He never liked it when people observed the obvious aloud, and here he was doing just that. He could not shake his feeling of discombobulation. Seeing Magnus here, in the middle of Jem's bedroom, was like seeing a faerie knight seated among the white-wigged barristers of the Old Bailey.

Magnus dropped his gloves on top of a table and moved toward the bed. He put out a hand to brace himself against one of the posts as he looked down at Jem, so still and white that he could have been carved on top of a tomb. "James Carstairs," he said, murmuring the words under his voice as if they had some incantatory power.

"He's dying," Will said.

"That much is evident." It could have sounded cold, but there were worlds of sadness in Magnus's voice, a sadness that Will felt with a jolt of familiarity. "I thought you believed he had a few days, a week perhaps."

"It is not just the lack of the drug." Will's voice sounded rusty; he cleared his throat. "In fact, we have a little of that, and have administered it. But there was a fight this afternoon, and he lost blood and was weakened. He is not strong enough, we fear, to recover himself."

Magnus reached out and with great gentleness lifted Jem's hand. There were bruises on his pale fingers, and the blue veins ran like a map of rivers under the skin of his wrist. "Is he suffering?"

"I don't know."

"Perhaps it would be better to let him die." Magnus looked at Will, his eyes dark gold-green. "Every life is finite, Will. And you knew, when you chose him, that he would die before you did."

Will stared ahead of him. He felt as if he were hurtling

down a dark tunnel, one that had no end, no sides to grip to slow his fall. "If you think that would be the best thing for him."

"Will." Magnus's voice was gentle but urgent. "Did you bring me here because you hoped I could help him?"

Will looked up blindly. "I don't know why I summoned you," he said. "I don't think it was because I believed there was anything you could do. I think rather I thought you were the only one who might understand."

Magnus looked surprised. "The only one who might understand?"

"You have lived so long," Will said. "You must have seen so many die, so many that you loved. And yet you survive and you go on."

Magnus continued to look astonished. "You summoned me here—a warlock to the Institute, just after a battle in which you were nearly all killed—to *talk*?"

"I find you easy to talk to," Will said. "I cannot say why."

Magnus shook his head slowly, and leaned against the post of the bed. "You are *so* young," he murmured. "But then again, I do not think a Shadowhunter has ever called upon me before simply to pass the watches of the night with him."

"I don't know what to do," Will said. "Mortmain has taken Tessa, and I believe now I know where she might be. There is a part of me that wants nothing more than to go after her. But I cannot leave Jem. I swore an oath. And what if he wakes in the night and finds I am not here?" He looked as lost as a child. "He will think I left him willingly, not caring that he was dying. He will not know. And yet if he could speak, would he not tell me to go after Tessa? Is that not what he would want?" Will dropped his face into his hands. "I cannot say, and it is tearing me in half."

Magnus looked at him silently for a long moment. "Does he know you are in love with Tessa?"

"No." Will lifted his face, shocked. "No. I have never said a word. It was not his burden to bear."

Magnus took a deep breath and spoke gently. "Will. You asked me for my wisdom, as someone who has lived many lifetimes and buried many loves. I can tell you that the end of a life is the sum of the love that was lived in it, that whatever you think you have sworn, being here at the end of Jem's life is not what is important. It was being here for every other moment. Since you met him, you have never left him and never not loved him. *That* is what matters."

"You really mean that," Will said wonderingly, and then, "Why are you being so kind to me? I owe you a favor still, don't I? I remember that, you know, though you have never called it in."

"Haven't I?" Magnus said, and then smiled at him. "Will, you treat me as a human being, a person like yourself; rare is the Shadowhunter who treats a warlock like that. I am not so heartless that I would call in a favor from a brokenhearted boy. One who I think, by the way, will be a very good man someday. So I will tell you this. I will stay here when you go, and I will watch over your Jem for you, and if he wakes, I will tell him where you went, and that it was for him. And I will do what I can to preserve his life: I do not have *yin fen*, but I do have magic, and perhaps there is something in an old spell book I might find that can help him."

"I would count it a great favor," Will said.

Magnus stood looking down at Jem. There was sadness etched on his face, that face that was usually so merry or sardonic or uncaring, a sadness that surprised Will. "*For whence had that former sorrow so easily penetrated to the quick, but that I had poured out my soul upon the dust, in loving one who must die?*" Magnus said.

Will looked up at him. "What was that?"

"*Confessions* of Saint Augustine," said Magnus. "You asked me how I, being immortal, survive so many deaths. There is no great secret. You endure what is unbearable, and you bear it. That is all." He drew away from the bed. "I will give you a moment alone with him, to say good-bye as you need. You can find me in the library."

Will nodded, speechless, as Magnus went to retrieve his gloves, then turned and left the room. Will's mind was spinning.

He looked again at Jem, motionless in the bed. *I must accept that this is the end,* he thought, and even his thoughts felt hollow and distant. *I must accept that Jem will never look at me, never speak to me again. You endure what is unbearable, and you bear it. That is all.*

And yet it still did not seem real to him, as if it were a dream. He stood up and leaned over Jem's still form. He touched his *parabatai*'s cheek lightly. It was cold.

"*Atque in pepetuum, frater, ave atque vale,*" he whispered. The words of the poem had never seemed so fitting: *Forever and ever, my brother, hail and farewell.*

Will began to straighten up, to turn away from the bed. And as he did, he felt something wrap tightly around his wrist. He glanced down and saw Jem's hand braceleting his own. For a moment he was too shocked to do anything but stare.

"I am not dead yet, Will," Jem said in a soft voice, thin but as strong as wire. "What did Magnus mean by asking you if I knew you were in love with Tessa?"

11

FEARFUL OF THE NIGHT

Though my soul may set in darkness, it will rise in perfect light;
I have loved the stars too fondly to be fearful of the night.
—Sarah Williams, "The Old Astronomer"

"Will?"

After so much time of silence, of only Jem's breaths, raggedly in and out, Will thought for a moment he was imagining it, his best friend's voice speaking to him out of the dimness. As Jem released his grip on Will's wrist, Will sank into the armchair beside the bed. His heart was pounding, half with relief and half with a sickly dread.

Jem turned his head toward him, against the pillow. His eyes were dark, their silver swallowed up by black. For a moment the two young men just stared at each other. It was like the calm just as one engaged in a battle, Will thought, when thought fled and inevitability took over.

"Will," Jem said again, and coughed, pressing his hand to his mouth. When he took it away, there was blood on his fingers. "Did I—have I been dreaming?"

Will started upright. Jem had sounded so clear, so sure— *What did Magnus mean by asking you if I knew you were in love with Tessa?*—but it was as if that burst of strength had fled from him, and now he sounded dizzy and bewildered.

Had Jem really heard what Magnus had said to him? And if he had, was there any chance it could be passed off as a dream, a feverish hallucination? The thought filled Will with a mixture of relief and disappointment. "Dream what?"

Jem looked down at his bloody hand, and slowly closed it into a fist. "The fight in the courtyard. Jessamine's death. And they took her, didn't they? Tessa?"

"Yes," Will whispered, and he repeated the words Charlotte had said to him earlier. They had brought him no comfort, but perhaps they would to Jem. "Yes, but I don't think they'll hurt her. Remember, Mortmain desired her unhurt."

"We must find her. You know that, Will. We must—" Jem struggled into a sitting position, and immediately began to cough again. Blood spattered the white coverlet. Will held Jem's frail and shaking shoulders until the coughing ceased to rack his frame, then took one of the damp cloths from the bedside table and began to clean Jem's hands. When he reached to wipe the blood from his *parabatai*'s face, Jem took the cloth gently from his grasp and looked at him gravely. "I am not a child, Will."

"I know." Will drew his hands back. He had not cleaned

them since the fight in the courtyard, and Jessamine's dried blood mixed with Jem's fresh blood on his fingers.

Jem took a deep breath. Both he and Will waited to see if it would produce another spasm of coughing, and when it did not, Jem spoke. "Magnus said you were in love with Tessa. Is it true?"

"Yes," Will said, with the feeling that he was falling off a cliff. "Yes, it's true."

Jem's eyes were wide and luminous in the darkness. *"Does she love you?"*

"No." Will's voice cracked. "I told her I loved her, and she never wavered from you. It is you she loves."

Jem's death grip on the cloth in his hands relaxed slightly. "You told her," he said. "That you were in love with her."

"Jem—"

"When was this, and what excess of desperation could have driven you?"

"It was before I knew you were engaged. It was the day I discovered there was no curse on me." Will spoke haltingly. "I went to Tessa and told her that I loved her. She was as kind as she could be in telling me that she loved you and not me, and that you two were engaged." Will dropped his gaze. "I do not know if this will make any difference to you, James. But I truly had no idea that you cared for her. I was entirely obsessed with my own emotions."

Jem bit his lower lip, bringing color to the white skin. "And—forgive me for asking this—it is not a passing fancy, a transient regard . . . ?" He broke off, looking at Will's face. "No," he murmured. "I can see that it is not."

"I love her enough that when she assured me that she

would be happy with you, I swore to myself I would never speak of my desires again, never indicate my regard by word or by gesture, never by action or speech violate her happiness. My feelings have not changed, and yet I care enough for her and for you that I would not say a word to threaten what you have found." The words spilled from Will's lips; there seemed no reason to keep them back. If Jem was going to hate him, he would hate him for the truth and not a lie.

Jem looked stricken. "I am so sorry, Will. So very, very sorry. I wish that I had known—"

Will slumped down in the chair. "What could you have done?"

"I could have called off the engagement—"

"And broken both your hearts? How would that have benefited me? You are as dear to me as another half of my soul, Jem. I could not be happy while you were unhappy. And Tessa—she loves *you*. What sort of awful monster would I be, delighting in causing the two people I love the most in the world agony simply that I might have the satisfaction of knowing that if Tessa could not be mine, she could not be anybody's?"

"But you are my *parabatai*. If you are in pain, I wish to lessen it—"

"This," Will said, "is the one thing you cannot give me comfort for."

Jem shook his head. "But how could I not have noticed? I told you, I saw that the walls about your heart were coming down. I thought—I thought I knew why; I told you I always knew you carried a burden, and I knew you had gone to see

Magnus. I had thought that perhaps you had made some use of his magic, to free yourself from some imaginary guilt. If I had ever known it was because of Tessa, you must know, Will, I would never have made my feelings known to her."

"How could you have guessed?" Miserable though Will was, he felt free, as if a heavy burden had been displaced from him. "I did all I could to hide and deny it. You—you never hid your feelings. Looking back, it was clear and plain, and yet I never saw it. I was astonished when Tessa told me that you were engaged. You've always been the source in my life of such good things, James. I never thought you would be the source of pain, and so, wrongly, I never thought of your feelings at all. And that is why I was so blind."

Jem closed his eyes. The lids were blue-shadowed, parchmentlike. "I am grieved for your pain," he said. "But I am glad that you love her."

"You are *glad*?"

"It makes it easier," Jem said. "To ask you to do what I wish you to do: leave me, and go after Tessa."

"Now? Like this?"

Jem, incredibly, smiled. "Is that not what you were doing when I caught at your hand?"

"But—I did not believe you would regain consciousness. This is different. I cannot leave you like this, not to face alone whatever you must face—"

Jem's hand came up, and for a moment Will thought he was going to reach for Will's hand, but he knotted his fingers in the material of his friend's sleeve instead. "You are my *parabatai*," he said. "You have said I could ask anything of you."

"But I *swore* to stay with you. 'If aught but death part thee and me—'"

"Death *will* part us."

"You know the words of the oath come from a longer passage," Will said. "'Entreat me not to leave thee, or to return from following after thee: for whither thou goest, *I will go.*'"

Jem cried out with all his remaining strength. "You cannot go where I am going! Nor would I want that for you!"

"Neither can I walk away and leave you to die!"

There. Will had said it, said the word, admitted the possibility. *Die.*

"No one else can be trusted with this." Jem's eyes were bright, feverish, almost wild. "Do you think I don't know that if you do not go after her, no one will? Do you think it doesn't kill me that I cannot go, or at least go with you?" He leaned toward Will. His skin was as pale as the frosted glass of a lamp shade, and like such a lamp, light seemed to shine through him from some inner source. He slid his hands across the coverlet. "Take my hands, Will."

Numbly Will closed his hands around Jem's. He imagined he could feel a flicker of pain in the *parabatai* rune on his chest, as if it knew what he did not and was warning him of coming pain, a pain so great he did not imagine he could bear it and live. *Jem is my great sin,* he had told Magnus, and this, now, was the punishment for it. He had thought losing Tessa was his penance; he had not thought of how it would be when he had lost both of them.

"Will," Jem said. "For all these years I have tried to give you what you could not give yourself."

Will's hands tightened on Jem's, which were as thin as a bundle of twigs. "And what is that?"

"Faith," said Jem. "That you were better than you thought you were. Forgiveness, that you need not always punish yourself. I always loved you, Will, whatever you did. And now I need you to do for me what I cannot do for myself. For you to be my eyes when I do not have them. For you to be my hands when I cannot use my own. For you to be my heart when mine is done with beating."

"No," said Will wildly. "No, no, no. I will not be those things. Your eyes will see, your hands will feel, your heart will continue to beat."

"But if not, Will—"

"If I could tear myself in half, I would—that half of me might remain with you and half follow Tessa—"

"Half of you would be no good to either of us," said Jem. "There is no other I could trust to go after her, no other who would give of his own life, as I would, to save hers. I would have asked you to undertake this mission even if I had not known your feelings, but being certain that you love her as I do—Will, I trust you above all, and believe in you above all, knowing that as always your heart is twinned with mine in this matter. *Wo men shi jie bai xiong di*—we are more than brothers, Will. Undertake this journey, and you undertake it not for yourself alone but for both of us."

"I cannot leave you to face death alone," Will whispered, but he knew he was beaten; the sands of his will had run out.

Jem touched the *parabatai* rune on his shoulder, through the thin material of his nightshirt. "I am not alone," he said. "Wherever we are, we are as one."

Will rose slowly to his feet. He could not believe he was doing what he was doing, but it was clear that he was, as clear as the silver rim around the black of Jem's eyes. "If there is a life after this one," he said, "let me meet you in it, James Carstairs."

"There *will* be other lives." Jem held his hand out, and for a moment they clasped hands, as they had done during their *parabatai* ritual, reaching across twin rings of fire to interlace their fingers with each other. "The world is a wheel," he said. "When we rise or fall, we do it together."

Will tightened his grip on Jem's hand. "Well, then," he said, through a tight throat, "since you say there will be another life for me, let us both pray I do not make as colossal a mess of it as I have this one."

Jem smiled at him, that smile that had always, even on Will's blackest days, eased his mind. "I think there is hope for you yet, Will Herondale."

"I will try to learn how to have it, without you to show me."

"Tessa," Jem said. "She knows despair, and hope as well. You can teach each other. Find her, Will, and tell her that I loved her always. My blessing, for all that it is worth, is on you both."

Their eyes met and held. Will could not bring himself to say good-bye, or to say anything at all. He only gripped Jem's hand one last time and released it, and then turned and walked out the door.

The horses were stabled out behind the Institute—Cyril's territory during the daytime, where the rest of them rarely ventured. The stable had once been an old parish house, and the floor was of uneven stone, swept scrupulously clean. Stalls lined the walls, though only two were occupied: one by Balios and the other by Xanthos, both fast asleep with their tails switching slightly, in the manner of dreaming equines. Their mangers were packed with fresh hay, and shining tack lined the walls, polished to bright perfection. Will determined that if he should return from his mission alive, he would make sure to tell Charlotte that Cyril was doing an excellent job.

Will woke Balios with gentle murmurings and drew him from his stall. He had been taught to saddle and bridle a horse as a boy, before he had ever come to the Institute, and so he let his mind wander as he did it now, running the stirrups up the leathers, checking both sides of the saddle, reaching carefully beneath Balios to capture the cinch.

He had left no notes behind him, no messages for anyone in the Institute. Jem would tell them where he had gone, and Will had found that now, in this time when he most needed the words he usually found so easily, he could not reach them. He could not quite conceive that he might be saying good-bye, and so he ran over and over in his mind what he had packed in the saddlebags: gear, a clean shirt and collar (who knew when he might need to look like a gentleman?), two steles, all the weapons that would fit, bread, cheese, dried fruit, and mundane money.

As Will fastened the cinch, Balios lifted his head and whickered. Will's head whipped around. A slight feminine figure stood in the doorway of the stable. As Will stared, she raised her right hand, and the witchlight in it flared up, illuminating her face.

It was Cecily, a blue velvet cloak wrapped around her, her dark hair loose and free around her face. Her feet were bare, peeking out beneath the hem of the cloak. He straightened up. "Cecy, what are you doing here?"

She took a step forward, then paused on the threshold, glancing down at her bare feet. "I could ask of you the same."

"I like to talk to the horses at night. They make good company. And you should not be out and about in your nightgown. There are Lightwoods wandering these halls."

"Very funny. Where are you going, Will? If you are going to seek more *yin fen*, take me with you."

"I am not going to seek more *yin fen*."

Understanding dawned in her blue eyes. "You are going after Tessa. You are going to Cadair Idris."

Will nodded.

"Take me," she said. "Take me with you, Will."

Will could not look at her; he went to get the bit and bridle, though his hands shook as he took them down and turned back to Balios. "I cannot take you with me. You cannot ride Xanthos—you have not the training—and an ordinary horse would only slow our journey down."

"The carriage horses are automatons. You cannot hope to catch them up—"

"I do not expect to. Balios may be the fastest horse in England, but he must rest and sleep. I am already resigned. I shall not reach Tessa on the road. I can only hope to arrive at Cadair Idris before it is too late."

"Then let me ride after you and do not worry if you outpace me—"

"Be reasonable, Cecy!"

"Reasonable?" she flared. "All I see is my brother going away from me again! It has been years, Will! Years, and I came to London to find you, and now that we are together again, you are leaving!"

Balios stirred uneasily as Will fitted the bit into his mouth and slid the bridle up over his head. Balios did not like shouting. Will gentled him with a hand on his neck.

"Will." Cecily sounded dangerous. "Look at me, or I shall go wake the household and stop you, I swear that I will."

Will leaned his head against the horse's neck and closed his eyes. He could smell hay and horse, and cloth and sweat and some of the sweet scent of smoke that still clung to his clothes, from the fire in Jem's room. "Cecily," he said. "I need to know that you are here and as safe as you can be, or I cannot leave. I cannot fear for Tessa ahead on the road, and you behind me, or the fear will break me down. Already too many that I love are in danger."

There was a long silence. Will could hear the beat of Balios's heart under his ear, but nothing else. He wondered if Cecily had left, walked out while he was speaking, perhaps to rouse the household. He lifted his head.

But no, Cecily was still standing where she had been, the witchlight burning in her hand. "Tessa said that you called out for me once," she said. "When you were ill. Why me, Will?"

"Cecily." The word was a soft exhale. "For years you were my—my talisman. I thought I had killed Ella. I left Wales to keep you safe. As long as I could imagine you thriving and happy and well, the pain of missing you and Mother and Father was worth it."

"I never understood why you left," Cecily said. "And I thought the Shadowhunters were monsters. I could not understand why you had come here, and I thought—I always thought—that when I was old enough, I would come, and pretend I wished to be a Shadowhunter myself, until I could convince you to come home. When I learned of the curse, I did not know what to think anymore. I understood why you had come but not why you stayed."

"Jem—"

"But even if he dies," she said, and he flinched, "you will not come home to Mam and Dad, will you? You are a Shadowhunter, through and through. As Father never was. It is why you have been so stubborn about writing to them. You do not know how to both ask forgiveness and also say that you are not coming home."

"I can't come home, Cecily, or at least, it is not my home any longer. I am a Shadowhunter. It is in my blood."

"You know I am your sister, do you not?" she said. "It is also in my blood."

"You said you were pretending." He searched her face for a moment and said slowly, "But you are not, are you? I have seen you, training, fighting. You feel it as I did. As if the floor of the Institute is the first really solid ground under your feet. As if you have found the place you belong. You *are* a Shadowhunter."

Cecily said nothing.

Will felt his mouth twist into a sideways smile. "I am glad," he said. "Glad there will be a Herondale in the Institute, even if I—"

"Even if you do not come back? Will, let me come with you, let me help you—"

"No, Cecily. Is it not enough that I accept that you will choose this life, a life of fighting and danger, though I have always wanted greater safety for you? No, I cannot let you come with me, even if you hate me for it."

Cecily sighed. "Don't be so dramatic, Will. Must you always insist that people hate you when they obviously don't?"

"I *am* dramatic," said Will. "If I had not been a Shadowhunter, I would have had a future on the stage. I have no doubt I would have been greeted with acclaim."

Cecily did not appear to find this amusing. Will supposed he could not blame her. "I am not interested in your rendition of *Hamlet*," she said. "If you will not let me go with you, then promise me that if you go now—promise that you will come back?"

"I cannot promise that," Will said. "But if I can come back to you, I will. And if I do come back, I will write to Mother and Father. I can promise that much."

"No," said Cecily. "No letters. Promise me that if you do come back, you will return to Mother and Father with me, and tell them why you left, and that you do not blame them, and that you love them still. I do not ask that you go home to stay. Neither you nor I can ever go home to stay, but to comfort them is little enough to ask. Do not tell me that it is against the rules, Will, because I know all too well that you enjoy breaking those."

"See?" Will asked. "You do know your brother a little after all. I give you my word, that if all those conditions are met, I will do as you ask."

Her shoulders and face relaxed. She looked small and defenseless with her anger gone, though he knew she was not. "And Cecy," he said softly, "before I go, I wish to give you one more thing."

He reached into his shirt and lifted over his head the necklace Magnus had given him. It swung, gleaming rich ruby red, in the dim lights of the stables.

"Your lady's necklace?" Cecily said. "Well, I confess it does not suit you."

He stepped toward Cecily and drew the glittering chain over her dark head. The ruby fell against her throat as if it were made for her. She looked at him over it, her eyes serious. "Wear it always. It will warn you when demons are coming," Will said. "It will help keep you safe, which is how I want you, and help you be a warrior, which is what you want."

She put her hand against his cheek. *"Da bo ti, Gwilym. Byddaf yn dy golli di."*

"And I you," he said. Without looking at her again, he turned to Balios and swung himself up into the saddle. She stepped back as he urged the horse toward the stable doors and, bending his head against the wind, galloped out into the night.

Out of dreams of blood and metal monsters, Tessa woke with a start and a gasp.

She lay crouched like a child on the bench seat of a large carriage, whose windows were entirely covered with thick velvet curtains. The seat was hard and uncomfortable, with springs reaching to poke her sides through the material of her dress, which itself was torn and stained. Her hair had come down and hung in lank handfuls around her face. Across from her, huddled in the opposite corner of the carriage, sat a still figure, entirely covered in a thick black fur traveling cloak, its hood pulled down low. There was no one else in the carriage.

Tessa struggled upright, fighting a bout of dizziness and nausea. She put her hands on her stomach and tried to breathe deeply, though the fetid air inside the carriage did little to calm her stomach. She put her hands against her chest, feeling the sweat trickle down the bodice of her dress.

"Not going to be sick, are you?" said a rusty voice. "Chloroform does have that side effect, sometimes."

The hooded face creaked toward her, and Tessa saw the face of Mrs. Black. She had been too shocked on the steps of the Institute to make a real study of the visage of her erstwhile captor, but now that she could see it up close, she shuddered. The skin had a greenish tint, the eyes were veined in black, and the lips sagged, showing a view of gray tongue.

"Where are you taking me?" Tessa demanded. It was always the first thing heroines in Gothic novels asked when they were kidnapped, and it had always annoyed her, but she realized now that it actually made good sense. In this sort of situation the first thing you wanted to know was where you were going.

"To Mortmain," said Mrs. Black. "And that's all the information you'll get out of me, girl. I have been given strict instructions."

It was nothing Tessa hadn't expected, but it tightened her chest and shortened her breath anyway. On impulse she leaned away from Mrs. Black and pulled back the curtain across her window.

Outside it was dark, with a half-hidden moon. The countryside was hilly and angular, without spots of light to be seen that might have meant habitation. Black heaps of rock dotted the land. Tessa reached as subtly as she could for the handle of the door and tried it; it was locked.

"Do not bother," said the Dark Sister. "You cannot unlock the door, and if you were to flee, I would catch you. I am much faster now than you recall."

"Is that how you disappeared on the steps?" Tessa demanded. "Back at the Institute?"

Mrs. Black gave a superior smile. "Disappeared to your eyes. I only moved swiftly away, and then back again. Mortmain has given me that gift."

"Is that why you're doing this?" Tessa spat. "Gratitude for Mortmain? He didn't think much of you. He sent Jem and Will to kill you when he thought you were going to get in his way."

The moment she said Jem's and Will's names, she blanched with memory. She had been carried off while the Shadowhunters had been fighting desperately for their lives on the Institute steps. Had they held out against the automatons? Had any of them been injured, or, God forbid it, killed? But surely she would know, be able to feel it, if anything like that had happened to Jem or to Will? She was so conscious of them both as pieces of her heart.

"No," said Mrs. Black. "To answer the question in your eyes, you wouldn't know if either of them were dead, those pretty Shadowhunter boys you like so much. So people always imagine, but unless there exists a magical tie like the *parabatai* bond, it is but a fanciful imagining. When I left, they were fighting for their lives." She grinned, and her teeth sparked, metallic in the dimness. "If I did not have orders from Mortmain to bring you to him unharmed, I would have left you there to be cut into strips."

"Why does he want you to bring me to him unharmed?"

"You and your questions. I had nearly forgotten how annoying it was. There is some information he wants that only you can provide him. And he still wants to marry you. The more fool him. Let you devil him all his life for all I mind; I want what I want from him, and then I will be gone."

"There's nothing I could possibly know that would interest Mortmain!"

Mrs. Black snorted. "You are so young and stupid. You are not human, Miss Gray, and there is very little you understand about what you can do. We might have taught you more, but you were recalcitrant. You will find Mortmain a less lenient instructor."

"Lenient?" Tessa snapped. "You beat me bloody."

"There are worse things than physical pain, Miss Gray. Mortmain has little mercy."

"Exactly." Tessa leaned forward, her clockwork angel beating double time under the bodice of her dress. "Why do what he asks you? You know you can't trust him, you know he would happily destroy you—"

"I need what he can give me," Mrs. Black said. "And I will do what I must do to obtain it."

"And what is that?" Tessa demanded.

She heard Mrs. Black laugh, and then the Dark Sister slipped back her hood and unfastened the collar of her cloak.

Tessa had read in history books about heads on spikes over London Bridge, but she had never imagined how horrific it would actually look. Obviously whatever decay Mrs. Black had suffered after her head had been severed had not been reversed, so ragged gray skin hung down around the spike of metal that impaled her skull. She had no body, only a smooth column of metal from which two sticklike jointed arms protruded. The gray kid gloves that covered whatever sort of hands jutted from the ends of the arms added the last macabre touch.

Tessa screamed.

12

GHOSTS ON THE ROAD

Oh ever beauteous, ever friendly! tell,
Is it, in Heav'n, a crime to love too well?
To bear too tender, or too firm a heart,
To act a lover's or a Roman's part?
Is there no bright reversion in the sky,
For those who greatly think, or bravely die?
—Alexander Pope,
"Elegy to the Memory of an Unfortunate Lady"

Will stood upon the crest of a low hill, his hands jammed into his pockets, gazing out impatiently over the placid countryside of Bedfordshire.

He had ridden with all the speed he and Balios could muster out of London toward the Great North Road. Leaving so near to dawn had meant that the streets had been fairly clear as he'd pounded through Islington, Holloway, and Highgate; he had passed a few costermonger carts and a pedestrian or two, but otherwise there had been nothing much to hold him up, and as Balios did not tire as quickly as an ordinary horse, Will had soon been out of Barnet and able to gallop through South Mimms and London Colney.

Will loved to gallop—flat to the horse's back, with the wind in his hair, and Balios's hooves eating up the road underneath him. Now that he was gone from London, he felt both a tearing pain and a strange freedom. It was odd to feel both at once, but he could not help it. Near Colney there were ponds; he had stopped to water Balios there before journeying on.

Now, almost thirty miles north of London, he could not help recalling coming through this way on his way to the Institute years ago. He had brought one of his father's horses part of the way from Wales, but had sold it in Staffordshire when he'd realized he did not have money for the toll roads. He knew now that he had gotten a very bad price, and it had been a struggle to say good-bye to Hengroen, the horse that he had grown up riding, and even more of a struggle to trudge the remaining miles to London on foot. By the time he'd reached the Institute, his feet had been bleeding, and his hands, too, where he had fallen on the road and scraped them.

He looked down at his hands now, with the memory of those hands laid over them. Thin hands with long fingers—all the Herondales had them. Jem had always said it was a shame he didn't have a bit of musical talent, as his hands were made to span a piano. The thought of Jem was like the stab of a needle; Will pushed the memory away and turned back to Balios. He had stopped here not just to water the horse but to feed him a handful of oats—good for speed and endurance—and let him rest. He had often heard of cavalry riding their horses until they died, but desperate as he was to get to Tessa, he could not imagine doing something so cruel.

There was a deal of traffic; carts on the road, dray horses with brewery wagons, dairy vans, even the odd horse-drawn omnibus. Really, did all these people *have* to be out and about in the middle of a Wednesday, cluttering up the roads? At least there were no highwaymen; railways, toll roads, and proper police had put an end to highway robbers decades ago. Will would have hated to have to waste time killing anybody.

He had skirted Saint Albans, not bothering to stop for lunch in his hurry to catch up to Watling Street—the ancient Roman road that now split at Wroxeter, with one half crossing up to Scotland and the other cutting through England to the port of Holyhead in Wales. There were ghosts on the road— Will caught whispers of old Anglo-Saxon on the winds, calling the road *Wæcelinga Stræt* and speaking of the last stand of the troops of Boadicea, who had been defeated by the Romans along this road so many years ago.

Now, with his hands in his pockets, staring out over the countryside—it was three o'clock and the sky was beginning to darken, which meant that Will would soon have to consider the nightfall, and finding an inn to stop at, rest his horse, and sleep—he could not help remembering when he had told Tessa that Boadicea proved that women could be warriors too. He had not told her then that he had read her letters, that he already loved the warrior soul in her, hidden behind those quiet gray eyes.

He remembered a dream he had had, blue skies and Tessa

sitting down beside him on a green hill. *You will always come first in my heart.* A fierce rage blossomed in his soul. How dare Mortmain touch her. She was one of them. She did not belong to Will—she was too much herself to belong to anyone, even Jem—but she belonged *with* them, and silently he cursed the Consul for not seeing it.

He would find her. He would find her and bring her back home, and even if she never loved him, it would be all right, he would have done this for her, for himself. He spun back toward Balios, who looked at him balefully. Will swung himself up into the saddle.

"Come on, old boy," he said. "The sun's going down, and we ought to make Hockliffe by nightfall, for it looks liable to rain." He dug his heels into the horse's sides, and Balios, as if he had understood his rider's words, took off like a shot.

"He has gone off to Wales *alone?*" Charlotte demanded. "How could you have let him do something so—so stupid?"

Magnus shrugged. "It is not my responsibility now, nor will it ever be my responsibility, to manage wayward Shadowhunters. In fact, I am not sure why I am to blame. I spent the night in the library waiting for Will to come and talk to me, which he never did. Eventually I fell asleep in the Rabies and Lycanthropy section. Woolsey bites on occasion, and I'm concerned."

No one really responded to this information, although Charlotte looked more upset than ever. It had been a quiet breakfast as it was, with quite a few of them missing from the table. Will's absence had not been surprising. They had assumed Will was at his *parabatai's* side. So it had not been until Cyril had burst in, breathless and agitated, to report that Balios was gone from his stall, that the alarm had been raised.

A search of the Institute turned up Magnus Bane asleep in a corner of the library. Charlotte had shaken him awake. On being asked where he thought Will might be, Magnus had replied quite candidly that he expected that Will had already left for Wales, with the object of discovering Tessa's whereabouts and bringing her back to the Institute, whether by stealth or main force. This information, much to his surprise, had thrown Charlotte into a panic, and she had convened a meeting in the library, at which all the Shadowhunters of the Institute, save Jem, were commanded to appear—even Gideon, who had arrived limping and leaning heavily on a stick.

"Does anyone know when Will left?" Charlotte demanded, standing at the head of a long table around which the rest of them were seated.

Cecily, her hands folded demurely before her, suddenly became very interested in the pattern of the carpet.

"That is a very fine gem you're wearing, Cecily," Charlotte noted, narrowing her eyes at the ruby about the girl's throat. "I don't recall you having that necklace yesterday. In fact, I recall *Will* wearing it. When did he give it to you?"

Cecily crossed her arms over her chest. "I will say nothing. Will's decisions are his own, and we already tried to explain to the Consul what needed to be done. Since the Clave will not help, Will took matters into his own hands. I don't know why you expected anything different."

"I did not think he would leave Jem," said Charlotte, and then she looked shocked that she had said it. "I . . . I cannot even imagine how we will tell him when he wakes."

"Jem knows—" Cecily began indignantly, but she was interrupted, to her surprise, by Gabriel.

"Of course he knows," he said. "Will is only doing his duty as a *parabatai*. He is doing what Jem would be doing if he could. He has gone in Jem's place. It is only what a *parabatai* should do."

"*You* are defending Will?" Gideon said. "After the way you've always treated him? After telling Jem on dozens of occasions that he had dismal taste in *parabatai*?"

"Will may be a reprehensible person, but at least this demonstrates that he is not a reprehensible Shadowhunter," said Gabriel, and then, catching Cecily's look, he added, "He might not be that reprehensible a person, either. In entirety."

"A very magnanimous statement, Gideon," said Magnus.

"I'm Gabriel."

Magnus waved a hand. "All Lightwoods look the same to me—"

"*Ahem,*" Gideon interrupted, before Gabriel could pick up something and throw it at Magnus. "Regardless of Will's personal qualities and failings or anyone's inability to tell one Lightwood from another, the question remains: Do we go after Will?"

"If Will had wanted help, he wouldn't have ridden off in the middle of the night without telling anyone," said Cecily.

"Yes," said Gideon, "because Will is well known for his carefully thought-out and prudent decision making."

"He did steal our fastest horse," Henry pointed out. "That bespeaks forethought, of a sort."

"We cannot allow Will to ride off to battle Mortmain alone. He'll be slaughtered," Gideon said. "If he really did leave in the midst of the night, we might yet be able to over-take him on the road—"

"Fastest horse," reminded Henry, and Magnus snorted under his breath.

"Actually, it is not an inevitable slaughter," Gabriel said. "We could all ride off after Will, certainly, but the fact is that such a force, sent against the Magister, would be more noticeable than one boy on horseback. Will's best hope is remaining undetected. After all, he is not riding off to war. He is going to save Tessa. Stealth and secrecy best behoove such a mission—"

Charlotte slammed her hand down on the table with such force that the sound reverberated through the room. "All of you *be silent*," she said, in such a commanding tone that even Magnus looked alarmed. "Gabriel, Gideon, you are both cor-rect. It is better for Will if we do not follow him, and we cannot allow one of our own to perish. It is also true that the Magister is beyond our reach; the Council will meet to decide on that matter. There is nothing we can do about that now. Therefore we must bend all our energies to saving Jem. He is dying, but not dead. Part of Will's strength relies on him, and he is one of our own. He has finally given us permission to seek a cure for him, and therefore we must do that."

"But—," Gabriel began.

"*Silence*," Charlotte said. "I am the head of the Institute; you will remember who saved you from your father and show me respect."

"That's putting Gideon in his place, all right," Magnus said with satisfaction.

Charlotte turned on him with blazing eyes. "And you,

too, Warlock; Will may have summoned you here, but you remain on my sufferance. It is my understanding that, as you told me this morning, you promised Will that you would do all you could to help find a cure for Jem while Will was gone. You will be telling Gabriel and Cecily where the shop is from which they might procure the ingredients you need. Gideon, since you are wounded, you will remain in the library and seek out whatever books Magnus requires; if you need help, myself or Sophie will provide it. Henry, perhaps Magnus can use your crypt as a laboratory, unless there is a project you are engaged in that would forbid it?" She looked at Henry with her eyebrows raised.

"There is," Henry said a bit hesitantly, "but it might also be turned to helping Jem, and I would welcome Mr. Bane's assistance. In return he can certainly make use of any of my scientific implements."

Magnus looked at him curiously. "What are you working on, exactly?"

"Well, you know that we do not perform magic, Mr. Bane," said Henry, looking delighted that anyone was taking an interest in his experiments, "but I am at work on a device a bit like the scientific version of a transportation spell. It would open a doorway into anyplace you wanted—"

"Including perhaps a storeroom full of *yin fen* in China?" Magnus said, with his eyes aglint. "That sounds very interesting, very interesting indeed."

"No, it doesn't," muttered Gabriel.

Charlotte fixed him with a dagger gaze. "Mr. Lightwood, enough. I believe you have all been assigned your tasks. Go forth and perform them. I wish to hear no more from any of you until you bring me back a report of some progress made. I will be with Jem." And with that, she swept from the room.

"What a very satisfying response," said Mrs. Black.

Tessa glared. She was crouched in her corner of the carriage, as far as she could get from the horrible sight of the creature that had once been Mrs. Black. She had screamed at the first sight of her, and hastily clapped a hand over her mouth; but it was too late. Mrs. Black had been plainly delighted by her terrified reaction.

"You were beheaded," Tessa said. "How is it that you live? Like *that?*"

"Magic," said Mrs. Black. "It was your brother who suggested to Mortmain that in my current form I could be of use to him. It was your brother who spilled the blood that made my continued existence possible. Lives for my life."

She grinned horribly, and Tessa thought of her brother, dying in her arms. *You don't know everything I've done, Tessie.* She swallowed back bile. After her brother was dead, she had tried to Change into him, to glean any information about Mortmain she could from his memories, but they had been only a gray swirl of anger and bitterness and ambition: she had found nothing solid within them. A fresh surge of hate welled in her for Mortmain, who had found her brother's weaknesses and exploited them. Mortmain, who held Jem's *yin fen* in a cruel attempt to make the Shadowhunters dance to his tune. Even Mrs. Black, in a way, was a prisoner of his manipulations.

"You are doing Mortmain's bidding because you think he will give you a body," Tessa said now. "Not that—that thing you have, but some sort of real, human body."

"Human." Mrs. Black snorted. "I expect better than *human*. But better than this as well, something that will allow me to pass undetected among mundanes and practice my craft again. As for the Magister, I know he will have the power to do it, because of you. He will soon be all-powerful, and you will help him get there."

"You are a fool to trust him to reward you."

Mrs. Black's gray lips wobbled with mirth. "Oh, but he will. He has sworn it, and I have done everything I promised. Here I am delivering his perfect bride—trained by me! By Azazel, I remember when you stepped off the boat from America. You seemed so purely mortal, so entirely useless, I despaired of ever training you to be any sort of use at all. But with enough brutality anything can be shaped. You will serve nicely now."

"Not all that is mortal is useless."

A snort. "You say that because of your association with the Nephilim. You have been with them rather than your own kind for far too long."

"What kind? I have no kind. Jessamine said my mother was a Shadowhunter—"

"She was a Shadowhunter," said Mrs. Black. "But your father was not."

Tessa's heart skipped a beat. "He was a demon?"

"He was no angel." Mrs. Black smirked. "The Magister will explain it all to you, in time—what you are, and why you live, and what you were created for." She settled back with a creak of automated joints. "I have to say that I was almost impressed when you ran off with that Shadowhunter boy, you know. It showed you had spirit. In fact, it turned out to the Magister's benefit that you have spent so much time with the Nephilim.

You are acquainted with Downworld now, and you have shown yourself equal to it. You have been forced to use your gift in arduous circumstances. Tests that I might have created for you would not have been as challenging and would not have yielded the same learning and confidence. I can see the difference in you. You will make a fine bride for the Magister."

Tessa made a sound of disbelief. "Why? I am being forced to marry him. What difference does it make if I have spirit or learning? What could he possibly care?"

"Oh, you are to be more than his bride, Miss Gray. You are to be the ruin of the Nephilim. That is why you were created. And the more knowledge of them you have, the more your sympathies lie with them, the more effective a weapon you will be to raze them to the ground."

Tessa felt as if the air had been knocked out of her. "I don't care what Mortmain does. I will not cooperate in harming the Shadowhunters. I would die or be tortured first."

"It does not matter what you want. You will find that there is no resistance you could mount against his will that would matter. Besides, there is nothing you need do to destroy the Nephilim other than be what you are. And be married to Mortmain, which requires no action on your part."

"I'm engaged to someone else," spat Tessa. "James Carstairs."

"Oh, dear," said Mrs. Black. "I'm afraid the Magister's claim supersedes his. Besides, James Carstairs will be dead by Tuesday. Mortmain has bought up all the *yin fen* in England and blocked any new shipments. Perhaps you should have thought of this sort of thing before you fell in love with an addict. Although I did think it would be the blue-eyed one," she mused. "Don't girls usually fall in love with their rescuers?"

Tessa felt the cloak of the surreal begin to descend. She could not believe that she was here, trapped in this carriage with Mrs. Black, and that the warlock woman seemed content to discuss Tessa's romantic tribulations. She turned toward the window. The moon was up, and she could see that they were riding along a narrow road—there were shadows about the carriage, and below, a rocky ravine fell away into darkness. "There are all sorts of ways of being rescued."

"Well," said Mrs. Black, with a glint of teeth as she smiled. "You can be assured that no one will be coming to rescue you now."

You are to be the ruin of the Nephilim.

"Then I will have to rescue myself," Tessa said. Mrs. Black's eyebrows drew together in puzzlement as she turned her head toward Tessa with a whir and a click. But Tessa was already gathering herself, gathering all her energy in her legs and body in the way that she had been taught, so that when she launched herself across the carriage at the door, it was with all the force she possessed.

She heard the lock on the door break and Mrs. Black scream, a high whine of rage. A metal arm raked Tessa's back, seizing the collar of her dress, which tore away, and Tessa was falling, slamming down onto the rocks by the side of the road, falling and sliding and tumbling into the ravine as the carriage hurtled away down the road, Mrs. Black screaming at the driver to stop. Wind rushed into Tessa's ears as she fell, her arms and hands windmilling wildly against the empty space all around her, and any hopes that the ravine was shallow or that the fall would be survivable were gone. As she fell, she glimpsed a narrow stream glinting far below her, twisting among jagged rocks, and she knew she would break against the ground like fragile china when she struck.

She closed her eyes and willed that the end be quick.

Will stood at the top of a high green hill and looked out over the sea. The sky and sea were both so intensely blue that they seemed to merge one into the other, so that there was no fixed point upon the horizon. Gulls and terns wheeled and shrieked above him, and the salt wind blew through his hair. It was as warm as summer, and his jacket lay discarded on the grass; he was in shirtsleeves and braces, and his hands were brown and tanned by the sun.

"Will!" He turned at the familiar voice and saw Tessa coming up the hill toward him. There was a small path cut along the side of the hill, lined with unfamiliar white flowers, and Tessa looked like a flower herself, in a white dress like the one she had worn to the ball the night he had kissed her on Benedict Lightwood's balcony. Her long brown hair blew in the wind. She had taken off her bonnet and held it in one hand, waving it at him and smiling as if she were glad to see him. More than glad. As if seeing him were all the joy of her heart.

His own heart leaped up at the sight of her. "Tess," he called, and reached out a hand as if he could pull her toward him. But she was still such a distance away—she seemed both very near and very far suddenly and at the same time. He could see every detail of her pretty upturned face but could not touch her, and so he stood, waiting and desiring, and his heart beat like wings in his chest.

At last she was there, close enough that he could see where the grass and flowers bent beneath the tread of her shoes. He reached out for her, and she for him. Their hands closed on each other's, and for a moment they stood smiling, and her fingers were warm in his.

"I've been waiting for you," Will said, and she looked up at him

with a smile that vanished from her face as her feet slipped and she tilted toward the edge of the cliff. Her hands tore out of his, and suddenly he was reaching for air as she fell away from him, silently fell, a white blur against the blue horizon.

Will sat bolt upright in bed, his heart slamming against his ribs. His room at the White Horse was half-full of moonlight, which clearly outlined the unfamiliar shapes of the furniture: the washstand and side table with its unread copy of Fordyce's *Sermons to Young Women*, the overstuffed chair by the fireplace, in which the flames had burned down to embers. The sheets of his bed were cold, but he was sweating; he swung his legs over the side and walked to the window.

There was a stiff bunch of arranged dried flowers in a vase on the sill. He pushed them out of the way and unlatched the pane with aching fingers. His whole body hurt. He had never ridden so far or so hard in his life before, and he was weary and saddle-sore. He would need *iratzes* before he started out on the road again tomorrow.

The window opened outward, and cold air blew against his face and hair, cooling his skin. There was an ache inside him, under his ribs, that had nothing to do with riding. Whether it was the separation from Jem or his anxiety over Tessa, he could not say. He kept seeing her falling away from him, their hands unclasping. He had never been one to believe in the prophetic meaning of dreams, and yet he could not undo the tight, cold knot inside his stomach, or regulate his harsh breathing.

In the dark pane of the window he could see the reflection of his face. He touched the window lightly, his fingertips leaving marks in the condensation on the glass. He wondered what he would say to Tessa when he found her, how he could tell her why it was that he was the one who had come after her, and not Jem. If there was grace in the world, perhaps at least they could grieve together. If she never truly believed he loved her, if she never returned his affection, at least mercy might grant that they be able to share their sadness. Nearly unable to bear the thought of how much he needed her quiet strength, he closed his eyes and leaned his forehead against the cold glass.

As they made their way through the East End's winding lanes from Limehouse Station toward Gill Street, Gabriel could not help but be aware of Cecily by his side. They were glamoured, which was useful, as their appearance in this poorer part of London would otherwise doubtless have excited comment, and perhaps resulted in their being hauled into a broker's shop willy-nilly to look at the goods on offer. As it was, Cecily was intensely curious, and paused often to gaze into shop-windows—not just milliners' and bonnet-makers', but shops selling everything from boot polish and books to toys and tin soldiers. Gabriel had to remind himself that she came from the countryside and had probably never seen a thriving market town, much less anything like London. He wished he could take her somewhere befitting a lady of her station—the shops of Burlington Arcade or Piccadilly, not these dark, close streets.

He did not know what he had expected from Will Herondale's sister. That she would be just as unpleasant as Will? That she would not look so disconcertingly like him, and yet at the same time be extraordinarily pretty? He had rarely looked at Will's face without wanting to hit it, but Cecily's face was endlessly fascinating. He found himself wanting to write poetry about how her blue eyes were like starlight and her hair like night, because "night" and "starlight" rhymed, but he had a feeling the poem wouldn't turn out that well, and Tatiana had rather frightened him off poetry as it was. Besides, there were things you couldn't put in poetry anyway, like the way that when a certain girl curved her mouth in a certain way, you wanted very much to lean forward and—

"Mr. Lightwood," Cecily said in an impatient tone that indicated that this was not the first time she had tried to get Gabriel's attention. "I do believe we have passed the shop already."

Gabriel cursed under his breath and turned back. They had indeed passed the number Magnus had given them; they retraced their steps until they found themselves standing before a dark, ill-favored shop with clouded windows. Through the murky glass he was able to see shelves on which sat a variety of peculiar items—jars in which dead serpents floated, their eyes white and open; dolls whose heads had been removed and replaced with small gold birdcages; and stacked bracelets made of human teeth.

"Oh, dear," said Cecily. "How decidedly unpleasant."

"Do you not wish to enter?" Gabriel turned to her. "I could go instead—"

"And leave me standing about on the cold pavement? How ungentlemanly. Certainly not." She reached for the knob and pushed the door open, setting a small bell somewhere in the shop tinkling. "After me, please, Mr. Lightwood."

Gabriel went blinking after her into the dim light of the shop. The inside was no more welcoming than the exterior. Long rows of dusty shelves led back toward a shadowy counter. The windows seemed to have been smeared with some dark unguent, blocking out much of the sunlight. The shelves themselves were a cluttered mass—brass bells with handles shaped like bones, fat candles whose wax was stuffed with insects and flowers, a lovely golden crown of such peculiar shape and diameter than it could never have fit a human head. There were shelves of knives, and copper and stone bowls whose basins were marked with peculiar brownish stains. There were stacks of gloves of all sizes, some with more than five fingers on each hand. An entire de-fleshed human skeleton hung from a thin cord toward the front of the shop, twisting in the air, though there was no breeze.

Gabriel looked quickly toward Cecily to see if she had quailed, but she had not. She looked irritated if anything. "Someone really ought to dust in here," she announced, and swept toward the back of the shop, the small flowers on her hat bouncing. Gabriel shook his head.

He caught up to Cecily just as she brought her gloved hand down on the brass bell on the counter, setting it to an impatient ringing. "Hello?" she called. "Is anyone here?"

"Directly in front of you, miss," said an irritable voice, downward and to the left. Both Cecily and Gabriel leaned over the counter. Just below the edge of it was the top of the head of a small man. No, not quite a man, thought Gabriel as the glamour peeled away—a satyr. He wore a waistcoat and trousers, though no shirt, and had the cloven feet and neatly curling horns of a goat. He also had a trimmed beard, a pointed jaw, and the rectangular-pupilled yellow eyes of a goat, half-hidden behind spectacles.

"Gracious," said Cecily. "You must be Mr. Sallows."

"Nephilim," observed the shop owner gloomily. "I detest Nephilim."

"Hmph," said Cecily. "Charmed, I'm sure."

Gabriel felt it was about time to intervene. "How did you know we were Shadowhunters?" he snapped.

Sallows raised his eyebrows. "Your Marks, sir, are clearly visible on your hands and throat," he said, as if talking to a child, "and as for the girl, she looks just like her brother."

"How would you know my brother?" Cecily demanded, her voice rising.

"We don't get many of your kind in here," said Sallows. "It's notable when we do. Your brother Will was in and out quite a bit about two months ago, running errands for that warlock Magnus Bane. He was down the Cross Bones too, bothering Old Mol. Will Herondale's well-known in Downworld, though he mostly keeps himself out of trouble."

"That *is* astonishing news," said Gabriel.

Cecily gave Gabriel a dark look. "We are here on the authority of Charlotte Branwell," she said. "Head of the London Institute."

The satyr waved a hand. "I don't care much for your Shadowhunter hierarchies, you know; none of the Fair Folk do. Just tell me what you want, and I'll give you a fair price for it."

Gabriel unrolled the paper Magnus had given him. "Thieves' vinegar, bat's head root, belladonna, angelica, damiana leaf, powdered mermaid scales, and six nails from a virgin's coffin."

"*Well,*" said Sallows. "We don't get much call for that sort of thing around here. I'll have to look in the back."

"Well, if you don't get much call for this sort of thing, what *do* you get call for?" asked Gabriel, losing his patience. "You're hardly a florist's shop."

"Mr. Lightwood," chided Cecily under her breath—but not quite enough under her breath, for Sallows heard her, and his spectacles bounced on his nose.

"Mr. *Lightwood?*" he said. "Benedict Lightwood's son?"

Gabriel could feel the blood heating his cheeks. He had spoken to almost no one about his father since Benedict's death—if one could even count the thing that had died in the Italian garden as his father. Once it had been he and his family against the world, the Lightwoods above all else, but now—now there was shame in the name of Lightwood as much as there had ever been pride, and Gabriel did not know how to speak of it.

"Yes," he said finally. "I am Benedict Lightwood's son."

"Wonderful. I have some of your father's orders here. I was beginning to wonder if he would ever come and pick them up." The satyr bustled into the back, and Gabriel busied himself studying the wall. There were landscape sketches hung on it, and maps on it, but as he looked more closely, not sketches or maps of any place he knew. There was Idris, of course, with Brocelind Forest and Alicante on its hill, but another map showed continents he had never seen before—and what was the Silver Sea? The Thorn Mountains? What sort of country had a *purple* sky?

"Gabriel," said Cecily beside him, in a low voice. It was the first time she had used his Christian name in addressing him, and he began to turn toward her, just as Sallows emerged from the back of the shop. In one hand he carried a tied parcel, which he handed over to Gabriel. It was quite lumpy—clearly the bottles of Magnus's ingredients. In the other hand Sallows clutched a stack of papers, which he set down on the counter.

"Your father's order," he said with a smirk.

Gabriel lowered his eyes to the papers—and his jaw dropped in horror.

"Gracious," Cecily said. "Surely that isn't possible?"

The satyr craned up to see what she was looking at. "Well, not with one person, but with a Vetis demon and a goat, most likely." He turned to Gabriel. "Now, have you got the money for these or not? Your father is behind on his payments, and he can't buy on tick forever. What's it going to be, Lightwood?"

"Has Charlotte ever asked you if you wanted to be a Shadowhunter?" Gideon asked.

Halfway down the ladder with a book in her hand, Sophie froze. Gideon was seated at one of the long library tables, near a bay window that looked out over the courtyard. Books and papers were spread out before him, and he and Sophie had passed several pleasant hours searching through them for lists and histories of spells, details about *yin fen*, and specifics of herb lore. Though Gideon's leg was rapidly healing, it was propped up on two chairs in front of him, and Sophie had cheerfully offered to do all the climbing up and down ladders to reach the highest books. She was holding one now called the *Pseudomonarchia Daemonum*, which had a rather slimy-feeling cover and which she was eager to put down, though Gideon's question had startled her enough to arrest her mid-descent. "What do you mean?" she said, resuming her climb down the ladder. "Why would Charlotte have asked me something like that?"

Gideon looked pale, or it might simply have been the cast of the witchlight on his face. "Miss Collins," he said. "You are one of the best fighters I have ever trained, Nephilim included. That is why I ask. It seems a shame to waste such talent. Though perhaps it is not something you would want?"

Sophie set the book down on the table, and sat down opposite Gideon. She knew she should hesitate, seem to think the question over, but the answer was on her lips before she could stop it. "To be a Shadowhunter is all I ever wanted."

He leaned forward, and the witchlight shone up into his eyes, washing out their color. "You are not worried about the danger? The older one is when one Ascends, the riskier the process. I have heard them speak about lowering the age of agreement to Ascension to fourteen or even twelve."

Sophie shook her head. "I have never feared the risk. I would take it gladly. It is only that I fear— I fear that if I applied for it, Mrs. Branwell would think I am ungrateful for all that she has done for me. She saved my life and raised me up. She gave me safety and a home. I would not repay her for all that by abandoning her service."

"No." Gideon shook his head. "Sophie—Miss Collins—you are a free servant in a Shadowhunter home. You have the Sight. You know all there is to know of Downworlders and the Nephilim already. You are the *perfect* candidate for Ascension." He placed his hand atop the demonology book. "I am a voice on the Council. I could speak for you."

"I can't," Sophie said in a soft thread of a voice. Didn't he understand what he was offering her, the temptation? "And certainly not *now*."

"No, not now, of course, with James so ill," Gideon said hurriedly. "But in the future? Perhaps?" His eyes searched her face, and she felt a blush begin to creep up from her collar. The most obvious and common way for a mundane to Ascend to Shadowhunter status was through marriage to a Shadowhunter. She wondered what it meant that he seemed very determined not to mention that. "But when I asked you, you spoke so strongly. You said that being a Shadowhunter was all you ever wanted. Why is that? It can be a brutal life."

"All life can be brutal," said Sophie. "My life before I came to the Institute was hardly sweet. I suppose in part I wish to be a Shadowhunter so that if another man ever comes at me with a knife in his hand, as my former employer did, I can kill him where he stands." She touched her cheek as she spoke, an unconscious gesture she could not help, feeling the ridged scar tissue under her fingertips.

She saw Gideon's expression—shock mixed with discomfort—and dropped her hand. "I did not know that was how you had been scarred," he said.

She looked away. "Now you will say that it is not so ugly, or that you do not even see it, or something like that."

"I see it," Gideon said in a low voice. "I am not blind, and we are a people of many scars. I see it, but it is not ugly. It is just another beautiful part of the most beautiful girl I have ever seen."

Now Sophie did blush—she could feel her cheeks burn—and as Gideon leaned forward across the table, his eyes an intense, storm-washed green, she took a deep breath of resolution. He was *not* like her former employer. He was Gideon. She would not push him away this time.

The door of the library flew open. Charlotte stood on the threshold, looking exhausted; there were damp splotches on her pale blue dress, and her eyes were shadowed. Sophie sprang to her feet instantly. "Mrs. Branwell?"

"Oh, Sophie," Charlotte sighed. "I was hoping you could sit with Jem for a bit. He hasn't woken up yet, but Bridget needs to make supper, and I think her dreadful singing is giving him nightmares in his sleep."

"Of course." Sophie hurried to the door, not looking at Gideon as she did so—although as the door closed behind her, she was fairly sure that she heard him swearing softly and with great frustration in Spanish.

"You know," Cecily said, "you really didn't have to throw that man through the window."

"He wasn't a man," Gabriel said, scowling down at the heap of objects in his arms. He had taken the parcel of Magnus's ingredients that Sallows had made up for them, and a few more useful-looking objects off the shelves besides. He had pointedly left all the papers his father had ordered on the counter where Sallows had put them—*after* Gabriel had tossed the satyr through one of the grimed-up windows. It had been very satisfying, with shattered glass everywhere. The force of it had even dislodged the hanging skeleton, which had come apart in a clatter of messy bones. "He was an Unseelie Court faerie. One of the nasty ones."

"Is that why you chased him down the street?"

"He had no business showing images like that to a lady," Gabriel muttered, though it had to be admitted that the lady in question had hardly turned a hair, and seemed more annoyed with Gabriel for his reaction than impressed by his chivalry.

"And I do think it was excessive to hurl him into the canal."

"He'll float."

The corners of Cecily's mouth twitched. "It was very wrong."

"You're laughing," Gabriel said in surprise.

"I am not." Cecily raised her chin, turning her face away, but not before Gabriel saw the grin that spread over her face. Gabriel was baffled. After her displayed disdain for him, her cheek and back talk, he had been quite sure that this latest outburst of his would prompt her to tell tales to Charlotte as soon as they returned to the Institute, but instead she seemed amused. He shook his head as they turned onto Garnet Street. He would never understand the Herondales.

"Hand over that vial there on the shelf, would you, Mr. Bane?" asked Henry.

Magnus did so. He was standing in the center of Henry's laboratory, looking around at the gleaming shapes on tables around him. "What are all these contraptions, if I might ask?"

Henry, who was wearing two pairs of goggles at the same time—one on his head and one over his eyes—looked both pleased and nervous to be asked. (Magnus presumed the two pairs of goggles was a fit of absentmindedness, but in case it was in pursuit of fashion, he decided not to ask.) Henry picked up a square brass object with multiple buttons. "Well, over here, this is a Sensor. It senses when demons are near." He moved toward Magnus, and the Sensor made a loud wailing noise.

"Impressive!" Magnus exclaimed, pleased. He lifted a construction of fabric with a large dead bird perched atop it. "And what is this?"

"The Lethal Bonnet," Henry declared.

"Ah," said Magnus. "In times of need a lady can produce weapons from it with which to slay her enemies."

"Well, no," Henry admitted. "That does sound like a rather better idea. I do wish you had been on the spot when I had the notion. Unfortunately this bonnet wraps about the head of one's enemy and suffocates them, provided that they are wearing it at the time."

"I imagine that it will not be easy to persuade Mortmain

into a bonnet," Magnus observed. "Though the color would be fetching on him."

Henry burst into laughter. "Very droll, Mr. Bane."

"Please, call me Magnus."

"I shall!" Henry tossed the bonnet over his shoulder and picked up a round glass jar of a sparkling substance. "This is a powder that when applied to the air causes ghosts to become visible," Henry said.

Magnus tilted the jar of shining grains up to the lamp admiringly, and when Henry beamed in an encouraging fashion, Magnus removed the cork. "It seems very fine to me," he said, and on a whim he poured it upon his hand. It coated his brown skin, gloving one hand in shimmering luminescence. "And in addition to its practical uses, it would seem to work for cosmetic purposes. This powder would make my very skin glimmer for eternity."

Henry frowned. "Not eternity," he said, but then he brightened. "But I could make you up another batch whenever you please!"

"I could shine at will!" Magnus grinned at Henry. "These are fascinating items, Mr. Branwell. You think differently about the world than any other Nephilim I have ever encountered. I confess I thought your people somewhat lacking in imagination, though high on personal drama, but you have given me a completely different opinion! Surely the Shadowhunter community must honor you and hold you in high esteem as a gentleman who has truly advanced their race."

"No," Henry said sadly. "Mostly they wish that I would stop suggesting new inventions and cease setting fire to things."

"But all invention comes with risk!" cried Magnus. "I have

seen the transformation wrought on the world by the invention of the steam engine, and the proliferation of printed materials, the factories and mills which have changed the face of England. Mundanes have taken the world into their hands and made of it a marvelous thing. Warlocks throughout the ages have dreamed up and perfected different spells to make themselves a different world. Would the Shadowhunters be the only ones to remain stagnant and changeless, and therefore doomed? How can they turn up their noses at the genius that you have displayed? It is like turning toward shadows and away from light."

Henry blushed a scarlet color. It was clear that no one had ever complimented his inventing before, except perhaps Charlotte. "You humble me, Mr. Bane."

"Magnus," the warlock reminded him. "Now may I see your work upon this portal you were describing? The invention that transports a living being from one spot to another?"

"Of course." Henry drew a heavy pile of notepaper from one corner of his cluttered table, and pushed it toward Magnus. The warlock took it and flicked through the pages with interest. Each page was covered with crabbed, spidery handwriting, and dozens and dozens of equations, blending mathematics and runes in a startling harmony. Magnus felt his heart beating faster as he flipped through the pages—this was genius, real genius. There was only one problem.

"I see what you are trying to do," he said. "And it is almost perfected, but—"

"Yes, almost." Henry ran his hands through his gingery hair, upsetting his goggles. "The portal can be opened, but there is no way to direct it. No way to know if you will step through it to your intended destination in this world or into another world altogether, or even into Hell. It is too risky, and therefore useless."

"You cannot do this with these runes," said Magnus. "You need runes other than the ones you are using."

Henry shook his head. "We can use only the runes from the Gray Book. Anything else is magic. Magic is not the way of the Nephilim. It is something we may not do."

Magnus looked at Henry for a long thoughtful moment. "It is something that *I* can do," he declared, and drew the stack of papers toward him.

Unseelie Court faeries did not like too much light. The first thing Sallows—whose name was not really that—had done upon returning to his shop had been to put up waxed paper over the window that the Nephilim boy had so heedlessly broken. His spectacles were gone too, lost in the waters of the Limehouse Cut. And no one, it seemed, was going to pay him for the very expensive papers he had ordered for Benedict Lightwood. Altogether it had been a very bad day.

He looked up peevishly as the shop bell tinkled, warning of the opening of the door, and he frowned. He thought he had locked it. "Back again, Nephilim?" he snapped. "Decided to throw me into the river not once but twice? I'll have you know I have powerful friends—"

"I don't doubt you do, trickster." The tall, hooded figure in the entryway reached around and pulled the door shut behind him. "And I am very interested in learning more about them." A cold iron blade flashed in the dimness, and the satyr's eyes widened in fear. "I have some questions to ask you," said the man in the doorway. "And I wouldn't try to run if I were you. Not if you want to keep your fingers attached to your body...."

13

THE MIND HAS MOUNTAINS

O the mind, mind has mountains; cliffs of fall
Frightful, sheer, no-man-fathomed. Hold them cheap
May who ne'er hung there. Nor does long our small
Durance deal with that steep or deep. Here! creep,
Wretch, under a comfort serves in a whirlwind: all
Life death does end and each day dies with sleep.
—Gerard Manley Hopkins, "No Worse, There Is None"

Tessa could never remember later if she had screamed as she had fallen. She remembered only a long and silent fall, the river and the rocks hurtling toward her, the sky at her feet. The wind tore at her face and hair as she twisted in the air, and she felt a sharp jerk at her throat.

Her hands flew up. Her angel necklace was lifting over her head, as if an enormous hand had reached down out of the sky to remove it. A metallic blur surrounded her, a pair of great wings opening like gates, and something caught at her, arresting her fall. Her eyes widened—it was impossible, unimaginable—but her angel, her clockwork angel, had grown somehow to the size of a living human being and was hovering over her, its great mechanical wings beating against the wind. She stared up into a blank, beautiful face, the face of a statue made of metal, as expressionless as ever—but the angel had hands, as articulate as her own, and they were holding her, holding her up as the wings beat and beat and beat and she fell slowly now, gently, like a puff of dandelion fluff blown on the wind.

Maybe I am dying, Tessa thought. And, *This cannot be.* But as the angel held her, and they drifted together toward earth, the ground came clearer and clearer into focus. She could see the individual rocks by the side of the stream now, the currents as they ran downstream, the reflection of the sun in the water. The shadow of wings appeared against the earth and grew wider and wider until she was falling into it, falling into the shadow, and she and the angel plunged together to the ground and landed in the soft dirt and scattered rocks at the side of the stream.

Tessa gasped as she landed, more from shock than impact, and reached up, as if she could cushion the angel's fall with her body—but it was shrinking already, growing smaller and smaller, its wings folding in on themselves, until it struck the ground by her side, the size of a toy once more. She reached out a shaking hand and seized it. She was lying on uneven rocks, half-in, half-out of the chilly water; it was already soaking through her skirts. She seized the pendant and crawled up the side of the stream with the remainder of her strength, and collapsed at last on dry ground with the angel pressed against her chest, ticking its familiar beat against her heart.

Sophie sat in the armchair by the side of Jem's bed that had always been Will's place, and watched Jem sleep.

There had been a time, she thought, when she would have been almost grateful for this opportunity, a chance to be so close to him, to place cold cloths against his forehead when he stirred and murmured and burned with fever. And though she no longer loved him as she once had—the way, she realized now, one loved someone one did not know at all, with admiration and distance—it still wrung her heart to see him like this.

One of the girls in the town where Sophie had grown up had died of consumption, and Sophie recalled how they had all talked of the way the disease had made her more beautiful before it killed her—made her pale and slender, and flushed her face with a hectic rosy glow. Jem had that fever in his cheeks now as he tossed against his pillows; his silvery-white hair was like frost, and his restless fingers twitched against the blanket. Every once in a while he spoke, but the words were in Mandarin, and she did not know them. He called out for Tessa. *Wo ai ni, Tessa. Bu lu run, he qing kuang fa sheng, wo men dou hui zai yi qi.* And he called out for Will as well, *sheng si zhi jiao,* in a way that made Sophie want to take his hand and hold it, though when she did reach to touch him, he was burning up with fever and snatched his hand away with a cry.

Sophie shrank back against the chair, wondering if she should call for Charlotte. Charlotte would want to know if Jem's condition worsened. She was about to rise to her feet, when Jem suddenly gasped and his eyes flew open. She sank back into the chair, staring. His irises were such a pale silver that they were nearly white. "Will?" he said. "Will, is that you?"

"No," she said, almost afraid to move. "It is Sophie."

He exhaled softly and turned his head toward her on the pillow. She saw him focus on her face with an effort—and then, incredibly, he smiled, that smile of great sweetness that had first won her heart. "Of course," he said. "Sophie. Will is not— I sent Will away."

"He has gone after Tessa," Sophie said.

"Good." Jem's long hands plucked at the blanket, contracted once into fists—and then relaxed. "I—am glad."

"You miss him," Sophie said.

Jem nodded slowly. "I can feel it—his distance, like a cord inside me pulled very, very tightly. I did not expect that. We have not been apart since we became *parabatai*."

"Cecily said you sent him away."

"Yes," said Jem. "He was difficult to persuade. I think if he were not in love with Tessa himself, I would not have been able to make him go."

Sophie's mouth fell open. "You *knew?*"

"Not for long," Jem said. "No, I would not be that cruel. If I had known, I would never have proposed. I would have stood back. I did not know. And yet, now, as everything is going away from me, all things appear in such a clear light that I think I would have come to know it, even if he had not told me. At the end of things, I would have known." He smiled a little at Sophie's stricken expression. "I am glad I did not have to wait until the end."

"You're not angry?"

"I am glad," he said. "They will be able to take care of each other when I am gone, or at least I can hope for it. He says she does not love him, but—surely she will come to love him in time. Will is easy to love, and he has given her his whole heart. I can see it. I hope she will not break it."

Sophie could not think of a word to say. She did not know what anyone could say in the face of love like this—so much forbearance, so much endurance, so much hope. There had been many times in these past months when she'd regretted that she had ever had a bad thought about Will Herondale, when she saw how he had stood back and allowed Tessa and Jem to be happy together, and she knew the agony that had come to Tessa along with the happiness, in the knowledge that she was hurting Will. Sophie alone, she thought, knew that Tessa called out for Will sometimes when she slept; she alone knew that the scar on Tessa's palm was not from an accidental encounter with a fireplace poker but a deliberate wound, inflicted on herself that she might, somehow, physically match the emotional pain she'd felt in denying Will. Sophie had held Tessa while she'd wept and torn the flowers out of her hair that were the color of Will's eyes, and Sophie had covered up with powder the evidence of tears and sleepless nights.

Should she tell him? Sophie wondered. Would it really be a kindness to say, *Yes, Tessa loves him too; she has tried not to, but she does?* Could any man honestly want to hear that about the girl he was going to marry? "Miss Gray has great regard for Mr. Herondale, and she would not break any heart lightly, I think," Sophie said. "But I wish you would not speak as if your death were inevitable, Mr. Carstairs. Even now Mrs. Branwell and the others are hopeful of finding a cure. I think you will live to old age with Miss Gray, and the both of you very happy."

He smiled as if he knew something she did not. "That is kind of you to say, Sophie. I know I am a Shadowhunter, and we do not pass easily from this life. We fight to the last. We come from the realm of angels, and yet we fear it. I think, though, that one can face the end and not be afraid without having bowed under to death. Death shall never rule me."

Sophie looked at him, a little worried; he sounded part delirious to her. "Mr. Carstairs? Shall I fetch Charlotte?"

"In a moment, but, Sophie—in your expression, just there, when I spoke—" He leaned forward. "Is it true, then?"

"Is what true?" she asked him in a small voice, but she knew what the question would be, and she could not lie to Jem.

Will was in a foul mood. The day had dawned foggy, wet, and dreadful. He had woken feeling sick to his stomach, and had only barely been able to choke down the rubbery eggs and cold bacon the landlord's wife had served him in the stuffy parlor; every part of his body had hummed to get back to the road and continue on his journey.

Bouts of rain had left him shivering in his clothes despite a liberal use of warming runes, and Balios disliked the mud that sucked at his hooves as they tried to make speed along the road, Will grumpily contemplating how it was possible that fog might actually condense upon the *inside* of one's clothes. He had at least made it to Northamptonshire, which was something, but he had covered barely twenty miles and flatly refused to stop, though Balios looked at him entreatingly as they passed through Towcester, as if begging for a warm room in a stable and some oats, and Will was almost inclined to give it to him. A sense of hopelessness had invaded his bones, as chill and inescapable as the rain. What did he think he was doing? Did he really think he would find Tessa this way? Was he a fool?

They were passing through disagreeable country now too, where the mud made the rocky pathway treacherous. A great cliff wall rose on one side of the road, blocking out the sky. On the other side of the path, the road fell away dramatically into a ravine full of sharp rocks. The distant water of a muddy stream glinted faintly at the ravine's bottom. Will kept Balios's head well pulled in, far from the drop-off, but the horse still seemed skittish and shy of the fall. Will's own head was down, tucked into his collar to avoid the cold rain; it was only by chance that, glancing for a moment to the side, he caught a glimpse of bright green and gold amid the rocks at the edge of the road.

He had pulled up Balios in an instant and was down and off the horse so quickly that he almost slipped in the mud. The rain was coming down more heavily now as he approached and knelt to examine the golden chain that had become caught around the sharp outcrop of a rock. He picked it up carefully. It was a jade pendant, circular, with characters stamped upon the back. He knew well enough what they meant.

When two people are as one in their inmost hearts, they shatter even the strength of iron or bronze.

Jem's bridal gift to Tessa. Will's hand tightened about it as he stood. He remembered facing her in the stairwell—the chain of the jade pendant at her throat winking at him like a cruel reminder of Jem as she'd said, *They say you cannot divide your heart, and yet—*

"Tessa!" he cried out suddenly, his voice echoing off the rocks. "*Tessa!*"

He stood for a moment, shuddering, at the side of the road. He did not know what he had expected—an answer? It was hardly as if she could be here, hiding among the sparse rocks. There was only silence and the sound of the wind and rain. Still, he knew without a shadow of a doubt that this was Tessa's necklace. Perhaps she had torn it from her throat and dropped it out the carriage window to mark the path for him, like Hansel and Gretel's trail of bread crumbs. It was what a story-book heroine would do, and therefore what his Tessa would do. Maybe there would be other markers too, if he kept on his way. For the first time hope flowed back into his veins.

With new resolve he strode toward Balios and swung himself up into the saddle. There would be no slowing down; they would make Staffordshire by evening. As he turned the horse's head back toward the road, he slipped the pendant into his pocket, where its engraved words of love and commitment seemed to burn like a brand.

Charlotte had never felt so tired. The coming child had exhausted her more than she had thought it would at first, and she had been awake all night and racing about all day. There were stains on her dress from Henry's crypt, and her ankles ached from going up and down the stairs and the ladders in the library. Nevertheless, when she opened the door of Jem's bedroom and saw him not only awake but sitting up and talking to Sophie, she forgot her tiredness and felt her face break into a helpless smile of relief. "James!" she exclaimed. "I had wondered—that is, I am glad you are awake."

Sophie, who was looking oddly flushed, rose to her feet. "Should I go, Mrs. Branwell?"

"Oh, yes, please, Sophie. Bridget's in one of her moods; she says she can't find the Bang Mary, and I haven't even the slightest what she's talking about."

Sophie almost smiled—she would have, if her heart hadn't been pounding with the knowledge that she might just have done something very dreadful. "The *bain-marie*," she said. "I will locate it for her." She moved toward the door, paused, and threw a peculiar look over her shoulder at Jem, who was resting back against his pillows, looking very pale but composed. Before Charlotte could say anything, Sophie was gone, and Jem was beckoning Charlotte forward with a tired smile.

"Charlotte, if you would not mind very much—could you bring me my violin?"

"Of course." Charlotte went over to the table by the window where the violin was stored in its square rosewood case, with its bow and small round box of rosin. She lifted the violin and brought it over to the bed, where Jem took it carefully from her arms, and she sank down gratefully in the chair beside him. "Oh—," she said a moment later. "I'm sorry. I forgot the bow. Did you want to play?"

"That's all right." He plucked gently at the strings with his fingertips, which produced a soft, vibrant noise. "This is pizzicato—the first thing my father taught me how to do when he showed me the violin. It reminds me of being a child."

You are still a child, Charlotte wanted to say, but she did not. He was only a few weeks short of his eighteenth birthday, after all, when Shadowhunters became adults, and if when she looked at him she still saw the dark-haired little boy who had arrived from Shanghai clutching his violin, his eyes huge in his pale face, that did not mean he had not grown up.

She reached for the box of *yin fen* on his bedside table. There was only a pale scatter left at the bottom, barely a teaspoonful. She swallowed against her tight throat, and tapped the powder into the bottom of a glass, then poured water from the carafe into it, letting the *yin fen* dissolve like sugar. When she handed it to Jem, he put the violin aside and took the glass from her. He stared down into it, his pale eyes thoughtful.

"Is this the last of it?" he asked.

"Magnus is working on a cure," Charlotte said. "We all are. Gabriel and Cecily are out purchasing ingredients for medicine to keep you strong, and Sophie and Gideon and I have been researching. Everything is being done. Everything."

Jem looked a little surprised. "I did not realize."

"But of course it is," Charlotte said. "We are your family; we would do anything for you. Please do not lose hope, Jem. I need you to keep your strength."

"What strength I have is yours," he said cryptically. He downed the *yin fen* solution, handing her back the empty glass. "Charlotte?"

"Yes?"

"Have you won the fight about what to call the child yet?"

Charlotte gave a startled laugh. It seemed odd to think about her child now, but then why not? *In death, we are in life.* It was something to think about that was not illness, or Tessa's disappearance, or Will's dangerous mission. "Not yet," she said. "Henry is still insisting on Buford."

"You'll win," Jem said. "You always do. You would make an excellent Consul, Charlotte."

Charlotte wrinkled her nose. "A woman Consul? After all the trouble I've had simply for running the Institute!"

"There must always be a first," said Jem. "It is not easy to be first, and it is not always rewarding, but it is important." He ducked his head. "You carry with you one of my few regrets."

Charlotte looked at him, puzzled.

"I would have liked to see the baby."

It was a very simple, wistful thing to say, but it lodged itself in Charlotte's heart like a sliver of glass. She began to cry, the tears slipping silently down her face.

"Charlotte," Jem said, as if comforting her. "You've always taken care of me. You'll take amazing care of this baby. You'll be a wonderful mother."

"You cannot give up, Jem," she said in a choked voice. "When they brought you to me, at first they said you would live only a year or two. You've lived nearly six. Please just live a few more days. A few more days for me."

Jem gave her a softly measured look. "I lived for you," he said. "And I lived for Will, and then I lived for Tessa—and for myself, because I wanted to be with her. But I cannot live for other people forever. No one can say that death found in me a willing comrade, or that I went easily. If you say you need me, I will stay as long as I can for you. I will live for you and yours, and go down fighting death until I am worn away to bone and splinters. But it would not be my choice."

"Then . . ." Charlotte looked at him hesitantly. "What would be your choice?"

He swallowed, and his hand dropped to touch the violin by his side. "I made a decision," he said. "I made it when I told Will to go." He ducked his head, and then looked up at Charlotte, his pale, blue-shadowed eyes fixed on her face as if willing her to understand. "I want it to stop," he said. "Sophie says everyone is still searching for a cure for me. I know I gave Will my permission, but I want everyone to cease looking now, Charlotte. It is over."

It was growing dark by the time Cecily and Gabriel returned to the Institute. To be out and about in the city with someone besides Charlotte or her brother had been a unique experience for Cecily, and she was astonished at what good company Gabriel Lightwood had been. He had made her laugh, though she had done her best to hide it, and he had quite obligingly carried all the parcels, though she would have expected him to protest at being treated like a harried footman.

It was true that he probably should not have thrown that faerie through the shopwindow—or into the Limehouse canal afterward. But she could hardly blame him. She knew perfectly well that it was not the fact that the satyr had shown her improper images that had snapped his temper, but the reminder of his father.

It was odd, she thought as they mounted the Institute steps, how unlike his brother he was. She had liked Gideon perfectly well since she had arrived in London, but found him quiet and contained. He did not speak much, and though he sometimes helped Will with her training, he was distant and thoughtful with everyone but Sophie. With her it was possible to see flashes of humor in him. He could be quite dryly funny when he wished to be, and had a darkly observant nature alongside his calm soul.

In bits and pieces gleaned from Tessa, Will, and Charlotte, Cecily had pieced together the story of the Lightwoods and had begun to understand why Gideon was so quiet. In a way like Will and herself, he had turned his back on his family deliberately, and he carried the scars of that loss. Gabriel's choice had been a different one. He had stayed by his father's side and watched the slow deterioration of his body and mind. What had he thought, while it was happening? At what point had he realized the choice he had made had been the wrong one?

Gabriel opened the Institute door, and Cecily went through; they were greeted by Bridget's voice floating down the steps.

> *"O see ye not yon narrow road,*
> *So thick beset with thorns and briers?*
> *That is the path of righteousness,*
> *Tho after it but few enquires.*

> *"And see not ye that broad, broad road*
> *That lies across the lily leven?*
> *That is the path of wickedness,*
> *Tho some call it the road to Heaven."*

"She's singing," said Cecily, starting up the steps. "Again."

Gabriel, balancing the parcels nimbly, made an equable noise. "I'm famished. I wonder if she'll scare me up some cold chicken and bread in the kitchen if I tell her I don't mind the songs?"

"Everyone minds the songs." Cecily looked at him sideways; he had an awfully fine profile. Gideon was good-looking as well, but Gabriel was all sharp angles, chin, and cheekbones, which she thought altogether more elegant. "It isn't your fault, you know," she said abruptly.

"What is not my fault?" They turned from the steps onto the corridor of the second floor. It seemed dark to Cecily, the witchlights turned down low. She could hear Bridget, still singing:

> "It was dark, dark night, there was no starlight,
> And they waded through red blood to the knee;
> For all the blood that's shed on earth
> Runs through the springs of that country."

"Your father," Cecily said.

Gabriel's face tightened. For a moment Cecily thought he was going to make an angry retort, but instead he said only: "It may or may not be my fault, but I chose to be blind to his crimes. I believed in him when it was wrong to do so, and he has disgraced the name of Lightwood."

Cecily was silent for a moment. "I came here because I believed Shadowhunters were monsters who had taken my brother. I believed it because my parents believed it. But they were wrong. We are not our parents, Gabriel. We do not have to carry the burden of their choices or their sins. You can make the Lightwood name shine again."

"That is the difference between you and me," he said, with not a little bitterness. "You chose to come here. I was driven out of my home—chased here by the monster that was once my father."

"Well," Cecily said kindly, "not chased all the way here. Only as far as Chiswick, I thought."

"What—"

She smiled at him. "I am Will Herondale's sister. You can't expect me to be serious *all* the time."

His expression at that was so comical that she giggled; she was still giggling when they pushed the library door open and entered—and both stopped dead in their tracks.

Charlotte, Henry, and Gideon were sitting around one of the long tables. Magnus stood a distance away, by the window, his hands clasped behind him. His back was rigid and straight. Henry looked wan and tired, Charlotte tearstained. Gideon's face was a mask.

The laughter died on Cecily's lips. "What is it? Has there been word? Is Will—"

"It is not Will," said Charlotte. "It is Jem." Cecily bit her lip, even as her heartbeat slowed with guilty relief. She had thought first of her brother, but of course it was his *parabatai* who was in more imminent peril.

"Jem?" she breathed.

"He is still alive," Henry said, in answer to her unspoken question.

"Well, then. We got everything," Gabriel said, putting the parcels down on the table. "Everything Magnus asked for—the damiana, the bat's head root—"

"Thank you." Magnus spoke from the window, without turning.

"Yes, thank you," Charlotte said. "You did all I asked, and I am grateful. But I am afraid your errand was in vain." She looked down at the parcel, and then back up again. It was clear that it was taking her a great effort to speak. "Jem has made a decision," she said. "He wishes us to cease searching for a cure. He has had the last of the *yin fen*; there is no more, and it is a matter of hours now. I have summoned the Silent Brothers. It is time to say good-bye."

It was dark in the training room. The shadows lay long upon the floor, and moonlight came in through the high arched windows. Cecily sat on one of the worn benches and stared down at the patterns the moonlight made on the splintered wooden floor.

Her right hand idly worried at the red pendant around her throat. She could not help but think of her brother. Part of her mind was there in the Institute, but the rest was with Will: on the back of a horse, leaning into the wind, riding hell-for-leather over the roads that separated London from Dolgellau. She wondered if he was frightened. She wondered if she would see him again.

So deep in thought was she that she started at the creak of the door as it opened. A long shadow was cast across the floor, and she looked up to see Gabriel Lightwood blinking at her in surprise.

"Hiding here, are you?" he said. "That's—awkward."

"Why?" She was surprised at how ordinary her voice sounded, even calm.

"Because I had intended to hide here myself."

Cecily was silent for a moment. Gabriel actually looked a little uncertain—it hung strangely on him; he was usually so confident. Though it was a more fragile confidence than his brother's. It was too dark for her to see the color of his eyes or hair, and for the first time she could actually see the resemblance between him and Gideon. They had the same determined set to their chins, the same wide-spaced eyes and careful stance. "You may hide here with me," she said, "if you wish."

He nodded, and crossed the room to where she sat, but instead of joining her he moved to the window and glanced outside. "The Silent Brothers' carriage is here," he said.

"Yes," said Cecily. She knew from her reading of the *Codex* that the Silent Brothers were both the doctors and the priests of the Shadowhunter world; one might expect to find them at deathbeds and sickbeds and childbed alike. "I thought I should see Jem. For Will. But I could—I could not bring myself. I am a coward," she added as an afterthought. It was not something she had ever thought about herself before.

"Then I am too," he replied. The moonlight fell across one side of his face, making him look as if he were wearing a half mask. "I had come up here to be alone and, frankly, to be away from the Brothers, for they give me the chills. I thought I might play solitaire. We could, if you'd like, have a game of Beggar My Neighbor."

"Like Pip and Estella in *Great Expectations*," said Cecily, with a flash of amusement. "But, no—I do not know how to play cards. My mother tried to keep cards out of the house, as my father . . . had a weakness for them." She looked up at Gabriel. "You know, in some ways we are the same. Our brothers left and we were alone without brother or sister, with a father who was deteriorating. Mine went a bit mad for a while after Will left and Ella died. It took him years to recover himself, and in the meantime we lost our home. Just as you lost Chiswick."

"Chiswick was taken from us," said Gabriel with an acidic

flash of bitterness. "And to be quite honest, I am both sorry and not. My memories of the place—" He shuddered. "My father locked himself in his study a fortnight before I came here for help. I should have come earlier, but I was too proud. I did not want to admit that I had been wrong about Father. For that two weeks I barely slept. I banged on the door of the study and begged my father to come out, to speak to me, but I heard only inhuman noises. I turned the lock on my door at night and in the morning there would be blood on the stairs. I told myself the servants had fled. I knew better. So no, we are not the same, Cecily, because you *left*. You were brave. I stayed until there was no choice but to leave. I stayed even though I knew it was wrong."

"You are a Lightwood," Cecily said. "You stayed because you were loyal to your family name. It is not cowardice."

"Wasn't it? Is loyalty still a commendable quality when it is misdirected?"

Cecily opened her mouth, and then closed it again. Gabriel was looking at her, his eyes shining in the moonlight. He seemed genuinely desperate to hear her answer. She wondered if he had anyone else to talk to. She could see how it might be terrifying to take one's moral qualms to Gideon; he seemed so staunch, as if he had never questioned himself in his life and would not understand those who did.

"I think," she said, choosing her words with care, "that any good impulse can be twisted into something evil. Look at the Magister. He does what he does because he hates the Shadowhunters, out of loyalty to his parents, who cared for him, and who were killed. It is not beyond the realm of under- standing. And yet nothing excuses the result. I think when we make choices—for each choice is individual of the choices we have made before—we must examine not only our reasons for making them but what result they will have, and whether good people will be hurt by our decisions."

There was a pause. Then, "You are very wise, Cecily Herondale," he said.

"Do not regret too much the choices you have made in the past, Gabriel," she said, aware that she was using his Christian name, but not able to help it. "Only make the right ones in future. We are ever capable of change and ever capable of being our better selves."

"That," said Gabriel, "would not be the self my father wanted me to be, and despite everything, I find myself reluctant to dismiss the hope of his approval."

Cecily sighed. "We can do our best, Gabriel. I tried to be the child my parents wanted, the lady they wished me to be. I left to bring Will back to them because I thought it was the right thing to do. I knew they were grieved he had chosen a different path—and it is the right one for him, for all that he came to it strangely. It is *his* path. Do not choose the path your father would have chosen or the path your brother would choose. Be the Shadowhunter you want to be."

He sounded very young when he replied. "How do you know that I will make the right choice?"

Outside the window horses' hooves sounded on the flagstones of the courtyard. The Silent Brothers, leaving. *Jem*, Cecily thought, with a pang in her heart. Her brother had always looked to him as a kind of North Star, a compass that would ever point him toward the right decision. She had never quite thought of her brother as lucky before, and certainly would not have expected to do so today, and yet—and yet in a way he had been. To always have someone to turn to like that, and not to worry constantly that one was looking to the wrong stars.

She tried to make her voice as firm and strong as it could be, for herself as much as for the boy at the window. "Perhaps, Gabriel Lightwood, I have faith in you."

14

PARABATAI

Peace, peace! he is not dead, he doth not sleep,
He hath awaken'd from the dream of life;
'Tis we, who lost in stormy visions, keep
With phantoms an unprofitable strife,
And in mad trance, strike with our spirit's knife
Invulnerable nothings. We decay
Like corpses in a charnel; fear and grief
Convulse us and consume us day by day,
And cold hopes swarm like worms within our living clay.
— Percy Bysshe Shelley,
"Adonais: An Elegy on the Death of John Keats"

The courtyard of the Green Man Inn was a churned mess of mud by the time Will drew up his spent horse and slid down from Balios's broad back. He was weary, stiff, and saddle-sore, and with the bad condition of the roads and the exhaustion of himself and his horse, he had made the last few hours in very bad time. It was already quite dark, and he was relieved to see a stable-boy hurrying toward him, boots splashed with mud to the knee and carrying a lantern that gave off a warm yellow glow.

"Oi, but it's a wet evening, sir," said the boy cheerfully as he grew nearer. He looked like an ordinary enough human boy, but there was something mischievous and a bit spritelike about him—faerie blood, sometimes, handed down over generations, could express itself in humans and even Shadowhunters with the curve of an eye or the bright shine of a pupil. Of course the boy had the Sight. The Green Man was a well-known Downworld way station. Will had been hoping to reach it by nightfall. He was tired of pretending in front of mundanes, tired of being glamoured, tired of hiding.

"Wet? You think?" Will muttered as water ran off his hair and into his eyelashes. He had his eyes on the front door of the inn, through which welcoming yellow light poured. Overhead almost all light had drained from the sky. Ponderous black clouds loomed overhead, heavy with the promise of more rain.

The boy took Balios by the bridle. "You've got one of them magic horses," he exclaimed.

"Yes." Will patted the horse's lathered side. "He needs a rubdown, and special care."

The boy nodded. "You a Shadowhunter, then? We don't get many of them around these parts. One a little while ago, but 'e were old an' disagreeable—"

"Listen," Will asked, "are there rooms available?"

"Not sure if there are any private ones, sir."

"Well, I'll be wanting a private one, so there'd better be. And a stable for the horse for the night, and a bath and a meal. Run along and get the horse put away, and I'll see what your landlord says."

The landlord was utterly obliging and, unlike the boy, made no comments on the Marks on Will's hands or at his throat, only asked the very usual sort of questions: "Do you want your meal in a private parlor or to take it in the common room, sir? And will you be wanting a bath before your supper, or after?"

Will, who felt encased in mud, opted for the bath first, though agreed to take dinner in the common room. He had brought a good amount of mundane money with him, but a private parlor for dining in was an unnecessary expense, especially when one did not care what one was eating. Food was fuel for the journey, and that was all.

Though the landlord had taken little notice of the fact that Will was Nephilim, there were others in the common area of the inn who did. As Will leaned against the counter, a group of young werewolves by the large fireplace, who had been indulging in cheap beer for most of the day, muttered among themselves. Will attempted not to notice them as he ordered hot water bottles for himself and a bran mash for his horse, like any high-handed young gentleman, but their sharp eyes on him were avid, taking in every detail from his dripping wet hair and muddy boots to the heavy coat that showed no sign of whether he wore the Nephilim's customary weapons belt beneath.

"Easy, boys," said the tallest of the group. He sat well back toward the fire, casting his face in heavy shadow, though the fire outlined his long fingers as he took out a fine majolica cigar box and tapped thoughtfully at the lock. "I know him."

"You know him?" one of the younger wolves asked in disbelief. "That Nephilim? A friend of yours, Scott?"

"Oh, not a friend. Not exactly." Woolsey Scott lit the tip of his cigar with a match and regarded the boy across the room over the small flame, a smile playing about his mouth. "But it's very interesting that he's here. Very interesting indeed."

"Tessa!" The voice echoed in her ear, a ragged shout. She sat bolt upright on the riverbank, her body trembling.

"Will?" She scrambled to her feet and looked around. The moon had passed behind a cloud. The sky above was like dark gray marble, shot through with veins of black. The river ran before her, dark gray in the poor light, and glancing around, she saw only gnarled trees, the steep cliff down which she had fallen, a broad swatch of countryside stretching away in the other direction—fields and stone fences, the occasionally distant dotting of a farmhouse or habitation. She could see nothing like a city or a town, not even a cluster of lights that might have indicated a tiny hamlet.

"Will," she whispered again, drawing her arms about herself. She was *sure* it had been his voice she had heard calling her name. No one else's voice sounded like his. But it was ridiculous. He was not here. He could not be. Perhaps, like Jane Eyre, who had heard Rochester's voice calling for her on the moors, she was half-dreaming.

At least it was a dream that had driven her out of her unconsciousness. The wind was like a knife of cold, cutting through her clothes—she wore only a thin dress, meant for indoors, and no coat or hat—and into her skin. Her skirts were still wet with river water, her dress and stocking ripped and stained with blood. The angel had saved her life, it seemed, but it had not protected her from injury.

She touched it now, hoping for guidance, but it was as still and mute as ever. As she took her hand away from her throat, though, she heard Will's voice in her head: *Sometimes, when I have to do something I don't want to do, I pretend I'm a character from a book. It's easier to know what they would do.*

A character from a book, Tessa thought, a good, sensible one, would follow the stream. A character from a book would know that human habitations and towns are often built by water, and would seek out help, rather than blundering into the woods. Resolutely she wrapped her arms about herself and began to trudge downstream.

By the time Will—well-bathed, shaved, and wearing a clean shirt and collar—returned to the common room for supper, the room was half-full of people.

Well, not exactly people. As he was shown to a table, he passed tables where trolls sat hunched together over pints of beer, looking like gnarled old men save for the tusks that protruded from their lower jaws. A thin warlock with a mop of brown hair and a third eye in the center of his forehead was sawing into a veal cutlet. A group sat huddled at a table by the fire—werewolves, Will sensed, from their packlike demeanor. The room smelled of damp and embers and cooking, and Will's stomach rumbled; he hadn't realized how hungry he was.

Will studied a map of Wales as he drank his wine (sour, vinegary) and ate the food he was brought (a tough cut of

venison with potatoes) and did his best to try to ignore the
stares of the other customers. He supposed the stable-boy had
been right; they *didn't* get many Nephilim here. He felt as if his
Marks were glowing like brands. When the plates were cleared
away, he took out paper and composed a letter:

> *Charlotte:*
> *I am sorry for leaving the Institute without your per-*
> *mission. I ask for your forgiveness; I felt I had no other*
> *choice.*
> *That, however, is not why I am sending this letter. By*
> *the side of the road I have found evidence of Tessa's pas-*
> *sage. Somehow she had managed to cast her jade necklace*
> *from the carriage window, I believe so that we might trace*
> *her by it. I have it with me now. It is proof undeniable*
> *that we were correct in our supposition about Mortmain's*
> *whereabouts. He must be in Cadair Idris. You must write*
> *to the Consul and demand that he send a full force to the*
> *mountain.*
> *Will Herondale*

Having sealed the letter, Will called over the landlord and
confirmed that for half a crown, the boy would bring it to the
night coach for delivery. Having made his payment, Will sat
back, considering whether he should force down another glass
of wine to ensure that he could sleep—when a sharp, stabbing pain shot through his chest. It felt like being shot with
an arrow, and Will jerked back. His wineglass crashed to the
floor and shattered. He lurched to his feet, leaning both hands
on the table. He was vaguely aware of stares, and the landlord's

anxious voice in his ear, but the pain was too great to think through, almost too great to breathe through.

The tightness in his chest, the one that he had thought of as one end of a cord tying him to Jem, had pulled so taut that it was strangling his heart. He stumbled away from his table, pushing through a knot of customers near the bar, and passed to the front door of the inn. All he could think of was air, getting air into his lungs to breathe.

He pushed the doors open and half-tumbled out into the night. For a moment the pain in his chest eased, and he fell back against the wall of the inn. Rain was sheeting down, soaking his hair and clothes. He gasped, his heart stuttering with a mixture of terror and desperation. Was this just the distance from Jem affecting him? He had never felt anything like this, even when Jem had been at his worst, even when he'd been injured and Will had ached with sympathetic pain.

The cord snapped.

For a moment everything went white, the courtyard bleaching through as if with acid. Will jackknifed to his knees, vomiting up his supper into the mud. When the spasms had passed, he staggered to his feet and blindly away from the inn, as if trying to outrace his own pain. He fetched up against the wall of the stables, beside the horse trough. He dropped to his knees to plunge his hands into the icy water—and saw his own reflection. There was his face, as white as death, and his shirt, and a spreading stain of red across the front.

With wet hands he seized at his lapels and jerked the shirt open. In the dim light that spilled from the inn, he could see that his *parabatai* rune, just over his heart, was bleeding.

His hands were covered in blood, blood mixed with rain,

the same rain that was washing the blood away from his chest, showing the rune as it began to fade from black to silver, changing all that had been sense in Will's life into nonsense.

Jem was dead.

Tessa had been walking for hours, and her thin shoes were cut through from the jagged rocks by the riverbed. She had started out almost running, but exhaustion and cold had overtaken her, and now she was limping slowly, if determinedly, downstream. The soaked material of her skirts dragged her down, feeling like an anchor that would pull her to the bottom of some terrible sea.

She had seen no sign of human habitation for miles, and was beginning to despair of her plan, when a clearing came into view. It had begun to rain lightly, but even through the drizzle she could see the outline of a low stone building. As she drew closer, she saw that it seemed to be a small house, with a thatched roof and overgrown path leading to the front door.

She picked up her pace, hurrying now, thinking of a kindly farmer and his wife, the kind in books who would take in a young girl and help contact her family, as the Rivers had done for Jane in *Jane Eyre*. As she drew closer, though, she noticed the dirty and broken windows and the grass growing on the thatched roof. Her heart sank. The house was deserted.

The door was already part open, the wood swelled with rain. There was something frightening about the house's emptiness, but Tessa was desperate for shelter from both the rain and any pursuers that Mortmain might have sent after her. She clung to the hope that Mrs. Black would think she had died in the fall, but she doubted that Mortmain would be so easily put off her trail. After all, if anyone knew what her clockwork angel could do, it would be him.

There was grass growing between the flagstones of the floor inside the house, and the hearth was dirty, with a blackened pot still hanging over the remains of the fire and the whitewashed walls dingy with soot and the passage of time. There was a tangle of what looked like farming implements near the door. One resembled a long metal stick with a curved forked end, the tines still sharp. Knowing she might need some means of defense, she caught it up, then moved from the entrance room into the only other room the house had: a small bedroom in which she was delighted to find a musty blanket on the bed.

She looked down hopelessly at her wet dress. It would take ages to remove without Sophie's help, and she was desperate for warmth. She wrapped the blanket around herself, wet clothes and all, and curled up on the prickly hay-stuffed mattress. It smelled of mold and probably had mice living in it, but at this moment it felt like the most luxurious bed Tessa had ever stretched herself upon.

Tessa knew it was wiser to stay awake. But despite everything, she could no longer withstand the demands of her battered and exhausted body. Clutching the metal weapon to her chest, she slid away into sleep.

"So this is him, then? The Nephilim?"

Will did not know how long he had been sitting slumped against the wall of the stable, growing ever wetter with the rain, when the growling voice came out of the darkness. He lifted his head, too late to ward off the hand reaching for him. A moment later it had grabbed his collar and hauled him to his feet.

He stared through eyes dimmed by rain and agony at a group of werewolves standing in a half circle around him. There were perhaps five of them, including the one who had him slammed up against the stable wall, a hand fisted in his bloody shirt. They were all dressed similarly, in black garb so wet with rain, it shone like oilskin. All were hatless, their hair—worn long as werewolves did—plastered to their heads.

"Get your hands off me," Will said. "The Accords forbid touching a Nephilim unprovoked—"

"Unprovoked?" The werewolf in front of him yanked him forward and slammed him back against the wall again. In ordinary circumstances it most likely would have hurt, but these were not ordinary circumstances. The physical pain of Will's *parabatai* rune had faded, but his whole body felt dry and hollow, all the meaning sucked out of the center of him. "I'd say it's provoked. If it wasn't for you Nephilim, the Magister never would have come after our lot with his dirty drugs and his filthy lies—"

Will looked at the werewolves with an emotion bordering on hilarity. Did they really think they could hurt him, after what he had lost? For five years it had been his absolute truth. Jem and Will. Will and Jem. Will Herondale lives, therefore Jem Carstairs lives also. *Quod erat demonstrandum.* To lose an arm or a leg would be painful, he imagined, but to lose the central truth of your life felt—fatal.

"Dirty drugs *and* filthy lies," Will drawled. "That *does*

sound unsanitary. Though, tell me, is it true that instead of bathing, werewolves just lick themselves once a year? Or do you all lick one another? Because that's what I've heard."

The hand in his shirt tightened. "You want to be a little more respectful, Shadowhunter."

"No," Will said. "No, I really don't."

"We've heard all about you, Will Herondale," said one of the other werewolves. "Always crawling to Downworlders for help. We'd like to see you crawl now."

"You'll have to cut me off at the knees, then."

"That," said the werewolf holding Will, "can be arranged."

Will exploded into action. He slammed his head into the face of the werewolf in front of him. He both heard and felt the sick crunch of the werewolf's nose breaking, hot blood spurting over the man's face as he staggered back across the courtyard and crumpled onto his knees on the cobblestones. His hands were pressed to his face, trying to stem the flow of blood.

A hand grasped Will's shoulder, claws piercing the fabric of Will's wet shirt. He whirled around to face the wolves and saw in this second werewolf's hand, silvery in the moonlight, the sharp gleam of a knife. His assailant's eyes shone through the rain, gold-green and menacing.

They did not come out here to taunt or hurt me, Will realized. *They came out here to kill me.*

For one black moment Will was tempted to let them. The thought of it seemed like an enormous relief—all pain gone, all responsibility gone, a simple submersion in death and forgetting. He stood without moving as the knife swung toward him. Everything seemed to be happening very slowly—the iron edge of the knife swinging toward him, the sneering face of the werewolf blurred by the rain.

The image he had dreamed the night before flashed before his eyes: Tessa, running up a green path toward him. Tessa. His hand came up automatically and grasped the werewolf's wrist in one hand as he ducked the blow, swinging under the wolf's arm. He brought the arm down hard, breaking the bone with a savage splintering. The lycanthrope screamed, and a dark bolt of glee shot through Will. The dagger fell to the cobblestones as Will kicked his opponent's legs out from under him, then slammed his elbow into the man's temple. The wolf went down in a heap and didn't move again.

Will snatched up the dagger and turned to face the others. There were only three of them standing now, and they looked decidedly less sure of themselves than they had before. He grinned, cold and terrible, and tasted the metal of rain and blood in his mouth. "Come and kill me," he said. "Come and kill me if you think you can." He kicked the unconscious werewolf at his feet. "You'll have to do better than your friends."

They lunged at him, claws out, and Will went down hard onto the cobblestones, his head cracking against the stone. A set of claws raked his shoulder; he rolled sideways under a flurry of blows and lashed upward with his dagger. There was a high yelp of pain that ended on a whine, and the weight on top of Will, which had been moving and struggling, went limp. Will rolled to the side and sprang to his feet, spinning around.

The wolf he had stabbed lay open-eyed, dead in a widening pool of blood and rainwater. The two remaining werewolves were struggling to their feet, caked in mud and drenched in water. Will was bleeding from his shoulder where one of them had dug deep furrows with his claws; the pain was glorious. He laughed through the blood and the mud as the rain sluiced the blood from the blade of his dagger. "Again," he said, and barely recognized his own voice, strained and cracked and deadly. "*Again.*"

One of the werewolves spun and bolted. Will laughed again and moved toward the last of them, who stood, frozen, clawed hands extended—with bravery or terror, Will wasn't sure, and didn't care. His dagger felt like an extension of his wrist, part of his arm. One good blow and a jerk upward, and he would rip through bone and cartilage, stabbing toward the heart—

"*Stop!*" The voice was hard, commanding, familiar. Will cut his eyes to the side. Striding across the courtyard, his shoulders hunched against the rain, his expression furious, was Woolsey Scott. "I command you, both of you, stop this instant!"

The werewolf dropped his hands to his sides instantly, his claws vanishing. He bent his head, the classic gesture of submission. "Master—"

A boiling tide of rage poured over Will, obliterating rationality, sense, everything but rage. He reached out and jerked the werewolf toward him, his arm wrapping the man's neck, blade against his throat. Woolsey, only a few feet away, came up short, his green eyes shooting daggers.

"Come any closer," Will said, "and I'll cut your little wolfling's throat."

"I told you to stop," Woolsey said in a measured tone. He was wearing, as he always was, a beautifully cut suit, a brocade riding coat atop it, everything now liberally soaked with rain. His fair hair, plastered to his face and neck, was colorless with water. "Both of you."

"But *I don't have to listen to you!*" Will shouted. "I was winning! *Winning!*" He glanced about the courtyard at the three scattered bodies of the wolves he had fought—two unconscious, one dead. "Your pack attacked me unprovoked. They broke the Accords. I was defending myself. They broke the *Law!*" His voice rose, harsh and unrecognizable. "I am owed their blood, and *I will have it!*"

"Yes, yes, buckets of blood," said Woolsey. "And what would you do with it if you had it? You don't care about this werewolf. Let him go."

"No."

"At least let him free so he can fight you," Woolsey said.

Will hesitated, then released his grip on the werewolf he held, who faced his pack leader, looking terrified. Woolsey snapped his fingers in the wolf's direction. "Run, Conrad," he said. "Fast. And now."

The werewolf didn't need to be told twice; he turned on his heels and darted away, vanishing behind the stables. Will turned back to Woolsey with a sneer.

"So your pack are all cowards," he said. "Five against one Shadowhunter? Is that how it is?"

"I didn't tell them to come out here after you. They're young. And stupid. And impetuous. And half their pack was killed by Mortmain. They blame your kind." Woolsey stepped a little closer, his eyes raking up and down Will, as cold as green ice. "I assume your *parabatai* is dead, then," he added with shocking casualness.

Will was not ready to hear the words at all, would never be ready. The battle had cleared his head of the pain for a moment. Now it threatened to return, all-encompassing and terrifying.

He gasped as if Woolsey had punched him, and took an involuntary step back.

"And you're trying to get yourself killed because of it, Nephilim boy? Is that what's going on?"

Will swiped his wet hair out of his face and looked at Woolsey with hatred. "Maybe I am."

"Is that how you respect his memory?"

"What does it matter?" Will said. "He's dead. He'll never know what I do or what I don't do."

"My brother is dead," Woolsey said. "I still struggle to fulfill his wishes, to continue the Praetor Lupus in his memory, and to live as he would have had me live. Do you think I'm the sort of person who would ever be found in a place like this, consuming pig swill and drinking vinegar, knee deep in mud, watching some tedious Shadowhunter brat destroy even more of my already diminished pack, if it weren't for the fact that I serve a greater purpose than my own desires and sorrows? And so do you, Shadowhunter. So do you."

"Oh, God." The dagger fell out of Will's hand and landed in the mud at his feet. "What do I do now?" he whispered.

He had no idea why he was asking Woolsey, except that there was no one else in the world to ask. Not even when he thought he was cursed had he felt so alone.

Woolsey looked at him coolly. "Do what your brother would have wanted," he said, then turned and stalked off back toward the inn.

15

STARS, HIDE YOUR FIRES

Stars, hide your fires;
Let not light see my black and deep desires.
—Shakespeare, Macbeth

Consul Wayland,
I write to you on a matter of the gravest import. One of
the Shadowhunters of my Institute, William Herondale,
is upon the road to Cadair Idris even as I write. He has
discovered along the way an unmistakable sign of Miss
Gray's passage. I enclose his letter for your perusal, but I
am sure you will agree that the whereabouts of Mortmain
are now established and that we must with all haste
assemble what forces we can and march immediately
upon Cadair Idris. Mortmain has shown in the past a
remarkable ability to slip from the nets we cast. We must

*take advantage of this moment and strike with all possible
haste and force. I await your speedy reply.*

    Charlotte Branwell

*The room was cold. The fire had long burned down in the grate, and
the wind outside was howling around the corners of the Institute,
rattling the panes of the windows. The lamp on the nightstand was
turned down low, and Tessa shivered in the armchair by the bed,
despite the shawl wrapped tightly around her shoulders.*

*In the bed Jem was asleep, his head pillowed on his hand. He
breathed just enough to move the blankets slightly, though his face
was as pale as the pillows.*

*Tessa stood, letting the shawl slip from her shoulders. She was
in her nightgown, the way she had been the first time she had ever
met Jem, bursting into his room to find him playing the violin by the
window. Will? he had said. Will, is that you?*

*He stirred and murmured now as she crawled into the bed with
him, drawing the blankets over them both. She cupped her hands
around his and held their joined hands between them. She tangled
their feet together and kissed his cool cheek, warming his skin with
her breath. Slowly she felt him stir against her, as if her presence were
bringing him to life.*

*His eyes opened and looked into hers. They were blue, achingly
blue, the blue of the sky where it meets the sea.*

*"Tessa?" Will said, and she realized it was Will in her arms, Will
who was dying, Will breathing out his last breath—and there was
blood on his shirt, just over his heart, a spreading red stain—*

Tessa sat bolt upright, gasping. For a moment she stared
about her, disoriented. The tiny, dark room, the musty blanket
wrapped around her, her own damp clothes and bruised body,

seemed foreign to her. Then memory came back in a flood, and with it a wave of nausea.

She missed the Institute piercingly, in a way she had never even missed her home in New York. She missed Charlotte's bossy but caring voice, Sophie's understanding touch, Henry's puttering, and of course—she could not help it—she missed Jem and Will. She was terrified for Jem, for his health, but she was frightened for Will as well. The battle in the courtyard had been bloody, vicious. Any of them could have been hurt or killed. Was that the meaning of her dream, Jem turning into Will? Was Jem ill, was Will's life in danger? Not either of them, she prayed silently. Please, let me die before harm comes to either of them.

A noise startled her out of her reverie—a sudden dry scraping that sent a brutal shiver down her spine. She froze. Surely it was just the scratching of a branch against the window. But, no—there it came again. A scraping, dragging noise.

Tessa was on her feet in a moment, the blanket still wrapped around her. Terror was like a live thing inside her. All the tales she had ever heard of monsters in the dark woods seemed to be fighting for space in her mind. She closed her eyes, drawing a deep breath, and saw the spindly automatons on the front steps of the Institute, their shadows long and grotesque, like human beings pulled out of shape.

She drew the blanket closer around herself, her fingers closing spasmodically on the material. The automatons had come for *her* on the Institute steps. But they were not very intelligent—able to follow simple commands, to recognize particular human beings. Still, they could not think for themselves. They were machines, and machines could be fooled.

The blanket was patchwork, the kind that would have been sewed by a woman, a woman who had lived in this house. Tessa drew in her breath and *reached*—reached into the blanket, searching for a flicker of ownership, the signature of whatever spirit had created and owned it. It was like plunging her hand into dark water and feeling around for an object. After what felt like an age of searching, she lit upon it—a flicker in the darkness, the solidity of a soul.

She concentrated on it, wrapping it around her like the blanket she clung to. The Change was easier now, less painful. She saw her fingers warp and change, becoming the clubbed, arthritic hands of an old woman. Liver spots rose on her skin, her back hunched, and her dress began to hang off her withered form. When her hair fell in front of her eyes, it was white.

The scraping sound came again. A voice echoed in the back of Tessa's mind, a querulous old woman's voice demanding to know who was in her house. Tessa stumbled for the door, her breath coming short, her heart fluttering in her chest, and made for the main room of the house.

For a moment she saw nothing. Her eyes were rheumy, filmed over; shapes looked blurred and distant. Then something rose from beside the fire, and Tessa bit back a scream.

It was an automaton. This one was built to look nearly human. It had a thick body, clothed in a dark gray suit, but the arms that protruded from beyond the cuffs were stick-thin, ending in spatulate hands, and the head that rose above the collar was smooth and egglike. Two bulbous eyes were set into the head, but the machine had no other features.

"Who are you?" Tessa demanded in the old woman's voice,

brandishing the sharp pick she had taken earlier. "What are you doing in my house, creature?"

The thing made a whirring, clicking noise, obviously confused. A moment later the front door opened and Mrs. Black swept in. She was wrapped in her dark cloak, her white face blazing under the hood. "What's going on here?" she demanded. "Did you find—" She broke off, staring at Tessa.

"What's going on?" Tessa demanded, her voice coming out in the old woman's high whine. "I ought to ask you that— breaking into perfectly decent folks' homes—" She blinked, as if to make it clear she couldn't see very well. "Get out of here, and take your friend"—she jabbed the object she held (A *frog pick*, said the voice of the old woman in her mind; *you use it for cleaning horse's hooves, silly girl*)—"with you. You'll find nothing here worth stealing."

For a moment she thought it had worked. Mrs. Black's face was expressionless. She took a step forward. "You haven't seen a young girl in these parts, have you?" she asked. "Very finely dressed, brown hair, gray eyes. She would have looked lost. Her people are looking for her and offering a handsome reward."

"A likely story, looking for some lost girl." Tessa sounded as surly as she could; it wasn't difficult. She had a feeling the old woman whose face she was wearing had been a naturally surly sort. "Get out I said!"

The automaton whirred. Mrs. Black's lips pressed suddenly together, as if she were holding back laughter. "I see," she said. "Might I say that's quite a fine necklace you're wearing, old woman?"

Tessa's hand flew to her chest, but it was already too late. The clockwork angel was there, clearly visible, ticking gently.

"Take her," said Mrs. Black in a bored voice, and the automaton lurched forward, reaching for Tessa. She dropped the blanket and backed away, brandishing her frog pick. She managed to rake quite a long gash down the automaton's front as it reached for her and knocked her arm aside. The frog pick clattered to the floor, and Tessa cried out in pain just as the front door burst open and a flood of automatons filled the room, their arms reaching for her, their mechanical hands closing on her flesh. Knowing she was overpowered, knowing it would not do a bit of good, she finally allowed herself to scream.

Sun on his face woke Will. He blinked, opening his eyes slowly.

Blue sky.

He rolled over and stretched stiffly into a sitting position. He was on the rise of a green hill, just out of sight of the Shrewsbury-Welshpool road. He could see nothing all around him but scattered farmhouses in the distance; he had passed only a few tiny hamlets on his frantic midnight ride away from the Green Man, riding until he literally slid from Balios's back in exhaustion and hit the dirt with bone-jarring force. Half-walking and half-crawling, he had let his exhausted horse nose him off the road and into a slight dip in the ground, where he had curled up and fallen asleep, heedless of the drizzle of cold rain that had still been falling.

Sometime between then and now the sun had come up, drying his clothes and hair, though he was still dirty, his shirt a mess of caked mud and blood. He rose to his feet, his whole body aching. He hadn't bothered with any kind of healing runes the previous night. He'd gone into the inn—tracking rain and mud behind him—only to retrieve his things, before returning to the stables to free Balios and hurtle off into the night. The injuries he'd sustained in his battle against Woolsey's pack still hurt, as did the bruises from falling off the horse. He limped stiffly to where Balios was cropping grass near the shade of a spreading oak tree. A rummage through the saddlebags yielded a stele and a handful of dried fruit. He used the one to trace himself with painkilling and healing runes in between taking bites of the other.

The events of the night before seemed a thousand miles away. He remembered fighting the wolves, the splinter of bones and the taste of his own blood, the mud and the rain. He remembered the pain of the severance from Jem, though he could no longer feel it. Instead of pain he felt hollowness. As if some great hand had reached down and cut everything that made him human out of his insides, leaving him a shell.

When he was done with his breakfast, he returned his stele to his saddlebag, stripped off his ruined shirt, and changed into a clean one. As he did so, he could not help but glance down at the *parabatai* rune on his chest.

It was not black, but silver-white, like a long-faded scar. Will could hear Jem's voice in his head, steady and serious and familiar: *"And it came to pass . . . that the soul of Jonathan was knit with the soul of David, and Jonathan loved him as his own soul. . . . Then Jonathan and David made a covenant, because he loved him as his own soul."* They were two warriors, and their souls were knit together by Heaven, and out of that Jonathan Shadowhunter took the idea of parabatai, *and encoded the ceremony into the Law.*

For years now this Mark and Jem's presence had been all Will had had in his life to assure him that he was loved by anybody. All that he'd had to know that he was real and existed. He traced his fingers over the edges of the faded *parabatai* rune. He had thought he would hate it, hate the sight of it in sunlight, but he found to his surprise that he didn't. He was glad the *parabatai* rune had not simply vanished off his skin. A Mark that spoke of loss was still a Mark, a remembrance. You could not lose something you had never had.

Out of the saddlebag he took the knife Jem had given him: a narrow blade with the intricate silver handle. In the shadow of the oak tree, he cut the palm of his hand and watched as the blood ran onto the ground, soaking the earth. Then he knelt and plunged the blade into the bloody ground. Kneeling, he hesitated, one hand on the hilt.

"James Carstairs," he said, and swallowed. It was always this way; when he needed words the most, he could not find them. The words of the biblical *parabatai* oath came into his head: *Entreat me not to leave thee, or to return from following after thee—for whither thou goest, I will go, and where thou lodgest, I will lodge. Thy people shall be my people, and thy God my God. Where thou diest, will I die, and there will I be buried. The Angel do so to me, and more also, if aught but death part thee and me.*

But no. That was what was said when you were joined, not when you were cut apart. David and Jonathan had been separated, too, by death. Separated but not divided.

"I told you before, Jem, that you would not leave me," Will said, his bloody hand on the hilt of the dagger. "And you are still with me. When I breathe, I will think of you, for without you I would have been dead years ago. When I wake up and when I sleep, when I lift up my hands to defend myself or when I lie down to die, you will be with me. You say we are born and born again. I say there is a river that divides the dead and the living. What I do know is that if we are born again, I will meet you in another life, and if there is a river, you will wait on the shores for me to come to you, so that we can cross together." Will took a deep breath and let go of the knife. He drew his hand back. The cut on his palm was already healing—the result of the half dozen *iratzes* on his skin. "You hear that, James Carstairs? We are bound, you and I, over the divide of death, down through whatever generations may come. *Forever*."

He rose to his feet and looked down at the knife. The knife was Jem's, the blood was his. This spot of ground, whether he could ever find it again, whether he lived to try, would be theirs.

He turned to walk toward Balios, toward Wales and Tessa. He did not look back.

> To: *Charlotte Branwell*
> From: *Consul Josiah Wayland*
> By footman

> *My Dear Mrs. Branwell,*
> *I am not certain that I perfectly understood your missive. It seems incredible to me that a sensible woman such as yourself should place such reliance on the bare word of a boy as notoriously reckless and unreliable as William Herondale has time and again proven himself to be. I certainly will not do so. Mr. Herondale has, as shown by his own letter, raced away on a wild chase without your knowledge. He is absolutely capable of fabrication in order to aid his cause. I will not send a large force of my Shadowhunters on the whim and careless word of a boy.*
> *Pray cease your peremptory rallying cries to Cadair*

Idris. Attempt to keep in mind that I am the Consul. I command the armies of the Shadowhunters, madam, not yourself. Fix your mind instead on an attempt to better keep your Shadowhunters in check.

> *Yours truly,*
> *Josiah Wayland, Consul*

"There's a man here to see you, Mrs. Branwell."

Charlotte glanced up wearily to see Sophie standing in the doorway. She looked tired, as they all did; the unmistakable traces of weeping were beneath her eyes. Charlotte knew the signs—she had seen them in her own mirror that morning.

She sat behind the desk in the drawing room, staring down at the letter in her hand. She had not expected Consul Wayland to be pleased by her news, but neither had she expected this blank contempt and refusal. *I command the armies of the Shadowhunters, madam, not yourself. Fix your mind instead on an attempt to better keep your Shadowhunters in check.*

Keep them in check. She fumed. As if they were all children and she no better than their governess or nursemaid, parading them in front of the Consul when they were washed and dressed, and hiding them in the playroom the rest of the time that he not be disturbed. They were *Shadowhunters*, and so was she. And if he did not think that Will was reliable, he was a fool. He knew of the curse; she had told him herself. Will's madness had always been like Hamlet's, half play and half wildness, and all driving toward a certain end.

The fire crackled in the grate; outside, the rain sheeted down, painting the windowpanes in silver lines. That morning she had passed Jem's bedroom, the door open, the bed divested of its linens, the possessions cleared away. It could have been anyone's room. All the evidence of his years with them, gone with the wave of a hand. She had leaned against the wall of the corridor, sweat beading on her brow, her eyes burning. *Raziel, did I do the right thing?*

She passed her hand over her eyes now. "Now, of all times? It isn't Consul Wayland, is it?"

"No, ma'am." Sophie shook her dark head. "It's Aloysius Starkweather. He says it is a matter of the greatest urgency."

"*Aloysius Starkweather?*" Charlotte sighed. Some days simply piled horror on horror. "Well, let him in, then."

She folded the letter she had written as a response to the Consul, and had just sealed it when Sophie returned and ushered Aloysius Starkweather into the room, before excusing herself. Charlotte did not rise from her desk. Starkweather looked much as he had the last time she had seen him. He seemed to have calcified, as if while he was getting no younger, he could get no older either. His face was a map of wrinkled lines, framed with a white beard and white hair. His clothes were dry; Sophie must have hung his overcoat downstairs. The suit he wore was at least ten years out of fashion, and he smelled faintly of old mothballs.

"Please be seated, Mr. Starkweather," said Charlotte as courteously as she could to someone who she knew disliked her, and had hated her father.

But he did not sit down. His hands were locked behind his back, and as he turned, surveying the room around him, Charlotte saw with a flash of alarm that one of the cuffs of his jacket was splattered with blood.

"Mr. Starkweather," she said, and now she did rise. "Are you hurt? Should I summon the Brothers?"

"Hurt?" he barked out. "Why would I be hurt?"

"Your sleeve." She pointed.

He drew his arm away and gazed at it before huffing out a laugh. "Not my blood," he said. "I was in a fight, earlier. He took objection . . ."

"Took objection to what?"

"To my cutting off all his fingers and then slitting his throat," said Starkweather, meeting her eyes. His own were gray-black, the color of stone.

"Aloysius." Charlotte forgot to be polite. "The Accords forbid unprovoked attacks on Downworlders."

"Unprovoked? I'd say this was provoked. His folk murdered my granddaughter. My daughter nearly died of grief. The house of Starkweather destroyed—"

"Aloysius!" Charlotte was seriously alarmed now. "Your house is not destroyed. There are still Starkweathers in Idris. I do not say that to minimize your sorrow, for some losses are with us always." *Jem*, she thought, unbidden, and the pain of the thought pushed her back into the chair. She rested her elbows on the table, her face in her hands. "I do not know why you came to tell me this now," she murmured. "Did you not see the runes upon the door of the Institute? This is a time of great sorrow for us—"

"I came to tell you because it's important!" Aloysius flared up. "It regards Mortmain, and Tessa Gray."

Charlotte lowered her hands. "What do you know of Tessa Gray?"

Aloysius had turned away. He stood facing the fire, his long shadow cast across the Persian rug on the floor. "I am not a man who thinks much of the Accords," he said. "You know it; you have been in Councils with me. I was brought up to believe that everything touched by demons was foul and corrupt. That it was the blood right of a Shadowhunter to kill these creatures and to take what they had as spoils and treasure. The spoils room of the Institute in York was left in my charge, and I kept it filled until the day the new Laws were passed." He scowled.

"Let me guess," said Charlotte. "You did not stop there."

"Of course not," said the old man. "What are man's Laws to the Angel's? I know the right way of doing things. I kept a lower profile, but I did not cease taking spoils, or destroying those Downworlders who crossed my path. One of those was John Shade."

"Mortmain's father."

"Warlocks cannot have children," snarled Starkweather. "Some human boy they found and trained up. Shade taught him his unholy tinkering ways. Won his trust."

"It's unlikely the Shades stole Mortmain from his parents," said Charlotte. "He was probably a boy who would have died in a workhouse otherwise."

"It was unnatural. Warlocks should not have human children to raise." Aloysius stared deep within the red embers of the fire. "That is why we raided Shade's house. We killed him and his wife. The boy escaped. Shade's *clockwork prince*." He snorted. "We took several of his items back with us to the Institute, but none of us could make head or tail of them. That was all there was to it—a routine raid. Everything according to plan. That is, until my granddaughter was born. Adele."

"I know that she died at her first rune ceremony," said

Charlotte, her hand unconsciously going to her own belly. "I am sorry. It is a great sorrow to have a sickly child—"

"She was not born sickly!" he barked. "She was a healthy infant. Beautiful, with my son's eyes. Everyone doted on her, until one morning my daughter-in-law woke us with a scream. She insisted that the child in her cradle was not her daughter, though they looked exactly alike. She swore she knew her own child and this was not it. We thought she had gone mad. Even when the baby's eyes changed from blue to gray—well, that happens often with infants. It wasn't until we tried to apply her first Marks that I began to realize my daughter-in-law had been right. Adele—the pain was excruciating for her. She screamed and screamed and writhed. Her skin burned where the stele touched her. The Silent Brothers did all they could, but by the next morning she was dead."

Aloysius paused and was silent for a long time, gazing, as if fascinated, into the fire.

"My daughter-in-law nearly went mad. She could not bear to remain in the Institute. I stayed. I knew she had been correct— Adele was *not* my granddaughter. I heard rumors of faeries and other Downworlders who boasted that they had had their revenge on the Starkweathers, had taken one of their children from them and replaced her with a sickly human. None of my investigations yielded anything concrete, but I was determined to find out where my granddaughter had gone." He leaned on the mantel. "I had nearly given up when Tessa Gray came to my Institute in the company of your two Shadowhunters. She could have been the ghost of my daughter-in-law, so similar did they look. But she did not appear to have any Shadowhunter blood. It was a mystery, but one I pursued.

"The faerie I interrogated today gave me the last bits of the puzzle. In her infancy my granddaughter was replaced with a kidnapped human child, a sickly creature who died when the Marks were applied, because she was not Nephilim." There was a hard crack in his voice now, a fissure in the flint. "My granddaughter was left with a mundane family to raise her, their sickly Elizabeth—chosen because of her superficial resemblance to Adele—replaced with our healthy girl. That was the Court's revenge on me. They believed I had killed their own, so they would kill mine." His eyes were cold as they rested on Charlotte. "Adele—Elizabeth—grew to womanhood in that mundane family, never knowing what she was. And then she married. A mundane man. His name was Richard. Richard Gray."

"Your granddaughter," Charlotte said slowly, "was Tessa's mother? Elizabeth Gray? Tessa's mother was a Shadowhunter?"

"Yes."

"These are crimes, Aloysius. You should go to the Council with this—"

"They do not care about Tessa Gray," said Starkweather roughly. "But you do. You will listen to my story because of it, and you may help me because of it."

"I may," said Charlotte, "if it is the right thing to do. I do not yet understand how Mortmain comes into this story."

Aloysius moved restlessly. "Mortmain learned of what had happened and determined that he would make use of Elizabeth Gray, a Shadowhunter who did not know she was a Shadowhunter. I believe that Mortmain courted Richard Gray as an employee in order to grant himself access to Elizabeth. I believe that he loosed an Eidolon demon upon her—my granddaughter—in the shape of her husband, and that he did it in order to get Tessa on her. Tessa was always the goal. The child of a Shadowhunter and a demon."

"But the offspring of demons and Shadowhunters are still-born," Charlotte said automatically.

"Even if the Shadowhunter does not know they are a Shadowhunter?" said Starkweather. "Even if they carry no runes?"

"I . . ." Charlotte closed her mouth. She had no idea what the answer was; as far as she knew, the situation had never occurred. Shadowhunters were marked when children, male and female, all of them.

But Elizabeth Gray had not been.

"I know the girl is a shape-shifter," said Starkweather. "But I do not believe that is why he wants her. There is something else he wants her to do. Something only she can do. She is the key."

"The key to what?"

"It was the last words the faerie spoke to me this afternoon." Starkweather glanced at the blood on his sleeve. "He said, 'She is to be our vengeance for all your wasteful death. She will bring ruin to the Nephilim, and London will burn, and when the Magister rules over all, you will be no more to him than cattle in a pen.' Even if the Consul does not wish to go after Tessa for her own sake, they ought to go after her to prevent that."

"If they believe it," said Charlotte.

"Coming from your lips, they must," said Starkweather. "If it came from me, they would laugh me off as a mad old man, as they have done for years."

"Oh, Aloysius. You far overestimate the trust the Consul

has in me. He will say I am a foolish, credulous woman. He will say the faerie lied to you—well, they cannot lie, but twisted the truth, or repeated the truth as he believed it."

The old man looked away, his mouth working. "Tessa Gray is the key to Mortmain's plan," he said. "I do not know how, but she is. I have come to you because I do not trust the Council with Tessa. She is part demon. I remember what in the past I have done to things that were part demon or supernatural."

"Tessa is not a thing," Charlotte said. "She is a girl, and she has been kidnapped and is probably terrified. Don't you think if I could have thought of a way to save her already, I would have done it?"

"I have done wrong," said Aloysius. "I want to make this right. My blood runs in that girl's veins, even if demon blood does as well. She is my great-granddaughter." He raised his chin, his watery, pale eyes rimmed with red. "I ask only one thing of you, Charlotte. When you find Tessa Gray, and you will find her, tell her she is welcome to the name of Starkweather."

Do not make me regret that I have trusted you, Gabriel Lightwood.

Gabriel sat at the desk in his room, writing paper spread out before him, pen in hand. The lamps in the room were not lit, and the shadows were dark in the corners, and long across the floors.

> *To: Consul Josiah Wayland*
> *From: Gabriel Lightwood*
>
> *Most Honored Consul,*
> *I write to you today at last with the news that you*

requested of me. I had expected it to come from Idris, but as chance would have it, its source is much closer to home. Today Aloysius Starkweather, head of the York Institute, came to call upon Mrs. Branwell.

He set the pen down and took a deep breath. He had heard the bell of the Institute ring earlier, had watched from the stairs as Sophie had ushered Starkweather into the house and up to the drawing room. It was easy enough after that to station himself at the door and listen to everything that passed within the room.

Charlotte did not, after all, expect to be spied on.

He is an old man gone mad with grief, and as such he has created an elaborate set of fabrications with which he explains to himself his great loss. He is certainly to be pitied, but not to be taken seriously, nor should the policy of the Council rest upon the words of the untrustworthy and the mad.

The floorboards creaked; Gabriel's head jerked up. His heart was pounding. If it was Gideon—Gideon would be horrified to discover what he was doing. They all would. He thought of the look of betrayal that would bloom across Charlotte's small face if she knew. Henry's bewildered anger. Most of all he thought of a pair of blue eyes in a heart-shaped face, looking at him with disappointment. *Maybe I have faith in you, Gabriel Lightwood.*

When he set the pen back to the letter, he did so with such ferocity that the pen nearly tore through the paper.

I regret to report this, but they spoke together of both Council and Consul with great disrespect. It is clear that Mrs. Branwell resents what she sees as unnecessary interference in her plans. She met Mr. Starkweather's wild claims, such as that Mortmain has bred demons and Shadowhunters together, a clear impossibility, with sheer credulousness. It appears that you were correct, and that she is far too head-strong and easily influenced to head an Institute properly.

Gabriel bit his lip and forced himself not to think of Cecily; instead he thought of Lightwood House, his birthright; the good name of the Lightwoods restored; the safety of his brother and sister. He was not really harming Charlotte. It was only a question of her position, not her safety. The Consul had no dark plans for her. Surely she would be happier in Idris, or in some country house, watching her children run over green lawns and not worrying constantly about the fate of all Shadowhunters.

Though Mrs. Branwell exhorts you to send a force of Shadowhunters to Cadair Idris, anyone who makes the opinions of madmen and hysterics the cornerstone of their policies lacks the objectivity to be trusted.

If necessary, I shall swear by the Mortal Sword that all this is true.

Yours in Raziel's name,

Gabriel Lightwood

16

THE CLOCKWORK PRINCESS

O Love! who bewailest
The frailty of all things here,
Why choose you the frailest
For your cradle, your home, and your bier?
—Percy Bysshe Shelley,
"Lines: When the Lamp Is Shattered"

To: Consul Josiah Wayland
From: Charlotte Branwell

Dear Consul Wayland,
I have but this moment received tidings of the gravest
import, which I hasten to impart to you. An informant,
whose name I cannot at this time disclose but whom I vouch
for as reliable, has relayed to me details that suggest to me

that Miss Gray is no mere passing fancy of Mortmain's but a key to his main objective: to wit, the utter destruction of us all.

He plots to construct devices of greater power than any we have yet before seen, and I deeply fear that Miss Gray's unique abilities will aid him in this endeavor. She would never intend harm to us, but we do not know what threats or indignities Mortmain will offer her. It is imperative that she be rescued at once, as much to save us all as to aid her.

In light of this new information, I once more implore you to gather what forces you may and march upon Cadair Idris.

Yours sincerely, and in sincere distress,
Charlotte Branwell

Tessa woke slowly, as if consciousness were at the end of a long, dark corridor and she were walking toward it at a snail's pace, her hand outstretched. Finally she reached it, and swung the door open to reveal—

Blinding light. It was golden light, not pale like witchlight. She sat up and looked around her.

She was in a simple brass bed, with a deep feather tick spread over a second mattress, and a heavy eiderdown quilt on top. The room she was in looked as if it had been hollowed out of a cave. There was a tall dresser, and a washstand with a blue jug on it; there was also a wardrobe, its door hanging open just enough that Tessa could see that garments hung inside. There were no windows in the room, though there was a fireplace in which a cheerful blaze burned. On either side of the fireplace were hung portraits.

She slid from the bed and winced as her bare feet encountered cold stone. It was not as painful as she would have expected, though, given her battered state. Glancing down, she had two quick shocks: the first was that she was wearing nothing but an oversize black silk dressing gown. The second was that her cuts and bruises seemed to have largely disappeared. She still felt slightly sore, but her skin, pale against the black silk, was unmarked. Touching her hair, she felt that it was clean and loose around her shoulders, no longer matted with mud and blood.

That did leave the question of who had cleaned her, healed her, and put her in this bed. Tessa remembered nothing beyond struggling with the automatons in the small farmhouse while Mrs. Black laughed. Eventually one of them had choked her into unconsciousness and a merciful darkness had come. Still, the idea of Mrs. Black undressing and bathing her was horrible, though not perhaps as horrible as the idea of Mortmain doing it.

Most of the furniture in the room was grouped on one side of the cave. The other side was largely bare, though she could see the black rectangle of a doorway cut into the far wall. After a brief glance around she made her way toward it—

Only to find herself, halfway across the room, brought up bruisingly short. She staggered back, gathering her dressing gown more tightly about her, her forehead stinging where she had smacked it on *something*. Gingerly she reached out, tracing the air in front of her.

And she felt solid hardness in front of her, as if a perfectly clear glass wall stood between her and the other side of the room. She flattened her hands against it. Invisible it might be, but it was as hard as adamant. She moved her hands up, wondering how high it could possibly go—

"I wouldn't bother," said a cold, familiar voice from the door. "The configuration stretches all the way across the cave, from wall to wall, from floor to ceiling. You are completely immured behind it."

Tessa had been stretching upward; at that, she dropped to her feet and backed up a step.

Mortmain.

He was exactly as she recalled him. A wiry man, not tall, with a weathered face and a neatly clipped beard. Extraordinarily ordinary, save for his eyes, as cold and gray as a winter snowstorm. He wore a dove-colored suit, not overly formal, the sort of thing a gentleman might wear to an afternoon at the club. His shoes were polished to a high shine.

Tessa said nothing, only drew the black dressing gown closer about her. It was voluminous, and concealed her whole body, but without the underpinnings of chemise and corset, stockings and bustle, she felt naked and exposed.

"Do not panic yourself," Mortmain went on. "You cannot reach me through the wall, but neither can I reach you. Not without dissolving the spell itself, and that would take time." He paused. "I wished for you to feel safer."

"If you wished me to be safe, you would have left me at the Institute." Tessa's tone was bone-chillingly cold.

Mortmain said nothing to that, only cocked his head and squinted at her, like a sailor squinting at the horizon. "My condolences on the death of your brother. I never meant for that to happen."

Tessa felt her mouth twist into a terrible shape. It had been two months since Nate had died in her arms, but she had not forgotten, or forgiven. "I don't want your pity. Or your good wishes. You made him a tool of yours, and then he died. It was your fault, as surely as if you had shot him in the street."

"I suppose it would avail little to point out that he was the one who sought me out."

"He was just a *boy*," Tessa said. She wanted to sink to her knees, wanted to pound against the invisible barrier with her fists, but she held herself upright and cold. "He was not even twenty."

Mortmain slid his hands into his pockets. "Do you know what it was like for me, when I was a boy?" he said, in as calm a tone as if he had been seated beside her at a dinner party and forced to make conversation.

Tessa thought of the images she had seen in Aloysius Starkweather's mind.

The man was tall, broad-shouldered—and as green-skinned as a lizard. His hair was black. The child he held by the hand, by contrast, seemed as normal as a child could be—small, chubby-fisted, pink-skinned.

Tessa knew the man's name, because Starkweather knew it.

John Shade.

Shade hoisted the child up onto his shoulders as through the door of the house spilled a number of odd-looking metal creatures, like a child's jointed dolls, but human-size, and with skin made of shining metal. The creatures were featureless. Though, oddly, they wore clothes—the rough workman's coveralls of a Yorkshire farmer on some, and on others plain muslin dresses. The automatons joined hands and began to sway as if they were at a country dance. The child laughed and clapped his hands.

"Look well on this, my son," said the green-skinned man, "for one day I shall rule a clockwork kingdom of such beings, and you shall be its prince."

"I know your adoptive parents were warlocks," she said. "I know that they cared for you. I know that your father invented the clockwork creatures with which you are so enamored."

"And you know what happened to them."

—*a room torn apart, cogs and cams and gears and ripped metal everywhere, fluid leaking as black as blood, and the green-skinned man and blue-haired woman lying dead among the ruins—*

Tessa looked away.

"Let me tell you about my childhood," Mortmain said. "Adoptive parents, you call them, but they were as much my parents as any amount of blood could make them. They raised me up with care and love, just as yours did you." He gestured toward the fireplace, and Tessa realized with a dull shock that the portraits that hung on either side were portraits of her own parents: her fair-haired mother, and her thoughtful-looking father with his brown eyes and tie askew. "And then they were killed by Shadowhunters. My father wanted to create these beautiful automatons, these *clockwork creatures*, as you call them. They would be the greatest machines ever invented, he dreamed, and they would protect Downworlders against the Shadowhunters who routinely murdered and stole from them. You saw the spoils in Starkweather's Institute." He spat the last words. "You saw pieces of my parents. He kept my mother's blood in a jar."

And the remains of warlocks. Mummified taloned hands, like Mrs. Black's. A stripped skull, utterly de-fleshed, human-looking save that it had tusks instead of teeth. Vials of sludgy-looking blood.

Tessa swallowed. *My mother's blood in a jar.* She could not say she did not understand his rage. And yet—she thought of Jem, his parents dying in front of him, his own life destroyed, and yet he had never sought revenge. "Yes, that was horrible," Tessa said. "But it does not excuse the things you've done."

A flicker of something deep in his eyes: rage, quickly tamped down. "Let me tell you what I've done," he said. "I have created an army. An army that, once the final piece of the puzzle is in place, will be invincible."

"And the final piece of the puzzle—"

"Is you," said Mortmain.

"You say that over and over, and yet you refuse to explain it," Tessa said. "You demand my cooperation and yet you tell me nothing. You have me imprisoned here, sir, but you cannot force my speech with you, or my willingness if I choose not to give it—"

"You are half-Shadowhunter, half-demon," Mortmain said. "That is the first thing you should know."

Tessa, already half-turned away from him, froze. "That is not possible. The offspring of Shadowhunters and demons are stillborn."

"Yes, they are," he said. "They are. The blood of a Shadowhunter, the runes on the body of a Shadowhunter, are death to a warlock child in the womb. But *your mother was not Marked.*"

"My mother was not a Shadowhunter!" Tessa looked wildly to the portrait of Elizabeth Gray over the fireplace. "Or are you saying she lied to my father, lied to everyone all her life—"

"She did not know," said Mortmain. "The Shadowhunters did not know it. There was no one to tell her. My father built your clockwork angel, you know. It was meant to be a gift for my mother. It contains within it a bit of the spirit of an angel, a rare thing, something he had carried with him since the Crusades. The mechanism itself was meant to be tuned to her life, so that every time her life was threatened the angel would intervene to protect her. However, my father never had a chance to finish it. He was murdered first." Mortmain began to pace. "My parents were not singled out for murder, of course. Starkweather and his kind delighted in slaughtering Downworlders—they grew rich off the spoils—and would take the slightest excuse to bring violence against them. For that he was hated by the Downworlder community. It was the faeries of the countryside who helped me escape when my parents were killed, and who hid me until the Shadowhunters stopped looking for me." He took a shuddering breath. "Years later, when they decided to have their revenge, I helped them. Institutes are protected against the ingress of Downworlders, but not against mundanes, and not, of course, against automatons."

He smiled a terrible smile.

"It was I, with the help of one of my father's inventions, who crept into the York Institute and switched the baby in the crib there for one of mundane descent. Starkweather's granddaughter, Adele."

"Adele," Tessa whispered. "I saw a portrait of her." *A very young girl with long, fair hair, dressed in an old-fashioned child's dress, a great ribbon surmounting her small head. Her face was thin and pale and sickly, but her eyes were bright.*

"She died when the first runes were put on her," said Mortmain with relish. "Died screaming, as so many Downworlders had before at the hands of Shadowhunters. Now they had killed one they had come to love. A fitting retribution."

Tessa stared at him in horror. How could anyone think that to die in agony was fitting retribution for an innocent child?

She thought of Jem again, his hands gentle on his violin.

"Elizabeth, your mother, grew up not knowing she was a Shadowhunter. No runes were given to her. I followed her progress, of course, and when she married Richard Gray, I made sure I employed him. I believed that the lack of runes on your mother meant that she could conceive a child who was half-demon, half-Shadowhunter, and to test that theory I sent a demon to her in the shape of your father. She never knew the difference."

Only the emptiness in Tessa's stomach kept her from being sick. "You—did *what*—to my mother? A demon? I am half-demon?"

"He was a Greater Demon, if that comforts you. Most of them were angels once. He was fair enough in his own aspect." Mortmain smirked. "Before your mother became pregnant, I had worked for years to finish my father's clockwork angel. I finished it, and after you were conceived, tuned it to *your* life. My greatest invention."

"But why would my mother be willing to wear it?"

"To save you," said Mortmain. "Your mother realized that something was wrong when she became pregnant. To carry a warlock child is not like carrying a human child. I came to her then and gave her the clockwork angel. I told her that wearing it would save her child's life. She believed me. I was not lying. You are immortal, girl, but you are not invulnerable. You can be killed. The angel is tuned to your life; it is *designed* to save you if you are dying. It may have saved you a hundred times before you were ever born, and it's saved you since. Think of the times you have been close to death. Think of the way it intervened."

Tessa thought back—the way her angel had flown at the automaton choking her, had fended off the blades of the creature that had attacked her near Ravenscar Manor, had kept her from being dashed to pieces on the rocks of the ravine. "But it did not save me from torture, nor injury."

"No. For those are part of the human condition."

"So is death," said Tessa. "I am not human, and you let the Dark Sisters torture me. I could never forgive you for that. Even if you convinced me my brother's death was his fault, that Thomas's death was justified, that your hatred was reasonable, I could never forgive you for that."

Mortmain lifted the box at his feet and upended it. There was a rattling crash as cogs fell from it—cogs and cams and gears, sheared-off bits of metal smeared with black fluid, and lastly, bouncing atop the rest of the rubbish like a child's red rubber ball, a severed head.

Mrs. Black's.

"I destroyed her," he said. "For you. I wished to show you I am sincere, Miss Gray."

"Sincere in what?" Tessa demanded. "Why did you do all this? *Why did you create me?*"

His lips twitched slightly; it was not a smile, not really. "For two purposes. The first is so that you could bear children."

"But warlocks cannot . . ."

"No," said Mortmain. "But you are no ordinary warlock. In you the blood of demons and the blood of angels has fought its own war in Heaven, and the angels have been victorious. You are not a Shadowhunter, but you are not a warlock, either. You are something new, something entirely other. *Shadowhunters*," he spat. "All Shadowhunter and demon hybrids die, and the Nephilim are proud of it, glad that their blood will never be filthied, their lineage tainted by magic. But *you*. You can do magic. You can have children like any other woman. Not for some years yet, but when you reach your full maturity. The greatest warlocks alive have assured me of it. Together we will start a new race, with the Shadowhunters' beauty and with no warlock mark. It will be a race that will break the Shadowhunters' arrogance by replacing them on this earth."

Tessa's legs gave out. She slumped to the floor, her dressing gown pooling around her like black water. "You—you want to use me to *breed your children?*"

Now he did grin. "I am not a man without honor," he said. "I offer you marriage. I always planned that." He gestured at the pitiful pile of ragged metal and flesh that had been Mrs. Black. "If I can have your willing participation, I would prefer it. And I can promise I shall deal thus with all your enemies."

My enemies. She thought of Nate, his hand closing on hers as he died, bloody, in her lap. She thought of Jem again, the way he never railed against his fate but faced it down bravely; she thought of Charlotte, who wept over Jessamine, though Jessie had betrayed her; and she thought of Will, who had laid down his heart for her and Jem to walk upon because he loved them more than he loved himself.

There was human goodness in the world, she thought—all caught up with desires and dreams, regrets and bitterness, resentments and powers, but it was there, and Mortmain would never see it.

"You will never understand," she said. "You say that you build, that you invent, but I know an inventor—Henry

Branwell—and you are nothing like him. He brings things to life; you just destroy. And now you bring me another dead demon, as if it were flowers rather than more death. You have no feelings, Mr. Mortmain, no empathy for anyone. If I had not known it before, it would have been made abundantly clear when you tried to use James Carstairs's illness to force me to come here. Though he is dying because of you, he wouldn't allow me to come—wouldn't take your *yin fen*. That's how *good* people behave."

She saw the look on his face. Disappointment. It was only there for a moment, though, before it was wiped away with a shrewd look. "Wouldn't allow you to come?" he said. "So I did not misjudge you; you would have done it. Would have come to me, here, out of love."

"Not love for you."

"No," he said thoughtfully, "not for me," and he drew from his pocket an object that Tessa recognized immediately.

She stared at the watch he held out to her, dangling on its gold chain. It was clearly unwound. The hands had long ago stopped spinning, the time seemingly frozen at midnight. The initials J.T.S. were carved on the back in elegant script.

"I said there were two reasons I created you," he said. "This is the second. There are shape-shifters in the world: demons and magicians who can take on the appearance of others. But only you can truly *become* someone else. This watch was my father's. John Thaddeus Shade. I beg of you to take this watch and Change into my father so I may speak with him one more time. If you do that, I will send all the *yin fen* I have in my possession—and it is a considerable amount—to James Carstairs."

"He will not take it," Tessa said immediately.

"Why not?" His tone was reasonable. "You are no longer a condition of the drug. It is a gift, freely given. It would be foolish to throw it away, and avail nothing. Whereas by doing this small thing for me, you may well save his life. What do you say to that, Tessa Gray?"

Will. Will, wake up.

It was Tessa's voice, unmistakably, and it brought Will bolt upright in the saddle. He caught at Balios's mane to steady himself and looked around blearily.

Green, gray, blue. The vista of Welsh countryside spread out before him. He had passed Welshpool and the England-Wales border sometime around dawn. He remembered little of his journey, only a continuous, tortuous progression of places: Norton, Atcham, Emstrey, Weeping Cross, diverting himself and his horse around Shrewsbury, and finally, finally the border and Welsh hills in the distance. They had been ghostly in the morning light, everything shrouded in mist that had burned off slowly as the sun had risen overhead.

He guessed he was somewhere near Llangadfan. It was a pretty road, laid over an old Roman byway, but almost empty of habitation apart from the occasional farm, and it seemed endlessly long, longer than the gray sky stretching overhead. At the Cann Office Hotel he had forced himself to stop and take some food, but only for moments. The journey was what mattered.

Now that he was in Wales, he could feel it—the draw in his blood toward the place where he had been born. Despite all Cecily's words, he had not felt the connection in him until now—breathing Welsh air, seeing the Welsh colors: the green of hills, gray of slate and sky, the pallor of whitewashed stone houses, the ivory dots of sheep against the grass. Pine and oak trees were dark emerald in the distance, higher up, but closer to the road the vegetation grew green-gray and ochre.

As he moved farther into the heart of the country, the soft green rolling hills grew starker, the road steeper, and the sun began to sink toward the rim of the distant mountains. He knew where he was now, knew when he passed into the Dyfi Valley, and the mountains in front of him thrust up, stark and ragged. The peak of Car Afron was on his left, a tumble of gray slate and shingle like broken gray spiderweb across its side. The road was steep and long, and as Will urged Balios up it, he slumped in the saddle and, against his will, drifted out of consciousness. He dreamed of Cecily and Ella running up and down hills not unlike these, calling after him, *Will! Come and run with us, Will!* And he dreamed of Tessa and her hands held out for him, and he knew he could not stop, could not stop until he reached her. Even if she never looked at him like that in waking life, even if that softness in her eyes was for someone else. And sometimes, as now, his hand would slip into his pocket and close around the jade pendant there.

Something struck him hard from the side; he released the pendant as he fell, jarringly, onto the rocky grass by the side of the road. Pain shot up his arm, and he rolled to the side just in time to avoid Balios crumpling to the earth beside him. It took him a moment, gasping, to realize that they had not been attacked. His horse, too exhausted to take another step, had collapsed beneath him.

Will heaved himself up to his knees and crawled to Balios's side. The black horse lay lathered in foam, his eyes rolling upward pitifully toward Will as Will neared him and flung an arm around his neck. To his relief the horse's pulse was steady and strong. "Balios, Balios," he whispered, stroking the animal's mane. "I am sorry. I should not have ridden you like that."

He remembered when Henry had bought the horses and was trying to decide what to name them. Will had been the one to suggest their names: Balios and Xanthos, after the immortal horses of Achilles. *We two can fly as swiftly as Zephyrus, who they say is the fleetest of all winds.*

But those horses had been immortal, and Balios was not. Stronger than an ordinary horse, and faster, but every creature had its limits. Will lay down, his head spinning, and stared up at the sky—like a gray sheet pulled tight, touched here and there with streaks of black cloud.

He had thought, once, in the brief moments between the lifting of the "curse" and the knowledge that Jem and Tessa were engaged, of bringing Tessa here to Wales, to show her the places he had been as a child. He had thought to take her down to Pembrokeshire, to walk around Saint David's Head and see the cliff-top flowers there, to see the blue sea from Tenby and find seashells at the tide lines. These all seemed the distant fancies of a child now. There was only the road ahead, more riding and more exhaustion, and probable death at the end of it.

With another reassuring pat on his horse's neck, Will heaved himself to his knees and then his feet. Fighting dizziness, he limped to the crest of the hill, and looked down.

A small valley lay below him, and within it was cradled a diminutive stone village, little bigger than a hamlet. He took his stele from his belt and wearily carved a Vision rune into his left wrist. It lent him enough power to see that the village had a square, and a small church. It would almost certainly have some sort of public house where he could rest for the night.

Everything in his heart screamed to go on, to *finish this*— he could not be more than twenty miles from his goal—but to go on would be to kill his horse and, he knew, to arrive at Cadair Idris himself in no fit state to do battle with anyone. He turned back toward Balios and with a measured appli-cation of coaxing and handfuls of oats managed to get the horse to its feet. Gathering the reins in his hand and squint-ing into the sunset, he began to lead Balios down the hill toward the village.

The chair Tessa sat in had a high, carved wooden back, ham-mered through with massive nails, the dull ends of which poked into her back. In front of her was a wide desk, weighed down by books on one end. Before her on the desk was a clean tablet of paper, a jar of ink, and a quill. Beside the paper sat John Shade's pocket watch.

On either side of her stood two massive automatons. Little effort had been expended to make them resemble humans. Each was nearly triangular, with thick arms protruding from either side of their bodies, each arm ending in a razor-sharp blade. They were frightening enough, but Tessa could not help but feel that if Will were there, he would have commented that they looked like turnips, and perhaps made up a song about it.

"Take up the watch," said Mortmain. "And Change."

He sat across from her, in a chair much like hers, with the same high curving back. They were in another cave room, which she had been led to by automatons; the only light in the room came from an enormous fireplace, large enough to roast an entire cow in. Mortmain's face was cast into shadows, his fingers steepled below his chin.

Tessa lifted the watch. It felt heavy and cool in her hands. She closed her eyes.

She had only Mortmain's word that he had sent the *yin fen*, and yet she believed him. He had no reason not to do it, after all. What difference did it make to him whether Jem Carstairs lived a little longer? It had only ever been a bargaining tool to get her into his hands, and here she was, *yin fen* or not.

She heard Mortmain's breath hiss out between his teeth, and she tightened her fingers' grip on the watch. It seemed to throb suddenly in her grasp, the way the clockwork angel sometimes did, as if it had its own life within it. She felt her hand jerk, and then suddenly the Change was on her—without her having to will it or reach for it as she usually did. She gave a little gasp as she felt the Change take her like a harsh wind, pushing her down and under. John Shade was suddenly all around her, his presence enveloping hers. Pain drove up her arm, and she let go of the watch. It thumped to the desk, but the Change was unstoppable. Her shoulders broadened under the dressing gown, her fingers turning green, the color spreading up her body like verdigris over copper.

Her head jerked upright. She felt heavy, as if an enormous weight were pressing on her. Looking down, she saw that she had a man's heavy arms, the skin a dark, textured green, the hands large and curved. A feeling of panic rose in her, but it was tiny, a small spark within an immense gulf of darkness. She had never been so lost inside a Change before.

Mortmain had sat upright. He was staring at her fixedly, his firm lips compressed, his eyes shining with a hard dark light. "Father," he said.

Tessa did not answer. Could not answer. The voice that rose within her was not hers; it was Shade's. "My clockwork prince," Shade said.

The light in Mortmain's eyes grew. He leaned forward, pushing the papers eagerly across the table toward Tessa. "Father," he said. "I need your help, and quickly. I have a Pyxis. I have the means to open it. I have the automaton bodies. I need only the spell you created, the binding spell. Write it down for me, and I will have the last piece of the puzzle."

The tiny flare of panic inside Tessa was growing and spreading. This was no touching reunion between father and son. This was something Mortmain wanted, needed from the warlock John Shade. She began to struggle, to try to extricate herself from the Change, but it held her with a grip like iron. Not since the Dark Sisters had trained her had she been unable to extricate herself from a Change, but though John Shade was dead, she could feel the steely hold of his will on her, keeping her prisoned in his body and forcing that body into action. In horror she saw her own hand reach for the pen, dip the nib in the ink, and begin to write.

The pen scratched across the paper. Mortmain leaned forward. He was breathing hard, as if running. Behind him the fire crackled, high and orange in the grate. "That is it," he said, his tongue licking over his bottom lip. "I can see how that would work, yes. Finally. That's it exactly."

Tessa stared. What was coming from her pen seemed a stream of gibberish to her: numbers, signs, and symbols she could not comprehend. Again she tried to struggle, succeeding only in blotting the page. There went the pen again—ink, paper, more scratching. The hand that held the pen was shaking violently, but the symbols continued to flow. Tessa began to bite her lip: hard, then harder. She tasted blood in her mouth. Some of the blood dripped onto the page. The pen continued to write through it, smearing scarlet fluid across the page.

"That is it," Mortmain said. "Father—"

The nib of the pen snapped, as loud as a gunshot, echoing off the walls of the cave. The pen fell broken from Tessa's hand, and she slumped back against the chair, exhausted. The green was draining from her skin, her body was shrinking, her own brown hair was tumbling loose over her shoulders. She could still taste blood in her mouth. "No," she gasped, and reached for the papers. "No—"

But her movements were made slow by pain and the Change, and Mortmain was faster. Laughing, he snatched the papers out from under her hand and rose to his feet. "Very good," he said. "Thank you, my little warlock girl. You have given me everything I need. Automatons, escort Miss Gray back to her room."

A metal hand closed on the back of Tessa's gown and lifted her to her feet. The world seemed to swing dizzily in front of her. She saw Mortmain reach down and lift up the gold watch that had fallen on the table.

He smiled at it, a feral, vicious smile. "I will make you proud, Father," he said. "Never doubt it."

Tessa, no longer able to bear watching, closed her eyes. *What have I done?* she thought as the automaton began to push her from the room. *My God, what have I done?*

17

Only Noble to be Good

Howe'er it be, it seems to me,
'Tis only noble to be good.
Kind hearts are more than coronets,
And simple faith than Norman blood.
—Alfred, Lord Tennyson, "Lady Clara Vere de Vere"

Charlotte's dark head was bent over a letter when Gabriel came into the drawing room. It was chilly in the room, the fire dead in the grate. Gabriel wondered why Sophie had not built it up—too much time spent training. His father wouldn't have had patience with that. He liked servants who were trained to fight, but he preferred them to acquire that knowledge before they entered his service.

Charlotte looked up. "Gabriel," she said.

"You wanted to see me?" Gabriel did his best to keep his voice even. He couldn't help the feeling that Charlotte's dark eyes could see through him, as if he were made of glass. His eyes flicked toward the paper on her desk. "What is that?"

She hesitated. "A letter from the Consul." Her mouth was twisted into a tight, unhappy line. She glanced down again and sighed. "All I ever wanted was to run this Institute as my father had. I never thought it would be quite so hard. I shall write to him again, but—" She broke off then, with a tight, false smile. "But I did not ask you here to talk about myself," she said. "Gabriel, you have looked tired these past few days, and tense. I know we are all distressed, and I fear that in that distress your—situation—may have been forgotten."

"My situation?"

"Your father," she clarified, rising from her chair and approaching him. "You must be grieving him."

"What of Gideon?" he said. "He was his father too."

"Gideon grieved your father some time ago," she said, and to his surprise she was standing at his elbow. "For you it must be new and raw. I did not want you to think I had forgotten."

"After everything that's happened," he said, his throat starting to close with bewilderment—and something else, something he did not want to identify too closely—"after Jem, and Will, and Jessamine, and Tessa, after your household has been very nearly cut in *half*, you do not wish me to believe that you have forgotten *me*?"

She laid a hand on his arm. "Those losses do not make your loss nothing—"

"That cannot be it," he said. "You cannot want to comfort me. You asked me to find out if my loyalty is still to my father, or to the Institute—"

"Gabriel, no. Nothing like that."

"I can't give you the answer you want," Gabriel said. "I cannot forget that he stayed with me. My mother died—and Gideon left—and Tatiana is a useless fool—and there was never anyone else, never anyone else to bring me up, and I had *nothing*, just my father, just the two of us, and now you, you and Gideon, you expect me to despise him, but I can't. He was my father, and I—" His voice broke.

"Loved him," she said gently. "You know, I remember you when you were just a little boy, and I remember your mother. And I remember your brother, always standing next to you. And your father's hand on your shoulder. If it matters, I do believe he loved you, too."

"It doesn't matter. Because I killed my father," Gabriel said in a shaking voice. "I put an arrow through his eye—I spilled his blood. Patricide—"

"It was not patricide. He wasn't your father anymore."

"If that was not my father, if I did not end my father's life, then *where is he?*" Gabriel whispered "Where is my father?" and felt Charlotte reach up to draw him down, to embrace him as a mother would, holding him as he choked dryly against her shoulder, tasting tears in his throat but unable to shed them. "Where is my father?" he said again, and when she tightened her hold on him, he felt the iron in her grip, the strength of her holding him up, and wondered how he had ever thought this small woman was weak.

To: *Charlotte Branwell*
From: *Consul Josiah Wayland*

My Dear Mrs. Branwell,
    An informant whose name you cannot at this time dis-
close? I would venture a guess that there is no informant,
and that this is all your own invention, a ploy to convince
me of your rightness.
    Pray cease your impression of a parrot witlessly repeat-
ing "March upon Cadair Idris at once" at all the hours of
the day, and show me instead that you are performing your
duties as leader of the London Institute. Otherwise I fear I
must suppose that you are unfit to do so, and will be forced
to relieve you of them at once.
    As a token of your compliance, I must ask that you
cease speaking of this matter entirely, and implore no
members of the Enclave to join you in your fruitless quest.
If I hear that you have brought this matter before any
other Nephilim, I shall consider it the gravest disobedience
and act accordingly.
    Josiah Wayland, Consul of the Clave

Sophie had brought Charlotte the letter at the breakfast
table. Charlotte pried it open with her butter knife, breaking
through the Wayland seal (a horseshoe with the C of the Consul
below it), and fairly tore it open in her eagerness to read.

The rest of them watched her, Henry with concern on his
bright, open face as two dark red spots bloomed slowly over
Charlotte's cheekbones while her eyes scanned the lines. The

others sat still, arrested over their meals, and Cecily could not help but think how it was strange in a way to see a group of men hanging upon the reaction of a woman.

Though a smaller group of men than it should have been. The absence of Will and Jem felt like a new wound, a clean white slice not yet filled in with blood, the shock almost too fresh for pain.

"What is it?" Henry said anxiously. "Charlotte, dear . . ."

Charlotte read the words of the message out with the emotionless beats of a metronome. When she was done, she pushed the letter away, still staring at it. "I simply cannot . . ." She began. "I do not understand."

Henry had flushed red beneath his freckles. "How dare he write to you like that," he said, with unexpected ferocity. "How dare he address you in that manner, dismiss your concerns—"

"Perhaps he is correct. Perhaps he is mad. Perhaps we all are," Charlotte said.

"We are not!" Cecily exclaimed, and she saw Gabriel look sideways at her. His expression was difficult to read. He had been pale since he had come into the dining room, and had barely spoken or eaten, staring instead at the tablecloth as if it held the answers to all the questions in the universe. "The Magister is in Cadair Idris. I am sure of it."

Gideon was frowning. "I believe you," he said. "We all do, but without the ear of the Consul, the matter cannot be placed before the Council, and without a Council there can be no assistance for us."

"The portal is nearly ready for use," said Henry. "When it works, we should be able to transport as many Shadowhunters as needed to Cadair Idris in a matter of moments."

"But there will be no Shadowhunters to transport," said Charlotte. "Look, here, the Consul forbids me to speak of this matter to the Enclave. Its authority supersedes mine. To overstep his command like that—we could lose the Institute."

"And?" Cecily demanded heatedly. "Do you care more for your position than you care for Will and Tessa?"

"Miss *Herondale*," Henry began, but Charlotte silenced him with a gesture. She looked very tired.

"No, Cecily, it is not that, but the Institute provides us protection. Without it our ability to help Will and Tessa is severely compromised. As the head of the Institute, I can provide them assistance that a single Shadowhunter could not—"

"No," Gabriel said. He had pushed away his plate, and his slim fingers were tense and white as he gestured. "You cannot."

"Gabriel?" said Gideon in a questioning tone.

"I will not stay silent," Gabriel said, and rose to his feet, as if he intended to either make a speech or sprint away from the table, Cecily was not sure. He turned a haunted green gaze on Charlotte. "The day that the Consul came here, when he brought me and my brother away for questioning, he threatened us until we promised to spy on you for him."

Charlotte paled. Henry began to stand up from the table. Gideon threw a hand out pleadingly.

"Charlotte," he said. "We never did it. We never told him a word. Nothing that was true, anyway," he amended, looking around as the rest of the occupants of the room stared at him. "Some lies. Misdirection. He stopped asking after only two letters. He knew there was no use in it."

"It's true, ma'am," came a small voice from the corner of the room. Sophie. Cecily almost hadn't noticed her there, pale under her white mobcap.

"Sophie!" Henry sounded utterly shocked. "You knew about this?"

"Yes, but—" Sophie's voice shook. "He threatened Gideon and Gabriel awfully, Mr. Branwell. He told them he would have the Lightwoods stricken off the Shadowhunter records, that he would have Tatiana turned out in the street. And still they didn't tell him anything. When he stopped asking, I thought he'd realized there was nothing to find out and given up. I'm so sorry. I just—"

"She didn't want to hurt you," Gideon said desperately. "Please, Mrs. Branwell. Do not blame Sophie for this."

"I don't," said Charlotte, her eyes dark and quick, moving from Gabriel to Gideon to Sophie, and back again. "But I rather imagine there is more to this story. Isn't there?"

"That is all there is, truly—," Gideon began.

"No," Gabriel said. "It isn't. When I came to you, Gideon, and told you that the Consul no longer wanted us to report to him about Charlotte, that was a lie."

"What?" Gideon looked horrified.

"He brought me aside on my own, the day of the attack on the Institute," Gabriel said. "He told me that if I helped him discover some wrongdoing on Charlotte's part, he would give back the Lightwood estate to us, restore the honor to our name, cover up what our father did . . ." He took a deep breath. "And I told him I would do it."

"*Gabriel*," Gideon groaned, and buried his face in his hands. Gabriel looked as if he were about to be sick, half-wavering on

his feet. Cecily was torn between pity and horror, remembering that night in the training room, how she had told him she
had faith in him that he would make the right choices.

"That is why you looked so frightened when I called you to
speak with me earlier today," Charlotte said, her gaze steady on
Gabriel. "You thought I had found you out."

Henry began to rise to his feet, his pleasant, open face dark-
ening with the first real anger Cecily thought she had ever seen
on it. "Gabriel Lightwood," he said. "My wife has shown you
nothing but kindness, and this is how you repay it?"

Charlotte put a restraining hand on her husband's arm.
"Henry, wait," she said. "Gabriel. What did you do?"

"I listened to your conversation with Aloysius Starkweather," Gabriel said in an empty voice. "I wrote a letter to
the Consul afterward, telling him that you were basing your
requests that he march on Wales on the words of a madman,
that you were credulous, too headstrong . . ."

Charlotte's eyes seemed to pierce through Gabriel like nails;
Cecily thought she would never want that gaze on her, not in
her life. "You wrote it," she said. "Did you send it?"

Gabriel took a long, gasping breath. "No," he said, and
reached into his sleeve. He drew out a folded paper and threw
it down onto the table. Cecily stared at it. It was smudged with
fingerprints and soft at the edges, as if it had been folded and
unfolded many times. "I could not do it. I did not tell him anything at all."

Cecily let out a breath she hadn't realized she'd been holding.

Sophie made a soft noise; she started toward Gideon, who
was looking as if he were recovering from being punched in
the stomach. Charlotte remained as calm as she had been

throughout. She reached out, picked up the letter, glanced over it, and then placed it back on the table.

"Why didn't you send it?" she said.

He looked at her, an odd shared look that passed between them, and said, "I had my reasons to reconsider."

"Why didn't you come to me?" Gideon said. "Gabriel, you are my brother. . . ."

"You cannot make all my choices for me, Gideon. Sometimes I have to make my own. As Shadowhunters we are meant to be selfless. To die for mundanes, for the Angel, and most of all for each other. Those are our principles. Charlotte lives by them; Father never did. I realized that I had been mistaken before in putting my loyalty to my bloodline above principle, above everything. And I realized the Consul was wrong about Charlotte." Gabriel stopped abruptly; his mouth was set in a thin, white line. "He was wrong." He turned to Charlotte. "I cannot take back what I have done in the past, or what I considered doing. I know of no way to make up to you my doubt in your authority, or my ungratefulness for your kindness. All I can do is tell you what I know: that you cannot wait for an approval from Consul Wayland that will never come. He will never march upon Cadair Idris for you, Charlotte. He does not want to agree to any plan that has your stamp of authority on it. He wishes you out of the Institute. Replaced."

"But he is the one who put me here," Charlotte said. "He supported me—"

"Because he thought you would be weak," said Gabriel. "Because he believes women are weak and easily manipulated, but you have proved not to be, and it has ruined all his planning. He does not just desire you discredited; he *needs* it. He was clear enough with me that even if I could not discover you engaged in any true wrongdoing, he was granting me the freedom to invent a lie that would convict you. As long as it was a convincing one."

Charlotte pressed her lips together. "Then he never had faith in me," she whispered. "Never."

Henry tightened his grip on her arm. "But he should have," he said. "He underestimated you, and that is not a tragedy. That you have proven to be better, cleverer, and stronger than anyone could have expected, Charlotte—it is a triumph."

Charlotte swallowed, and Cecily wondered, just for a moment, what it would be like to have someone look at her as Henry looked at Charlotte—as if she were a wonder on the earth. "What do I do?"

"What you think best, Charlotte darling," said Henry.

"You are the leader of the Enclave, and of the Institute," said Gabriel. "We have faith in you, even if the Consul does not." He ducked his head. "You have my loyalty from this day forward. For whatever it is worth to you."

"It is worth a great deal," Charlotte said, and there was something in her voice, a quiet authority that made Cecily want to rise and proclaim her own loyalty, simply to win the balm of Charlotte's approval. Cecily couldn't imagine feeling that way, she realized, about the Consul. *And that is why the Consul hates her*, she thought. *Because she is a woman, and yet he knows she can command loyalty in a way he never could.* "We proceed as if the Consul does not exist," Charlotte went on. "If he is determined to remove me from my place here, then I have nothing to safeguard. It is simply a matter of doing what we must before he has a chance to stop us. Henry, how long before your invention is ready?"

"Tomorrow," Henry said promptly. "I shall work through the night—"

"It will be the first time it is ever used," said Gideon. "Does that not seem a bit risky?"

"We have no other way of getting to Wales in time," said Charlotte. "Once I send my message, we will have only a short time before the Consul comes to relieve me of my place."

"What message?" Cecily asked, bewildered.

"I am going to send a message to all the members of the Clave," Charlotte said. "At once. Not the Enclave. The *Clave*."

"But only the Consul is allowed—," Henry began, then shut his mouth like a box. "Ah."

"I will tell them the situation as it stands and ask for their assistance," said Charlotte. "I am not sure what response we can count on, but surely some will stand with us."

"*I* will stand with you," said Cecily.

"And I, of course," Gabriel said. His expression was resigned, nervous, considering, determined. Never had Cecily liked him more.

"And I," said Gideon, "though"—and his gaze, as it passed over his brother, was worried—"a mere six of us, one only barely trained, against whatever force Mortmain has mustered . . ." Cecily was caught between pleasure that he had counted her as one of them and annoyance that he had said she was barely trained. "It could be a suicide mission."

Sophie's soft voice spoke again. "You may have only six *Shadowhunters* on your side, but you have at least nine fighters. I am trained as well, and I would like to fight alongside you. So will Bridget and Cyril."

Charlotte looked half-pleased, half-startled. "But, Sophie, you have only just begun to be trained—"

"I have been trained longer than Miss Herondale," said Sophie.

"Cecily is a Shadowhunter—"

"Miss Collins has a natural talent," said Gideon. He spoke slowly, the conflict clear on his face. He did not want Sophie in the fighting, in danger, and yet would not lie about her abilities. "She should be allowed to Ascend and become a Shadowhunter."

"Gideon—," Sophie began, startled, but Charlotte was already looking at her with a keen dark gaze.

"Is that what you want, Sophie, dear? To Ascend?"

Sophie stammered. "I—it is what I have always wanted, Mrs. Branwell, but not if it meant I had to leave your service. You have been so kind to me, I would not wish to repay that by abandoning you—"

"Nonsense," Charlotte said. "I can find another maid; I cannot find another Sophie. If being a Shadowhunter was what you wanted, my girl, I wish you had spoken. I could have gone to the Consul before I was at odds with him. Still, when we return—"

She broke off, and Cecily heard the words beneath the words: *If we return.*

"When we return, I will put you forward for Ascension," Charlotte finished.

"I will speak out for her case as well," Gideon said. "After all, I have my father's place on the Council—his friends will listen to me; they still owe loyalty to our family—and besides, how else can we be married?"

"*What?*" said Gabriel with a wild hand gesture that accidentally flipped the nearest plate onto the floor, where it shattered.

"Married?" said Henry. "You're marrying your father's friends on the Council? Which of them?"

Gideon had gone an odd sort of greenish color; clearly he had not meant those words to escape him, and he did not know what to do now that they had. He was staring at Sophie in horror, but it didn't seem she was likely to be much help either. She looked as shocked as a fish that had been stranded unexpectedly on land.

Cecily stood up and dropped her serviette onto her plate. "All right," she said, doing her best to approximate the commanding tones her mother used when she needed something done about the house. "Everyone out of the room."

Charlotte, Henry, and Gideon began to rise to their feet. Cecily threw her hands up. "Not *you*, Gideon Lightwood," she said. "Honestly! But you"—she pointed at Gabriel—"do stop staring. And come along." And taking him by the back of the jacket, she half-dragged him from the room, Henry and Charlotte hard on their heels.

The moment they had left the dining room, Charlotte strode off toward the drawing room with the announced purpose of composing a message for the Clave, Henry by her side. (She paused at the turn of the corridor to look back at Gabriel with an amused quirk of her mouth, but Cecily suspected he did not see it.) Cecily put it out of her mind quickly, regardless. She was too busy pressing her ear up against the dining room door, trying to hear what was going on inside.

Gabriel, after a moment's pause, leaned back against the wall beside the door. He was in equal parts pale and flushed, his pupils dilated with shock. "You shouldn't do that," he said finally. "Eavesdropping is most incorrect behavior, Miss Herondale."

"It's *your* brother," Cecily whispered, ear against the wood. She could hear murmurs inside but nothing definite. "I should think you'd want to know."

He ran both his hands through his hair and exhaled like someone who'd been running a long distance. Then he turned to her and took a stele from his waistcoat pocket. He carved a rune quickly into his wrist, then placed his hand flat against the door. "I do, at that."

Cecily's gaze darted from his hand to the thoughtful expression on his face. "Can you *hear* them?" she demanded. "Oh, that is not at all fair!"

"It's all very romantic," Gabriel said, and then frowned. "Or it would be, if my brother could get a word out without sounding like a choking frog. I fear he will not go down in history as one of the world's great wooers of women."

Cecily crossed her arms in vexation. "I do not see why you are being so difficult," she said. "Or are you bothered that your brother wishes to marry a servant girl?"

The expression Gabriel turned on her was fierce, and Cecily suddenly regretted tweaking him after what he had just been through. "Nothing I can think of him doing would be worse than what my father did. At least his taste runs to human women."

And yet it was so difficult *not* to tweak him. He was so *aggravating*. "That is hardly a great endorsement for a woman as fine as Sophie."

Gabriel looked as if he were about to deliver a sharp retort, but then he thought better of it. "I did not mean it like that. She is a fine girl and will be a fine Shadowhunter when she Ascends. She will bring honor to our family, and the Angel knows we need it."

"I believe you will bring honor to your family too," Cecily said quietly. "What you just did, what you confessed to Charlotte—that took courage."

Gabriel was still for a moment. Then he reached out his hand toward her. "Take my hand," he said. "You will be able to hear what is going on in the dining room, through me, if you desire."

After a moment's hesitation Cecily took Gabriel's hand. It was warm and rough in hers. She could feel the thrum of his blood through his skin, oddly comforting—and indeed, through him, as if she had her own ear pressed to the door, she could hear the low rumble of spoken words: Gideon's soft hesitant voice, and Sophie's delicate one. She closed her eyes and listened.

"Oh," said Sophie faintly, and sat down in one of the chairs. "Oh, my."

She could not help but sit; her legs felt wobbly and uneasy. Gideon, meanwhile, was standing by the sideboard, looking panicked. His blond-brown hair was tousled wildly as if he had been running his hands through it. "My dear Miss Collins—," he began.

"This is," Sophie began, and paused. "I don't— This is quite unexpected."

"Is it?" Gideon moved away from the sideboard and leaned on the table; his shirtsleeves were rolled up slightly, and Sophie found herself staring at his wrists, downed with faint blond hair and marked with the white memories of Marks. "Surely you must have been able to see the respect and esteem I had for you. The admiration."

"Well," Sophie said. "Admiration." She managed to make it sound like a very pale word indeed.

Gideon flushed. "My dear Miss Collins," he began again. "It is true that my feelings for you go far beyond admiration. I would describe them as the most ardent affection. Your kindness, your beauty, your generous heart—they have quite overset me, and it is to that alone that I can ascribe my behavior of this morning. I do not know what came over me, to speak the dearest wishes of my heart aloud. Please do not feel obligated to accept my proposal simply because it was public. Any embarrassment over the matter would and should be mine."

Sophie looked up at him. Color was coming and going in his cheeks, making his agitation clear. "But you haven't proposed,"

Gideon looked startled. "I— What?"

"You haven't proposed," Sophie said with equanimity. "You did announce to the whole breakfast table that you intended to marry me, but that is not a proposal. That is only a declaration. A proposal is when you ask *me*."

"Now *that's* putting my brother in his place," said Gabriel, looking delighted in that manner that younger siblings did when their brothers or sisters were entirely set down.

"Oh, shush!" whispered Cecily, squeezing his hand hard. "I want to hear what Mr. Lightwood says!"

"Very well, then," said Gideon, in the decided (yet slightly terrified) manner of Saint George setting off to fight the dragon. "A proposal it shall be."

Sophie's eyes tracked him as he crossed the room toward her and knelt down at her feet. Life was an uncertain thing, and there were some moments one wished to remember, to imprint upon one's mind that the memory might be taken out later, like a flower pressed between the pages of a book, and admired and recollected anew.

She knew she would not want to forget the way Gideon reached for her hand with his own hand trembling, or the way he bit his lip before he spoke. "My dear Miss Collins," he said. "Please forgive me for my untoward outburst. It is simply that I have such—such strong esteem—no, not esteem, *adoration*—for you that I feel as if it must blaze from me every moment of the day. Ever since I came to this house, I have been struck more forcibly each day by your beauty, your courage, and your nobility. It is an honor I could never deserve but most earnestly aspire to if you could only be mine—that is, if you would consent to be my wife."

"Gracious," Sophie said, startled out of all countenance. "Have you been *practicing* that?"

Gideon blinked. "I assure you it was entirely extemporaneous."

"Well, it was lovely." Sophie squeezed his hands. "And yes. Yes, I love you, and yes, I will marry you, Gideon."

A brilliant smile broke out over his face, and he startled

both of them by reaching for her and kissing her soundly on the mouth. She held his face between her hands as they kissed—he tasted slightly of tea leaves, and his lips were soft and the kiss entirely sweet. Sophie floated in it, in the prism of the moment, feeling safe from all the rest of the world.

Until Bridget's voice broken in on her happiness, drifting lugubriously from the kitchen.

> *"On a Tuesday they were wed*
> *And by Friday they were dead*
> *And they buried them in the churchyard side by side,*
> *Oh, my love,*
> *And they buried them in the churchyard side by side."*

Breaking away from Gideon with some reluctance, Sophie rose to her feet and dusted off her dress. "Please forgive me, my dear Mr. Lightwood—I mean Gideon—but I must go and murder the cook. I shall be directly back."

"Ohhh," Cecily breathed. "That was *so* romantic!"

Gabriel took his hand away from the door and smiled down at her. His face quite changed when he smiled: all the sharp lines were softened, and his eyes went from the color of ice to the green of leaves in spring sunshine. "Are you crying, Miss Herondale?"

She blinked damp eyelashes, suddenly aware that her hand was still in his—she could still feel the soft pulse beat in his wrist against hers. He leaned toward her, and she caught the early-morning scent of him: tea and shaving soap—

She pulled away hastily, freeing her hand. "Thank you for

allowing me to listen," she said. "I must—I need to go to the library. There is something I must do before tomorrow."

His face crinkled in confusion. "Cecily—"

But she was already hurrying away down the corridor, without looking back.

To: Edmund and Branwen Herondale
Ravenscar Manor
West Riding, Yorkshire

Dear Mam and Dad,

I have started this letter to you so many times and never sent it. At first it was guilt. I knew I had been a willful, disobedient girl in leaving you, and I could not face the evidence of my wrongdoing in stark black letters on a page.

After that it was homesickness. I missed you both so much. I missed the rich green hills sweeping up from the manor, and the heather all purple in the summer, and Mam singing in the garden. It was cold here, all black and brown and gray, pea-soup fogs and choking air. I thought I might die of loneliness, but how could I tell you that? After all, it was what I had chosen.

And then it was sorrow. I had planned to come here and bring Will back with me, to make him see where his duty lay, and bring him home. But Will has his own ideas about duty, and honor, and the promises he has made. And I came to see that I could not bring someone home when they were already there. And I did not know how to tell you that.

And then it was happiness. That may seem so very

strange to you, as it did to me, that I would not be able to return home because I had found contentment. As I trained to become a Shadowhunter, I felt the stirring in my blood, the same stirring Mam always spoke of feeling every time we came from Welshpool into sight of the Dyfi Valley. With a seraph blade in my hand, I am more than just Cecily Herondale, youngest of three, daughter of good parents, someday to make an advantageous marriage and give the world children. I am Cecily Herondale, Shadowhunter, and mine is a high and glorious position.

Glory. Such an odd word, something women are not supposed to want, but is not our queen triumphant? Was not Queen Bess called Gloriana?

But how could I tell you I had chosen glory over peace? The hard-bought peace you left the Clave to provide for me? How could I say I was happy as a Shadowhunter without it causing you the gravest unhappiness? This is the life you turned away from, the life from whose dangers you sought to shelter Will and me and Ella. What could I tell you that would not break your hearts?

Now—now it is understanding. I have come to realize what it means to love someone more than you love yourself. I realize now that all you ever wanted was, not for me to be like you but to be happy. And you gave me—you gave us—a choice. I see those who have grown up in the Clave, and who never had a choice about what they wished to be, and I am grateful for what you did. To have chosen this life is a very different thing from having been born into it. The life of Jessamine Lovelace has taught me that.

And as for Will, and bringing him home: I know, Mam, you feared that the Shadowhunters would take all the love out of your gentle boy. But he is loved and loving. He has not changed. And he loves you, as do I. Remember me, for I will always remember you.

Your loving daughter,
Cecily

To: Members of the Clave of the Nephilim
From: Charlotte Branwell

My Dear Brothers and Sisters in Arms,

It is my sad duty to relate to you all that despite the fact that I have presented Consul Wayland with incontrovertible proof provided by one of my Shadowhunters that Mortmain, the gravest threat the Nephilim has faced in our times, is resident at Cadair Idris in Wales—our esteemed Consul has mysteriously decided to ignore this information. I myself regard knowledge of the location of our enemy and the opportunity to defeat his plans for our destruction as of the deepest importance.

By means provided to me by my husband, the renowned inventor Henry Branwell, the Shadowhunters at my disposal in the London Institute will be proceeding with utmost dispatch to Cadair Idris, there to lay down our lives in an attempt to stop Mortmain. I am most grieved to leave the Institute undefended, but if Consul Wayland can be roused to any action at all, he is most welcome to send guards to defend a deserted building. There are but nine of our number, three of them not even Shadowhunters but brave mundanes trained by us at the Institute who have volunteered to fight beside us. I cannot say that our hopes at this time are high, but I believe the attempt must be made.

Obviously I cannot compel any of you. As Consul Wayland has reminded me, I am not in a position to command the forces of the Shadowhunters, but I would be most obliged if any of you who agree with me that Mortmain must be fought and fought now will come to the London Institute tomorrow at midday and render us your assistance.

Yours truly,
Charlotte Branwell, head of the London Institute

18

For This Alone

For this alone on Death I wreak
The wrath that garners in my heart:
He put our lives so far apart
We cannot hear each other speak.
—Alfred, Lord Tennyson, "In Memoriam A.H.H."

Tessa stood at the edge of a precipice in a country she did not know. The hills about her were green, dropping off sharply into cliffs that sheered down toward a blue sea. Seabirds wheeled and cawed above her. A gray path wound like a snake along the edge of the cliff top. Just ahead of her, on the path, stood Will.

He wore black gear, and over it a long black riding coat, spattered with mud at the hem as if he had been walking a long way. He was without hat or gloves, and his dark hair was tousled by the wind off the sea. The wind lifted Tessa's hair as well, bringing the scent of salt

and brine, of the wet things that grow at the edge of the sea, a smell
that reminded her of her sea voyage on the Main.

"Will!" she called out. There was something so lonely about the
figure he cut, like Tristan watching across the Irish Sea for the ship
that would bear Isolde back to him. Will did not turn at the sound of
her voice, only raised his arms, his coat lifting in the wind, sweeping
out behind him like wings.

Fear rose up in her heart. Isolde had come for Tristan, but it had
been too late. He had died of grief. "Will!" she called again.

He stepped forward, off the cliff. She raced to the edge and looked
down, but there was nothing there, only plunging gray-blue water
and white surf. The tide seemed to carry his voice to her with each
surge of water. "Awake, Tessa. Awake."

"Awake, Miss Gray. Miss Gray!"

Tessa jerked upright. She had fallen asleep in the chair by
the fireplace in her small prison; a coarse blue blanket was
drawn over her, though she did not remember procuring it.
The room burned with torchlight and the coals of the fire were
low. It was impossible to tell if it was day or night.

Mortmain stood before her, and beside him was an automaton. It was one of the more humanoid that Tessa had seen.
It was even clothed, as not many of them were, this one in a
military tunic and trousers. The clothes made the head that
rose above the stiff collar look even more uncanny, with its
too-smooth features and bald metallic scalp. And its eyes—she
knew they were glass and crystal, the irises red in the firelight,
but the way they seemed to fix on her—

"You're cold," Mortmain said.

Tessa exhaled, and her breath came out in a white puff.

"The warmth of your hospitality leaves something to be desired."

He smiled, thin-lipped. "Very amusing." He himself was wearing a heavy astrakhan coat over a gray suit, ever the businessman. "Miss Gray, I do not wake you lightly. I came because I wish you to see what your kind assistance with my father's memories has allowed me to accomplish." He gestured proudly at the automaton by his side.

"Another automaton?" Tessa said without interest.

"How rude of me." Mortmain's eyes flicked to the creature. "Introduce yourself."

The creature's mouth opened; Tessa caught a flash of brass. It spoke. "I am Armaros," it said. "For a billion years I rode the winds of the great abysses between the worlds. I fought Jonathan Shadowhunter on the plains of Brocelind. For a thousand more years I lay trapped within the Pyxis. Now my master has freed me and I serve him."

Tessa rose, the blanket sliding to her feet, unheeded. The automaton was watching her. Its eyes—its eyes were full of a dark intelligence, a consciousness that no automaton she had seen before had ever possessed.

"What is this?" she said in a whisper.

"An automaton body animated by a demon spirit. Downworlders already have their ways of capturing demon energies and using them. I used them myself to power the automatons you've seen before. But Armaros and his brothers are different. They are demons with the carapaces of automatons. They can think and reason. They are not easily outwitted. And they are very difficult to kill."

Armaros reached across its body—Tessa could not help

but note that it moved fluidly, smoothly, without the jerkiness of the automatons she had seen before. It moved like a person. It drew the sword that hung at its side and handed it to Mortmain. The blade was covered in the runes that Tessa had become so familiar with over the last months, the runes that decorated the blades of all Shadowhunter weapons. The runes that made them Shadowhunter weapons. The runes that were deadly to demons. Armaros should barely have been able to look upon the blade, much less hold it.

Her stomach clenched. The demon gave the sword to Mortmain, who handled it with the precision of a longtime naval officer. He spun the blade, swept it forward, and drove it into the demon's chest.

There was a sound of tearing metal. Tessa was used to seeing automatons crumple when attacked, or spurt black fluid, or stagger. But the demon stood its ground, unblinking and unmoving, like a lizard in the sun. Mortmain twisted the hilt savagely, then jerked the weapon free.

Its blade crumbled to ash, like a log burned away in a fire.

"You see," said Mortmain. "They are an army designed to destroy Shadowhunters."

Armaros was the only automaton Tessa had ever seen smile; she did not even know their faces had been built to accomplish such a purpose. The demon said, "They have destroyed many of my kind. It will be a pleasure to kill them all."

Tessa swallowed hard but tried not to let the Magister see it. His gaze was flicking back and forth from her to the demon automaton, and it was hard for her to say which he looked more delighted to lay eyes on. She wanted to scream, to throw herself at him and claw his face. But the invisible wall lay between them, shimmering slightly, and she knew she could not breach it.

Oh, you are to be more than his bride, Miss Gray, Mrs. Black had said. *You are to be the ruin of the Nephilim. That is why you were created.*

"The Shadowhunters will not be so easily destroyed," she said. "I have seen them cut apart your automatons. Perhaps these cannot be felled by their runed weapons, but any blade can shear metal and cut wires."

Mortmain shrugged. "Shadowhunters are not used to battling creatures against whom their runed weapons are useless. It will slow them. And there are countless of these automatons. It will be like trying to beat back the tide." He cocked his head to the side. "You see, now, the genius of what I have invented? But I must thank you, Miss Gray, for that last piece of the puzzle. I thought perhaps even you might be . . . admiring . . . of what we have created together."

Admiring? She looked in his eyes for mockery, but there was something of a sincere question there, curiosity mixed with the coldness. She thought of how long it must have been since he had had the praise of another human being, and took a deep breath.

"You are obviously a great inventor," she said.

Mortmain smiled, pleased.

Tessa was aware of the gaze of the mechanical demon on her, its tension and readiness, but she was more aware of Mortmain. Her heart was beating hard inside her chest. She seemed, as she had in her dream, poised on the edge of a precipice. To speak to Mortmain like this was chancy, and she would either fall or fly. But she must take the chance. "I see why you have brought me here," she said. "And it is not just because of your father's secrets."

There was anger in his eyes, but also a certain confusion. She was not behaving as he had expected her to behave. "What do you mean?"

"You are lonely," she said. "You have surrounded yourself with creatures that are not real, that do not live. We see our own souls in the eyes of others. How long has it been since you have seen that you have a soul?"

Mortmain's eyes narrowed. "I had a soul. It has been burned away by what I have dedicated my life to: the pursuit of justice and recompense."

"Do not seek revenge and call it justice."

The demon gave a low chuckle, though there was contempt in it, as if he were watching the antics of a kitten. "You would let her speak to you like that, Master?" he said. "I can cut out her tongue for you, silence her forever."

"It would serve nothing to mutilate her. She has powers you know not of," said Mortmain, his eyes still on Tessa. "There is an old saying in China—perhaps your beloved fiancé familiarized you with it—that states. 'A man may not live under the same Heaven with the slayer of his father.' I shall erase the Shadowhunters from under Heaven; they will not longer live upon the earth. Do not seek to appeal to my better nature, Tessa, for I have none."

Tessa could not help herself—she thought of *A Tale of Two Cities*, of Lucie Manette's appeals to Sydney Carton's better nature. She had always thought of Will as Sydney, consumed by sin and despair against his own better knowledge, even against his own desire. But Will was a good man, a much better one than Carton had ever been. And Mortmain was barely a man at all. It was not his better nature she appealed to but his vanity: All men thought of themselves as good in the end, surely. No one believed themselves a villain. She took a breath. "Surely that is not so—surely you might again be worthy and good. You have done what you set out to do. You have brought life and intelligence to these—these Infernal Devices of yours. You have created that which might destroy the Shadowhunters. All your life you have pursued justice because you believed the Shadowhunters were corrupt and vicious. Now, if you stay your hand, you win the greatest victory. You show that you are better than they."

She searched Mortmain's face with her eyes. Surely there was some hesitation there—surely the thin lips were shaking slightly, surely there was the tension of doubt in his shoulders?

His mouth quirked into a smile. "You think, then, that I can be a better man? And if I were to do as you say, to stay my hand, you would have me believe that you would stay with me out of admiration, that you would not return to the Shadowhunters?"

"Why, yes, Mr. Mortmain. I swear it." She swallowed against the bitterness in her throat. If she had to remain with Mortmain in order to save Will and Jem, to save Charlotte and Henry and Sophie, she would do it. "I believe you can find your better self; I believe we all can."

His thin lips turned up at the corners. "It is afternoon already, Miss Gray," he said. "I did not wish to wake you earlier. Come with me now, outside the mountain. Come and see this day's work, for there is something that I wish to show you."

A finger of ice touched her spine. She straightened. "And what is that?"

His smile spread across his face. "What I have been waiting for."

To: *Consul Josiah Wayland*
From: *Inquisitor Victor Whitelaw*

Josiah: Forgive my informality, for I write in haste. I am certain that this will not be the only letter you will receive on this subject; in fact, it is likely not even the first. I myself have already received many. Each touches upon the same question that burns in my mind: Is Charlotte Branwell's information correct? For if so, it seems to me that there is a more than likely chance that the Magister is indeed in Wales. I know of your doubts in the veracity of William Herondale, but we both knew his father. A hasty soul, and too greatly ruled by his passions, but a more honest man you could not find. I do not think the younger Herondale a liar.

Regardless, as a result of Charlotte's message, the Clave is in chaos. I insist that we hold a dedicated Council meeting immediately. If we do not, the trust of the Shadowhunters in their Consul and their Inquisitor will be irrevocably eroded. I leave the announcement of the meeting in your hands, but this is not a request. Send out the call for the Council, or I shall resign my position and let it be known why.

Victor Whitelaw

Will was awoken by screams.

Years of training made themselves known instantly: He was

on the floor in a crouch before he was even properly awake. Glancing around, he saw that the small room of the inn was empty save for himself, and the furniture—narrow bed and plain deal table, barely visible in the shadows—was undisturbed.

The screams came again, louder. They were emanating from outside the window. Will rose to his feet, crossed the room soundlessly, and twitched one of the curtains back to look out.

He barely remembered walking into town, leading Balios behind him, the horse clopping slowly in exhaustion. A small Welsh town, like other small Welsh towns, unremarkable in any particular way. He had found the local public house easily and turned Balios over to the ministrations of the stableboy, ordering the horse rubbed down and fed a hot bran mash to revive him. The fact that he spoke Welsh had seemed to relax the innkeeper, and he had been shown quickly to a private room, where he had collapsed almost immediately, fully clothed, onto the bed and fallen into dreamless sleep.

The moon was bright above, its position indicating that it was not yet late in the evening. A gray haze seemed to hang over the town. For a moment Will thought it was mist. Then, inhaling, he realized it was smoke. Patches of bright red leaped up among the houses in the town. He narrowed his eyes. Figures were darting back and forth within the shadows. More screams—a flash that could only be blades—

He was out the door with his boots half-laced in barely a moment, seraph blade in hand. He pounded down the steps and into the main room of the inn. It was dark and cold—there was no fire, and several of the windows had been smashed in, letting in the chill night air. Glass littered the floor like chunks of ice. The door hung open, and as Will slipped through it, he saw that the upper hinges were nearly torn out of their mooring, as if someone had tried to rip the door free. . . .

He slipped out the door and round the side of the inn, where the stables were. The smell of smoke hung thicker here, and he darted ahead—and nearly tripped over a humped figure on the ground. He dropped to his knees. It was the stable-boy, his throat cut, the ground under him a sodden mess of blood and dirt. His eyes were open, staring, his skin already cold. Will swallowed back bile and straightened up.

He moved toward the stables mechanically, his mind racing over the possibilities. A demon attack? Or had he stumbled into the middle of something non-supernatural, some feud between townsfolk, or God only knew what? No one seemed to be looking for him in particular, that much was clear.

He could hear Balios's anxious whickering as he let himself into the stable. It appeared undisturbed, from the plaster ceiling to the cobbled floor crisscrossed with drainage ditches. No other horses were stabled there that night, which was lucky, for the moment he opened the stall door, Balios plunged forward, nearly knocking Will over. Will was only just able to dart out of the way as the horse hurtled past him and out the door.

"*Balios!*" Will swore and took off after his horse, pounding around the side of the inn and into the main road of the town.

He stopped dead. The street was in chaos. Bodies lay crumpled, discarded at the side of the road like so much rubbish. Homes stood with their doors ripped open, windows smashed in. People were running in and out of the shadows haphazardly, screaming and calling for one another. Several of the houses were burning. As Will stared in horror, he saw a family spill from the door of a burning house, the father in a nightshirt, coughing and choking, a woman behind him holding the hand of a small girl.

They had barely staggered into the street when shapes rose up out of the shadows. Moonlight sparked off metal.

Automatons.

They moved fluidly, without faltering or jerkiness. They wore clothes—a motley assortment of military uniforms, some recognizable to Will and some not. But their faces were bare metal, as were their hands, which gripped long-bladed swords. There were three of them; one, in a torn red army tunic, moved ahead, laughing—*laughing?*—as the father of the family tried to push his wife and daughter behind him, stumbling over the bloody cobblestones of the road.

It was all over in moments, too fast even for Will to move. Blades flashed, and three more bodies joined the heaps in the streets.

"That's it," said the automaton in the ragged tunic. "Burn their houses and smoke them out like rats. Kill them when they run—" It raised its head, and seemed to see Will. Even across the space that separated them, Will felt the force of that gaze.

Will raised his seraph blade. *"Nakir."*

The shimmer of the blade blazed up, illuminating the street, a beam of white light amid the red of flames. Through blood and fire Will saw the automaton in the red tunic stride toward him. A longsword was gripped in its left hand. The hand was metal, jointed, articulate; it curved around the hilt of the blade like a human hand.

"Nephilim," the creature said, stopping a mere foot from Will. "We did not expect your kind here."

"Clearly," Will said. He took a step forward and rammed the seraph blade into the automaton's chest.

There was a faint sizzling sound, as of bacon frying in a pan. As the automaton gazed down in bemusement, Nakir crumbled away to ash, leaving Will's hand clutched around a vanished hilt.

The automaton chuckled, raising its gaze to Will. Its eyes crackled with life and intelligence, and Will knew with a sinking in his heart that he was looking at something he had never seen before—not just a creature that could turn a seraph blade to ash but a kind of machine that had will and cleverness and strategy enough to burn a village to the ground in order to murder the inhabitants as they fled.

"And now you see," said the demon, for that was what it was, standing before him. "Nephilim, all these years you have driven us from this world with your runed blades. Now we have bodies that your weapons will not work on, and this world *will be ours*."

Will sucked in his breath as the demon raised the longsword. He took a step back— The blade swung over and down— He ducked away, just as something hurtled alongside him in the road, something huge and black that reared and kicked and knocked the automaton aside.

Balios.

Will reached up, blindly scrabbling for his horse's mane. The demon sprang up from the mud and leaped for him, blade flashing, just as Balios bolted forward, Will swinging himself up and over onto the horse's back. They plunged down the cobblestone street together, Will crouched down low on Balios, the wind tearing through his hair and drying the wetness on his face—whether it was blood or tears, he didn't know.

Tessa sat on the floor of her room in Mortmain's stronghold, staring numbly into the fire.

The flames played over her hands, the blue dress she wore. Both were stained with blood. She did not know how it had happened; the skin at her wrist was ragged, and she had some memory of an automaton seizing her there, tearing her skin with its sharp metal fingers as she tried to break away.

She could not rid her mind of the images that dominated it—the memories of the destruction of the village in the valley. She had been taken there blindfolded, carried by automatons, before being unceremoniously dumped onto an outcropping of gray rock with a view directly down into the town.

"Watch," Mortmain had said, not looking at her, only gloating. "Watch, Miss Gray, and then speak to me of redemption."

Tessa had stood prisoned, an automaton holding her from behind, a hand over her mouth, Mortmain murmuring softly under his breath the things he would do to her if she dared to look away from the village. She had watched helplessly as the automatons had marched into the town, cutting down innocent men and women in the streets. The moon had risen tinged red as the clockwork army had methodically set fire to house after house, slaughtering the families as they poured forth in confusion and terror.

And Mortmain had laughed.

"You see now," he had said. "These creatures, these creations, they are capable of thought and reason and strategy.

Like humans. And yet they are indestructible. Look, there, at that fool with the rifle."

Tessa had not wanted to look, but she had had no choice. She had watched, dry-eyed and grim, as a distant figure had raised a rifle to defend himself. The blasts had knocked some of the automatons back but had not disabled them. They had kept coming at him, knocking his rifle from his hand, pushing him down into the street.

And then they had torn him apart.

"Demons," Mortmain had murmured. "They are savage and they love to destroy."

"Please," Tessa had choked. "Please, no more, no more. I shall do whatever you desire, but please, spare the village."

Mortmain had chuckled dryly. "Clockwork creatures have no hearts, Miss Gray," he'd said. "They do not have mercy, any more than fire or water do. You might as well beg a flood or a forest fire to cease its destruction."

"I am not begging them," she'd said. From the corner of her eye, she'd thought she'd seen a black horse pounding through the streets of the village, a rider on its back. Someone escaping the carnage, she'd prayed. "I am begging *you*."

He'd turned his cold eyes on her, and they'd been as empty as the sky. "There is no mercy in my heart either. You appealed, tiresomely, to my better self earlier. I brought you here to show you the futility of such action. I have no better self to appeal to; it was burned away years ago."

"But I have done what you asked," she'd said desperately. "There is no need for this, not for me—"

"It is not for you," he'd said, flicking his gaze away from her. "The automatons had to be tested before they were sent into battle. That is simple science. They have intelligence now. Strategy. Nothing can stand before them."

"They will turn on you, then."

"They will not. Their lives are linked to mine. If I die, so are they destroyed. They must protect me to endure." His look had been cold and faraway. "Enough. I brought you here to show you that I am what I am, and you will accept it. Your clockwork angel protects your life, but the lives of other innocents are in my hands—in *your* hands. Do not test me, and there will not be a second such village. I wish to hear no more tiresome protests."

Your clockwork angel protects your life. She put her hand on it now, feeling the familiar ticking beneath her fingers. She closed her eyes, but terrible images lived behind her eyelids. She saw in her mind the Nephilim driven before the automatons as the villagers had been, Jem torn apart by clockwork monsters, Will stabbed through with metal blades, Henry and Charlotte burning . . .

Her hand tightened savagely around the angel, and she tore it from her throat, casting it to the uneven rock floor just as a log fell in the fire, sending up a spitting column of red sparks. In their illumination she saw the palm of her left hand, saw the faint scar of the burn she had given herself the day she had told Will she was engaged to Jem.

As it had then, her hand went to the fireplace poker. She lifted it, feeling its weight in her hand. The fire had climbed higher. She saw the world through a golden haze as she raised the poker and brought it down on the clockwork angel.

Iron though the poker was, it burst into metallic powder, a cloud of shining filaments that sifted to the floor, dusting the surface of the clockwork angel, which lay, untouched and undamaged, on the ground before her knees.

And then the angel began to shift and change. Its wings trembled, and its closed eyelids opened on bits of whitish quartz. From them poured thin beams of whitish light. Like in paintings of the star over Bethlehem, the light rose and rose, radiating spikes of light. Slowly it began to coalesce into a shape—the form of an angel.

It was a shimmering blur of light so bright, it was difficult to look at directly. Tessa could see, through the light, the faint outline of something like a man. She could see eyes that were without iris or pupil—inset bits of crystal that gleamed in the firelight. The angel's wings were broad, spreading out from its shoulders, each feather tipped with gleaming metal. Its hands were folded over the hilt of a graceful sword.

Its blank shining eyes rested on her. *Why do you try to destroy me?* Its voice was sweet, echoing in her mind like music. *I protect you.*

She thought of Jem suddenly, propped on his bed of pillows, his face pale and gleaming. *There is more to life than living.* "It is not you I seek to destroy, but myself."

But why would you do that? Life is a gift.

"I seek to do right," she said. "In keeping me alive you are allowing great evil to exist."

Evil. The musical voice was thoughtful. *I have been so long in my clockwork prison that I have forgotten good and evil.*

"Clockwork prison?" Tessa whispered. "But how can an angel be prisoned?"

It was John Thaddeus Shade who imprisoned me. He caught my soul inside a spell and trapped it within this mechanical body.

"Like the Pyxis," Tessa said. "Only entrapping an angel instead of a demon."

I am an angel of the divine, said the angel, hovering before her. *I am brother to the Sijil, Kurabi, and the Zurah, the Fravashis and Dakinis.*

"And—is this your true form? Is this what you look like?"

You see here only a fraction of what I am. In my true form I am deadly glory. Mine was the freedom of Heaven, before I was trapped and bound to you.

"I am sorry," she whispered.

You are not the one to blame. You did not imprison me. Our spirits are bound, it is true, but even as I protected you in the womb, I knew you were blameless.

"My guardian angel."

Few can claim a single angel who guards them. But you can.

"I don't want to claim you," Tessa said. "I want to die on my own terms, not be forced to live on Mortmain's."

I cannot let you die. The angel's voice was full of grief. Tessa was reminded of Jem's violin, playing out the music of his heart. *It is my mandate.*

Tessa raised her head. The firelight struck through the angel like sunlight through crystal, casting a radiance of color against the walls of the cave. This was no foul contraption; this was goodness, twisted and bent to Mortmain's will, but in its nature divine. "When you were an angel," she said, "what was your name?"

My name, said the angel, *was Ithuriel.*

"Ithuriel," Tessa whispered, and held out her hand to the angel, as if she could reach him, comfort him somehow. But her fingers met only empty air. The angel shimmered and faded, leaving behind only a glow, a starburst of light against the inside of her eyelids.

A wave of cold struck Tessa, and she jerked upright, her eyes flying open. She was half-lying on the cold stone floor in front of the nearly dead fire. The room was dark, barely lit by the reddish embers in the grate. The poker was where it had been before. Her hand flew to her throat—and found the clockwork angel there.

A dream. Tessa's heart fell. It had all been a dream. There was no angel to bathe her in its light. There was only this cold room, the encroaching darkness, and the clockwork angel steadily ticking down the minutes to the end of everything in the world.

Will stood atop Cadair Idris, the reins of his horse in his hand.

As he had ridden toward Dolgellau, he had seen the massive wall of Cadair Idris towering above the Mawddach estuary, and the breath had gone out of him in a gasp—he was here. He had climbed this mountain before, as a child, with his father, and those memories stayed with him as he left the Dinas Mawddwy road and pounded toward the mountain on the back of Balios, who seemed still to be fleeing the flames of the village they had left behind them. They had continued through a weedy tarn—the silvery sea could be seen in one direction, and the peak of Snowdon in the other—up to the Nant Cadair valley. The village of Dolgellau below, sparkling with occasional light, made a pretty picture, but Will was not admiring the view. The Night Vision rune he had given himself allowed him to track the footsteps of the clockwork creatures. There were enough of them that the ground was torn where they had walked down the mountain, and he followed with a pounding heart the path of ruination toward the peak of the mountain.

Their tracks led up past a tumble of massive boulders Will remembered were called the moraine. They formed a partial wall that protected Cwm Cau, a small valley atop the mountain in whose heart rested Llyn Cau, a clear glacial lake. The tracks of the clockwork army led from the edge of the lake—

And vanished.

Will stood, looking down at the cold, clear waters. In the daylight, he recalled, this view was magnificent: Llyn Cau pure blue, surrounded by green grass, and the sun touching the razor-sharp edges of Mynydd Pencoed, the cliffs surrounding the lake. He felt a million miles from London.

The reflection of the moon gleamed up at him from the water. He sighed. The water lapped gently at the edge of the lake, but it could not erase the marks of the automatons' tracks. It was clear where they had come from. He reached back and patted Balios's neck.

"Wait for me here," he said. "And if I do not return, take yourself back to the Institute. They will be glad to see you again, old boy."

The horse whickered gently and bit at his sleeve, but Will only drew in his breath and waded into Llyn Cau. The cold liquid lapped up over his boots and hit his trousers, soaking through to freeze his skin. He gasped with the shock of it.

"Wet again," he said glumly, and plunged forward into the icy waters of the lake. They seemed to pull him in, like quicksand—he barely had time to gasp in a breath before the freezing water dragged him down into darkness.

* * *

To: *Charlotte Branwell*
From: *Consul Wayland*

Mrs. Branwell,

You are relieved of your position as head of the Institute. I could speak of my disappointment with you, or the broken faith that exists between us now. But words, in the face of a betrayal of the magnitude of that which you have offered me, are futile. On my arrival in London tomorrow, I will expect you and your husband to have already departed the Institute and removed your belongings. Failure to comply with this request will be met with the harshest penalties available under the Law.

Josiah Wayland, Consul of the Clave

19

To Lie and Burn

Now I will burn you back, I will burn you through,
Though I am damned for it we two will lie
And burn.
—Charlotte Mew, "In Nunhead Cemetery"

It was dark for only moments. The icy water sucked Will down, and then he was falling—he curled in on himself just as the ground rose up to slam into him, knocking the breath from his body.

He choked and rolled over onto his stomach, pulling himself to a kneeling position, his hair and clothes streaming water. He reached for his witchlight, then dropped his hand; he didn't want to illuminate anything if that might call attention to him. The Night Vision rune would have to do.

It was enough to show him that he was in a rocky cavern.

If he looked above him, he could see the swirling waters of the lake, held in abeyance as if by glass, and a blurred bit of moonlight. Tunnels led off the cavern, with no markings to show where they might lead. He rose to his feet and blindly chose the leftmost tunnel, moving carefully ahead into the shadowy darkness.

The tunnels were wide, with smooth floors that showed no mark where the clockwork creatures might have passed. The sides were rough volcanic rock. He remembered climbing Cadair Idris with his father, years ago. There were many legends about the mountain: that it had been a chair for a giant, who had sat upon it and regarded the stars; that King Arthur and his knights slept beneath the hill, waiting for the time when Britain would awake and need them again; that anyone who spent the night on the mountainside would awake a poet or a madman.

If only it was known, Will thought as he turned through the curve of a tunnel and emerged into a larger cave, how strange the truth of the matter was.

The cave was wide, opening out to a greater space at the far end of the room, where a dim light gleamed. Here and there Will caught a silvery glint that he thought was water running in streams down the black walls, but on closer examination it turned out to be veins of crystalline quartz.

Will moved toward the dim light. He found that his heart was beating rapidly inside his chest, and he tried to breathe steadily to quell it. He knew what was speeding his pulse. Tessa. If Mortmain had her, then she was here—close. Somewhere in this honeycomb of tunnels he might find her.

He heard Jem's voice in his head, as if his *parabatai* stood at his side, advising him. He had always said that Will rushed toward the end of a mission rather than proceeding in a measured manner, and that one must look at the next step on the path ahead, rather than the mountain in the distance, or one would never reach one's goal. Will closed his eyes for a moment. He knew that Jem was right, but it was hard to remember, when the goal that he sought was the girl that he loved.

He opened his eyes and moved toward the dim light at the far end of the cavern. The ground beneath him was smooth, without rocks or pebbles, and veined like marble. The light ahead flared up—and Will came to a dead stop, only his years of Shadowhunter training keeping him from tumbling forward to his death.

For the rock floor ended in a sheer drop. He was standing on an outcropping, looking down at a round amphitheater. It was full of automatons. They were silent, unmoving and still, like mechanical toys that had wound down. They were dressed, as those in the village had been, in scraps of military uniforms, lined up one by one, for all the world like life-size lead soldiers.

In the center of the room was a raised stone platform, and on the table lay another automaton, like a corpse on an autopsy table. Its head was bare metal, but there was pale human skin stretched taut over the rest of its body—and on that skin was inked runes.

As he stared, Will recognized them, one after another: Memory, Agility, Speed, Night Vision. They would never work, of course, not on a contraption made of metal and human skin. It might fool Shadowhunters from a distance, but . . .

But what if he used Shadowhunter skin? a voice in Will's mind whispered. *What could he create then? How mad is he, and when will he stop?* The thought, and the sight of the runes of Heaven inscribed on such a monstrous creature, twisted Will's stomach; he jerked away from the edge of the outcropping and stumbled back, fetching up against a cold rock wall, his hands clammy with sweat.

He saw the village again in his mind, the dead bodies in the streets, heard the mechanical hiss of the clockwork demon as it spoke to him:

All these years you have driven us from this world with your runed blades. Now we have bodies that your weapons will not work on, and this world will be ours.

Rage poured through Will like fire in his veins. He tore himself away from the wall and plunged headlong down a narrow tunnel, away from the cavern room. As he went, he thought he heard a sound behind him—a whirring, as if the mechanism of a great watch were starting up—but when he turned, he saw nothing, only the smooth walls of the cave, and the unmoving shadows.

The tunnel he was following narrowed as he walked, until eventually he was squeezing sideways past an outcropping of quartz-laden rock. If it narrowed further, he knew, he would have to turn around and go back to the cavern; the thought made him push himself forward with renewed vigor, and he slid forward, almost falling, as the passage suddenly opened into a wider corridor.

It was almost like a hallway at the Institute, only made all of smoothed stone, with torches at intervals set into metal brackets. Beside each torch was an arched door, also of stone. The first two stood open on empty dark rooms.

Beyond the third door was Tessa.

Will did not see her immediately when he walked into the room. The stone door swung partly shut behind him, but he found that he was not in darkness. There was a flickering light—the dimming flames of a blaze in a stone fireplace at the far end of the room. To his astonishment it was furnished like a room in an inn, with a bed and washstand, rugs on the ground, even curtains on the walls, though they hung over bare stone, not windows.

In front of the fire was a slim shadow, crouched on the ground. Will's hand went automatically to the hilt of the dagger at his waist—and then the shadow turned, hair slipping over her shoulder, and he saw her face.

Tessa.

His hand fell away from the dagger as his heart lurched inside his chest with an impossible, painful force. He saw her expression change: curiosity, astonishment, disbelief. She rose to her feet, her skirts tumbling around her as she straightened, and he saw her hold her hand out.

"Will?" she said.

It was like a key turning the lock of a door, releasing him; he started forward. There had never been a greater distance than the distance that separated him from Tessa at that moment. It was a large room; at the moment, the distance between London and Cadair Idris seemed nothing to the distance across it. He felt a shudder, as of some sort of resistance, as he crossed the room. He saw Tessa hold out her hand, her mouth shaping words—and then she was in his arms, the breath half-knocked out of both of them as they collided with each other.

She was up on her toes, her arms around his shoulders,

whispering his name: "Will, Will, *Will*—" He buried his face against her neck, where her thick hair curled; she smelled of smoke and violet water. He clutched her even more tightly as her fingers curled against the back of his collar, and they clung together. For just that moment the grief that had clenched him like an iron fist since Jem's death seemed to relax and he could breathe.

He thought of the hell he had been in since he'd left London—the days of riding without stopping, the sleepless nights. Blood and loss and pain and fighting. All to bring him here. To Tessa.

"Will," she said again, and he looked down into her tearstained face. There was a bruise across her cheekbone. Someone had hit her there, and his heart swelled with rage. He would find out who it was, and he would kill them. If it was Mortmain, he would kill him only after he had burned his monstrous laboratory to the ground, that the madman might see the ruin of all his creation—"Will," Tessa said again, interrupting his thoughts. She sounded almost breathless. "Will, you *idiot*."

His romantic notions came to a screeching halt like a hackney cab in traffic on Fleet Street. "I— What?"

"Oh, Will," she said. Her lips were trembling; she looked as if she couldn't decide whether to laugh or cry. "Do you remember when you told me that the handsome young gentleman who came to rescue you was never wrong, not even if he said the sky was purple and made of hedgehogs?"

"The first time I ever saw you. Yes."

"Oh, my Will." She drew gently away from his embrace, smoothing a tangled lock of hair behind her ear. Her eyes remained fixed on his. "I cannot imagine how you came to find me, how difficult it must have been. It is incredible. But—do you really think Mortmain would leave me unguarded in a room with an open door?" She turned away and moved a few feet forward, then stopped abruptly. "Here," she said, and raised her hand, spreading her fingers wide. "The air is as solid as a wall here. This is a prison, Will, and now you are in it alongside me."

He moved to stand beside her, already knowing what he would find. He recalled the resistance he had felt as he crossed the room. The air rippled slightly when he touched it with his finger but was harder than a frozen lake. "I know this configuration," he said. "The Clave uses a version of it sometimes." His hand curled itself into a fist, and he slammed it against the solid air, hard enough to bruise the bones in his hand. *"Uffern gwaedlyd,"* he swore in Welsh. "All the bloody way across the country to get to you, and I can't even do *this* right. The moment I saw you, all I could think of was running to you. By the Angel, Tessa—"

"Will!" She caught at his arm. "Don't you *dare* apologize. Do you understand what it means to me that you are here? It is like a miracle or the direct intervention of Heaven, for I had been praying to see the faces of those I cared for again before I died." She spoke simply, straightforwardly—it was one of the things he had always loved about Tessa, that she did not hide or dissemble, but spoke her mind without embellishment. "When I was in the Dark House, there was no one who cared enough to search for me. When you found me, it was an accident. But now—"

"Now I have condemned us both to the same fate," he said

in a low voice. He drew a dagger from his belt and drove it against the invisible wall before him. The runed silver blade of the dagger shattered, and Will cast the broken hilt aside and cursed again, under his breath.

Tessa put a light hand on his shoulder. "We are not condemned," she said. "Surely you have not come by yourself, Will. Henry, or Jem, will find us. From the other side of the wall, we can be freed. I have seen how Mortmain does it, and . . ."

Will did not know what happened then. His expression must have changed at the mention of Jem's name, for he saw some of the color leave her face. Her hand tightened on his arm.

"Tessa," he said. "I *am* alone."

The word "alone" came out broken, as if he could taste the bitterness of loss on his tongue and struggled to speak around it.

"Jem?" she said. It was more than a question. Will said nothing; his voice seemed to have fled. He had thought to spirit her from this place before he told her about Jem, had imagined telling her somewhere safe, somewhere where there would be space and time to comfort her. He knew now he had been a fool to think it, to imagine that what he had lost would not be written all over his face. The remaining color drained from her skin; it was like watching a fire flicker and go out. "No," she whispered.

"Tessa . . ."

She took a step back from him, shaking her head. "No, it's not possible. I would have known—it can't be possible."

He reached out a hand to her. "Tess—"

She had begun to shake violently. "No," she said again. "No, *don't* say it. If you don't say it, it won't be true. It can't be true. It isn't fair."

"I'm sorry," he whispered.

Her face crumpled, shattered like a dam under too much pressure. She sank to her knees, folding in on herself. Her arms went around her body. She was holding herself tightly, as if she could keep from breaking apart. Will felt a fresh wave of the helpless agony he had experienced in the courtyard of the Green Man. What had he done? He had come here to save her, but instead of saving her he had only succeeded in inflicting agony. It was as if he were truly cursed—capable only of bringing suffering to those he loved.

"I am sorry," he said again, with all his heart in the words. "So sorry. I would have died for him if I could."

At that, she looked up. He braced himself for the accusation in her eyes, but it was not there. Instead she reached up her hand to him silently. In wonder and surprise he took it, and let her draw him down until he was kneeling opposite her.

Her face was streaked with tears, surrounded by the tumble of her hair, outlined in gold by the firelight. "I would have too," she said. "Oh, Will. This is all my fault. He threw away his life for me. If he had taken the drug more sparingly—if he had allowed himself to rest and be ill instead of pretending good health for my sake—"

"No!" He took her by the shoulders, turning her toward him. "It's not your fault. No one could imagine that it was—"

She shook her head. "How can you bear to have me near you?" she said in despair. "I took your *parabatai* from you. And now we will both die here. Because of me."

"Tessa," he whispered, shocked. He could not remember

the last time he had been in this position, the last time he had had to comfort someone whose heart was broken, and had genuinely been *allowed* to, rather than forcing himself to turn away. He felt as clumsy as he had as a child, dropping knives from his hands before Jem had taught him how to use them. He cleared his throat. "Tessa, come here." He drew her toward him, until he was sitting on the ground and she was leaning against him, her head on his shoulder, his fingers threading through her hair. He could feel her body shaking against him, but she did not pull away. Instead she clung to him, as if truly his presence gave her comfort.

And if he thought of how warm she was in his arms or the feel of her breath on his skin, it was only for a moment, and he could pretend that it wasn't at all.

Tessa's grief, like a storm, spent itself slowly over the course of hours. She wept, and Will held her and did not let go, except for once when he rose and built up the fire. He returned swiftly and sat down beside her again, their backs against the invisible wall. She touched the place on his shoulder where her tears had soaked through the fabric.

"I'm sorry," she said. She couldn't count the number of times she'd told him she was sorry over the past hours, as they'd shared the tales of what had happened to them since their separation at the Institute. He'd spoken to her of his farewell to Jem and Cecily, his ride across the countryside, the moment he had realized Jem was gone. She'd told him of what Mortmain had demanded of her, that she Change into his father, and give him the last bit of the puzzle that would turn his automaton army into an unstoppable force.

"You have nothing to be sorry for, Tess," Will said now. He was looking toward the fire, the only light in the room. It painted him in shades of gold and black. The shadows under his eyes were violet, the angle of his cheekbones and collarbones sharply outlined. "You have suffered, just as I have. Seeing that village destroyed—"

"We were both there at the same time," she said, wonderingly. "If I had known you were near—"

"If I had known *you* were near, I would have charged Balios directly up the hill to you."

"And been murdered by Mortmain's creatures in the process. It is better that you did not know." She followed his gaze to the fire. "You found me in the end; that is what matters."

"Of course I found you. I promised Jem I would find you," he said. "Some promises cannot be broken."

He took a shallow breath. She felt it against her side: she was curled half against him, and his hands were shaking, almost imperceptibly, as he held her. Distantly she knew that she should not let herself be held like this by any boy who was not her brother or fiancé—but her brother and her fiancé were both dead, and tomorrow Mortmain would find them and punish them both. She could not bring herself, in the face of all that, to care much about propriety.

"What was the point of all that pain?" she asked. "I loved him so much, and I wasn't even there when he died."

Will's hand smoothed down her back—light and quick, as if he were afraid she would draw away. "Neither was I," he said. "I was in the courtyard of an inn, halfway to Wales, when I knew. I felt it. The bond between us being severed. It was as if a great pair of scissors had cut my heart in half."

"Will . . . ," Tessa said. His grief was so palpable, it mixed with her own to create a sharp sadness, lighter for being shared, though it was hard to say who was comforting who now. "You were always half his heart as well."

"I am the one who asked him to be my *parabatai*," Will said. "He was reluctant. He wanted me to understand that I was tying myself in what was meant to be a life bond to someone who would not live much of a life. But I wanted it, blindly wanted it, some proof that I wasn't alone, some way to show him what I owed him. And he gave way gracefully to what I wanted in the end. He always did."

"Don't," said Tessa. "Jem wasn't a martyr. It was no punishment for him, being your *parabatai*. You were like a brother to him—better than a brother, for you had chosen him. When he spoke of you, it was with loyalty and love, unclouded by any doubt."

"I confronted him," Will went on. "When I found he had been taking more of the *yin fen* than he should. I was so angry. I accused him of throwing his life away. He said, 'I can choose to be as much for her as I can be, to burn as brightly for her as I wish.'"

Tessa made a small sound in her throat.

"It was his choice, Tessa. Not something you forced upon him. He was never as happy as when he was with you." Will was not looking at her, but at the fire. "Whatever else I have ever said to you, no matter what, I am glad he had that time with you. You should be as well."

"You do not sound glad."

Will was still looking into the fire. His black hair had been damp when he had come into the room, and it had dried in loose curls against his temples and forehead. "I disappointed him," he said. "He entrusted this to me, this one task, to follow you and to find you, to bring you home safely. And now I fail at the final hurdle." He finally turned to look at her, his blue eyes unseeing. "I would not have left him. I would have stayed with him if he had asked, until he died. I would have stood by my oath. But he asked me to go after you . . ."

"Then you only did what he asked. You did not disappoint him."

"But it was also what was in my heart," Will said. "I cannot separate selfishness from selflessness now. When I dreamed of saving you, the way you would look at me—" His voice dropped off abruptly. "I am well punished for that hubris, at any rate."

"But I am rewarded." Tessa slipped her hand into his. His calluses were rough against her palm. She saw his chest hitch with surprised breath. "For I am not alone; I have you with me. And we should not give up all hope. There might still be a chance for us. To overpower Mortmain, or slip past him. If anyone can conjure a way to do it, you can."

He turned his gaze on her. His lashes shadowed his eyes as he said, "You are a wonder, Tessa Gray. To have such faith in me, though I have done nothing to earn it."

"Nothing?" Her voice rose. "Nothing to earn it? Will, you saved me from the Dark Sisters, you pushed me away to save me, you've saved me over and over again. You are a good man, one of the best I've ever known."

Will looked as stunned as if she had pushed him. He licked his dry lips. "I wish you wouldn't say that," he whispered.

She leaned toward him. His face was shadows, angles and planes; she wanted to touch him, touch the curve of his mouth, the arc of his lashes against his cheek. Fire reflected in his eyes, pinpricks of light. "Will," she said. "The first time I saw you, I thought you looked like a hero from a storybook. You joked that you were Sir Galahad. Remember that? And for so long I tried to understand you that way—as if you were Mr. Darcy, or Lancelot, or poor miserable Sydney Carton—and that was just a disaster. It took me so long to understand, but I did, and I do now—you are not a hero out of a book."

Will gave a short, disbelieving laugh. "It's true," he said. "I am no hero."

"No," Tessa said. "You are a person, just like me." His eyes searched her face, mystified; she held his hand tighter, lacing her fingers with his. "Don't you see, Will? You're a person *like* me. You are *like me*. You say the things I think but never say out loud. You read the books I read. You love the poetry I love. You make me laugh with your ridiculous songs and the way you see the truth of everything. I feel like you can look inside me and see all the places I am odd or unusual and fit your heart around them, for you are odd and unusual in just the same way." With the hand that was not holding his, she touched his cheek, lightly. "We are the same."

Will's eyes fluttered closed; she felt his lashes against her fingertips. When he spoke again, his voice was ragged but controlled. "Don't say those things, Tessa. Don't say them."

"Why not?"

"You said I am a good man," he said. "But I am not *that* good a man. And I am—I am *catastrophically* in love with you."

"Will—"

"I love you so much, so incredibly much," he went on, "and when you're this close to me, I forget who you are. I forget you're Jem's. I'd have to be the worst sort of person to think what I'm thinking right now. But I am thinking it."

"I loved Jem," she said. "I love him still, and he loved me, but I am not anybody's, Will. My heart is my own. It is beyond you to control it. It has been beyond *me* to control it."

Will's eyes were still closed. His chest was rising and falling swiftly, and she could hear the hard thump of his heart, rapid beneath the solidity of his rib cage. His body was warm against hers, and alive, and she thought of the automatons' cold hands on her, and Mortmain's colder eyes. She thought of what would happen if she lived and Mortmain succeeded in what he wanted and she was shackled to him all her life—a man she did not love and in fact despised.

She thought of the feel of his cold hands on her, and if those would be the only hands that would ever touch her again.

"What do you think will happen tomorrow, Will?" she whispered. "When Mortmain finds us. Tell me honestly."

His hand moved carefully, almost unwillingly, to slide down her hair and come to rest at the juncture of her neck. She wondered if he could feel the pounding of her pulse, answering his. "I think Mortmain will kill me. Or to be precise, he will have those creatures kill me. I am a decent Shadowhunter, Tess, but those automatons—they cannot be stopped. Runed blades serve as no better than ordinary weapons upon them, and seraph blades not at all."

"But you are not afraid."

"There are so many worse things than death," he said. "Not to be loved or not to be able to love: that is worse. And to go down fighting as a Shadowhunter should, there is no dishonor in that. An honorable death—I have always wanted that."

A shiver passed through Tessa. "There are two things I want," she said, and was surprised by the steadiness of her own voice. "If you think Mortmain will try to kill you tomorrow, then I wish to be given a weapon. I shall divest myself of my clockwork angel, and I shall fight by your side, and if we go down, we go down together. For, I too, wish an honorable death, like Boadicea."

"Tess—"

"I would rather die than be the Magister's tool. Give me a weapon, Will."

She felt his body shudder against hers. "I can do that for you," he said at last, subdued. "What was the second thing? That you wanted?"

She swallowed. "I want to kiss you one more time before I die."

His eyes flew wide. They were blue, blue like the sea and sky in her dream where he had fallen away from her, blue as the flowers Sophie had put in her hair. "Don't—"

"Say anything I don't mean," she finished for him. "I know. I am not. I mean it, Will. And I know it is entirely beyond the bounds of propriety to ask it. I know I must seem a bit mad." She glanced down, and then up again, gathering her courage. "And if you can tell me that you can die tomorrow without our lips ever touching again, and you will not regret it at all, then tell me, and I will desist in asking, for I know I have no right—"

Her words were cut off, for he had caught hold of her and pulled her against him, and crushed his lips down against hers. For a split second it was almost painful, sharp with desperation and thinly controlled hunger, and she tasted salt and heat in her mouth and the gasp of his breath. And then he gentled, with a force of restraint she could *feel* all through her body, and the slide of lips against lips, the interplay of tongue and teeth, altered from pain to pleasure in the sliver of a moment.

On the balcony at the Lightwoods', he had been so careful, but he was not being careful now. His hands slid roughly down her back, tangling in her hair, fisting in the loose fabric at the back of her dress. Half-lifting her so their bodies collided; he was against her, the long slim length of his body, hard and fragile at the same time. Her head slanted to the side as he parted her lips with his and they were not so much kissing as devouring each other. Her fingers gripped his hair tightly, hard enough that it must have hurt, and her teeth grazed his bottom lip. He groaned and pulled her tighter, making her gasp for air.

"Will—," she whispered, and he stood up, lifting her in his arms, still kissing her. She held tight to his back and shoulders as he carried her over to the bed and laid her down on it. She was already barefoot; he kicked off his boots and climbed up beside her. Part of her training had been in how to remove gear, and her hands were light and quick on his gear, undoing the clasps and pulling it aside like a shell. He batted it aside impatiently, and knelt upright to undo his weapons belt.

She watched him, swallowing hard. If she was going to tell him to stop, now was the moment. His scarred hands were nimble, undoing the fastenings, and as he turned to drop the belt over the side of the bed, his shirt—damp with sweat, and sticking to him—slid up and showed her the hollow curve of his stomach, the arched bone of his hip. She had always thought Will was beautiful, his eyes and lips and face, but she had never particularly thought of his body that way. But the shape of him was lovely, like the planes and angles of Michelangelo's *David*. She reached out to touch him, to run her fingers, as soft as spider silk, across the flat hard skin of his stomach.

His response was immediate and startling. He sucked in his breath and closed his eyes, his body going very still. She ran her fingers along the waistband of his trousers, her heart pounding, hardly knowing what she was doing—there was an instinct here, driving her, that she couldn't identify or explain. Her hand curved about his waist, thumb flicking against his hipbone, drawing him down.

He slid down over her, slowly, elbows resting on either side of her shoulders. Their eyes met, held; they were touching all along their bodies, but neither of them spoke. Her throat ached: adoration, heartbreak, in equal measure. "Kiss me," she said.

He lowered himself slowly, slowly, until their lips just brushed. She arched upward, wanting to meet his mouth with hers, but he drew back, nuzzling at her cheek, now his lips pressing the corner of her mouth—and then along her jaw and down her throat, sending little shocks of astonished pleasure through her body. She had always thought of her arms, her hands, her neck, her face, as separate—not that her skin was all the same delicate envelope, and that a kiss placed on her throat might be felt all the way down to the bottom of her feet.

"Will." Her hands pulled at his shirt, and it came away, the buttons tearing, his head shaking free of the fabric, all wild dark hair, Heathcliff on the moors. His hands were less sure on her dress, but it came away as well, off over her head, and was cast aside, leaving Tessa in her chemise and corset. She went motionless, shocked at being so undressed in front of anyone but Sophie, and Will took a wild look at her corset that was only part desire.

"How—," he said. "Does it come off?"

Tessa couldn't help herself; despite everything, she giggled. "It laces," she whispered. "In the back." And she guided his hands around her until his fingers were on the strings of the corset. She shivered then, and not from cold but from the intimacy of the gesture. Will pulled her against him, gentle now, and kissed the line of her throat again, and her shoulder where the chemise bared it, his breath soft and hot against her skin until she was breathing just as hard, her hands smoothing up and over his shoulders, his arms, his sides. She kissed the white scars the Marks had left on his skin, winding herself around him until they were a heated tangle of limbs and she was swallowing down the gasps he made against her mouth.

"Tess," he whispered. "Tess—if you want to stop—"

She shook her head silently. The fire in the grate had nearly burned down again; Will was all angles and shadows and soft and hard skin against her. *No.*

"You want this?" His voice was hoarse.

"Yes," she said. "Do you?"

His finger traced the outline of her mouth. "For this I would have been damned forever. For this I would have given up everything."

She felt the burn behind her eyes, the pressure of tears, and blinked wet eyelashes. "Will . . ."

"Dw i'n dy garu di am byth," he said. "I love you. Always." And he moved to cover her body with his own.

Late in the night or early in the morning, Tessa woke. The fire had burned down entirely, but the room was lit by the peculiar torchlight that seemed to go on and off without rhyme or reason.

She drew back, propping herself on her elbow. Will was asleep beside her, immured in the unmoving slumber of the utterly exhausted. He looked at peace, though—more so than she had ever seen him before. His breath was regular, his eyelashes fluttering slightly in dreams.

She had fallen asleep with her head on his arm, the clockwork angel, still around her throat, resting against his shoulder, just to the left of his collarbone. As she moved away, the clockwork angel slipped free and she saw to her surprise that where it had lain against his skin it had left a mark behind, no bigger than a shilling, in the shape of a pale white star.

20

THE INFERNAL DEVICES

Like wire-pulled automatons,
Slim silhouetted skeletons
Went sidling through the slow quadrille,
Then took each other by the hand,
And danced a stately saraband;
Their laughter echoed thin and shrill.
—Oscar Wilde, "The Harlot's House"

"It's *beautiful*," Henry breathed.

The Shadowhunters of the London Institute—along with Magnus Bane—stood in a loose half circle in the crypt, staring at one of the bare stone walls—or, more precisely, at something that had *appeared* on one of the bare stone walls.

It was a glowing archway, about ten feet in height, and perhaps five across in width. It was not carved into the stone but rather was made of glowing runes that twined into one another like the vines of a trellis. The runes were not from the Gray Book—Gabriel would have recognized them if they had been—but were runes he had never seen before. They had the foreign look of another language, yet each was distinct and beautiful and spoke a murmuring song of travel and distance, of whirling dark space and the distance between worlds.

They glowed green in the darkness, pale and acidic. Within the space created by the runes the wall was not visible—only darkness, impenetrable, as if of a great dark pit.

"It truly is amazing," Magnus said.

All but the warlock were dressed in their gear and were bristling with weapons—Gabriel's favorite double-edged long-sword was slung over his back, and he was itching to get his gloved hands on the hilt. Though he liked the bow and arrow, he had been trained in the longsword by a master who could trace his own masters back to Lichtenauer, and Gabriel fancied the longsword his specialty. Besides, a bow and arrow would be much less use against automatons than a weapon that could chop them into component parts.

"All down to you, Magnus," Henry said. He was glowing—or, Gabriel thought, it could have been the reflection of the lighted runes against his face.

"Not at all," Magnus replied. "If not for your genius, this could never have been created."

"While I am enjoying this exchange of pleasantries," Gabriel said, seeing that Henry was about to respond, "there do remain a few—central—questions about this invention."

Henry looked at him blankly. "Such as what?"

"I believe, Henry, that he is inquiring whether this . . . doorway—," Charlotte began.

"We've called it a Portal," said Henry. The capitalization of the word was very clear in his tone.

"Whether it works," Charlotte finished. "Have you tried it?"

Henry looked stricken. "Well, no. There hasn't been time. But I assure you, our calculations are faultless."

Everyone but Henry and Magnus looked at the Portal with refreshed alarm. "Henry . . . ," Charlotte began.

"Well, I think Henry and Magnus should go first," Gabriel said. "They invented the blasted thing."

Everyone turned on him. "It's like he's replaced Will," said Gideon, eyebrows up. "They say all the same sort of things."

"I am *not* like Will!" Gabriel snapped.

"I should hope not," said Cecily, though so quietly that he wondered if anyone else had heard her. She was looking especially pretty today, though he had no idea why. She was dressed in the same plain black woman's gear as Charlotte; her hair was secured demurely behind her head, and the ruby necklace at her throat glowed against her skin. However, Gabriel reminded himself sternly, since they were most likely about to direct themselves all into mortal danger, thinking about whether Cecily was pretty ought not to be foremost on his mind. He told himself to stop immediately.

"I am *nothing* like Will Herondale," he repeated.

"I am perfectly willing to go through first," Magnus said, with the long-suffering air of a schoolmaster in a room full of ill-behaved schoolboys. "There are a few things I need. We are hoping Tessa will be there; Will may be also; I should like some extra gear and weapons to bring through. I plan, of course, to wait for you on the other side, but should there be any—unexpected developments, it is always good to prepare."

Charlotte nodded. "Yes—of course." She glanced down for a moment. "I cannot believe no one has come to assist us. I thought, after my letter, at least a few—" She broke off, swallowing, and raised her chin. "Let me get Sophie. She can put together the things you need, Magnus. And she and Cyril and Bridget are meant to join us shortly." She vanished up the steps, Henry looking after her with worried fondness.

Gabriel could not blame him. It was obviously a severe blow to Charlotte that no one had answered her call and come to aid them, though he could have told her they would not. People were intrinsically selfish, and many hated the idea of a woman in charge of the Institute. They would not put themselves at risk for her. Only a few weeks ago he would have said the same thing about himself. Now, knowing Charlotte, he realized to his surprise, the idea of risking himself for her seemed an honor, as it would be to most Englishmen to risk themselves for the queen.

"How *does* one make the Portal work?" Cecily asked, glancing at the glowing archway as if it were a painting in a gallery, her dark head cocked to the side.

"It will transport you instantly from one place to another," said Henry. "But the trick is—well, that part is magic." He said the word a little nervously.

"You need to be picturing the place you're going to," said Magnus. "It won't work to take you to a place you have never been and cannot imagine. In this case, to get to Cadair Idris, we are going to need Cecily. Cecily, how close to Cadair Idris do you believe you can bring us?"

"To the very top," Cecily said confidently. "There are several paths that will bring you up the mountain, and I have walked two of them with my father. I can remember the crest of the mountain."

"Excellent," Henry said. "Cecily, you will stand before the Portal and visualize our destination—"

"But she's not going first, is she?" Gabriel demanded. The moment the words were out of his mouth, he was startled. He hadn't meant to say them. Ah, well, in for a penny, in for a pound, though, he thought. "I meant: She is the least trained of us all; it wouldn't be safe."

"I can go through first," Cecily said, looking as if she were not in the least grateful for Gabriel's support. "I see no reason why—"

"Henry!" It was Charlotte, reappearing at the foot of the steps. Behind her were the servants of the Institute, all in training gear—Bridget, looking as if she were out for a morning stroll; Cyril, set and determined; and Sophie, carrying a large leather bag.

Behind them were three more men. Tall men, in parchment robes, moving with peculiar gliding motions.

Silent Brothers.

Unlike any other Silent Brothers that Gabriel had seen before, though, these were armed. Weapons belts were cinched around their waists, over their robes, and from their belts hung long, curved blades, their hilts made of shimmering *adamas*, the same material used to make steles and seraph blades.

Henry looked up, puzzled—then guiltily, from the Portal, to the Brothers. His lightly freckled face paled. "Brother Enoch," he said. "I—"

Calm yourself. The Silent Brother's voice rang out in all their minds. *We have not come to warn you of any possible breach of the Law, Henry Branwell. We have come to fight with you.*

"To fight with us?" Gideon looked amazed. "But Silent Brothers don't— I mean, they aren't warriors—"

That is incorrect. Shadowhunters we were and Shadowhunters we remain, even when changed to become Brothers. We were founded by Jonathan Shadowhunter himself, and though we live by the book, we may yet die by the sword if we so choose.

Charlotte was beaming. "They learned of my message," she said. "They came. Brother Enoch, Brother Micah, and Brother Zachariah."

The two Brothers behind Enoch inclined their heads silently. Gabriel fought off a shiver. He had always found the Silent Brothers eerie, though he knew they were an integral part of Shadowhunter life.

"Brother Enoch also told me why no one else came," Charlotte said, the smile vanishing from her face. "Consul Wayland convened a Council meeting this morning, though he told us nothing of it. Attendance for all Shadowhunters was mandatory by Law."

Henry's breath hissed out through his teeth. "That ba—bad man," he finished, with a quick glance at Cecily, who rolled her eyes. "What's the Council meeting about?"

"Replacing us as heads of the Institute," Charlotte said. "He still believes Mortmain's attack will come against London, and that a strong leader here is needed to stand against the clock-work army."

"Mrs. Branwell!" Sophie, in the act of handing to Magnus the bag she had been carrying, nearly dropped it. "They can't do that!"

"Oh, they very well can," said Charlotte. She looked around at all their faces, and raised her chin. In that moment, despite her small size, Gabriel thought, she seemed taller than the Consul. "We all knew this would come," she said. "It does not matter. We are Shadowhunters, and our duty is to each other and to what we think is right. We believe Will, and we believe in Will. Faith has brought us this far; it will bring us a little farther. The Angel watches over us, and we shall win out."

Everyone was silent. Gabriel looked around at their faces—determined, every one—and even Magnus seemed, if not moved or convinced, considering and respectful. "Mrs. Branwell," he said at last. "If Consul Wayland does not consider you a leader, he is a fool."

Charlotte inclined her head toward him. "Thank you," she said. "But we should waste no more time—we must go, and quickly, for this matter can wait on us no longer."

Henry looked for a long moment at his wife, and then toward Cecily. "Are you ready?"

Will's sister nodded, and moved forward to stand before the Portal. Its gleaming light cast the shadow of unfamiliar runes across her small, determined face.

"Visualize," said Magnus. "Imagine as hard as you can that you are looking at the top of Cadair Idris."

Cecily's hands clenched at her sides. As she stared, the Portal began to move, the runes to ripple and change. The darkness within the archway lightened. Suddenly Gabriel was no longer looking at shadow. He was gazing at a portrait of a landscape that could have been painted within the Portal—the green curve of the top of a mountain, a lake as blue and deep as the sky.

Cecily gave a little gasp—and then, unprompted, stepped forward, and vanished through the archway. It was like watching a sketch being erased. First her hands vanished into the Portal, and then her arms, outstretched, and then her body.

And she was gone.

Charlotte gave a little shriek. "Henry!"

There was a buzzing in Gabriel's ears. He could hear Henry reassuring Charlotte that this was the way the Portal was meant to function, that nothing untoward had happened, but it was like a song half-heard from another room, the words a rhythm without meaning. All he knew was that Cecily, braver than all of them, had stepped through the unknown doorway and was gone. And he could not let her go alone.

He moved forward. He heard his brother call his name, but he ignored him; pushing past Gideon, he reached the Portal, and stepped through it.

For a moment there was nothing but blackness. Then a great hand seemed to reach out of the darkness and snatch hold of him, and he was pulled into the whirling inky maelstrom.

The great Council room was full of people shouting.

On the raised platform at the center stood Consul Wayland, staring out at the shouting throng with a look of furious impatience on his face. His dark eyes raked the Shadowhunters congregated in front of him: George Penhallow was locked in a screaming match with Sora Kaidou of the Tokyo Institute; Vijay Malhotra was jabbing a thin finger into the chest of Japheth Pangborn, who rarely left his manor house in the Idris countryside these days, and who had turned as red as a tomato at the indignity of it all. Two of the Blackwells had cornered

Amalia Morgenstern, who was snapping at them in German. Aloysius Starkweather, all in black, stood beside one of the wooden benches, his wiry limbs nearly bent up around his ears as he glared up at the podium with sharp old eyes.

The Inquisitor, standing beside Consul Wayland, slammed his wooden staff down against the floor hard enough to nearly shatter the floorboards. "That is ENOUGH!" he roared. "All of you will be silent, and you will be silent *now*. SIT DOWN."

A ripple of shock went through the room—and, to the Consul's evident surprise, they sat. Not quietly, but they sat— all who had room to sit. The chamber was filled to bursting; this many Shadowhunters rarely appeared at any one meeting. There were representatives here from all the Institutes— New York, Bangkok, Geneva, Bombay, Kyoto, Buenos Aires. Only the London Shadowhunters, Charlotte Branwell and her cohorts, were absent.

Only Aloysius Starkweather remained standing, his ragged dark cloak flapping about him like crow's wings. "Where is Charlotte Branwell?" he demanded. "It was understood from the message you sent out that she would be here to explain the contents of her message to the Council."

"I will explain the contents of her message," said the Consul through gritted teeth.

"It would be preferable to hear it from her," said Malhotra, his dark eyes keen as he looked from the Consul to the Inquisitor and back. Inquisitor Whitelaw looked drawn, as if he had been suffering recent sleepless nights; his mouth was tight at the corners.

"Charlotte Branwell is overreacting," said the Consul. "I take full responsibility for having put her in charge of the

London Institute. It was something I should never have done. She has been relieved of her position."

"I have had occasion to meet and speak with Mrs. Branwell," said Starkweather in his hoarse Yorkshire tones. "She does not strike me as someone who would easily overreact."

Looking as if he remembered exactly why he had been so glad Starkweather had ceased attending Council meetings, the Consul said tightly: "She is in a delicate way, and I believe she has become . . . overset."

Chatter and confusion. The Inquisitor looked over at Wayland and gave him a narrow glance of disgust. The Consul returned his look with a glare. It was clear that the two men had been arguing: The Consul was flushed with anger, the look he bent toward the Inquisitor in return filled with betrayal. It was clear that Whitelaw did not agree with the Consul's words.

A woman rose to her feet from the crowded benches. She had white hair piled high on her head and an imperious manner. The Consul looked as if he were groaning inwardly. Callida Fairchild, Charlotte Branwell's aunt. "If you are suggesting," she said in a frozen voice, "that my niece is making hysterical and unreasonable decisions because she is carrying one of the next generation of Shadowhunters, Consul, I suggest you think again."

The Consul ground his teeth. "There is no evidence that Charlotte Branwell's statements that Mortmain is in Wales have any truth to them," he said. "It all stems from the reports of Will Herondale, who is only a boy, and a reprehensibly irresponsible one at that. All evidence, including the journals of Benedict Lightwood, point to an attack on London, and it is there we must marshal our forces."

A buzz went through the room, the words "an attack on London" repeated over and over. Amalia Morgenstern fanned herself with a lace handkerchief, while Lilian Highsmith, her fingers stroking the haft of a dagger protruding from the wrist of one glove, looked delighted.

"Evidence," snapped Callida. "My niece's word *is* evidence—"

There was another rustle, and a young woman rose to her feet. She wore a bright green dress and a defiant expression. The last time the Consul had seen her, she had been sobbing in this same Council room, demanding justice. Tatiana Blackthorn, née Lightwood.

"The Consul is right about Charlotte Branwell!" she exclaimed. "Charlotte Branwell and William Herondale are the reason my husband is dead!"

"Oh?" It was Inquisitor Whitelaw, his tone dripping with sarcasm. "Who exactly killed your husband? Was it Will?"

There was a murmur of astonishment. Tatiana looked outraged. "It was not my father's fault—"

"On the contrary," interrupted the Inquisitor. "This was kept from public knowledge, Mrs. Blackthorn, but you force my hand. We opened an investigation into the matter of your husband's death, and it was determined that your father was indeed at fault, most grievous fault. If it were not for the actions of your brothers—and of William Herondale and Charlotte Branwell, among the others of the London Institute—the name of Lightwood would be stricken from the Shadowhunter records and you would be living the rest of your life as a friendless mundane."

Tatiana turned beet red and clenched her fists. "William

Herondale has—he has offered me insults unspeakable to a lady—"

"I fail to see how that is germane to the matter at hand," said the Inquisitor. "One may be rude in one's personal life but also correct about larger matters."

"You took our house!" Tatiana screeched. "I am forced to rely on the generosity of my husband's family like some starving beggar—"

The Inquisitor's eyes were glittering to match the stones in his rings. "Your house was confiscated, Mrs. Blackthorn, not stolen. We searched the Lightwood family house," he went on, raising his voice. "It was full of evidence of the elder Mr. Lightwood's connections to Mortmain, journals detailing acts vile and filthy and unspeakable. The Consul cites the man's journals as evidence that there will be an attack on London, but by the time Benedict Lightwood died, he was mad with demon pox. Nor is it likely Mortmain would have confided his true plans to him, even had he been sane."

Looking nearly desperate, Consul Wayland interrupted. "The matter of Benedict Lightwood is closed—closed, and irrelevant. We are here to discuss the matters of Mortmain and the Institute! First, as Charlotte Branwell has been removed from the position, and the situation facing us is centered most heavily upon London, we require a new leader of the London Enclave. I am going to throw the floor open. Does anyone wish to step forward as her replacement?"

There was a rustle and murmur. George Penhallow had begun to rise to his feet—when the Inquisitor burst in furiously: "This is ridiculous, Josiah. There is no proof yet that Mortmain is not where Charlotte says he will be. We have not even begun to discuss sending reinforcements after her—"

"After her? What do you mean after her?"

The Inquisitor swept an arm out at the throng. "She is not here. Where do you think the inhabitants of the London Institute are? They have gone to Cadair Idris, after the Magister. And yet, instead of discussing whether we shall give them aid, we convene a Council to discuss Charlotte's *replacement?*"

The Consul's temper snapped. "There will be no aid!" he roared. "There will *never* be aid for those who—"

But the Council never found out who was destined to go unaided, for at that moment a steel blade, deadly sharp, whipped through the air behind the Consul and neatly severed his head from his body.

The Inquisitor jerked back, reaching for his staff, as blood sheeted across him; the Consul's body fell, tumbling to the ground in two severed parts: his body slumping to the blood-wet floor of the podium while his severed head rolled away like a tennis ball. As he collapsed, revealed behind him was an automaton—as spindly as a human skeleton, dressed in the ragged remains of a red military tunic. It grinned like a skull as it retracted its scarlet-drenched blade and looked out upon the silent, stunned crowd of Shadowhunters.

The only other sound in the room came from Aloysius Starkweather, who was laughing, steadily and softly, apparently to himself. "She told you," he wheezed. "She *told* you what would happen—"

A moment later the automaton had moved forward, its clawed hand shooting out to close about Aloysius's throat. Blood burst from the old man's throat as the creature lifted him off his feet, still grinning. The Shadowhunters began to shout—and then the doors burst open and a flood of clockwork creatures poured into the room.

"Well," said a very amused voice. "This *is* unexpected."

Tessa sat bolt upright, pulling the heavy coverlet around her. Beside her, Will stirred, propping himself up on his elbows, eyelids fluttering open slowly. "What—"

The room was filled with bright light. The torches had come on at full strength, and it was like the place was lit with daylight. Tessa could see the wreck of the room that they had made: their clothes scattered across the floor and the bed, the rug before the fireplace rucked up, the bedclothes wound about them. On the other side of the invisible wall was lounging a familiar figure in an elegant dark suit, one thumb hooked into the waistband of his trousers. His cat-pupilled eyes glimmered with mirth.

Magnus Bane.

"You might want to get up," he said. "Everyone will be here quite soon to rescue you, and you may prefer to have clothes on when they arrive." He shrugged. "I would, at any rate, but then, I am well known to be remarkably shy."

Will swore in Welsh. He was sitting up now, the covers tucked about his waist, and had done his best to move his body to shield Tessa from Magnus's gaze. He was without a shirt, of course, and in the brighter light Tessa could see where the tan on his hands and face faded into the paler white of his chest and shoulders. The white star mark on his shoulder gleamed out like a light, and she saw Magnus's eyes go to it, and narrow.

"Interesting," he said.

Will made an incoherent noise of protest. "*Interesting?* By the Angel, Magnus—"

Magnus gave him a wry look. There was something in it— something that made Tessa feel as if Magnus knew something they didn't. "If I were a different person, I would have a lot to say to you right now," he said.

"I appreciate your restraint."

"You won't soon," said Magnus shortly. Then he reached up as if he were knocking on a door, and tapped the invisible wall between them. It was like watching someone plunge their hand into water—ripples spread out from the place where his fingers touched, and suddenly the wall slid away and was gone, in a shower of blue sparks. "Here," the warlock said, and tossed a tied leather sack onto the foot of the bed. "I brought gear. I thought you might be in need of clothing, but I didn't realize quite *how* in need."

Tessa glared at him around Will's shoulder. "How did you find us here? How did you know—which of the others are with you? Are they all right?"

"Yes. Quite a few of them are, hurrying through this place, looking for you. Now get dressed," he said, and turned his back, giving them privacy. Tessa, mortified, reached for the sack on the bed, scrabbled through it until she found her gear, and then stood up with the sheet wrapped around her body and dashed behind the tall Chinese screen in the corner of the room.

She did not look at Will as she went; she couldn't bring herself to. How could she look at him without thinking of what they'd done? Wondering if he was horrified, if he couldn't believe either of them would do such a thing after Jem—

Viciously she yanked on the gear. Thank goodness that gear, unlike dresses, could be assembled on the body without recourse to help from anyone else. Through the screen she heard Magnus explaining to Will that he and Henry had managed, through a combination of magic and invention, to create a Portal that would transport them from London to Cadair Idris. She could see them only in silhouette, but she saw Will nodding in relief as Magnus listed those who had come with him—Henry, Charlotte, the Lightwood brothers, Cyril, Sophie, Cecily, Bridget, and a group of the Silent Brothers.

At the mention of his sister's name, Will began to pull on his clothes with even greater haste, and by the time Tessa stepped out from behind the screen, he was entirely dressed in gear, his boots laced up, his hands buckling on his weapons belt. As he saw her, his face broke into a tentative smile.

"The others have all spread out through the tunnels to find you," Magnus said. "We were meant to take a half hour to search and then meet up in a central chamber. I will give you two a moment to—collect yourselves." He smirked, and pointed to the door. "I shall be outside in the corridor."

The moment the door closed behind him, Tessa was in Will's arms, her hands locked about his neck. "Oh, by the Angel," she said. "That was mortifying."

Will slid his hands into her hair and was kissing her, kissing her eyelids and her cheeks and then her mouth, quickly but with fervor and concentration, as if nothing could be more important. "Listen to you," he said. "You said 'by the Angel.' Like a Shadowhunter." He kissed the side of her mouth. "I love you. God, I love you. I waited so long to say it."

She curved her hands about the sides of his waist, holding

him there, the material of his gear rough beneath her finger-tips. "Will," she said hesitantly. "You're not—sorry?"

"Sorry?" He looked at her in disbelief. "*Nage ddim*—you're mad if you think I'm sorry, Tess." His knuckle brushed her cheek. "There is more, so much more I want to say to you—"

"No," she teased. "Will Herondale, with more to say?"

He ignored this. "*But* now is not the time—not with Mortmain breathing down our necks, most likely, and Magnus outside the door. Now is the time to finish this. But when it is over, Tess, I will say everything to you I have always wanted to say. As for now—" He kissed her temple, and released her, his eyes searching her face. "I need to know you believe me when I say I love you. That is all."

"I believe everything you say," Tessa said with a smile, her hands creeping down from his waist to his weapons belt. Her fingers closed on the hilt of a dagger, and she yanked it from the belt, smiling as he looked down at her in surprise. She kissed his cheek and stepped back. "After all," she said, "you weren't lying about that tattoo of the dragon of Wales, were you?"

The room reminded Cecily of the inside of Saint Paul's dome, which Will had taken her to see on one of his less disagreeable days, after she had first come to London. It was the grandest building she had ever been inside. They had tested the echo of their voices in the interior Whispering Gallery and read the inscription left by Christopher Wren: *Si monumentum requiris, circumspice.* "If you seek his monu-ment, look about you."

Will had explained to her what it meant, that Wren pre-ferred to be remembered by the works he had built rather than any tombstone. The whole of the cathedral was a monument to his craft—as, in a way, the whole of this labyrinth beneath the mountain, and this room especially, was a monument to Mortmain's.

There was a domed ceiling here, too, though there were no windows, only an upward-reaching hollow in the stone. A circular gallery ran around the upper part of the dome, and there was a platform on it, from which, presumably, one could stand and look down at the floor, which was smooth stone.

There was an inscription on the wall here, too. Four sentences, cut into the wall in glittering quartz.

> THE INFERNAL DEVICES ARE WITHOUT PITY.
> THE INFERNAL DEVICES ARE WITHOUT REGRET.
> THE INFERNAL DEVICES ARE WITHOUT NUMBER.
> THE INFERNAL DEVICES WILL NEVER STOP COMING.

On the stone floor, lined up in rows, were hundreds of automatons. They wore a motley assortment of military uniforms and were deadly still, their metal eyes closed. Tin soldiers, Cecy thought, grown to human size. The Infernal Devices. Mortmain's great creation—an army bred to be unstoppable, to slaughter Shadowhunters and to move onward without remorse.

Sophie had been the first to discover the room; she had screamed, and the others had all rushed to find out why. They had found Sophie standing, shaking, amid the unmoving mass of clockwork creatures. One of them lay at her feet; she had cut its legs out from under it with a sweep of her blade, and it had crumpled like a puppet whose strings had been cut. The others had not moved or awakened despite the fate of their associate, which had given the Shadowhunters the boldness to go forward among them.

Henry was on his knees now, beside the carapace of one of the still unmoving automatons; he had slit open its uniform and opened its metal chest and was studying what was within. The Silent Brothers stood about him, as did Charlotte, Sophie, and Bridget. Gideon and Gabriel had returned as well, their explorations having proved fruitless. Only Magnus and Cyril had not yet returned. Cecily could not fight down her mounting unease—not at the presence of the automatons but at the absence of her brother. No one had found him yet. Could it be that he was not here to *be* found? She said nothing, however. She had promised herself that as a Shadowhunter she would not fuss, or scream, whatever happened.

"Look at this," Henry murmured in a low voice. Inside the chest of the clockwork creature was a mess of wires and what looked to Cecily like a metal box, the kind that might hold tobacco. Carved onto the outside of the box was the symbol of a serpent swallowing its own tail. "The *ourobouros*. The symbol of the containment of demon energies."

"As on the Pyxis." Charlotte nodded.

"Which Mortmain stole from us," Henry confirmed. "It had concerned me that this was what Mortmain was attempting."

"That *what* was what he was attempting?" Gabriel demanded. He was flushed, his green eyes bright. Bless Gabriel, Cecily thought, for always asking exactly the question that was on his mind.

"Animating the automatons," Henry said absently, reaching for the box. "Giving them consciousness, even will—"

He broke off as his fingers touched the box and it flared suddenly into light. Light, like the illumination of a witchlight rune-stone, poured from the box and through the *ourobouros*. Henry jerked back with a cry, but it was already too late. The creature sat up, lightning fast, and seized hold of him. Charlotte shrieked and threw herself forward, but she was not fast enough. The automaton, its chest still hanging grotesquely open, caught Henry under the arms and cracked his body like a whip.

There was a terrible snapping sound, and Henry went limp. The automaton tossed Henry aside and turned to cuff Charlotte brutally across the face. She crumpled beside her husband's body as the clockwork creature took a step forward, and seized hold of Brother Micah. The Silent Brother slammed his staff down on the automaton's hand, but the creature did not even seem to notice. With a rumble of machinery that sounded like a laugh, it reached out and tore the Silent Brother's throat open.

Blood sprayed across the room, and Cecily did exactly what she had promised herself she would not do, and screamed.

21

BURNING GOLD

Bring me my bow of burning gold:
Bring me my arrows of desire:
Bring me my spear: O clouds unfold!
Bring me my chariot of fire!
—William Blake, "Jerusalem"

Tessa's training at the Institute had never addressed how difficult it was to run with a weapon strapped to your side. With every stride she took, the dagger slapped against her leg, its point scratching her skin. She knew it ought to have been sheathed—and on Will's belt, probably had been—but there was no use in hindsight now. Will and Magnus were running pell-mell down the rocky corridors inside Cadair Idris, and she was doing her level best to keep up.

It was Magnus who was leading the way, as he seemed

to have the best idea where they were going. Tessa had gone nowhere inside the morass of twisty corridors without being blindfolded, and Will admitted he remembered little of his solitary journey of the night before.

The tunnels narrowed and widened again haphazardly as the three of them made their way through the labyrinth, with no seeming rhyme or reason to the pattern. At last, as they moved into a wider tunnel, they heard something—the sound of a distant cry of horror.

Magnus went tense all over. Will's head jerked up. *"Cecily,"* he said, and then he was running twice as fast as he had been, both Magnus and Tessa racing to keep up. They hurtled by strange chambers: one whose door seemed splashed with blood, another Tessa recognized as the room with the desk where Mortmain had forced her to Change, and another where a great lattice of metal and copper twisted in an invisible wind. As they raced forward, the sounds of cries and battle grew louder, until finally they burst into a massive circular chamber.

It was full of automatons. Row upon row of them, as many as had poured down on the village the night before while Tessa had watched helplessly. Most of them were still, but a group of them, in the center of the room, were moving—moving and engaged in a fierce battle. It was like seeing all over again what had happened on the steps of the Institute as she had been dragged away—the Lightwood brothers fighting side by side, Cecily swinging a shimmering seraph blade, the body of a Silent Brother crumpled on the floor. Tessa registered distantly that two other Silent Brothers were fighting alongside the Shadowhunters, anonymous in their hooded parchment robes, but her attention was not on them. It was on Henry, who lay, still and unmoving, on the floor. Charlotte, crumpled on her knees, had her arms about him as if she could shield him from the churning battle going on all around them, but Tessa guessed from the whiteness of his face and the stillness of his body that it was too late to shield Henry from anything.

Will darted forward. "No seraph blades!" he cried. "Fight them with other weapons! The angel blades are useless!"

Cecily, hearing him, jerked back even as her seraph blade connected with the automaton she was fighting—and crumbled away like dry frost, its fire gone. She had the presence of mind to duck beneath the creature's swinging arm, just as Cyril and Bridget plunged toward her, Cyril laying about him with a stout staff. The automaton went down under Cyril's assault, as Bridget, a flying menace of red hair and steely blades, sliced her way past Cecily to Charlotte's side, shearing the arms off two automatons with her sword before whirling about, her back to Charlotte, as if she meant to protect the head of the Institute with her life.

Will's hands were suddenly tight on Tessa's upper arms. She caught a glimpse of his white, set face as he pushed her toward Magnus, hissing: *"Stay with her!"* Tessa began to protest, but Magnus caught hold of her, drawing her back even as Will dashed into the melee, fighting his way toward his sister.

Cecily was fending off a massive, barrel-chested automaton with two arms on its right side. Seraph blade abandoned, she had only a short sword to defend herself. Her hair began to slip free of its fastenings as she lunged forward, stabbing at the creature's shoulder. It roared like a bull, and Tessa shuddered. God, these creatures made such *sounds*; before Mortmain had changed them, they had been silent—they had been *things*;

now they were *beings*. Malevolent, murderous beings. Tessa started forward as the automaton fighting Cecily seized the blade of her weapon and jerked it out of her grasp, pulling her forward—she heard Will call out his sister's name—

And Cecily was caught and thrown to the side by one of the Silent Brothers. In a whirl of parchment robes, he spun to face the creature, staff held before him. As the automaton lurched toward him, the Brother swung out with the staff, with such speed and force that the automaton was knocked back, its chest dented inward. It tried to move forward again, but its body was too badly bent. It gave an angry whir, and Cecily, scrambling back up to her feet, cried out a warning.

Another automaton had loomed up beside the first. As the Silent Brother turned, the second automaton knocked the staff from his hand and seized him, lifting him off his feet, wrapping its metal arms around his body from behind, in the parody of an embrace. The Brother's hood fell back, and his silvery hair shone out in the dim chamber like starlight.

All the air rushed out of Tessa's lungs in a single instant. The Silent Brother was Jem.

Jem.

It was as if the world had stopped. Every figure was still, even the automatons, frozen in time. Tessa stared across the room at Jem, and he looked back at her. Jem, in the parchment robes of a Silent Brother. Jem, whose silvery hair, tumbling over his face, was threaded through with black. Jem, whose cheeks were scarred with two matching red cuts, one over each cheekbone.

Jem, who was not dead.

Tessa, jerked from her frozen shock, heard Magnus say something to her, felt him reach for her arm, but she tore away from him and plunged into the melee. He shouted after her, but all she saw was Jem—Jem seizing at the automaton's arm where it wrapped his throat, his scrabbling fingers unable to find a purchase on the smooth metal. Its grip tightened, and Jem's face began to suffuse with blood as he strangled. She drew her dagger, slashing out in front of her to clear a path, but she knew it was impossible, knew she couldn't get to him in time—

The automaton gave a roar and toppled forward. Its legs had been sliced clean through from behind, and as it fell, Tessa saw Will rising from a crouch, a long-bladed sword in his hand. He reached out for the automaton as if he could catch it, prevent its fall, but it had already crashed to the floor, half on top of Jem, whose staff had rolled from his hand. Jem lay still, pinned by the massive machine above him.

Tessa darted forward, ducking under the outstretched arm of a clockwork creature. She heard Magnus shout something from behind her but ignored it. If she could get to Jem before he was badly hurt, even crushed—but as she ran, a shadow fell across her vision. She skidded to a stop, and looked up into the face of a leering automaton, reaching for her with clawed fingers.

The force of the fall and the weight of the automaton on his back knocked the air from Jem's lungs as he hit the ground, bruisingly hard. For a moment stars danced across his vision and he fought for breath, his chest spasming.

Before he had become a Silent Brother, before they had

put the first ritual knife to his skin and cut the lines into his face that would begin the process of his transformation, the fall, the injury, might have killed him. Now, as he sucked the air back into his lungs, he found himself twisting, reaching for his staff, even as the creature's hand closed on his shoulder—

And a shudder went through its body, along with the ring of metal on metal. Jem seized up his staff and jabbed it upward, knocking the automaton's head sideways even as the top half of its body was lifted off him and thrown to the side. He kicked out at the weight still pinning his legs, and then that was gone too and Will was on his knees beside him where he lay on the ground. Will's face was as white as ashes.

"Jem," he said.

There was a stillness around them both, a gap in the battle, an eerie timeless silence. The weight of a thousand things was in Will's voice: disbelief and amazement, relief and betrayal. Jem began to struggle up onto his elbows just as Will's sword, smeared with black oil, riven with dents, clattered to the ground.

"You're dead," Will said. "I *felt* you die." And he put his hand over his heart, on his bloodstained shirt, where his *parabatai* rune was. "Here."

Jem scrabbled for Will's hand, caught it in his, and pressed the fingers of his blood brother's hand to the inside of his own wrist. He willed his *parabatai* to understand. *Feel my pulse, the beat of blood under the skin; Silent Brothers have hearts, and they beat.* Will's blue eyes widened. "I did not die. I changed. If I could have told you—if there was a way—"

Will stared at him, his chest rising and falling quickly. The automaton had clawed one side of Will's face. He was bleeding from several deep scratches, but he didn't appear to notice. He drew his hand back from Jem's grasp and exhaled softly. "*Roeddwn i'n meddwl dy fod wedi mynd am byth,*" he said. He spoke, without thinking, in Welsh, but Jem understood the words regardless. The runes of the Silent Brothers meant that no language was unknown to him.

I thought you were gone forever.

"I am still here," Jem said, and then there was a flicker at the corner of his eye, and he moved swiftly, spinning aside. A metal axe whistled down through the space where he had just been, and clanged against the stone floor. Automatons had surrounded them, a ring of whirring metal.

And Will was on his feet, sword in hand, and they were back-to-back, and Will was saying: "There is no rune effective against them; they must be hacked apart by main force—"

"I gathered that." Jem gripped his staff and swung it hard, knocking one automaton back into a nearby wall. Sparks flew from its metal carapace.

Will struck with his blade, slicing through the jointed knees of two creatures. "I like that stick of yours," he said.

"It's a staff." Jem swung out to knock another automaton sideways. "Made by the Iron Sisters, only for Silent Brothers."

Will lunged forward, slicing his blade cleanly through the neck of another automaton. Its head rolled to the ground, and a mixture of oil and vapor poured from its ragged throat. "Anyone can sharpen a stick."

"It's a *staff,*" Jem repeated, and saw Will's quicksilver smile out of the corner of his eye. Jem wanted to grin back—there was a time he would have grinned back naturally, but something in the change that had been wrought in him put what felt like the distance of years between him and such simple mortal gestures.

The room was a mass of moving bodies and swinging weapons; Jem could see none of the other Shadowhunters clearly. He was aware of Will next to him, matching his stride to Jem's, matching him blow for blow. As metal rang on metal, some inner part of Jem, some part that had been lost without his even knowing it was lost, felt the pleasure of fighting together with Will one last time.

"Whatever you say, James," said Will. "Whatever you say."

Tessa swung around, bringing her dagger up, and plunged it into the creature's metal carapace. The blade punched through with an ugly ripping sound, followed by—her heart sank—a gravelly laugh. "Miss Gray," said a deep voice, and she looked up to see the smooth face of Armaros. "Surely you know better than that. No weapon that small can cut me apart, nor do you have the strength."

Tessa opened her mouth to scream, but his clawed hands seized her, and he swung her up in his arms, clamping his hand over her mouth to stifle her cry. Through the haze of movement in the room, the flash of swords and metal, she saw Will cutting apart the automaton that had fallen on Jem. He reached to move it, just as Armaros snarled into her ear: "I may be made of metal, but I have the heart of a demon, and my demon's heart yearns to feast on your flesh."

Armaros began to carry Tessa backward, through the fighting, even as she kicked at him with her boots. He tore her head to the side, his sharp fingers ripping the skin of her cheek.

"You can't kill me," she gasped. "The angel I wear protects my life—"

"Oh, no. It's true I cannot kill you, but I can hurt you. And I can hurt you most exquisitely. I have no flesh with which to feel pleasure, so the only pleasures left to me are causing pain. While the angel at your throat protects you—as do the orders of the Magister—I must stay my hand, but were the angel's power to fail—should it ever fail—I would rip you apart in my metal jaws."

They were outside the circle of the fighting now, and the demon was carrying her into an alcove, part hidden by a pillar of stone.

"Do it. I'd rather die by your hands than be married to Mortmain."

"Don't worry," he said, and while he spoke without breath, his words still felt like a whisper against her skin, making her shudder in horror. Cold metal fingers circled her arms like manacles as he drew her into the shadows. "I will make sure of both."

Cecily saw her brother slice out at the automaton attacking Brother Zachariah. The roar of metal as it collapsed forward tore her eardrums. She started toward Will, seizing a dagger from her belt—and then toppled forward as something closed about her ankle, jerking her off her feet.

She hit the ground on knees and elbows and twisted about to see that what had caught at her was the disembodied hand of an automaton. Sliced off at the wrist, black fluid pumping from the wires that still protruded from the jagged metal, its fingers were digging into her gear. She twisted and pivoted, hacking at the thing until its fingers loosened and separated and it clattered to the ground like a dead crab, twitching faintly.

She groaned in disgust and staggered to her feet, only to find that she could no longer see Will or Brother Zachariah. The room was a chaotic blur of motion. She saw Gabriel, back-to-back with his brother, a pile of dead automatons at their feet. Gabriel's gear was torn at the shoulder and he was bleeding. Cyril lay crumpled on the ground. Sophie had moved to be near him, slashing out in a circle with her sword, her scar livid in her pale face. Cecily could not see Magnus, but she could see the trail of blue sparks in the air that indicated his presence. And then there was Bridget, visible in flashes between the moving bodies of clockwork creatures, her weapon a blur, her red hair like a burning banner. And at her feet . . .

Cecily began to fight her way through the crowd toward them. Halfway there she dropped her dagger, picking up a long-handled axe that one of the automatons had dropped. It was surprisingly light in her grasp, and made a very satisfying *crunch* when she drove the blade into the chest of a mechanical demon that had reached to seize her, sending the automaton spinning backward.

And then she was leaping over a crumpled pile of fallen automatons, most of which had been hacked apart, their limbs scattered—no doubt the source of the hand that had seized her ankle. At the far end of the pile was Bridget, whirling this way and that as she beat back the tide of clockwork monsters threatening to advance on Charlotte and Henry. Bridget spared Cecily only a glance as the younger girl darted by her and dropped to her knees beside the head of the Institute.

"Charlotte," Cecily whispered.

Charlotte looked up. Her face was white with shock, her pupils so wide, they seemed to have swallowed the light brown of her eyes. Her arms were wrapped around Henry, his head lolling back against her fragile shoulder, her hands locked about his chest. He seemed entirely limp.

"Charlotte," Cecily said again. "We cannot win this fight. We must retreat."

"I cannot move Henry!"

"Charlotte—he is past our help now."

"No, he's not," Charlotte said wildly. "I can still feel his pulse."

Cecily reached out a hand. "Charlotte—"

"I am not mad! He is alive! He is alive, and I will not leave him!"

"Charlotte, the baby," Cecily said. "Henry would want you to save yourselves."

Something flickered in Charlotte's eyes—she tightened her grip on Henry. "Without Henry we cannot leave," she said. "We cannot make a Portal. We are trapped in this mountain."

Cecily's breath went out of her in a little gasp. She had not thought of that. Her heart pounded a sharp message through her veins: *We're going to die. We are all going to die.* Why had she chosen this? My God, what had she done? She raised her head, saw a familiar flash of blue and black at the corner of her vision—Will? The blue reminded her of something—of sparks rising above the smoke—

"Bridget," she said. "Get Magnus."

Bridget shook her head. "If I leave you, you will be dead in five minutes," she said. As if to illustrate her point, she brought her blade down on a charging automaton as if she were split-ting kindling. The creature fell to both slides, sliced down the middle in two equal parts.

"You don't understand," Cecily said. "We need Magnus—"

"I'm here." And he was, appearing above Cecily so suddenly and soundlessly that she stifled a scream. There was a long cut along his collar, shallow but bloody. Warlocks bled as red as humans did, it seemed. His gaze fell on Henry, and a terrible, fathomless sadness crossed his face. It was the look of a man who had seen hundreds die, who had lost and lost and lost and was facing loss once more. "God," he said. "He was a good man."

"No," Charlotte said. "I am telling you, I felt his pulse—do not speak of him as if he is gone already—"

Magnus dropped to his knees and reached a hand out to touch Henry's eyelids. Cecily wondered if he planned to say "*ave atque vale*," the requisite farewell for Shadowhunters, but instead he jerked his hand back, his eyes narrowing. A moment later his fingers were against Henry's throat. He muttered something in a language Cecily didn't understand, then slid closer, his hand rising to cup Henry's jaw. "Slow," he said, half to himself, "slow, but his heart *is* beating."

Charlotte took a ragged breath. "I told you."

Magnus's eyes flicked up to her. "You did. I'm sorry for not listening." His gaze dropped back down to Henry. "Now be quiet, everyone." He raised the hand that was not pressed to Henry's throat, and snapped his fingers. Instantly the air around them seemed to thicken and warp like old glass. A solid dome had appeared over them, trapping Henry, Charlotte, Cecily, and Magnus in a shimmering bubble of silence. Through it Cecily could still see the room around them, the battling automatons, Bridget laying waste right and left with her black-smeared blade. Inside, all was quiet.

She looked quickly at Magnus. "You've made a protective wall."

"Yes." His attention was on Henry. "Very good."

"Couldn't you just make one around all of us and keep it that way? Keep us all protected?"

Magnus shook his head. "Magic takes energy, little one. I could hold such a protection together for only a short time, and when it fell apart, *they* would fall upon *us*." He leaned forward, murmuring something, and a spark of blue leaped from his fingertips to Henry's skin. The pale blue fire seemed to burrow in, striking a sort of fire through Henry's veins, for as if Magnus had touched a match to one end of a line of gunpowder, trails of fire burned up his arms, tracing his neck and face. Charlotte, holding him, gasped as his body spasmed, his head jerking forward.

Henry's eyes flew open. They were tinted with the same blue fire that burned through his veins. "I—" His voice was rough. "What happened?"

Charlotte burst into tears. "Henry! Oh, my darling Henry." She clutched at him and kissed him frantically, and he threaded his fingers into her hair and held her there, and both Magnus and Cecily looked away.

When at last Charlotte let Henry go, still stroking his hair and murmuring, he struggled to sit up, and slumped back down. His eyes met Magnus's. Magnus looked down and away, his eyelids drooping with exhaustion and something else. Something that made Cecily's heart tighten.

"Henry," Charlotte said, sounding a little frightened, "is the pain bad? Can you stand?"

"There's little pain," Henry said. "But I cannot stand. I cannot feel my legs at all."

Magnus was still staring at the floor. "I am sorry," he said. "There are some things magic cannot do, some injuries it cannot touch."

The look on Charlotte's face was awful to see. *"Henry—"*

"I can still make a Portal," Henry interrupted. Blood trickled from the corner of his mouth; he wiped it away with his sleeve. "We can escape this place. We must retreat." He tried to turn, to look about him, and winced, whitening. "What is happening?"

"We are far outnumbered," said Cecily. "Everyone is fighting for their lives—"

"For their lives, but not to win?" Henry asked.

Magnus shook his head. "We cannot win. There is no hope. There are too many of them."

"And Tessa and Will?"

"Will found her," Cecily said. "They are here, in the room."

Henry closed his eyes, breathed in hard, then opened them again. The blue tinge had already begun to fade. "Then we must make a Portal. But first we must get everyone's attention—separate them from the automatons so that we are not all sucked through the Portal to the Institute together. The last thing we need is any of those Infernal Devices winding up in London." He looked at Magnus. "Reach into the pocket of my coat."

As Magnus reached out, Cecily saw that his hand was

trembling slightly. Clearly the effort of keeping the protective wall solid around them was beginning to take its toll on him.

He withdrew his hand from Henry's pocket. In it was a small golden box, with no visible hinges or opening.

Henry's words came with difficulty. "Cecily—take it, please. Take it, and throw it. As hard and far as you can."

Magnus handed over the box to Cecily with shaking fingers. It felt warm against her hand, though she could not tell if that was from some heat inside it or simply the result of its having been in Henry's pocket.

She glanced down at Magnus. His face was drawn. "I'm letting the wall down now," he said. "Throw, Cecily."

He raised his hands. Sparks flew; the wall shimmered and vanished. Cecily drew her arm back and threw the box.

For a moment nothing happened. Then there was a dull implosion—a vanishing inward of sound, as if everything in the room were being sucked down an enormous drain. Cecily's ears popped, and she sank to the ground, clapping her hands to the sides of her head. Magnus was also on his knees, and their small group huddled together as what seemed like a massive wind blew through the room.

The wind roared, and joining the sound of the wind was the sound of creaking, tearing metal as the clockwork creatures in the room began to stagger and stumble. Cecily saw Gabriel dart out of the way as an automaton fell at his feet and began spasming, its iron arms and legs flailing as if it were in the throes of a fit. Her eyes darted to Will and the Silent Brother he fought beside, whose hood had fallen back. Even among everything else that was happening, Cecily felt a shock go through her. Brother Zachariah was—*Jem*. She had known, they had all known, that Jem had gone to the Silent City to become a Silent Brother or die trying, but that he would be well enough to be here now, with them, fighting beside Will as he used to, that he would have the strength . . .

There was a crash as a clockwork monster crumpled to the ground between Will and Jem, forcing them to spring apart. The air smelled like the air just before a storm.

"*Henry*—" Charlotte's hair blew about her face.

Henry's face was tight with pain. "It's—a sort of Pyxis. Meant to detach demon souls from their bodies. Before death. I haven't had time—to perfect it. But it seemed worth trying."

Magnus staggered to his feet. His voice rose over the sound of crumpling metal and the high shrieks of demons. "Come here! All of you! *Gather, Shadowhunters!*"

Bridget stood her ground, still fighting two automatons whose movements had become jerky and uneven, but the others began to run toward them: Will, Jem, Gabriel . . . but Tessa, where was Tessa? Cecily saw Will realize Tessa's absence at the same time that she did; he turned, his hand on Jem's arm, his blue eyes scanning the room. She saw his lips form the word "Tessa," though she could hear nothing over the ever-louder shrieking of the wind, the shuddering of metal—

"*Stop.*"

A bolt of silvery light shot down, like a fork of lightning, from the top of the dome, and exploded through the room like the sparks of a Catherine wheel. The wind stilled and stopped, leaving the room filled with a ringing silence.

Cecily looked up. On the gallery halfway up the dome stood a man in a well-cut dark suit, a man she recognized instantly.

It was Mortmain.

* * *

"Stop."

The voice echoed through the room, sending chills through Tessa's veins. Mortmain. She knew his speech, his voice, even though she could see nothing past the stone pillar that hid the alcove Armaros had dragged her into. The demon automaton had kept a tight hold on her, even as a dull explosion had rocked the room, followed by a biting, vicious wind that had blown past their alcove, leaving them untouched.

Silence had fallen now, and Tessa wanted desperately to tear away from the metal arms that held her, to run into the room and see if any of her friends, those she loved, had been harmed, even killed. But struggling against him was like struggling against a wall. She kicked out anyway, just as Mortmain's voice rang through the room again:

"Where is Miss Gray? Bring her to me."

Armaros made a rumbling noise, and lurched into motion. Lifting Tessa by the arms, he carried her from the alcove into the main room.

It was a scene of chaos. The automatons stood frozen, looking up at their master. Many were crumpled on the ground, or hacked into pieces. The floor was slippery with a mixture of blood and oil.

In the center of the room, in a circle, stood the Shadowhunters and their companions. Cyril was kneeling upon the ground, a torn piece of bloody bandage wrapped around his leg. Near him was Henry, half-sitting and half-lying down in Charlotte's arms. He was pale, so pale. . . . Tessa's eyes met Will's as he raised his head and saw her. A look of dismay passed over his face, and he started forward. Jem seized his sleeve. His eyes were on Tessa too; they were wide and dark and full of horror.

She looked away from both of them, away and up at Mortmain. He stood at the railing of the gallery above them, like a preacher at a pulpit, and smirked down. "Miss Gray," he said. "So good of you to join us."

She spat, tasting blood in her mouth where the automaton's fingers had raked her cheek.

Mortmain raised an eyebrow. "Set her down," he said to Armaros. "Keep your hands on her shoulders."

The demon obeyed with a low chuckle. As soon as Tessa's boots touched the ground, she straightened her spine, raising her chin and glaring viciously at Mortmain. "It's bad luck to see the bride before the wedding day," she said.

"Indeed," Mortmain said. "But bad luck for whom?"

Tessa did not look around. The sight of so many automatons, and the ragtag band of Shadowhunters who were all that stood before them, was too painful. "The Nephilim have already entered your fortress," she said. "There will be others behind them. They will swarm your automatons and destroy them. Surrender now, and perhaps you will keep your life."

Mortmain threw his head back and laughed. "Brava, madam," he said. "You stand there surrounded by defeat, and demand my surrender."

"We are not defeated—," Will began, and Mortmain hissed out a breath through his teeth, audible in the echoing room. As one, all the automatons in the room snapped their heads toward Will—a terrifying synchronicity.

"Not a word from you, Nephilim," Mortmain said. "The

next time one of you speaks will be the last time you ever draw breath."

"Let them go," Tessa said. "This is nothing to do with them. Let them go, and keep me."

"You bargain with nothing in your hands," Mortmain said. "You are wrong if you think other Shadowhunters are coming to help you. At this very moment a significant part of my army is cutting your Council to pieces." Tessa heard Charlotte gasp, a short, stifled noise. "Clever of the Nephilim to handily assemble themselves all in one place, that I might wipe them out in one fell swoop."

"Please," Tessa said. "Turn your hand from them. Your grievances against the Nephilim are just. But if they are all dead, who will be lessoned by your vengeance? Who will atone? If there is no one to learn from the past, there is no one to carry on its lessons. Let them live. Let them carry your teachings into the future. They can be your legacy."

He nodded thoughtfully, as though he were weighing her words. "I *will* spare them—I will keep them here, as our prisoners. Their captivity will keep you pleasant, and it will keep you obedient"—his voice hardened—"because you love them, and if you ever even try to escape, I will kill them *all*." He paused. "What do you say, Miss Gray? I have been generous, and now I am owed thanks."

The only sound in the room was the creak of the automatons and Tessa's own blood pounding in her ears. She realized now what Mrs. Black had meant by her words in the carriage. *And the more knowledge of them you have, the more your sympathies lie with them, the more effective a weapon you will be to raze them to the ground.* Tessa had become one of the Shadowhunters, if not entirely like them. She cared for them and loved them, and Mortmain would use that caring and that love to force her hand. In saving the few she loved, she would doom them all. And yet to condemn Will and Jem, Charlotte and Henry, Cecily and the others to death was unthinkable.

"Yes." She heard Jem—or was it Will—make a muffled sound. "Yes, I will take that bargain." She looked up. "Tell the demon to let me go, and I will come up to you."

She saw Mortmain's eyes narrow. "No," he said. "Armaros, bring her to me."

The demon's hands tightened on her arms; Tessa bit her lip with the pain. As if in sympathy, the clockwork angel at her throat twitched.

Few can claim a single angel who guards them. But you can.

Her hand went to her throat. The angel seemed to thrum under her fingers, as if it were breathing, as if it were trying to communicate something to her. Her hand tightened on it, the points of the wings cutting into her palm. She thought of her dream.

Is this what you look like?

You see here only a fraction of what I am. In my true form I am deadly glory.

Armaros's hands closed on Tessa's arms.

Your clockwork angel contains within it a bit of the spirit of an angel, Mortmain had said. She thought of the white star mark the clockwork angel had left on Will's shoulder. She thought of the smooth, beautiful, unmoving face of the angel, the cool hands that had held her as she had fallen from Mrs. Black's carriage toward the churning water below.

The demon began to lift her.

Tessa thought of her dream.

She took a deep breath. She did not know if what she was about to do was even possible, or simply madness. As Armaros raised her with his hands, she closed her eyes, reaching out with her mind, reaching *into* the clockwork angel. She tumbled for a moment through dark space, and then a gray limbo, seeking that light, that spark of spirit, that *life*—

And there it was, a sudden blaze, a bonfire, brighter than any spark she had ever seen before. She reached for it, wrapping it about herself, coils of white fire that burned and scorched her skin. She screamed aloud—

And Changed.

White fire blasted through her veins. She shot upward, her gear ripping and tearing and falling away, light blazing all around her. She was fire. She was a falling star. Armaros's arms were torn from her body—soundlessly he melted and dissolved, scorched by the heavenly fire that blazed through Tessa.

She was flying—flying upward. No, she was rising, *growing*. Her bones stretched and elongated, a lattice being pulled outward and upward as she grew impossibly. Her skin had turned gold, and it stretched and tore as she hurtled upward like the bean stalk from the old fairy tale, and where her skin tore, golden ichor leaked from the wounds. Curls like shavings of hot white metal sprang from her head, surrounding her face. And from her back burst wings—massive wings, greater than any bird's.

She supposed that she should be terrified. Glancing down, she saw the Shadowhunters staring up at her, their mouths open. The whole room was filled with blinding light, light that poured from *her*. She had *become* Ithuriel. The divine fire of angels was blazing through her, scorching her bones, searing her eyes. But she felt only a steely calm.

She stood twenty feet high now. She was eye to eye with Mortmain, who was frozen with terror, his hands gripping the railing of the balcony. The clockwork angel, after all, had been his gift to her mother. He must never have imagined that it would ever be put to this use.

"It's not possible," he said hoarsely. "Not possible—"

You have entrapped an angel of Heaven, Tessa said, though it was not her voice speaking but Ithuriel's speaking through her. His voice echoed through her body like the ringing of a gong. Distantly she wondered if her heart was beating—did angels have hearts? Would this kill her? If it did, it was worth it. *You have tried to create life. Life is the province of Heaven. And Heaven does not take kindly to usurpers.*

Mortmain turned to run. But he was slow, as all humans were slow. Tessa reached out her hand, Ithuriel's hand, and closed it about him as he ran, lifting him off his feet. He screamed as the angel's grip scorched him. He was writhing, already burning, as Tessa tightened her grip, crushing his body to a jelly of scarlet blood and white bones.

She opened her fingers. Mortmain's crushed body fell, crashing to the ground among his own automatons. There was a shuddering, a great creaking scream of metal as of a building collapsing, and the automatons began to fall, one by one, crumpling to the ground, lifeless without their Magister to animate them. A garden of metal flowers, withering and dying one by one, and the Shadowhunters stood in the center of them, looking about themselves in wonder.

And then Tessa realized that she did still have a heart, for it leaped in joy to see them alive and safe. Yet even as she reached for them with her golden hands—one stained with scarlet now, Mortmain's blood mixing with Ithuriel's golden ichor—they shrank back from the blaze of light around her. *No, no,* she wanted to say, *I would never hurt you,* but the words would not come. She could not speak; the burning was too great. She struggled to find her way back to herself, to Change into Tessa again, but she was lost in the blaze of the fire, as if she had fallen into the heart of the sun. An agony of flames exploded through her, and she felt herself begin to fall, the clockwork angel a red-hot lariat about her throat. *Please,* she thought, but everything was fire and burning, and she fell, senseless, into the light.

22

THUNDER IN THE TRUMPET

For till the thunder in the trumpet be,
Soul may divide from body, but not we
One from another
—Algernon Charles Swinburne, "Laus Veneris"

Clockwork creatures clawed at Tessa out of black mists. Fire ran through her veins, and when she looked down, her skin was cracked and blistering, golden ichor running in sheets down her arms. She saw the endless fields of Heaven, saw a sky constantly on fire with a blaze that would have blinded any human. She saw silver clouds with edges like razors, and felt the icy emptiness that hollowed the hearts of angels.

"*Tessa.*" It was Will; she would have known his speech anywhere. "*Tessa, wake up, wake up. Tessa, please.*"

She could hear the pain in his voice and wanted to reach

out for him, but as she lifted her arms, the flames rose and charred her fingers. Her hands turned to ash and blew away on the hot wind.

Tessa tossed on her bed in a delirium of fever and nightmares. The sheets, twisted around her, were soaked with sweat, her hair plastered to her temples. Her skin, always pale, was near-translucent, showing the mapping of veins beneath her skin, the shape of her bones. Her clockwork angel was at her throat; every once in a while she would catch at it, and then cry out in a lost voice, as if the touch pained her.

"She's in so much agony." Charlotte dipped a cloth in cool water and pressed it to Tessa's burning forehead. The girl made a soft protesting sound at the touch but didn't move to bat Charlotte's hand away. Charlotte would have liked to think it was because the cool cloths were helping, but she knew that it was more likely that Tessa was simply becoming too exhausted. "Isn't there anything more we can do?"

The angel's fire is leaving her body. Brother Enoch, standing at Charlotte's side, spoke in his eerie omnidirectional whisper. *It will take the time it takes. She will be free of pain when it is gone.*

"But she will live?"

She has survived thus far. The Silent Brother sounded grim. *The fire should have killed her. It would have killed any normal human. But she is part Shadowhunter and part demon, and she was protected by the angel whose fire she drew on. It shielded her even in those last moments as it blazed up and burned away its own corporeal form.*

Charlotte could not help but remember the circular room under Cadair Idris, Tessa stepping forward and transforming from girl into flame, blazing up like a column of fire, her hair turning to tendrils of sparks, the light of it blinding and terrifying. Crouched on the floor by Henry's body, Charlotte had wondered how even angels could burn like that and live.

When the angel had left Tessa, she had collapsed, her clothes hanging in tatters and her skin covered in marks as if she had been scorched. Several Shadowhunters had rushed to her side between the crumpling automatons, though it had been something of a blur to Charlotte—scenes viewed through the wavering lens of her terror over Henry: Will lifting Tessa in his arms; the Magister's stronghold beginning to close itself up behind them, doors slamming closed as they raced through the corridors, Magnus's blue fire lighting them a path to escape. The creation of a second Portal. More Silent Brothers waiting for them at the Institute, scarred hands and scarred faces, shutting out even Charlotte as they closed themselves in with Henry and Tessa. Will turning to Jem, his expression stricken. He had reached out for his *parabatai*.

"James," he had said. "You can find out—what they're doing to her—if she'll live—"

But Brother Enoch had stepped between them. *His name is not James Carstairs*, he had said. *It is Zachariah now.*

Will's look, the way he had lowered his hand. "Let him speak for himself."

But Jem had only turned, turned and walked away from all of them, out of the Institute, Will watching him go in disbelief, and Charlotte had remembered the first time they had ever met: *Are you really dying? I am sorry.*

It was Will, still looking stunned and disbelieving, who had explained to them all, haltingly, Tessa's story: the function of the clockwork angel, the tale of the ill-fated Starkweathers, and the unorthodox manner of Tessa's conception. Aloysius had been right, Charlotte reflected. Tessa was his great-granddaughter. A descendant he would never know, for he had been slain in the Council massacre.

Charlotte couldn't stop herself from imagining what it must have been like when the doors of the Council room had opened and the automatons had poured in. Councils were not required to be unarmed, but they were not prepared to fight. Nor had most Shadowhunters ever faced an automaton. Even to imagine the slaughter chilled her. She was overwhelmed by the enormity of the loss to the Shadowhunter world, though it would have been much greater had Tessa not made the sacrifice she did. All the automatons had fallen with Mortmain's death, even the ones in the Council rooms, and the majority of the Shadowhunters had survived, though there had been heavy losses—including the Consul.

"Part demon and part Shadowhunter," Charlotte murmured now, gazing down at Tessa. "What does that make her?"

Nephilim blood is dominant. A new kind of Shadowhunter. New is not always a bad thing, Charlotte.

It was because of that Nephilim blood that they had gone so far as to try healing runes upon Tessa, but the runes had simply sunk into her skin and vanished, like words written in water. Charlotte reached out now to touch Tessa's collarbone, where the rune had been inked. Her skin was hot to the touch.

"Her clockwork angel," Charlotte observed. "It has stopped its ticking."

The angel's presence has left it. Ithuriel is free, and Tessa unprotected, though with the Magister dead, and as a Nephilim herself, she will likely be safe. As long as she does not attempt to transform herself into an angel a second time. It would certainly kill her.

"There are other dangers."

We all must face dangers, said Brother Enoch. It was the same cool, unruffled mental voice he had used when he had told her that though Henry would live, he would never walk again.

On the bed Tessa stirred, crying out in a dry voice. In her sleep, since the battle, she had called out names. She had called for Nate, and for her aunt, and for Charlotte. "Jem," she whispered now, clutching fitfully at her coverlet.

Charlotte turned away from Enoch as she reached for the cool cloth again and laid it across Tessa's forehead. She knew she should not ask, and yet—

"How is he? Our Jem? Is he—adjusting to the Brotherhood?"

She felt Enoch's reproach. You know I cannot tell you that. He is no longer your Jem. He is Brother Zachariah now. You must forget him.

"Forget him? I cannot forget him," Charlotte said. "He is not as your other Brothers, Enoch; you know that."

The rituals that make a Silent Brother are our deepest secrets.

"I am not asking to know of your rituals," Charlotte said. "Yet I know that most Silent Brothers sever their ties to their mortal lives before they enter the Brotherhood. But James could not do that. He still has that which tethers him to this world." She looked down at Tessa, her eyelids fluttering as she breathed harshly. "It is a cord that ties each of them to the other, and unless it is dissolved properly, I fear it may harm them both."

"'She is coming, my own, my sweet;
Were it ever so airy a tread,
My heart would hear her and beat,

Were it earth in an earthy bed;
My dust would hear her and beat,
Had I lain for a century dead;
Would start and tremble under her feet,
And blossom in purple and red."'

"Oh, for goodness' sake," Henry said irritably, pushing up the ink-stained sleeves of his dressing gown. "Can't you read something less depressing? Something with a good battle in it."

"It's Tennyson," said Will, sliding his feet off the ottoman near the fire. They were in the drawing room, Henry's chair pulled up near the fire, a sketchbook open on his lap. He was still pale, as he had been since the battle at Cadair Idris, though he was beginning to get his color back. "It will improve your mind."

Before Henry could reply, the door opened, and Charlotte came in, looking tired, the lace-edged sleeves of her sack dress stained with water. Will immediately set his book down, and Henry, too, looked up inquiringly from his sketchbook.

Charlotte glanced from one of them to the other, noting the book on the side table beside the silver tea service. "Have you been reading to Henry, Will?"

"Yes, some dreadful thing, all full of poetry." Henry had a pen in one hand and papers scattered all over the lap rug drawn up around his knees.

Henry had met with his usual fortitude the news that even the Silent Brothers' healing would not let him walk again. And a conviction that he must build himself a chair, like a sort of Bath chair but better, with self-propelling wheels and all manner of other accoutrements. He was determined that it be able to go up and down stairs, so that he could still get to his inventions in the crypt. He had been scribbling designs for the chair the whole hour that Will had been reading to him from "Maud," but then poetry had never been Henry's area of interest.

"Well, you are released from your duties, Will, and, Henry, you are released from further poetry," said Charlotte. "If you like, darling, I can help you gather your notes—" She slipped around behind her husband's chair and reached over his shoulders, helping scoop his scattered papers into a neat pile. He took her wrist as she moved, and looked up at her—a gaze of such trust and adoration that it made Will feel as if tiny knives were cutting at his skin.

It was not as if he begrudged Charlotte and Henry their happiness—far from it. But he could not help but think of Tessa. Of the hopes he had cherished once and repressed later. He wondered if she had ever looked at him like that. He did not think so. He had worked so hard to destroy her trust, and though all he wanted was a true chance to rebuild it for her, he could not help but fear—

He pushed the dark thoughts back and rose to his feet, about to explain that he intended to go see Tessa. Before he could speak, there was a knock at the door, and Sophie came in, looking unaccountably anxious. The anxiety was explained a moment later when the Inquisitor followed her into the room.

Will, used to seeing him in his ceremonial robes at Council meetings, almost didn't recognize the stern-looking man in the gray morning coat and dark trousers. There was a livid scar on his cheek that had not been there before.

"Inquisitor Whitelaw." Charlotte straightened up, her

expression suddenly serious. "To what do we owe the honor of your visit?"

"Charlotte," said the Inquisitor, and he held out his hand. There was a letter, sealed with the seal of the Council. "I have brought a message for you."

Charlotte looked at him in bewilderment. "You could not simply have sent it through the post?"

"This letter is of grave importance. It is imperative that you read it now."

Slowly Charlotte reached out and took it. She pulled at the flap, then frowned and crossed the room to take a letter opener from her bureau. Will took the opportunity to stare at the Inquisitor covertly. The man was frowning at Charlotte and ignoring Will entirely. He could not help but wonder if the scar on the Inquisitor's cheek was a relic of the Council's battle with Mortmain's automatons.

Will had been sure that they were all going to die, together, there under the mountain, until Tessa had blazed up in all the glory of the angel and struck down Mortmain like lightning striking down a tree. It had been one of the most wondrous things he had ever seen, but his wonder had been consumed quickly by terror when Tessa had collapsed after the Change, bleeding and insensible, however hard they'd tried to wake her. Magnus, near exhaustion, had barely been able to open a Portal back to the Institute with Henry's help, and Will remembered only a blur after that, a blur of exhaustion and blood and fear, more Silent Brothers summoned to tend the wounded, and the news coming from the Council of all who had been killed in battle before the automatons had disintegrated upon Mortmain's death. And Tessa—Tessa not speaking, not waking, being carried off to her room by the Silent Brothers, and he had not been able to go with her. Being neither brother nor husband he could only stand and stare after her, closing and unclosing his bloodstained hands. Never had he felt more helpless.

And when he had turned to find Jem, to share his fear with the only other person in the world who loved Tessa as much as he did—Jem had been gone, back to the Silent City on the orders of the Brothers. Gone without even a word of good-bye.

Though Cecily had tried to soothe him, Will had been angry— angry with Jem, and with the Council and the Brotherhood themselves, for allowing Jem to become a Silent Brother, though Will knew that was unfair, that it had been Jem's choice and the only way to keep him alive. And yet since their return to the Institute, Will had felt constantly seasick—it was like having been a ship at anchor for years and being cut free to float on the tides, with no idea which direction to steer in. And Tessa—

The sound of tearing paper interrupted his thoughts, as Charlotte opened the letter and read it, the color draining from her face. She lifted her eyes and stared at the Inquisitor. "Is this some sort of jest?"

The Inquisitor's frown deepened. "There is no jest, I assure you. Do you have an answer?"

"Lottie," said Henry, looking up at his wife, even his tufts of gingery hair radiating anxiety and love. "Lottie, what is it, what's wrong?"

She looked at him, and then back at the Inquisitor. "No," she said. "I don't have an answer. Not yet."

"The Council does not wish—," he began, and then seemed to see Will for the first time. "If I could speak to you in private, Charlotte."

Charlotte straightened her spine. "I will not send either Will or Henry away."

The two of them glared at each other, eyes locked. Will knew that Henry was looking at him anxiously. In the aftermath of Charlotte's disagreement with the Consul, and the Consul's death, they had all waited breathlessly for the Council to hand down some sort of retributive judgment. Their hold on the Institute felt precarious. Will could see it in the minute trembling of Charlotte's hands, and the set of her mouth.

He wished suddenly that Jem or Tessa were here, someone he could speak to, someone he could ask what he should do for Charlotte, to whom he owed so much.

"It's all right," he said, rising to his feet. He wanted to see Tessa, even if she would not open her eyes, not recognize him. "I had meant to go anyway."

"Will—," Charlotte protested.

"It's all right, Charlotte," Will said again, and he pushed past the Inquisitor to the door. Once out in the corridor, he leaned against the wall for a moment, recovering himself. He couldn't help remembering his own words—God, it seemed a million years ago now, and no longer in the least bit funny: *The Consul? Breaking up our breakfast time? Whatever next? The Inquisitor over for tea?*

If the Institute was taken from Charlotte . . .

If they all lost their home . . .

If Tessa . . .

He could not finish the thought. Tessa would live; she must live. As he set off down the corridor, he thought of the blues and greens and grays of Wales. Perhaps he could return there, with Cecily, if the Institute was lost, make some kind of life for themselves in their home country. It would not be a Shadowhunting life, but without Charlotte, without Henry, without Jem or Tessa or Sophie or even the bloody Lightwoods, he did not want to be a Shadowhunter. They were his family, and precious to him—just another realization, he thought, that had come to him all at once and yet too late.

"Tessa. Wake up. Please, wake up."

Sophie's voice now, cutting through the darkness. Tessa struggled, forcing her eyes open for a split second. She saw her bedroom at the Institute, the familiar furniture, the drapes pulled back, weak sunlight casting squares of light on the floor. She fought to hold on to it. It was like this, brief periods of lucidity in between fever and nightmares—never enough, never enough time to reach out, to speak. *Sophie,* she fought to whisper, but her dry lips would not pass the words. Lightning shivered down through her vision, splitting the world apart. She cried out soundlessly as the Institute broke into pieces and rushed away from her into the dark.

It was Cyril who finally told Gabriel that Cecily was in the stables, after the younger Lightwood brother had spent much of the day searching fruitlessly—though, he hoped not obviously—through the Institute for her.

Twilight had come, and the stable was full of warm yellow lantern light and the smell of horses. Cecily was standing by Balios's stall, her head against the neck of the great black horse. Her hair, nearly the same inky color, was loose over her shoulders. When she turned to look at him, Gabriel saw the wink of the red ruby around her throat.

A look of concern passed across her face. "Has something happened to Will?"

"Will?" Gabriel was startled.

"I just thought—the way you looked—" She sighed. "He has been so distraught these past few days. If it were not enough that Tessa is ill and injured, to know what he does about Jem—" She shook her head. "I have tried to speak to him about it, but he will say nothing."

"I think he is speaking to Jem now," Gabriel said. "I confess I do not know his state of mind. If you wish, I could—"

"No." Cecily's voice was quiet. Her blue eyes were fixed on something far away. "Let him be."

Gabriel took a few steps forward. The soft yellow glow of the lantern at Cecily's feet laid a faint golden sheen over her skin. Her hands were bare of gloves, very white against the horse's black hide. "I . . . ," he began. "You seem to like that horse very much."

Silently he cursed himself. He remembered his father once saying that women, the gentler sex, liked to be wooed with charming words and pithy phrases. He wasn't sure exactly what a pithy phrase was, but he was sure that "You seem to like that horse very much" was not one.

Cecily seemed not to mind, though. She gave the horse's hide an absent pat before turning to face him. "Balios saved my brother's life."

"Are you going to leave?" Gabriel said abruptly.

Her eyes widened. "What was that, Mr. Lightwood?"

"No." He held his hand up. "Don't call me Mr. Lightwood,

please. We are Shadowhunters. I am Gabriel to you."

Her cheeks pinked. "Gabriel, then. Why did you ask me if I am leaving?"

"You came here to bring your brother home," said Gabriel. "But it is clear he is not going to go, isn't it? He is in love with Tessa. He is going to stay wherever she is."

"She might not stay here," Cecily said, her eyes unreadable.

"I think she will. But even if she does not, he will go where she is. And Jem—Jem has become a Silent Brother. He is still Nephilim. If Will hopes to see him again, and I think we know he does, he will remain. The years have changed him, Cecily. His family is here now."

"Do you think you are telling me anything I have not observed for myself? Will's heart is here, not in Yorkshire, in a house he has never lived in, with parents he has not seen for years."

"Then, if he cannot go home—I thought perhaps that you would."

"So that my parents are not alone. Yes. I can see why you would think that." She hesitated. "You know, of course, that in a few years I would be expected to be married, and to leave my parents regardless."

"But not to never speak to them again. They are exiled, Cecily. If you remain here, you will be cut off from them."

"You say it as if you wish to convince me to return home."

"I say it because I am afraid you will." The words were out of his mouth before he could recapture them; he could only look at her as a flush of embarrassment heated his face.

She took a step toward him. Her blue eyes, upturned to his,

were wide. He wondered when they had stopped reminding him of Will's eyes; they were just Cecily's eyes, a shade of blue he associated with her alone. "When I came here," she said, "I thought the Shadowhunters were monsters. I thought I had to rescue my brother. I thought that we would return home together, and my parents would be proud of us both. That we would be a family again. Then I realized—you helped me realize—"

"I helped you? How?"

"Your father did not give you choices," she said. "He demanded that you be what he wanted. And that demand broke your family apart. But my father, he chose to leave the Nephilim and marry my mother. That was *his* choice, just as staying with the Shadowhunters is Will's. Choosing love or war: both are brave choices, in their own ways. And I do not think my parents would grudge Will his choice. Above all, what matters to them is that he be happy."

"But what of you?" Gabriel said, and they were very close now, almost touching. "It is your choice to make now, to stay or return."

"I will stay," Cecily said. "I choose the war."

Gabriel let out the breath he hadn't realized he was holding. "You will give up your home?"

"A drafty old house in Yorkshire?" Cecily said. "This is London."

"And give up what is familiar?"

"Familiar is dull."

"And give up seeing your parents? It is against the Law . . ."

She smiled, the glimmer of a smile. "Everyone breaks the Law."

"Cecy," he said, and closed the distance between them, though it was not much, and then he was kissing her—his hands awkward around her shoulders at first, slipping on the stiff taffeta of her gown before his fingers slid behind her head, tangling in her soft, warm hair. She stiffened in surprise before softening against him, the seam of her lips parting as he tasted the sweetness of her mouth. When she drew away at last, he felt light-headed. "Cecy?" he said again, his voice hoarse.

"Five," she said. Her lips and cheeks were flushed, but her gaze was steady.

"Five?" he echoed blankly.

"My rating," she said, and smiled at him. "Your skill and technique may, perhaps, require work, but the native talent is certainly there. What you require is *practice*."

"And you are willing to be my tutor?"

"I should be very insulted if you chose another," she said, and leaned up to kiss him again.

When Will came into Tessa's room, Sophie was sitting by her bed, murmuring in a soft voice. She swung around as the door closed behind Will. The corners of her mouth looked pinched and worried.

"How is she?" Will asked, pushing his hands deep into his trouser pockets. It hurt to see Tessa like this, hurt as if a sliver of ice had lodged itself under his ribs and was digging into his heart. Sophie had plaited Tessa's long brown hair neatly so that it would not tangle when she tossed her head fitfully against the pillows. She breathed quickly, her chest rising and falling fast, her eyes visibly moving beneath her pale eyelids. He wondered what she was dreaming.

"The same," Sophie said, rising gracefully to her feet and ceding him the chair beside the bed. "She has been calling out again."

"For anyone particular?" Will asked, and then was immediately sorry he had asked. Surely his motives would be ridiculously transparent.

Sophie's dark hazel eyes darted away from his. "For her brother," she said. "If you wish a few moments alone with Miss Tessa . . ."

"Yes, please, Sophie."

She paused at the door. "Master William," she said.

Having just settled himself in the armchair beside the bed, Will glanced over at her.

"I am sorry I have thought and spoken so ill of you for all these years," Sophie said. "I understand now that you were only doing what we all try to do. Our best."

Will reached out and placed his hand over Tessa's left one, where it plucked feverishly at the coverlet. "Thank you," he said, unable to look at Sophie directly; a moment later he heard the door softly close behind her.

He looked at Tessa. She was momentarily quiet, her lashes fluttering as she breathed. The circles beneath her eyes were dark blue, her veins a delicate filigree at her temples and the insides of her wrists. When he remembered her blazing up in glory, it was impossible to believe her fragile, yet here she was. Her hand felt hot in his, and when he brushed his knuckles against her cheek, her skin was burning.

"Tess," he whispered. "Hell is cold. Do you remember when you told me that? We were in the cellars of the Dark House. Anyone else would have been panicking, but you were as calm as a governess, telling me Hell was covered in ice. If it is the fire of Heaven that takes you from me, what a cruel irony that would be."

She breathed in sharply, and for a moment his heart leaped—had she heard him? But her eyes remained firmly shut.

His hand tightened on hers.

"Come back," he said. "Come back to me, Tessa. Henry said that perhaps, since you had touched the soul of an angel, that you dream of Heaven now, of fields of angels and flowers of fire. Perhaps you are happy in those dreams. But I ask this out of pure selfishness. Come back to me. For I cannot bear to lose all my heart."

Her head turned slowly toward him, her lips parting as if she were about to speak. He leaned forward, heart leaping.

"Jem?" she said.

He froze, unmoving, his hand still wrapped about hers. Her eyes fluttered open—as gray as the sky before rain, as gray as the slate hills of Wales. The color of tears. She looked at him, through him, not seeing him at all.

"Jem," she said again. "Jem, I am so sorry. It is all my fault."

Will leaned forward again. He could not help himself. She was speaking, and comprehensibly, for the first time in days. Even if not to him.

"It's not your fault," he said.

She returned the pressure of his hand hotly; each of her individual fingers seemed to burn through his skin. "But it is," she said. "It is because of me that Mortmain deprived you of your *yin fen*. It is because of me that all of you were in danger. I was meant to love you, and all I did was shorten your life."

Will took a ragged breath. The splinter of ice was back in his heart, and he felt as if he were breathing around it. And yet it was not jealousy, but a sorrow more profound and deeper than any he thought he had known before. He thought of Sydney Carton. *Think now and then that there is a man who would give his life, to keep a life you love beside you.* Yes, he would have done that for Tessa—died to keep the ones she needed beside her—and so would Jem have done that for him or for Tessa, and so would Tessa, he thought, do that for both of them. It was a near incomprehensible tangle, the three of them, but there was one certainty, and that was that there was no lack of love between them.

I am strong enough for this, he told himself, lifting her hand gently. "Life is not just surviving," he said. "There is also happiness. You know your James, Tessa. You know he would choose love over the span of his years."

But Tessa's head only tossed fretfully on the pillow. "Where are you, James? I search for you in the darkness, but I cannot find you. You are my intended; we should be bound by ties that cannot sever. And yet when you were dying, I was not there. I have never said good-bye."

"What darkness? Tessa, where are you?" Will gripped her hand. "Give me a way to find you."

Tessa arched back on the bed suddenly, her hand clamping down on his. "I'm sorry!" she gasped. "Jem—I am so sorry—I have wronged you, wronged you horribly—"

"Tessa!" Will bolted to his feet, but Tessa had already collapsed bonelessly onto the mattress, breathing hard.

He could not help it. He cried out for Charlotte like a child who had woken from a nightmare, as he had never permitted himself to cry out when he truly was a child, waking in the then unfamiliar Institute and longing for comfort but knowing he must not take it.

Charlotte came running through the Institute, as he had always known she would come running for him if he called. She arrived, breathless and frightened; she took one look at Tessa on the bed, and Will clasping her hand, and he saw the terror leave her face, replaced by a look of wordless sorrow. "Will . . ."

Will gently detached his hand from Tessa's, turning toward the door. "Charlotte," he said. "I have never asked you to use your position as head of the Institute to help me before—"

"My position cannot heal Tessa."

"It can. You must bring Jem here."

"I cannot demand that," Charlotte said. "Jem has only just begun his term of service in the Silent City. New Initiates are not meant to leave at all for the first year—"

"He came to the battle."

Charlotte pushed a stray curl from her face. Sometimes she looked very young, as she did now, though earlier, facing the Inquisitor in the drawing room, she had not. "That was Brother Enoch's choice."

Certainty straightened Will's spine. For so many years he had doubted the contents of his own heart. He did not doubt them now. "Tessa needs Jem," he said. "I know the Law, I know he cannot come home, but—the Silent Brothers are meant to sever every bond that ties them to the mortal world before they join the Brotherhood. That is also the Law. The bond between Tessa and Jem was not severed. How is she to rejoin the mortal world, then, if she cannot even see Jem one last time?"

Charlotte was silent for a space of time. There was a shadow over her face, one he could not define. Surely she would want this, for Jem, for Tessa, for both of them? "Very well," she said at last. "I shall see what I can do."

"They lighted down to take a drink
Of the spring that ran so clear,
And there she spied his bonny heart's blood,
A-running down the stream.
'Hold up, hold up, Lord William,' she said,
'For I fear that you are slain;'
"Tis nought but the dye of my scarlet clothes,
That is sparkling down the stream.'"

"Oh, for goodness' sake," Sophie muttered as she passed the kitchen. Did Bridget really have to be so morbid in all her songs, and did she have to use Will's *name*? As if the poor boy hadn't suffered enough—

A shadow materialized out of the darkness. "Sophie?"

Sophie screamed and nearly dropped her carpet brush. Witchlight flared up in the dim corridor, and she saw familiar gray-green eyes.

"Gideon!" she exclaimed. "Heavens above, you nearly frightened me to death."

He looked penitent. "I apologize. I only wished to wish you good night—and you were smiling as you walked along. I thought . . ."

"I was thinking about Master Will," she said, and then smiled again at his dismayed expression. "Only that a year ago, if you had told me that someone was tormenting him, I would have been delighted, but now I find myself in sympathy with him. That is all."

He looked sober. "I am in sympathy with him as well. Every day that Tessa does not wake, you can see a bit of the life drain out of him."

"If only Master Jem were here . . ." Sophie sighed. "But he is not."

"There is much that we must learn to live without, these days." Gideon touched her cheek lightly with his fingers. They were rough, the fingers callused. Not the smooth fingers of a gentleman. Sophie smiled at him.

"You didn't look at me at dinner," he said, dropping his voice. It was true—dinner had been a quick affair of cold roast chicken and potatoes. No one had seemed to have much appetite, save Gabriel and Cecily, who'd eaten as if they had spent the day training. Perhaps they had.

"I have been concerned about Mrs. Branwell," Sophie confessed. "She has been so worried, about Mr. Branwell, and about Miss Tessa, she is wasting away, and the baby—" She bit her lip. "I am concerned," she said again. She could not bring herself to say more. It was hard to lose the reticence of a lifetime of service, even if she *was* engaged to a Shadowhunter now.

"Yours is a gentle heart," Gideon said, sliding his fingers down her cheek to touch her lips, like the lightest of kisses. Then he drew back. "I saw Charlotte go alone into the drawing room, only a few moments ago. Perhaps you could have a word with her about your concern?"

"I couldn't—"

"Sophie," Gideon said. "You are not just Charlotte's maid; you are her friend. If she will talk to anyone, it will be to you."

* * *

The drawing room was cold and dark. There was no fire in the grate, and none of the lamps were lit against the cloak of night, which cast the chamber into gloom and shadow. It took Sophie a moment to even realize that one of the shadows was Charlotte, a small silent figure in the chair behind the desk.

"Mrs. Branwell," she said, feeling a great awkwardness come upon her, despite Gideon's encouraging words. Two days ago she and Charlotte had fought side by side at Cadair Idris. Now she was a servant again, here to clean the grate and dust the room for the next day's use. A bucket of coals in one hand, tinderbox in her apron pocket. "I am sorry—I did not mean to interrupt."

"You are not interrupting, Sophie. Not anything important." Charlotte's voice—Sophie had never heard her sound like that before. So small, or so defeated.

Sophie set the coals down by the fire and approached her mistress hesitantly. Charlotte was seated with her elbows on the desk, her face resting in her hands. A letter was on the desk, with the seal of the Council broken open. Sophie's heart sped suddenly, remembering how the Consul had ordered them all out of the Institute before the battle at Cadair Idris. But surely it had been proved that they were correct? Surely their defeat of Mortmain would have canceled out the Consul's edict, especially now that he was dead? "Is—is everything all right, ma'am?"

Charlotte gestured toward the paper, a hopeless flutter of her hand. Her insides turning cold, Sophie hurried to Charlotte's side and took the letter from the desk.

Mrs. Branwell,
Considering the nature of the correspondence you had

entered into with my late colleague, Consul Wayland, you may well be surprised to receive this missive. The Clave, however, finds itself in the position of requiring a new Consul, and when put to a vote, the foremost choice among us was yourself.

I can well understand that you may be satisfied with the running of the Institute, and that you may not wish the responsibility of this position, especially considering the injuries sustained by your husband in your brave battle against the Magister. However, I felt it incumbent upon me to offer you this opportunity, not only because you are clearly the desired choice of the Council, but because, given what I have seen of you, I think you would make one of the finer Consuls it has been my privilege to serve beside.

Yours with the highest regard,
Inquisitor Whitelaw

"*Consul!*" Sophie gasped, and the paper fluttered from her fingers. "They want to make you Consul?"

"So it seems." Charlotte's voice was lifeless.

"I—" Sophie reached for what to say. The idea of a London Institute not run by Charlotte was dreadful. And yet the position of Consul was an honor, the highest the Clave had to give, and to see Charlotte covered in the honor she had so dearly earned . . . "There is no one more deserving of this than you," she said at last.

"Oh, Sophie, no. I was the one who chose to send us all to Cadair Idris. It is my fault Henry will never walk again. *I* did that."

"He cannot blame you. He does not blame you."

"No, he does not, but I blame myself. How can I be the Consul and send Shadowhunters into battle to die? I do not want that responsibility."

Sophie took Charlotte's hand in hers and pressed it. "Charlotte," she said. "It is not just sending Shadowhunters into battle; sometimes it is a matter of holding them back. You have a compassionate heart and a thoughtful mind. You have led the Enclave for years. Of course your heart is broken for Mr. Branwell, but to be the Consul it is not a matter only of taking lives but also of saving them. If it had not been for you, if there had been only Consul Wayland, how many Shadowhunters would have died at the hands of Mortmain's creatures?"

Charlotte looked down at Sophie's red, work-roughened hand clasping hers. "Sophie," she said. "When did you become so wise?"

Sophie blushed. "I learned wisdom from you, ma'am."

"Oh, no," Charlotte said. "A moment ago you called me Charlotte. As a future Shadowhunter, Sophie, you shall be calling me Charlotte from now on. And we shall be bringing on another maid, to take your place, so that your time will be free to prepare for your Ascension."

"Thank you," Sophie whispered. "So will you accept the offer? Become the Consul?"

Charlotte gently freed her hand from Sophie's and took up her pen. "I will," she said. "On three conditions."

"What will those be?"

"The first is that I am allowed to lead the Clave from the Institute, here, and not move myself and my family to Idris, at least for the first few years. For I do not want to leave you all, and besides, I wish to be here to train Will to take over the Institute for me when I do depart."

"*Will?*" said Sophie in astonishment. "Take over the Institute?"

Charlotte smiled. "Of course," she said. "That is the second condition."

"And the third?"

Charlotte's smile faded, replaced by a look of determination. "That, you shall see the result of as soon as tomorrow, if it is accepted," she said, and bent her head to begin writing.

23

THAN ANY EVIL

Come; let us go: your cheeks are pale;
But half my life I leave behind:
Methinks my friend is richly shrined;
But I shall pass; my work will fail. . . .
I hear it now, and o'er and o'er,
Eternal greetings to the dead;
And "Ave, Ave, Ave," said,
"Adieu, adieu," for evermore.
—Alfred, Lord Tennyson, "In Memoriam A.H.H."

Tessa shivered; the cold water rushed around her in the darkness. She thought she might be lying at the bottom of the universe, where the river of forgetfulness split the world in two, or perhaps she was still in the stream where she had collapsed after falling from the Dark Sister's carriage, and everything that had happened since had been a dream. Cadair Idris, Mortmain, the clockwork army, Will's arms about her—

Guilt and sorrow drove through her like a spear, and she arched backward, her hands scrabbling for purchase in the darkness. Fire ran through her veins, a thousand branching streams of agony. She gasped for breath, and suddenly there was something cold against her teeth, parting her lips, and her mouth was full of a freezing sourness. She swallowed hard, choking—

And felt the fire in her veins subside. Ice shuddered through her. Her eyes flew open as the world spun and righted itself. The first thing she saw was pale, slim hands withdrawing a vial—*the coldness in her mouth, the bitter taste on her tongue*—and then the contours of her bedroom at the Institute.

"Tessa," said a familiar voice. "This will keep you lucid for a time, but you must not let yourself fall back into darkness and dreams."

She froze, not daring to look.

"Jem?" she whispered.

The sound of the vial being set down on the bedside table. A sigh. "Yes," he said. "Tessa. Will you look at me?"

She turned, and looked. And drew in her breath.

It was Jem, and not Jem.

He wore the parchment robes of a Silent Brother, open at the throat to show the collar of an ordinary shirt. His hood was thrown back, revealing his face. She could see the changes in him, where she had only barely seen them in the noise and confusion of the battle at Cadair Idris. His delicate cheekbones were scarred with the runes she had noticed before, one on each, long slashes of scars that did not look like ordinary Shadowhunter runes. His hair was no longer pure silver—streaks of it had darkened to black-brown, no doubt the color he had been born with. His eyelashes, too, had darkened to black. They looked like fine strands of silk against his pale skin—though he was no longer as pale as he had been.

"How is it possible?" she whispered. "That you are here?"

"I was called from the Silent City by the Council." His voice was not the same either. There was an undertone of something cool to it, something that had not been there before. "Charlotte's influence, I was given to understand. I am allowed an hour with you, no more."

"An hour," Tessa echoed, stunned. She put a hand up to push her hair from her face. What a fright she must look, in her crumpled nightgown, her hair hanging in tangled plaits, her lips dry and cracked. She reached for the clockwork angel at her neck—a familiar, habitual gesture, meant to comfort, but the angel was no longer there. "Jem. I thought you were *dead*."

"Yes," he said, and there was that remoteness in his voice still, a distance that reminded her of the icebergs she had seen off the side of the *Main*, floes drifting far out in icy water. "I'm sorry. I'm sorry I couldn't somehow—that I couldn't tell you."

"I thought you were dead," Tessa said again. "I can't believe you're real, now. I dreamed of you, over and over. There was a dark corridor and you were walking away from me, and however I called out, you could not, would not, turn to see me. Perhaps this is only another dream."

"This is no dream." He rose to his feet and stood in front of her, his pale hands interlaced in front of him, and she could not forget that this was how he had proposed to her—standing, as she sat upon the bed, looking up at him, incredulous, as she was now.

He opened his hands slowly, and on the palms, as on his cheeks, she saw great black runes scored. She was not familiar enough with the *Codex* to recognize them, but she knew instinctively that they were not the runes of an ordinary Shadowhunter. They spoke of a power beyond that.

"You told me it was impossible," she whispered. "That you could not become a Silent Brother."

He turned away from her. There was something to his motions now that was different, something of the gliding softness of the Silent Brothers. It was both lovely and chilling. What was he doing? Could he not bear to look at her?

"I told you what I believed," he said, his face turned toward the window. In profile, she could see that some of the painful thinness of his face had faded. His cheekbones were no longer so pronounced, the hollows at his temples no longer so dark. "And what was true. That the *yin fen* in my blood prevented the runes of the Brotherhood from being placed upon me." She saw his chest rise and fall beneath the parchment robes, and it almost startled her: It seemed so human, the need to draw breath. "Every effort that had ever been made to wean me slowly from the *yin fen* had nearly killed me. When I ceased to take it because there was no more, I felt my body begin to break, from the inside out. And I thought that I had nothing more to lose." The intensity in Jem's voice warmed it—was that a tone of humanity there, a crack in the armor of the Brotherhood? "I begged Charlotte to call the Silent Brothers and asked them to place the runes of the Brotherhood on me at the very last possible moment, the moment when the life was leaving my body. I knew that the runes might mean I died in agony. But it was the only chance."

"You said that you did not wish to become a Silent Brother. Did not wish to live forever . . ."

He had taken a few steps across the room and was beside her vanity table. He reached down and lifted something metallic and glittering from a shallow jewelry dish. She realized with a shock of surprise that it was her clockwork angel.

"It no longer ticks," he said. She could not read his voice; it was distant, as smooth and cool as stone.

"Its heart is gone. When I changed into the angel, I freed it from its clockwork prison. It no longer lives within. It no longer protects me."

His hand closed around the angel, the wings digging hard into the flesh of his palm. "I must tell you," he said. "When I received Charlotte's demand that I come here, it was against my wishes."

"You did not wish to see me?"

"No. I did not want you to look at me as you are looking at me now."

"Jem—" She swallowed, tasting on her tongue the bitterness of the tisane he had given her. A whirl of memories, the darkness under Cadair Idris, the town on fire, Will's arms around her—*Will*. But she had thought Jem was dead. "Jem," she said again. "When I saw you alive, there below Cadair Idris, I thought it was a dream or a lie. I had thought you dead. It was the darkest moment of my life. Believe me, please believe me, that my soul rejoices to see you again when I thought that I never would. It's just that . . ."

He released his grip on the metal angel, and she saw the lines of blood on his hand, where the tips of the wings had cut him, scored across the runes on his palm. "I am strange to you. Not human."

"You will always be human to me," she whispered. "But I cannot quite see my Jem in you now."

He closed his eyes. She was used to dark shadows on his lids, but they were gone now. "I had no choice. You were gone, and in my stead Will had gone after you. I did not fear death, but I feared deserting you both. This, then, was my only recourse. To live, to stand and fight."

A little color had come into his voice: There was passion there, under the cold detachment of the Silent Brothers.

"But I knew what I would lose," he said. "Once you understood my music. Now you look at me as though you do not know me at all. As though you never loved me."

Tessa slid out from beneath the coverlet and stood. It was a mistake. Her head swam suddenly, her knees buckling. She threw out a hand to catch at one of the posts of the bed, and found herself with a handful of Jem's parchment robes instead. He had darted toward her with the graceful quiet tread of the Brothers that was like smoke unfurling, and his arms were around her now, holding her up.

She went still in his arms. He was close, close enough that she should have been able to feel warmth coming off his body, but she did not. His usual scent of smoke and burned sugar was gone. There was only the faint scent of something dry and as cold as old stone, or paper. She could feel the muffled beat of his heart, see the pulse in his throat. She stared up at him in wonder, memorizing the lines and angles of his face, the scars on his cheekbones, the rough silk of his eyelashes, the bow of his mouth.

"Tessa." The word came out on a groan, as if she had hit him. There was the faintest trace of color in his cheeks, blood under snow. "Oh, God," he said, and buried his face in the crook of her neck, where the curve of her shoulder began, his cheek against her hair. His palms were flat against her back, pressing her harder against him. She could feel him trembling.

For a moment she was unmoored by the heady relief of it, the feeling of Jem under her hands. Perhaps you did not really believe in a thing until you could touch it. And here was Jem, who she had thought was dead, holding her, and breathing, and *alive.*

"You feel the same," she said. "And yet you look so different. You *are* different."

He broke away from her at that, with an effort that made him bite his lip and corded the muscles in his throat. Holding her gently by the shoulders, he guided her to sit down again upon the edge of the bed. When he released her, his hands curled into fists. He took a step back. She could see him breathing, see the pulse going in his throat.

"I am different," he said in a low voice. "I am changed. And not in a way that can be undone."

"But you are not entirely one of *them* yet," she said. "You can speak—and see—"

He exhaled slowly. He was still staring at the post of the bed as if it held the universe's secrets. "There is a process. A series of rituals and procedures. No, I am not quite a Silent Brother yet. But I will be soon."

"So the *yin fen* did not prevent it."

"Almost. There was—pain when I made the transition. Great pain, that nearly killed me. They did what they could. But I shall never be like other Silent Brothers." He looked down, his lashes veiling his eyes. "I shall not be—quite as they are. I will be less powerful, for there are some runes, still, that I cannot withstand."

"Surely they can just wait now for the *yin fen* to leave your body completely?"

"It will not. My body has been arrested in the state it was in when they put these first runes on me here." He indicated the scars on his face. "Because of it, there will be skills I cannot achieve. It will take me much longer to master their vision and speech of the mind."

"Does that mean they will not take your eyes—sew your lips shut?"

"I don't know." His voice was soft now, almost entirely the voice of the Jem she knew. There was a flush across his cheekbones, and she thought of a pale column of hollow marble slowly filling with human blood. "They will have me for a long time. Perhaps forever. I cannot say what will happen. I have given myself over to them. My fate is in their hands now."

"If we could free you from them—"

"Then the *yin fen* that remains in me would burn again, and I would be as I was. An addict, dying. This is my choice, Tessa, because it is death otherwise. You know that it is. I do not want to leave you. Even knowing that becoming a Silent Brother could ensure my survival, I fought it as if it were a prison sentence. Silent Brothers cannot marry. They cannot have *parabatai*. They can live only in the Silent City. They do not laugh. They cannot play music."

"Oh, Jem," Tessa said. "Perhaps the Silent Brothers cannot play music, but neither can the dead. If this is the only way you can live, then I rejoice in my soul for you, even as my heart sorrows."

"I know you too well to think that you would feel another way."

"And I know you well enough to know that you feel bowed by guilt. But why? You have done nothing wrong."

He bent his head so that his forehead rested on the bedpost. He closed his eyes. "This is why I did not want to come."

"But I am not angry—"

"I did not think you would be *angry*," Jem burst out, and it was like ice cracking across a frozen waterfall, freeing a torrent. "We were *engaged*, Tessa. A proposal—an offer of marriage—is a promise. A promise to love and care for someone always. I did not mean to break mine to you. But it was that or die. I wanted to wait, to be married to you and live with you for years, but that wasn't possible. I was dying too fast. I would have given it up—all of it up—to be married to you for a day. A day that would never have come. You are a reminder—a reminder of everything I am losing. The life I will not have."

"To give up your life for one day of marriage—it would not have been worth it," Tessa said. Her heart was pounding out a message that spoke to her of Will's arms around her, his lips on hers in the cave under Cadair Idris. She didn't deserve Jem's gentle confessions, his penitence, or his longing. "Jem, I must tell you something."

He looked at her. She could see the black in his eyes, threads of black alongside the silver, beautiful and strange.

"It's about Will. About Will, and me."

"He loves you," Jem said. "I know he loves you. We spoke of it before he left here." Though the coldness had not returned to his voice, he sounded suddenly almost unnaturally calm.

Tessa was shocked. "I didn't know you had ever talked of it with each other. Will did not say."

"Nor did you ever tell me of his feelings, though you knew for months. We all have our secrets that we keep because we do not want to hurt the people who love us." There was a sort of warning in his voice, or was she imagining it?

"I do not want to keep secrets from you any longer," Tessa said. "I thought you were dead. Will and I both did. In Cadair Idris—"

"Did you love me?" he interrupted. It seemed an odd question, and yet he asked it without implication or hostility, and waited quietly for her answer.

She looked at him, and Woolsey's words came back to her, like the whisper of a prayer. *Most people never find one great love in their life. You are lucky enough to have found two.* For a moment she put aside her confession. "Yes. I loved you. I love you still. I love Will, too. I cannot explain it. I didn't know it when I agreed to marry you. I loved you, I still love you, I never loved you less for all that I love him. It sounds mad, but if anyone might ever understand—"

"I do," Jem said. "There is no need to tell me more about yourself and Will. There's nothing you could have done that would cause me to cease loving either of you. Will is myself, my own soul, and if I am not to have the keeping of your heart, then there is no other I would rather have that honor. And when I am gone, you must help Will. This will be—it will be hard for him."

Tessa searched his face with her gaze. The blood had left his cheeks; he was pale, but composed. His jaw was set. It said all she needed to understand: *Do not tell me more. I do not want to know.*

Some secrets, she thought, were better told; some were better left the burden of the carrier, that they might not cause pain to others. It was why she had not told Will she loved him, when there was nothing either of them could do about it.

She closed her mouth on what she had been intending to say, and said instead: "I do not know how I will manage without you."

"I ask myself the same thing. I do not want to leave you. I cannot leave you. But if I stay, I die here."

"No. You must not stay. You will not stay. Jem. Promise you will go. Go and be a Silent Brother, and live. I would tell you I hated you if I thought you would believe me, if it would make you go. I want you to live. Even if it means I shall never see you again."

"You will see me," he said quietly, raising his head. "In fact, there is a chance—only a chance, but—"

"But what?"

He paused—hesitated, and seemed to make his mind up about something. "Nothing. Foolishness."

"Jem."

"You will see me again, but not often. I have only just begun my journey, and there are many Laws that govern the Brotherhood. I will be moving away from my previous life. I cannot say what abilities or what scars I will have. I cannot say how I will be different. I fear I will lose my self and my music. I fear I will become something other than wholly human. I *know* I will not be your Jem."

Tessa could only shake her head. "But the Silent Brothers— they visit—they mingle with other Shadowhunters. . . . Can you not . . ."

"Not during their time of training. And even when they are done, rarely. You see us when someone is ill or dying, when a child is born, for the rituals of the first runes or of *parabatai* . . . but we do not grace the homes of Shadowhunters without a summoning."

"Then Charlotte will summon you."

"She called me here this once, but she cannot do it over and over again, Tessa. A Shadowhunter cannot summon a Silent Brother for no reason."

"But I am not a Shadowhunter," Tessa said. "Not truly."

There was a long silence as they looked at each other. Both stubborn. Both unmoving. At last Jem spoke:

"Do you remember when we stood together on Blackfriars Bridge?" he asked softly, and his eyes were like that night had been, all black and silver.

"Of course I remember."

"It was the moment I first knew I loved you," Jem said. "I will make you a promise. Every year, Tessa, on one day, I will meet you on that bridge. I will come from the Silent City and I will meet you, and we will be together, if only for an hour. But you must tell no one."

"An hour every year," Tessa whispered. "It is not much." She recollected herself then, and took a deep breath. "But you will live. You will live. That is what is important. I will not be visiting your grave."

"No. Not for a long, long time," he said, and the distance was back in his voice.

"Then that is a miracle," Tessa said. "And one does not question miracles, or complain that they are not constructed perfectly to one's liking." She reached up and touched the jade pendant about her throat. "Shall I return this to you?"

"No," he said. "I will marry no one else, now. And I shall not take my mother's bridal gift to the Silent City." He reached out and touched her face lightly, a brush of skin on skin. "When I am in the darkness, I want to think of it in the light, with you," he said, and straightened, and turned to walk toward the door. The parchment robes of the Silent Brothers moved around him as he moved, and Tessa watched him, paralyzed, every pulse of her heart beating out the words she could not say: *Good-bye. Good-bye. Good-bye.*

He paused at the door. "I shall see you on Blackfriars Bridge, Tessa."

And he was gone.

If Will closed his eyes, he could hear the sounds of the Institute coming to life early in the morning around him, or at least he could imagine them: Sophie setting the breakfast table, Charlotte and Cyril helping Henry to his chair, the Lightwood brothers sparring sleepily in the corridors, Cecily no doubt looking for him in his room, as she had several mornings in a row now, trying—and failing—to conceal her obvious worry.

And in Tessa's room, Jem and Tessa, talking.

He knew Jem was here, because the carriage of the Silent

Brothers was drawn up in the courtyard. He could see it from the training room windows. But that was not something he could think about. It was what he had wanted, what he had asked Charlotte for, but now that it was transpiring, he found he could not bear to think on it too closely. So he had taken himself to the room where he always went when his mind was troubled; he had been throwing knives at the wall since the sun had come up, and his shirt was soaked with sweat and sticking to his back.

Thunk. Thunk. Thunk. The knives hit the wall, each one in the center of the target. He remembered when he had been twelve, and getting the knife anywhere near its goal had seemed an impossible dream. Jem had helped him, showed him how to hold a blade, how to line up the point and throw. Of all the places in the Institute, the training room was the one he most associated with Jem—save Jem's own room, and that had been stripped of Jem's belongings. It was just another empty Institute room now, waiting for another Shadowhunter to fill it. Even Church did not seem to want to go into it; he would stand by the door sometimes, and wait as cats did, but he no longer slept on the bed as he had when Jem had lived there.

Will shivered—the training room was cold in the early morning grayness; the fire in the grate was burning down, a fanged shadow of red and gold spitting colorful embers. Will could see two boys in his mind, sitting on the floor in front of the fire in this same room, one with black, black hair, and one whose hair was as fair as snow. He had been teaching Jem how to play *ecarte* with a deck of cards he had stolen from the drawing room.

At one point, disgruntled upon losing, Will had thrown the cards into the fire and watched in fascination as they'd burned one by one, the fire punching holes in the glossy white paper. Jem had laughed. "You can't win like that."

"Sometimes it's the only way to win," Will had said. "Burn it all down."

He went to retrieve the knives from the wall, scowling. *Burn it all down.* His whole body still hurt. As he plucked the blades free, he saw that there were greenish-blue bruises on his arms despite the *iratzes*, and scars from the Cadair Idris battle that he would have forever. He thought of fighting beside Jem in the battle. Maybe he had not appreciated it at the time. *The last, last time.*

Like an echo of his thoughts, a shadow fell across the doorway. Will looked up—and nearly dropped the knife he was holding.

"Jem?" he said. "Is it you, James?"

"Who else?" Jem's voice. As he stepped forward into the light of the room, Will could see that the hood of his parchment robes was down, his gaze level with Will's. His face, eyes, all familiar. But Will had always been able to sense Jem before, sense his approach and his presence. The fact that Jem had startled him this time was a sharp reminder of the change in his *parabatai*.

Not your parabatai *any longer*, said a small voice in the back of his mind.

Jem came into the room with the soundless tread of the Silent Brothers, closing the door behind him. Will did not move from where he stood. He did not feel that he could. The sight of Jem in Cadair Idris had been a shock that had gone through his system like a terrible and wonderful incandescence—Jem was *alive*, but he was changed; he lived, but was lost.

"But," he said. "You are here to see Tessa."

Jem looked at him levelly. His eyes were gray-black, like slate shot through with streaks of obsidian. "And you did not think I would take the chance, whatever chance I could, to see you, too?"

"I did not know. You left, after the battle, without a farewell."

Jem took a few steps forward, into the room. Will felt his spine tighten. There was something strange, something bone-deep and different about the way Jem moved now; this was not the Shadowhunter's grace Will had trained himself over so many years to mimic, but something strange and alien and new.

Jem must have seen something in Will's expression, for he paused. "How could I say farewell," he said, "to you?"

Will let the knife fall from his hand. It stuck, point-down, in the wood of the floor. "As Shadowhunters do? *Ave atque vale.* And forever, brother, hail and farewell."

"But those are the words of death. Catullus spoke them over his brother's grave, did he not? *Multas per gentes et multa per aequora vectus advenio has miseras, frater, ad inferias—*"

Will knew the words. *Through many waters borne, brother, I am come to thy sad grave, that I may give these last gifts to the dead. Forever and ever, brother, hail. Forever and ever, farewell.* He stared. "You—memorized the poem in Latin? But you were always the one who would memorize music, not words—" He broke off with a short laugh. "Never mind. The rituals of the Brotherhood would have changed that." He turned and paced a few steps away, then spun abruptly to face Jem. "Your violin is in the music room. I thought you might have taken it with you—you cared for it so."

"We can take nothing with us to the Silent City but our own bodies and minds," said Jem. "I left the violin here for some future Shadowhunter who might wish to play it."

"Not for me, then."

"I would be honored if you would take it and care for it. But I left something else for you. In your room is my *yin fen* box. I thought that you might want it."

"That seems a cruel sort of gift," Will said. "That I might be reminded . . ." *What took you away from me. What made you suffer. What I searched for and could not find. How I failed you.*

"Will, no," said Jem, who, as always, understood without Will having to explain. "It was not always a box that held my drugs. It was my mother's. Kwan Yin is the goddess depicted on the front. It is said that when she died and reached the gates of paradise, she paused and heard the cries of anguish from the human world below and could not leave it. She remained to give aid to mortals, when they cannot aid themselves. She is the comfort of all suffering hearts."

"A box will not comfort me."

"Change is not loss, Will. Not always."

Will pushed his hands through his damp hair. "Oh, yes," he said bitterly. "Perhaps in some other life, beyond this one, when we have passed beyond the river, or turned upon the Wheel, or whatever kind words you want to use to describe leaving this world, I shall find my friend again, my *parabatai*. But I have lost you *now*—now, when I need you more than I ever did!"

Jem had moved across the room—like a flicker of shadow, the Silent Brother's grace light upon him—and now stood beside the fire. The firelight illuminated his face, and Will could see that something seemed to shine through him: a sort of light that had not been there before. Jem had always shone, with fierce life and fiercer goodness, but this was something different. The light in Jem seemed to burn now; it was a distant light and a lonely one, like the light of a star. "You don't need me, Will."

Will looked down at himself, at the knife at his feet, and remembered the knife he had buried at the base of the tree on the Shrewsbury-Welshpool road, stained with his blood and Jem's. "All my life, since I came to the Institute, you were the mirror of my soul. I saw the good in me in you. In your eyes alone I found grace. When you are gone from me, who will see me like that?"

There was a silence then. Jem stood as still as a statue. With his gaze Will searched for, and found, the *parabatai* rune on Jem's shoulder; like his own, it had faded to a pale white.

At last Jem spoke. The cool remoteness had left his voice. Will breathed in hard, remembering how much that voice had shaped the years of his growing up, its steady kindness a light-house beacon in the dark. "Have faith in yourself. You can be your own mirror."

"What if I can't?" Will whispered. "I don't even know how to be a Shadowhunter without you. I have only ever fought with you by my side."

Jem stepped forward, and this time Will did not move to discourage him. He came close enough to touch—Will thought distractedly that he had never stood so close to a Silent Brother before, that the fabric of the parchment robes was woven of a strange, tough, pale fabric like the bark of a tree, and that cold seemed to emanate from Jem's skin the way stone held a chill even on a hot day.

Jem put his fingers under Will's chin, forcing Will to look directly at him. His touch was cold.

Will bit at his lip. This was the last time Jem, as Jem, might ever touch him. The sharp memory went through him like a knife—of years of Jem's light tap on his shoulder, his hand reaching to help Will up when he fell, Jem holding him back when he was furious, Will's own hands on Jem's thin shoulders as Jem coughed blood into his shirt. "Listen to me. I am leaving, but I am *living*. I will not be gone from you entirely, Will. When you fight now, I will be still by you. When you walk in the world, I will be the light at your side, the ground steady under your feet, the force that drives the sword in your hand. We are bound, beyond the oath. The Marks did not change that. The oath did not change that. It merely gave words to something that existed already."

"But what of you?" said Will. "Tell me what I can do, for you are my *parabatai*, and I do not wish you to go into the shadows of the Silent City alone."

"I have no choice. But if there is one thing I could ask of you, it is that you be happy. I want you to have a family and grow old with those who love you. And if you wish to marry Tessa, then do not let the memory of me keep you apart." Jem hesitated a moment before continuing. "She and I have plans to meet once a year. I trust you with that secret. It is a small thing, and yet enormous. It will remind me of who I am. Who I was. You and Tessa must find your own way to each other. Form your own bond."

"She may not want me, you know," Will said.

Jem smiled, fleetingly. "Well, that part is up to you, I think."

Will smiled back, and for just that moment they were Jem-and-Will again. Will could see Jem, but also *through* him, to the past. Will remembered the two of them, running through the dark streets of London, jumping from rooftop to rooftop, seraph blades gleaming in their hands; hours in the training room, shoving each other into mud puddles, throwing snowballs at Jessamine from behind an ice fort in the courtyard, asleep like puppies on the rug in front of the fire.

Ave atque vale, Will thought. *Hail and farewell*. He had not given much thought to the words before, had never thought about why they were not just a farewell but also a greeting. Every meeting led to a parting, and so it would, as long as life was mortal. In every meeting there was some of the sorrow of parting, but in every parting there was some of the joy of meeting as well.

He would not forget the joy.

"We spoke of how to say good-bye," Jem said. "When Jonathan bid farewell to David, he said, 'Go in peace, for as much as we have sworn, both of us, saying the Lord be between me and thee, forever.' They did not see each other again, but they did not forget. So it will be with us. When I am Brother Zachariah, when I no longer see the world with my human eyes, I will still be in some part the Jem you knew, and I will see you with the eyes of my heart."

"Wo men shi sheng si ji jiao," said Will, and he saw Jem's eyes widen, fractionally, and the spark of amusement inside them. "Go in peace, James Carstairs."

They stayed looking at each other for a long moment, and

then Jem drew up his hood, hiding his face in shadow, and turned away.

Will closed his eyes. He could not hear Jem go, not anymore; he did not want to know the moment when he left and Will was alone, did not want to know when his first day as a Shadowhunter without a *parabatai* truly began. And if the place over his heart, where his *parabatai* rune had been, flared up with a sudden burning pain as the door closed behind Jem, Will told himself it was only a stray ember from the fire.

He leaned back against the wall, then slowly slid down it until he was sitting on the floor, beside his throwing knife. He did not know how long he sat there, but he could hear the noise of horses in the courtyard, the rattle of the Silent Brothers' carriage pulling out of the drive. The clang of the gate as it shut. *We are dust and shadows.*

"Will?" He looked up; he had not noticed the slight figure in the doorway of the training room until she spoke. Charlotte took a step forward and smiled at him. There was kindness in her smile, as there always was, and he fought to not close his eyes against the memories—Charlotte in the doorway of this very room. *Didn't you recall what I told you yesterday, that we were welcoming a new arrival to the Institute today? . . . James Carstairs . . .*

"Will," she said, again, now. "You were correct."

He lifted his head, his hands dangling between his knees. "Correct about what?"

"About Jem and Tessa," she said. "Their engagement is ended. And Tessa is awake. She is awake, and well, and asking for you."

* * *

When I am in the darkness, I will think of it in the light, with you.

Tessa sat upright against the pillows Sophie had carefully arranged for her (the two girls had embraced, and Sophie had brushed the tangles from Tessa's hair and said "bless, bless" so many times that Tessa had had to ask her to stop before she made them both cry) and looked down at the jade pendant in her hands.

She felt as if she were split into two different people. One was counting her blessings over and over that Jem was alive, that he would survive to see the sun rise again, that the poisonous drug he had suffered from so long would not burn the life out of his veins. The other—

"Tess?" A soft voice at the door; she looked up and saw Will there, silhouetted in the light from the corridor.

Will. She thought of the boy who had come into her room at the Dark House and distracted her from her terror by chattering about Tennyson and hedgehogs and dashing fellows who come to rescue one, and how they were never wrong. She had thought him handsome then, but now she thought him something else entirely. He was *Will*, in all his perfect imperfection; Will, whose heart was as easy to break as it was carefully guarded; Will, who loved not wisely but entirely and with everything he had.

"Tess," he said again, hesitating at her silence, and came in, half-closing the door behind him. "I—Charlotte said you wished to speak with me—"

"Will," she said, and she knew she was too pale, and her skin was blotchy with tears, her eyes still red, but it didn't matter, because it was Will, and she put her hands out, and he came immediately and took them, closing them in his own warm, scarred fingers.

"How are you feeling?" he asked, his eyes searching her face. "I must speak with you, but I do not wish to burden you until you are in full health again."

"I am well," she said, returning the pressure of his fingers with her own. "Seeing Jem has eased my mind. Did it ease yours?"

His eyes darted away from hers, though his grip on her hands did not slacken. "It did," he said, "and it did not."

"Your mind was eased," she said, "but not your heart."

"Yes," he said. "Yes. That is exactly it. You know me so well, Tess." He gave a rueful smile. "He is alive, and for that I am grateful. But he has chosen a path of great loneliness. The Brotherhood—they eat alone, and walk alone, rise alone and face the night alone. I would spare him that if I could."

"You have spared him everything you could spare him," Tessa said quietly. "As he spared you, and we all tried so hard to spare one another. In the end we must all make our own choices."

"Are you saying I should not grieve?"

"No. Grieve. We both shall. Grieve, but do not blame yourself, for in this you bear no responsibility."

He glanced down at their joined hands. Very gently he stroked the tops of her knuckles with his thumbs. "Perhaps not," he said. "But there are other things I do bear responsibility for."

Tessa took a quick, shallow breath. His voice had lowered, and there was a roughness to it she had not heard since—

his breath soft and hot against her skin until she was breathing just as hard, her hands smoothing up and over his shoulders, his arms, his sides . . .

She blinked hastily and withdrew her hands from his. She was not looking at him now but seeing the firelight against the walls of the cave, and hearing his voice in her ear, and it had all seemed like a dream at the time, moments drawn out of real life, as if they were taking place in some other world. Even now she could barely believe that it had happened at all.

"Tessa?" His voice was hesitant, his hands still outstretched. A part of her wanted to take them, to draw him down beside her and kiss him, to forget herself in Will as she had before. For he was as effective as any drug.

And then she remembered Will's own clouded eyes in the opium den, the dreams of happiness that crashed into ruins the moment the effects of the smoke wore away. No. Some things could be managed only by facing them. She took a breath, and looked up at Will.

"I know what you would say," she said. "You are thinking of what happened between us in Cadair Idris, because we thought Jem was dead, and that we, too, would die. You are an honorable man, Will, and you know what you must do now. You must offer me marriage."

Will, who had been very still, proved that he could still surprise her, and laughed. It was a soft laugh, and rueful. "I did not expect you to be so forthright, but I suppose I should have. I know my Tessa."

"I am your Tessa," she said. "But, Will. I do not want you to speak now. Not of marriage, of lifelong promises—"

He sat down on the edge of the bed. He was in training gear, the loose shirt pushed up around his elbows, the throat open, and she could see the healing scars of the battle on his skin, the white remembrance of healing runes. She could see the beginning of hurt, too, in his eyes. "You regret what happened between us?"

"Can one regret a thing that, however unwise, was beautiful?" she said, and the hurt in his eyes softened into confusion.

"Tessa. If you are afraid that I feel reluctant, obligated—"

"No." She put up her hands. "It is only that I feel your heart must be a tangle of grief and despair and relief and happiness and confusion, and I do not wish you to make pronouncements when you are so overwhelmed. And do not tell me you are not overwhelmed, for I can see it upon you, and I feel it myself. We are both overwhelmed, Will, and neither of us is in any fit state to make decisions."

For a moment he hesitated. His fingers hovered over his heart, where the *parabatai* rune had been, touching it lightly— she wondered if he was even aware he was doing it—and then he said, "Sometimes I fear you may be too wise, Tessa."

"Well," she said. "One of us has to be."

"Is there nothing I can do?" he said. "I would rather not leave your side. Unless you wish me to."

Tessa let her gaze fall to the bedside table, where the books she had been reading before the automaton attack on the Institute—it felt like a thousand years ago—lay stacked. "You could read to me," she said. "If you would not mind."

Will looked up at that and smiled. It was a raw, strange smile, but it was real, and it was Will. Tessa smiled back. "I do not mind," he said. "Not at all."

Which was how, some quarter of an hour later, Will came to be sitting in an armchair, reading from *David Copperfield*, when Charlotte pushed the door of Tessa's room gently open with her fingers and peered inside. She could not help but be anxious—Will had looked so desperate slumped on the floor of the training room, so very much alone, and she remembered the fear she had always harbored, that if Jem ever left them, he would take all the best of Will with him when he went. And Tessa, too, was still so fragile. . . .

Will's soft voice filled the room, along with the muted glow of the light from the fire in the grate. Tessa was lying on her side, her brown hair spread over the pillow, watching Will, whose face was bent over the pages, with a look of tenderness in her eyes, a tenderness mirrored in the softness of Will's voice as he read. It was a tenderness so intimate and so profound that Charlotte stepped away immediately, letting the door fall noiselessly shut behind her.

Still, Will's voice followed her down the corridor as she walked away, her heart a great deal lighter than it had been moments ago.

"*. . . and cannot watch over him, if that is not too bold a thing to say, as closely as I would. But if any fraud or treachery is practicing against him, I hope that simple love and truth will be strong in the end. I hope that real love and truth are stronger in the end than any evil or misfortune in the world. . . .*"

24

THE MEASURE OF LOVE

The measure of love is to love without measure.
—attributed to Saint Augustine

The Council room was full of light. A great double circle had been painted upon the raised dais at the front of the room, and in the space between the circles were runes: runes of binding, runes of knowledge, runes of skill and craft, and the runes that symbolized Sophie's name. Sophie knelt in the center of the circles. Her dark hair was unbound and fell to her waist, a ripple of dark curls against her darker gear. She looked very beautiful in the light that streamed from the skylighted dome above, the scar on her cheek red as a rose.

The Consul stood above her, her white hands upraised, the Mortal Cup held within them. Charlotte wore simple scarlet robes that billowed around her. Her small face was serious and severe. "Take the Cup, Sophia Collins," she said, and the room was breathlessly silent. The Council chamber was not full, but the row Tessa sat at the end of was: Gideon and Gabriel, Cecily and Henry, and her and Will, all leaning forward eagerly, waiting for Sophie to Ascend. At each end of the dais stood a Silent Brother, their heads bent, their parchment robes looking as if they had been carved out of marble.

Charlotte lowered the Cup, and held it out to Sophie, who took it carefully.

"Do you swear, Sophia Collins, to forsake the mundane world and follow the path of the Shadowhunter? Will you take into yourself the blood of the Angel Raziel and honor that blood? Do you swear to serve the Clave, to follow the Law as set forth by the Covenant, and to obey the word of the Council? Will you defend that which is human and mortal, knowing that for your service there will be no recompense and no thanks but honor?"

"I swear," said Sophie, her voice very steady.

"Can you be a shield for the weak, a light in the dark, a truth among falsehoods, a tower in the flood, an eye to see when all others are blind?"

"I can."

"And when you are dead, will you give up your body to the Nephilim to be burned, that your ashes may be used to build the City of Bones?"

"I will."

"Then drink," said Charlotte. Tessa heard Gideon draw in his breath. This was the dangerous part of the ritual. This was the part that could kill the untrained or unworthy.

Sophie bent her dark head and set the Cup to her lips. Tessa sat forward, her chest tight with apprehension. She felt Will's hand slide over hers, a warm, comforting weight. Sophie's throat moved as she swallowed.

The circle that surrounded her and Charlotte flared up once with a cold, blue-white light, obscuring them both. When it faded, Tessa was left blinking stars from her eyes as the light dwindled. She blinked hastily, and saw Sophie hold up the Cup. There was a glow about the Cup she held as she handed it back to Charlotte, who smiled broadly.

"You are Nephilim now," she said. "I name you Sophia Ashdown, of the blood of Jonathan Shadowhunter, child of the Nephilim. Arise, Sophia."

And Sophie rose, amid the cheering of the crowd, Gideon's cheers the loudest among many. Sophie was smiling, her whole face shining in the winter sunlight that gleamed down through the clear skylight. Shadows moved across the floor, darting and quick. Tessa looked up in wonder—whiteness streaked the windows, swirling gently beyond the glass.

"Snow," Will said softly in her ear. "Merry Christmas, Tessa."

That night was the night of the Enclave's annual Christmas party. It was the first time Tessa had seen the great ballroom at the Institute thrown open and filled with people. The enormous windows glowed with reflected light, casting a golden sheen across the polished floor. Beyond the dark glass, one could see the snow falling, in great soft white flakes, but inside the Institute all was warm and golden and secure.

Christmas among Shadowhunters was not Christmas as Tessa had come to know it. There were no advent wreaths, no carols sung, no Christmas crackers. There *was* a tree, though it was not decorated in the traditional fashion. A massive fir, it rose to nearly touch the ceiling at the far end of the ballroom. (When Will asked Charlotte how on earth it had gotten in there, she had only waved her hands and said something about Magnus.) Candles balanced on each branch, though Tessa could not see how they were fastened or supported. They cast even more golden light over the room.

Tied to the branches of the tree—and dangling from sconces, from the candelabras on tables, the knobs of doors— were crystalline glittering runes, each one as clear as glass yet refracting light, throwing glimmering rainbows through the room. The walls were decorated with intertwined wreaths of holly and ivy, the red berries glowing against the green leaves. Here and there were white-berried sprigs of mistletoe. There was even one tied to the collar of Church, who was hovering under one of the Christmas tables and looking furious.

Tessa didn't think she had ever seen so much food. The tables were laden with carved chicken and turkey, game birds and hare, Christmas hams and pies, wafer-thin sandwiches, ices and trifles and blancmanges and cream puddings, jewel-colored jellies, tipsy-cake and Christmas puddings flamed with brandy, iced sherbet, mulled wine and great silver bowls containing Bishop Christmas punch. There were horns of plenty spilling treats and candies, and Saint Nicholas's bags, each containing a lump of coal, a bit of sugar, or a lemon drop, to tell the receiver whether their behavior that year had been mischievous, sweet, or sour. There had been tea and presents earlier just for the inhabitants of the Institute, the group of them exchanging their gifts before the guests arrived—Charlotte, balanced on Henry's lap as he sat in his rolling chair, opening gift after gift for the baby due to arrive in April. (Whose name, it had been decided, was going to be Charles. "Charles Fairchild," Charlotte had said proudly, holding up the small blanket that Sophie had knitted for her, with a neat *C.F.* in the corner.)

"Charles *Buford* Fairchild," Henry had corrected.

Charlotte had made a face. Tessa, laughing, had asked, "Fairchild? Not Branwell?"

Charlotte had given a shy smile. "I am the Consul. It has been decided that in this case the child will take my name. Henry doesn't mind, do you, Henry?"

"Not at all," Henry had said. "Especially as Charles Buford Branwell would have sounded rather silly, but Charles Buford Fairchild has an excellent ring to it."

"*Henry . . .*"

Tessa smiled now at the memory. She was standing near the Christmas tree, watching the members of the Enclave in all their finery—women in the deep jewel tones of winter, dresses of red satin and sapphire silk and gold taffeta, men in elegant evening dress—as they milled and laughed. Sophie stood with Gideon, glowing and relaxed in an elegant green velvet gown; there was Cecily in blue, dashing here and there, delighted to be looking at everything, and Gabriel following her, all long limbs and tousled hair and adoring amusement. A massive Yule log, wound round with wreaths of ivy and holly, burned in the enormous stone fireplace, and hanging above the fireplace were nets containing golden apples, walnuts, colored popcorn, and candies. There was music, too, soft and haunting, and Charlotte seemed finally to have found a use for Bridget's singing, for it rose above the sound of the instruments, lilting and sweet.

> *"Alas, my love, ye do me wrong*
> *To cast me off discourteously.*
> *And I have loved you so long,*
> *Delighting in your company.*
>
> *Greensleeves was all my joy;*
> *Greensleeves was my delight;*
> *Greensleeves was my heart of gold,*
> *And who but Lady Greensleeves?"*

"'Let the sky rain potatoes,'" said a musing voice. "'Let it thunder to the tune of Greensleeves.'"

Tessa started and turned. Will had appeared somehow at her elbow, which was vexing, as she had been looking for him since she had come into the room and had seen no sign of him. As always, the sight of him in evening dress—all blue and black and white—took her breath away, but she hid the hitch in her chest with a smile. "Shakespeare," she said. "*The Merry Wives of Windsor.*"

"Not one of the better plays," Will said, narrowing his blue eyes as he took her in. Tessa had chosen to wear rose-colored silk that night, and no jewelry save a velvet ribbon, wrapped twice about her throat and hanging down her back. Sophie had done her hair—as a favor, now, not as a lady's maid—and woven small white berries in among the upswept curls. Tessa felt very fancy, and conspicuous. "Though it has its moments."

"Always a literary critic," Tessa sighed, gazing away from

him, across the room, to where Charlotte was in conversation with a tall, fair-haired man Tessa did not recognize.

Will leaned in toward her. He smelled faintly of something green and wintry, fir or lime or cypress. "Those are mistletoe berries in your hair," he said, his breath ghosting across her cheek. "Technically, I believe that means anyone can kiss you at any time."

She widened her eyes at him. "Do you think they're likely to try?"

He touched her cheek lightly; he was wearing white chamois gloves, but she felt it as if it were his skin on hers. "I'd kill anyone who did."

"Well," Tessa said. "It wouldn't be the first time you did something scandalous at Christmas."

Will paused for a moment and then grinned, that rare grin of his that lit up his face and changed the whole nature of it. It was a smile Tessa had worried once was gone forever, gone with Jem down into the darkness of the Silent City. Jem was not dead, but some bit of Will had gone with him when he'd left, some bit chiseled out of Will's heart and buried down there among the whispering bones. And Tessa had worried, for that first week just after, that Will would not recover, that he would always be a sort of ghost, wandering about the Institute, not eating, always turning to speak to someone who was not there, the light in his face dying as he remembered and fell silent.

But she had been determined. Her own heart had been broken, but to mend Will's, she was sure, would mean to mend her own somehow. As soon as she'd been strong enough, she had set herself to bring him tea he did not want, and books that he did, and harried him, in and out of the library, and demanded his help with training. She told Charlotte to stop treating him like glass that would break and to send him out into the city to fight, as he had been sent before, with Gabriel or Gideon instead of Jem. And Charlotte had done it, uneasily, but Will had come back from them bloody and bruised, but with his eyes alive and alight.

"That was clever," Cecily had said to her later, as they'd stood by the window, watching Will and Gabriel talking in the courtyard. "Being Nephilim gives my brother a purpose. Shadowhunting will mend the cracks in him. Shadowhunting, and you."

Tessa had let the curtain fall closed, thoughtfully. She and Will had not spoken of what had happened in Cadair Idris, the night they had spent together. Indeed, it seemed as distant as a dream. It was like something that had happened to another person, not her, not Tessa. She did not know if Will felt the same way. She knew Jem had known, or guessed, and forgave them both, but Will had not approached her again, not said he loved her, not asked if she loved him since the day Jem had left.

It seemed that endless ages went by, though it was only about a fortnight, before Will came and found her alone in the library, and asked her—rather abruptly—if she would go for a carriage ride with him the next day. Puzzled, Tessa had agreed, privately wondering if there was some other reason he wanted her company. A mystery to investigate? A confession to make?

But no, it had been a simple carriage ride through the park. The weather had been growing colder, and ice was riming the edges of the ponds. The bare branches of the trees were bleak and lovely, and Will made polite conversation with her about the weather and city landmarks. He seemed determined to take up where Jem had left off her London education. They went to the British Museum and the National Gallery, to Kew Gardens and to Saint Paul's Cathedral, where Tessa finally lost her temper.

They had been standing in the famous Whispering Gallery, Tessa leaning on the railing and gazing down into the cathedral below. Will was translating the Latin inscription on the wall of the crypt where Christopher Wren was buried—"*if you seek his monument, look about you*"—when Tessa absently reached to slip her hand into his. He immediately drew back, flushing.

She looked at him in surprise. "Is something wrong?"

"No," he said, too quickly. "I simply—I did not bring you here that I might maul you in the Whispering Gallery."

Tessa exploded. "I am not *asking* you to maul me in the Whispering Gallery! But by the Angel, Will, would you stop being so *polite*?"

He looked at her in amazement. "But wouldn't you rather—"

"I would not rather. I don't want you to be polite! I want you to be Will! I don't want you to indicate points of architectural interest to me as if you were a Baedeker guide! I want you to say dreadfully mad, funny things and make up songs and be—" *The Will I fell in love with,* she almost said. "And be Will," she finished instead. "Or I shall hit you with my umbrella."

"I am trying to court you," Will said in exasperation. "Court you *properly*. That's what all this has been about. You know that, don't you?"

"Mr. Rochester never courted Jane Eyre," Tessa pointed out.

"No, he dressed up as a woman and terrified the poor girl out of her wits. Is that what you want?"

"You would make a very ugly woman."

"I would not. I would be stunning."

Tessa laughed. "There," she said. "There is Will. Isn't that better? Don't you think so?"

"I don't know," Will said, eyeing her. "I'm afraid to answer that. I've heard that when I speak, it makes American women wish to strike me with umbrellas."

Tessa laughed again, and then they were both laughing, their smothered giggles bouncing off the walls of the Whispering Gallery. After that, things were decidedly easier between them, and Will's smile when he helped her down from the carriage on their return was bright and real.

That night there had been a soft tap on Tessa's door, and when she had gone to open it, she had found nobody there, only a book resting on the corridor floor. *A Tale of Two Cities*. An odd present, she had thought. There was a copy of the book in the library, which she could read as often as she wanted, but this one was brand-new, with a receipt from Hatchards marking the title page. It was only when she took it to bed with her that she realized that there was an inscription on the title page as well.

> *Tess, Tess, Tessa.*
>
> *Was there ever a more beautiful sound than your name? To speak it aloud makes my heart ring like a bell. Strange to imagine that, isn't it—a heart ringing? But when you touch me, that is what it is like, as if my heart is ringing in my chest and the sound shivers down my veins and splinters my bones with joy.*
>
> *Why have I written these words in this book? Because of you. You taught me to love this book, where I had scorned it.*

When I read it for the second time, with an open mind and heart, I felt the most complete despair and envy of Sydney Carton—yes, Sydney, for even if he had no hope that the woman he loved would love him, at least he could tell her of his love. At least he could do something to prove his passion, even if that thing was to die.

I would have chosen death for a chance to tell you the truth, Tessa, if I could have been assured that death would be my own. And that is why I envied Sydney, for he was free.

And now at last I am free, and I can finally tell you, without fear of danger to you, all that I feel in my heart.

You are not the last dream of my soul.

You are the first dream, the only dream I ever was unable to stop myself from dreaming. You are the first dream of my soul, and from that dream I hope will come all other dreams, a lifetime's worth.

With hope at last,

Will Herondale

She had sat up for a long time after that, holding the book without reading it, watching the dawn come up over London. In the morning she had fairly flown to get dressed, before she'd seized up the book and dashed downstairs with it. She caught Will coming out of his bedroom, hair still damp from the pitcher, and hurled herself at him, catching his lapels and pulling him to her, burying her face in his chest. The book thumped to the floor between him as he reached to hold her, smoothing her hair down her back, whispering softly, "Tessa, what is it, what's wrong? Did you not like—"

"No one has ever written me anything so beautiful," she

said, her face pressed against his chest, the soft beat of his heart steady beneath his shirt and jacket. "Not ever."

"I wrote it just after I discovered the curse was false," Will said. "I had meant to give it to you then, but—" His hand tightened in her hair. "When I found out you were engaged to Jem, I put it away. I did not know when I could, when I should, give it to you. And then yesterday, when you wanted me to be myself, I had hope enough to take out those old dreams again, to dust them off and give them to you."

They went to the park that day, though it was as cold as it was bright, and there were not many people about. The Serpentine was bright under the wintry sun, and Will pointed out the place where he and Jem had fed poultry pies to the mallards. It was the first time she saw him smile while talking about Jem.

She knew she could not be Jem for Will. No one could. But slowly the hollow places in his heart were filling in. Having Cecily about was a joy for Will; Tessa could see that when they sat together before the fire, speaking Welsh softly, and his eyes glowed; he had even grown to like Gabriel and Gideon, and they were friends for him, though no one could be a friend as Jem had been. And of course, Charlotte's and Henry's love was as steadfast as ever. The wound would never go away, Tessa knew, not for herself and not for Will, either, but as the weather grew colder and Will smiled more and ate more regularly and the haunted look faded from his eyes, she began to breathe more easily, knowing that look was not a mortal one.

"Hmm," he said now, rocking back on his heels slightly as he surveyed the ballroom floor. "You may be right. I think it was round about Christmas when I got my Welsh dragon tattoo."

At that, Tessa had to try very hard not to blush. "How *did* that happen?"

Will made an airy gesture with his hand. "I was drunk . . ."

"Nonsense. You were never really drunk."

"On the contrary—in order to learn how to pretend to be inebriated, one must become inebriated at least once, as a reference point. Six-Fingered Nigel had been at the mulled cider—"

"You can't mean there's truly a Six-Fingered Nigel?"

"Of course there is—," Will began with a grin, which suddenly faded; he was looking past Tessa, out at the ballroom. She turned to follow his gaze and saw the same tall, fair-haired man who had been talking to Charlotte earlier shouldering his way through the crowd toward them.

He was stocky, perhaps in his late thirties, with a scar that ran along his jaw. Tousled, fairish hair, and blue eyes, and skin tanned by the sun. It looked even darker against his starched white shirtfront. There was something familiar about him, something that teased at the edges of Tessa's memories.

He came to a stop in front of them. His eyes flicked to Will. They were a paler blue than Will's, almost the color of corn-flowers. The skin around them was tanned and lined with faint crow's-feet. He said, "You are William Herondale?"

Will nodded without speaking.

"I am Elias Carstairs," the man said. "Jem Carstairs was my nephew."

Will turned white, and Tessa realized what it was about the man that seemed familiar—there was something about him, something about the way he carried himself and the shape of his hands, that reminded her of Jem. Since Will seemed unable to speak, Tessa said:

"Yes, this is Will Herondale. And I am Theresa Gray."

"The shape-changer girl," said the man—Elias, Tessa reminded herself; Shadowhunters used each other's given names. "You were engaged to James before he became a Silent Brother."

"I was," Tessa said quietly. "I love him very much."

He gave her a look—not hostile or challenging, only curious. Then he turned his gaze to Will. "You were his *parabatai*?"

Will found his voice. "I am still," he said, and set his jaw stubbornly.

"James spoke of you," said Elias. "After I left China, when I returned to Idris, I asked if he would come and live with me. We had sent him away from Shanghai, considering it unsafe for him there while Yanluo's minions ran free, still seeking vengeance. But when I asked him if he would come to me in Idris, he said no, he could not. I asked him to reconsider. Told him I was his family, his blood. But he said he could not leave his *parabatai*, that there were some things more important than blood." Elias's light blue eyes were steady. "I have brought you a gift, Will Herondale. Something I intended to give to him, when he was of age, because his father no longer lived to give it to him. But I cannot give it to him now."

Will was tense all over, a bowstring strung too tight. He said: "I have not done anything to deserve a gift."

"I think you have." Elias drew from the belt at his waist a short sword in an intricate scabbard. He held it out to Will, who, after a moment, took it. The scabbard was covered in intricate designs of leaves and runes, carefully worked, gleaming under the golden light. With a decisive gesture Will pulled the sword free and held it up in front of his face.

The hilt was covered with the same pattern of runes and leaves, but the blade itself was simple and bare, save for a line of words that ran down its center. Tessa leaned in to read the words upon the metal.

I am Cortana, of the same steel and temper as Joyeuse and Durendal.

"Joyeuse was Charlemagne's sword," said Will, his voice still stiff in that way that Tessa knew now meant that he was forcing down emotion. "Durendal was Roland's. This sword is—it is of legend born."

"Forged by the first Shadowhunter weapons maker, Wayland the Smith. It has a feather from the wing of the Angel in its hilt," said Elias. "It has been in the Carstairs family for hundreds of years. I was instructed by Jem's father to give it to him when he reached eighteen. But the Silent Brothers cannot accept gifts." He looked at Will. "You were his *parabatai*. You should have it."

Will slammed the sword back into its scabbard. "I cannot take it. I will not."

Elias looked stunned. "But you must," he said. "You were his *parabatai*, and he loved you—"

Will held the sword back out toward Elias Carstairs, hilt-first. After a moment Elias took it, and Will turned and walked away, vanishing into the crowd.

Elias looked after him in bewilderment. "I did not intend to cause offense."

"You spoke of Jem in the past tense," said Tessa. "Jem is not with us, but he is not dead. Will—he cannot bear that Jem be thought of as lost, or forgotten."

"I did not mean to forget him," said Elias. "I meant simply

that the Silent Brothers do not have emotions like we do. They do not feel as we do. If they love—"

"Jem still loves Will," Tessa said. "Whether he is a Silent Brother or not. There are things no magic can destroy, for they are magic in themselves. You never saw them together, but I did."

"I meant to give him Cortana," Elias said. "I cannot give it to James, so I thought his *parabatai* ought to have it."

"You mean well," Tessa said. "But, forgive my impertinence, Mr. Carstairs—do you never mean to have any children of your own?"

His eyes widened. "I had not thought—"

Tessa looked at the shimmering blade, and then at the man holding it. She could see Jem in him a little, as if she were looking at the reflection of what she loved in rippling water. That love, remembered and present, made her voice gentle when she spoke. "If you are not sure," she said, "then keep it. Keep it for your own heirs. Will would prefer that. For he does not need a sword to remember Jem by. However illustrious its lineage."

It was cold on the Institute steps, cold where Will stood without a coat or hat, looking out into the frost-dusted night. The wind blew tiny drifts of snow against his cheeks, his bare hands, and he heard, as he always did, Jem's voice in the back of his head, telling him not to be ridiculous, to get back inside before he gave himself the flu.

Winter had always seemed the purest season to Will— even the smoke and dirt of London caught by the chill, frozen hard and clean. That morning he had broken a layer of ice that had formed on his water jug, before splashing the icy fluid onto his face and shivering as he looked in the mirror, his wet hair painting his face in black stripes. *First Christmas morning without Jem in six years.* The purest cold, bringing the purest pain.

"*Will.*" The voice was a whisper, of a very familiar kind. He turned his head, an image of Old Molly rising in his mind—but ghosts so rarely strayed from where they had died or were buried, and besides, what would she want with him now?

A gaze met his, level and dark. The rest of her was not so much transparent as edged by silver: the blond hair, the doll-pretty face, the white gown she had died in. Blood, red like a flower, on her chest.

"Jessamine," he said.

"*Merry Christmas, Will.*"

His heart, which had stopped for a moment, began to beat again, the blood running fast in his veins. "Jessamine, why— what are you doing here?"

She pouted a little. "I am here because I died here," she said, her voice growing in strength. It was not unusual for a ghost to achieve a greater solidity and auditory power when they were close to a human, especially one who could hear them. She indicated the courtyard at their feet, where Will had held her in her dying moments, her blood running onto the flagstones. "Are you not pleased to see me, Will?"

"Should I be?" he said. "Jessie, usually when I see ghosts, it is because there is some unfinished business or some sorrow that holds them to this world."

She raised her head, looking up at the snow. Though it fell all around her, she was as untouched by it as if she stood under glass. "And if I had a sorrow, would you help me cure it? You never cared for me much in life."

"I did," Will said. "And I am truly sorry if I gave the impression that I cared nothing for you, or hated you, Jessamine. I think you reminded me more of myself than I wished to admit, and therefore I judged you with the same harshness I would have judged myself."

At that, she did look at him. "Why, was that straightforward honesty, Will? How you *have* changed." She took a step back, and he saw that her feet made no impression in the dusting of snow on the steps. "I am here because in life I did not wish to be a Shadowhunter, to guard the Nephilim. I am charged now with the guard of the Institute, for as long as it needs guarding."

"And you do not mind?" he asked. "Being here, with us, when you could have passed over . . ."

She wrinkled her nose. "I did not care to pass over. So much was demanded of me in life, the Angel knows what it might be like afterward. No, I am happy here, watching you all, quiet and drifting and unseen." Her silvery hair shone in the moonlight as she inclined her head toward him. "Though *you* are near to driving me mad."

"I?"

"Indeed. I always said you would be a dreadful suitor, Will, and you are nigh on proving it."

"Truly?" Will said. "You have come back from death like the ghost of Old Marley, but to nag me about my romantic prospects?"

"What prospects? You've taken Tessa on so many carriage rides, I'd wager she could draw a map of London from memory, but have you proposed to her? You have not. A lady cannot propose to herself, William, and she cannot tell you she loves you if you do not state your intentions!"

Will shook his head. "Jessamine, you are incorrigible."

"I am also right," she pointed out. "What is it you are afraid of?"

"That if I do state my intentions, she will say she does not love me back, not the way she loved Jem."

"She will not love you as she loved Jem. She will love you as she loves *you*, Will, an entirely different person. Do you wish she had not loved Jem?"

"No, but neither do I wish to marry someone who does not love me."

"You must ask her to find that out," said Jessamine. "Life is full of risks. Death is much simpler."

"Why have I not seen you before tonight, when you have been here all this time?" he asked.

"I cannot enter the Institute yet, and when you are out in the courtyard, you are always with someone else. I have tried to go through the doors, but a sort of force prevents me. It is better than it was. At first I could go only a few steps. Now I am as you see me." She indicated her position on the stairs. "One day I shall be able to go inside."

"And when you do, you shall find that your room is as it ever was, and your dolls as well," said Will.

Jessamine smiled a smile that made Will wonder if she had always been so sad, or if death had changed her more than he had thought ghosts could be changed. Before he could speak again, though, a look of alarm crossed her face, and she vanished within a swirl of snow.

Will turned to see what had frightened her off. The doors of the Institute had opened, and Magnus had emerged. He wore an astrakhan wool greatcoat, and his tall silk hat was already being spotted by the falling snowflakes.

"I should have known I'd find you out here, doing your best to turn yourself into an icicle," Magnus said, descending the steps until he stood beside Will, looking out at the courtyard.

Will did not feel like mentioning Jessamine. Somehow he thought she would not have wanted him to. "Were you leaving the party? Or just looking for me?"

"Both," Magnus said, pulling on a pair of white gloves. "In fact, I am leaving London."

"Leaving London?" Will said in dismay. "You can't mean that."

"Why wouldn't I?" Magnus flicked a finger at an errant snowflake. It sparked blue and vanished. "I am not a Londoner, Will. I have been stopping with Woolsey for some time, but his home is not my home, and Woolsey and I wear out each other's company after not much duration."

"Where will you go?"

"New York. The New World! A new life, a new continent." Magnus threw his hands up. "I may even take your cat with me. Charlotte says he has been mourning since Jem left."

"Well, he bites everyone. You're welcome to him. Do you think he'll like New York?"

"Who knows? We will find out together. The unexpected is what keeps me from stagnating."

"Those of us who do not live forever do not like change perhaps as much as those of you who do. I am tired of losing people," Will said.

"So am I," Magnus said. "But it is as I said, isn't it? You learn to bear it."

"I have heard sometimes that men who lose an arm or a leg still feel the pain in those limbs, though they are gone," said Will. "It is like that sometimes. I can feel Jem with me, though he is gone, and it is like I am missing a part of myself."

"But you are not," Magnus said. "He is not dead, Will. He lives because you let him go. He would have stayed with you and died, if you had asked it, but you loved him enough to prefer that he live, even if that life is separate from yours. And that above all things proves that you are not Sydney Carton, Will, that yours is not the kind of love that can be redeemed only through destruction. It is what I saw in you, what I have always seen in you, what made me want to help you. That you are not despairing. That you have in you an infinite capacity for joy." He put one gloved hand under Will's chin and lifted Will's face. There were not many people Will had to raise his head to look in the eye, but Magnus was one. "Bright star," Magnus said, and his eyes were thoughtful, as if he were remembering something, or someone. "Those of you who are mortal, you burn so fiercely. And you fiercer than most, Will. I will not ever forget you."

"Nor I you," said Will. "I owe you a great deal. You broke my curse."

"You were not cursed."

"Yes, I was," Will said. "I was. Thank you, Magnus, for all you did for me. If I did not say it before, I am saying it now. Thank you."

Magnus dropped his hand. "I don't think a Shadowhunter has ever thanked me before."

Will smiled crookedly. "I would try not to become too accustomed to it. We are not a thankful sort."

"No." Magnus laughed. "No, I won't." His bright cat's eyes narrowed. "I leave you in good hands, I think, Will Herondale."

"You mean Tessa."

"I do mean Tessa. Or do you deny that she holds your heart?" Magnus had begun to descend the stairs; he paused, and looked back at Will.

"I do not," Will said. "But she will be sorry that you have left without saying good-bye to her."

"Oh," Magnus said, turning at the bottom of the steps, with a curious smile. "I don't think that will be necessary. Tell her I will see her again."

Will nodded. Magnus turned away, hands in the pockets of his coat, and began to walk toward the gates of the Institute. Will watched until his retreating figure faded into the whiteness of the falling snow.

Tessa had slipped out of the ballroom without anyone noticing. Even the usually keen-eyed Charlotte was distracted, sitting beside Henry in his wheeled chair, her hand in his, smiling at the antics of the musicians.

It did not take Tessa long to find Will. She had guessed where he would be, and she was correct—standing on the front steps of the Institute, without a coat or hat, letting the snow fall on his head and shoulders. There was a white dusting of it all over the courtyard, like icing sugar, frosting the line of carriages waiting there, the black iron gates, the flagstones upon which Jessamine had died. Will was staring intently ahead of him, as if trying to discern something through the descending flakes.

"Will," Tessa said, and he turned to look up at her. She had caught up a silk wrap, but nothing heavier, and she felt the cool sting of snowflakes against the bare skin of her neck and shoulders.

"I should have been more polite to Elias Carstairs," Will said by way of reply. He was looking up at the sky, where a pale crescent of moon darted in between thick sweeps of cloud and fog. Flakes of white snow had fallen and mixed with his black hair. His cheeks and lips were flushed with the cold. He looked more handsome than she had ever remembered him. "Instead I behaved as I would have—before."

Tessa knew what he meant. For Will there was only one before and after.

"You are allowed to have a temper," she said. "I have told you before, I do not want you to be perfect. Only to be Will."

"Who will never be perfect."

"Perfect is dull," Tessa said, descending the last step to stand beside him. "They are playing 'complete the poetic quotation' inside now. You could have made quite a showing. I do not think there is anyone there who could challenge your knowledge of literature."

"Other than you."

"I would be difficult competition indeed. Perhaps we could make ourselves a team of sorts, and divide the winnings."

"That seems bad form." Will spoke absently, tilting back his head. The snow circled whitely about them, as if they stood at the bottom of a whirlpool. "Today, when Sophie Ascended . . ."

"Yes?"

"Is that something that you would have wanted?" He turned

to look at her, white snowflakes caught in his dark lashes. "For yourself?"

"You know that isn't possible for me, Will. I am a warlock. Or at least, that is the closest approximation of what I am. I cannot ever be fully Nephilim."

"I know." He looked down at his hands, opening his fingers to let snowflakes settle, melting, on his palms. "But in Cadair Idris you said that you had hoped to be a Shadowhunter—that Mortmain had dashed those hopes—"

"I did feel that way at the time," she allowed. "But when I became Ithuriel—when I Changed and destroyed Mortmain— how could I hate something that allowed me to protect the ones I care about? It is not easy to be different, and even less so to be unique. But I begin to think I was never meant for an easy road."

Will laughed. "The easy road? No, not for you, my Tessa."

"Am I your Tessa?" She drew her wrap closer around herself, pretending her shiver was just the cold. "Are *you* bothered by what I am, Will? That I am not like you?"

The words hung between them, unspoken: *There is no future for a Shadowhunter who dallies with warlocks.*

Will paled. "Those things I said on the roof, so long ago— you know I did not mean them."

"I know—"

"I do not wish you other than you are, Tessa. You are what you are, and I love you. I do not love just the parts of you that meet with the Clave's approval—"

She raised her eyebrows. "You are willing to endure the rest?"

He raked a hand through his dark, snow-dampened hair.

"No. I am misspeaking. There is nothing about you that I can imagine *not* loving. Do you really think it is so important to me that you be Nephilim? My mother isn't a Shadowhunter. And when I saw you Change into the angel—when I saw you blaze forth with the fire of Heaven—it was glorious, Tess." He took a step toward her. "What you are, what you can do, it is like some great miracle of the earth, like fire or wildflowers or the breadth of the sea. You are unique in the world, just as you are unique in my heart, and there will never be a time when I do not love you. I would love you if you were not in any part a Shadowhunter at all—"

She gave him a shaky smile. "But I am glad that I am, if only by half," she said, "since it means that I may stay with you, here, in the Institute. That the family I have found here can remain my family. Charlotte said that if I chose, I could cease to be a Gray and take the name my mother should have had before she was married. I could be a Starkweather. I could have a true Shadowhunter name."

She heard Will exhale a breath. It came out a puff of white in the cold. His eyes were blue and wide and clear, fixed on her face. He wore the expression of a man who had steeled himself to do a terrifying thing, and was carrying it through. "Of course you can have a true Shadowhunter name," Will said. "You can have mine."

Tessa stared at him, all black and white against the black-and-white snow and stone. "Your name?"

Will took a step toward her, till they stood face-to-face. Then he reached to take her hand and slid off her glove, which he put into his pocket. He held her bare hand in his, his fingers curved around hers. His hand was warm and callused, and his touch made her shiver. His eyes were steady and blue; they were everything Will was: true and tender, sharp and witty, loving and kind. "Marry me," he said. "Marry me, Tess. Marry me and be Tessa Herondale. Or be Tessa Gray, or be whatever you wish to call yourself, but marry me and stay with me and never leave me, for I cannot bear another day of my life to go by that does not have you in it."

The snow was swirling down around them, white and cold and perfect. The clouds above had parted, and through the gaps she could see the stars.

"Jem told me what Ragnor Fell said about my father," Will went on. "That for my father there was only ever one woman he loved, and it was her for him, or nothing. You are that for me. I love you, and I will only ever love you until I die—"

"Will!"

He bit his lip. His hair was thick with snow, his lashes starred with flakes. "Was that too grand a statement? Did I frighten you? You know how I am with words—"

"Oh, I do."

"I recall what you said to me once," Will went on. "That words have the power to change us. Your words have changed me, Tess; they have made me a better man than I would have been otherwise. Life is a book, and there are a thousand pages I have not yet read. I would read them together with you, as many as I can, before I die—"

She put her hand against his chest, just over his heart, and felt its beat against her palm, a unique time signature that was all its own. "I only wish you would not speak of dying," she said. "But even for that, yes, I know how you are with your words, and, Will—I love *all* of them. Every word you say. The silly ones, the mad ones, the beautiful ones, and the ones that are only for me. I love them, and I love you."

Will began to speak, but Tessa covered his mouth with her hand.

"I love your words, my Will, but hold them for a moment," she said, and smiled into his eyes. "Think of all the words I have held inside all this time, while I did not know your intentions. When you came to me in the drawing room and told me that you loved me, it was the hardest thing I have ever done to send you away. You said you loved the words of my heart, the shape of my soul. I remember. I remember every word you said from that day to this. I will never forget them. There are so many words I wish to say to you, and so many I wish to hear you say to me. I hope we have all our lives to say them to each other."

"Then you will marry me?" Will said, looking dazed, as if he did not quite believe in his good fortune.

"Yes," she said—the last, the simplest, and most important word of all.

And Will, who had words for every occasion, opened his mouth and closed it on silence, and instead reached for her to pull her against him. Her wrap fell onto the stairs, but his arms were warm around her, and his mouth hot against hers as he slanted his head down to kiss her. He tasted like snowflakes and wine, like winter and Will and London. His mouth was soft against hers, his hands in her hair, scattering white berries across the stone steps. Tessa held fast to Will as the snow swirled around them. Through the windows of the Institute, she could hear the faint sound of the music playing in the ballroom: the pianoforte, the cello, and rising above it all, like sparks leaping toward the sky, the sweet, celebratory strains of the violin.

* * *

"I can't believe we're really going home," Cecily said. Her hands were clasped in front of her, and she was bouncing up and down in her white kid boots. She was bundled into a red winter coat, the brightest thing in the dark crypt except the Portal itself, great and silver and shining against the far wall.

Through it Tessa could catch a glimpse, like a glimpse in a dream, of blue sky (the sky outside the Institute was a spitting London gray) and snow-dusted hills. Will stood beside her, his shoulder brushing hers. He looked pale and nervous, and she longed to take his hand. "We're not *going home*, Cecy," he said. "Not to stay. We're visiting. I wish to introduce our parents to my fiancée"—and at that his pallor faded slightly, his lips curving into a smile—"that they might know the girl I am going to marry."

"Oh, pish tosh," said Cecily. "We can use the Portal to see them whenever we want! Charlotte is the Consul, so we cannot possibly get in trouble."

Charlotte groaned. "Cecily, this is a singular expedition. It is not a toy. You cannot simply use the Portal whenever you like, and this excursion must be kept a secret. None but we here can know you visited your parents, that I allowed you to break the Law!"

"I won't tell anyone!" Cecily protested. "And neither will Gabriel." She glanced at the boy at her side. "You won't, will you?"

"Why are we bringing him along, again?" Will inquired, of the world in general as well as his sister.

Cecily put her hands on her hips. "Why are you bringing Tessa?"

"Because Tessa and I are going to be *married*," Will said, and Tessa smiled; the way that Will's little sister could ruffle his feathers like no one else was still amusing to her.

"Well, Gabriel and I might well be married," Cecily said. "Someday."

Gabriel made a choking noise, and turned an alarming shade of purple.

Will threw up his hands. "You can't be married, Cecily! You're only fifteen! When I get married, I'll be eighteen! An adult!"

Cecily did not look impressed. "We may have a long engagement," she said. "But I cannot see why you are counseling me to marry a man my parents have never met."

Will sputtered. "I am not counseling you to marry a man your parents have never met!"

"Then we are in agreement. Gabriel must meet Mam and Dad." Cecily turned to Henry. "Is the Portal ready?"

Tessa leaned close to Will. "I do love the way she manages you," she whispered. "It is quite entertaining to watch."

"Wait until you meet my mother," Will said, and slipped his hand into hers. His fingers were cold; his heart must have been racing. Tessa knew he had been up all night. The idea of seeing his parents after so many years was as terrifying to him as it was joyful. She knew that admixture of hope and fear, infinitely worse than just one alone.

"The Portal is quite ready," said Henry. "And remember, in an hour I shall open it again, that you may return through it."

"And understand that this is just this once," Charlotte said anxiously. "Even if I am the Consul, I cannot allow you to visit your mundane family—"

"Not even at Christmas?" said Cecily, with large, tragic eyes. Charlotte weakened visibly. "Well, perhaps Christmas . . ."

"And birthdays," said Tessa. "Birthdays are special."

Charlotte put her hands over her face. "Oh, by the Angel."

Henry laughed, and swept an arm toward the door. "Go on through," he said, and Cecily went first, vanishing through the Portal as if she had stepped through a waterfall. Gabriel followed, and then Will and Tessa, holding tightly to each other's hands. Tessa concentrated on the warmth of Will's hand, the pulse of blood through his skin, as the cold and darkness took them, whirling them about for breathless, ageless moments. Lights burst behind her eyes, and she emerged from the darkness suddenly, blinking and stumbling. Will caught her to him, keeping her from falling.

They were standing on the wide curved drive in front of Ravenscar Manor. Tessa had seen the place only from above, when she and Jem and Will had visited Yorkshire together, not realizing that Will's family inhabited the house now. She recalled that the manor was held in the cup of a valley, with hills sweeping up on either side, covered in gorse and heather—patched now with a dusting of snow. The trees had been green then; they were leafless now, and from the dark slate roof of the manor hung sparkling icicles.

The door was dark oak, a heavy brass knocker set in the center. Will looked at his sister, who nodded minutely at him, then squared his shoulders and reached to lift and release it. The resultant crash seemed to echo through the valley, and Will swore under his breath.

Tessa touched his wrist lightly with her hand. "Be brave," she said. "It's not a duck, is it?"

He turned to smile at her, dark hair falling in his eyes, just as the door opened to reveal a neatly dressed parlor maid in a black dress and white mobcap. She took one look at the group on the doorstep, and her eyes widened like saucers.

"Miss *Cecily*," she gasped, and then her eyes went to Will. She clapped a hand over her mouth, turned, and bolted back into the house.

"Oh, dear," said Tessa.

"I have that effect on women," Will said. "I probably should have warned you before you agreed to marry me."

"I can still change my mind," Tessa said sweetly.

"Don't you dare—," he began with a breathless half laugh, and then suddenly there were people at the door—a tall man, broad-shouldered, with a mass of fair hair streaked with gray, and light blue eyes. Just behind him was a woman: slender and startlingly beautiful, with Will and Cecily's ink-black hair and blue eyes as dark as violets. She cried out the moment her gaze fell on Will, and her hands came up, fluttering like white birds startled by a gust of wind.

Tessa released Will's hand. He seemed frozen, like a fox when the hounds were almost on him. "Go on," Tessa said softly, and he stepped forward, and then his mother was embracing him, saying, "I knew you'd come back. I *knew* you would," followed by a torrent of Welsh, of which Tessa could discern only Will's name. Their father was stunned but smiling, holding out his arms for Cecily, who went into them as agreeably as Tessa had ever seen her do anything.

For the next few moments Tessa and Gabriel stood awkwardly on the doorstep, not quite looking at each other but not quite sure where else to look either. After a long moment Will drew away from his mother, patting her gently on the shoulder. She laughed, though her eyes were full of tears, and said something in Welsh that Tessa strongly suspected was a comment on the fact that Will was now taller than she was.

"Little mother," he said affectionately, confirming Tessa's suspicions, and he swung around just as his mother's gaze fell on Tessa, and then Gabriel, her eyes widening. "Mam and Dad, this is Theresa Gray. We are engaged to be married, next year."

Will's mother gave a gasp—though she sounded more surprised than anything else, to Tessa's relief—and Will's father's gaze went immediately to Gabriel, and then to Cecily, his eyes narrowing. "And who is the gentleman?"

Will's grin widened. "Oh, him," he said. "This is Cecily's— friend, Mr. Gabriel Lightworm."

Gabriel, half in the act of stretching out his hand to greet Mr. Herondale, froze in horror. "Lightwood," he sputtered. "Gabriel Lightwood—"

"*Will!*" Cecily said, breaking away from her father to glare at her brother.

Will looked at Tessa, his blue eyes shining. She opened her mouth to remonstrate with him, to say *Will!* as Cecily had just done, but it was too late—she was already laughing.

EPILOGUE

I say the tomb which on the dead is shut
Opens the Heavenly hall;
And what we here for the end of all things put
Is the first step of all.
—Victor Hugo, "At Villequier"

London, Blackfriars Bridge, 2008.

The wind was sharp, blowing grit and stray rubbish—crisps packets, stray pages of newspaper, old receipts—along the pavement as Tessa, glancing quickly from side to side to check for traffic, dashed across Blackfriars Bridge.

To any onlooker she would have looked like an ordinary girl in her late teens or early twenties: jeans tucked into boots, a blue cashmere top she'd gotten for half off during the January sales, and long brown hair, curling just a bit in the damp weather, tumbling haphazardly down her back. If they were particularly sharp-eyed about fashion, they would have assumed the paisley Liberty-print scarf she wore was a knockoff instead of a hundred-year-old original, and that the bracelet around her wrist was vintage, rather than a gift that had been given to her by her husband on their thirtieth wedding anniversary.

Tessa's steps slowed as she reached one of the stone recesses in the wall of the bridge. Cement benches had been built into them now, so that you could sit and look at the gray-green water below sloshing up against the bridge pilings, or at Saint Paul's in the distance. The city was alive with noise—the sounds of traffic: honking horns, the rumble of double-decker buses; the ringing of dozens of mobiles; the chatter of pedestrians; the faint sounds of music leaking from white iPod earbuds.

Tessa sat down on the bench, pulling her legs up under her. The atmosphere was shockingly clean and clear—the smoke and pollution that had rendered the air yellow and black when she had been a girl here were gone, and the sky was the color of a blue-gray marble. The eyesore that had been the Dover and Chatham railway bridge was gone too; only the pilings were still sticking up out of the water as an odd reminder of what had once been. Yellow buoys bobbed in the water now, and tourist boats chugged by, the amplified voices of tour guides blaring from their speakers. Buses as red as candy hearts sped by along the bridge, sending dead leaves fluttering to the curb.

She glanced down at the watch on her wrist. Five minutes to noon. She was a little early, but then she always was for this, their yearly meeting. It gave her a chance to think—to think and to remember, and there was no place better for doing either than here, on Blackfriars Bridge, the first place they had ever really talked.

Beside the watch was the pearl bracelet she always wore. She never took it off. Will had given it to her when they had been married thirty years, smiling as he'd fastened it on. He had had gray in his hair then, she knew, though she had never really seen it. As if her love had given him his own shape-shifting ability, no matter how much time had passed, when she looked at him, she saw always the wild, black-haired boy she had fallen in love with.

It still seemed incredible to her sometimes that they had managed to grow old together, herself and Will Herondale, whom Gabriel Lightwood had once said would not live to be older than nineteen. They had been good friends with the Lightwoods too, through all those years. Of course Will could hardly not be friends with the man who was married to his sister. Both Cecily and Gabriel had seen Will on the day he died, as had Sophie, though Gideon had himself passed away several years before.

Tessa remembered that day clearly, the day the Silent Brothers had said there was nothing more they could do to keep Will alive. He had been unable to leave their bed by then. Tessa had squared her shoulders and gone to give the news to their family and friends, trying to be as calm for them as she could, though her heart had felt as if it were being ripped out of her body.

It had been June, the bright hot summer of 1937, and with the curtains thrown back the bedroom had been full of sunlight, sunlight and her and Will's children, their grand-children, their nieces and nephews—Cecy's blue-eyed boys, tall and handsome, and Gideon and Sophie's two girls—and those who were as close as family: Charlotte, white-haired and upright, and the Fairchild sons and daughters with their curling red hair like Henry's had once been.

All day Tessa had sat on the bed with Will beside her, leaning on her shoulder. The sight might have been strange to others, a young woman lovingly cradling a man who looked old enough to be her grandfather, her hands looped through his, but to their family it was only familiar—it was only Tessa and Will. And because it was Tessa and Will, the others came and went all day, as Shadowhunters did at a deathbed, telling stories of Will's life and all the things he and Tessa had done through their long years together.

The children had spoken fondly of the way he had always loved their mother, fiercely and devotedly, the way he had never had eyes for anyone else, and how their parents had set the model for the sort of love they hoped to find in their own lives. They spoke of his regard for books, and how he had taught them all to love them too, to respect the printed page and cherish the stories that those pages held. They spoke of the way he still cursed in Welsh when he dropped something, though he rarely used the language otherwise, and of the fact that though his prose was excellent—he had written several histories of the Shadowhunters when he'd retired that had been very well respected—his poetry had always been awful, though that had never stopped him from reciting it.

Their oldest child, James, had spoken laughingly about

Will's unrelenting fear of ducks and his continual battle to keep them out of the pond at the family home in Yorkshire.

Their grandchildren had reminded him of the song about demon pox he had taught them—when they were much too young, Tessa had always thought—and that they had all memorized. They sang it all together and out of tune, scandalizing Sophie.

With tears running down her face, Cecily had reminded him of the moment at her wedding to Gabriel when he had delivered a beautiful speech praising the groom, at the end of which he had announced, "Dear God, I thought she was marrying Gideon. I take it all back," thus vexing not only Cecily and Gabriel but Sophie as well—and Will, though too tired to laugh, had smiled at his sister and squeezed her hand.

They had all laughed about his habit of taking Tessa on romantic "holidays" to places from Gothic novels, including the hideous moor where someone had died, a drafty castle with a ghost in it, and of course the square in Paris in which he had decided Sydney Carton had been guillotined, where Will had horrified passersby by shouting "I can see the blood on the cobblestones!" in French.

At the end of the day, as the sky had darkened, the family had come around Will's bed and kissed him each in turn and left one by one, until Will and Tessa were alone together. Tessa had lain down beside him and slid her arm beneath his head, and put her head on his chest, listening to the everweakening beat of his heart. And in the shadows they'd whispered, reminding each other of the stories only they knew. Of the girl who had hit over the head with a water jug the boy who had come to rescue her, and how he had fallen in love with her in that instant. Of a ballroom and a balcony and the moon sailing like a ship untethered through the sky. Of the flutter of the wings of a clockwork angel. Of holy water and blood.

Near midnight the door had opened and Jem had come in. Tessa supposed she should have thought of him as Brother Zachariah by then, but neither Will nor Tessa had ever called him that. He had come in like a shadow in his white robes, and Tessa had taken a deep breath when she had seen him, for she had known that this was what Will had been waiting for, and that the hour was now.

He did not come to Will at once, but crossed the room to a rosewood box that sat upon the top of the dresser. They had always kept Jem's violin for him, as Will had promised. It was kept clean and in order, and the hinges of the box did not creak as Jem opened it and lifted the instrument out. They watched as he rosined the bow with his familiar slim fingers, his pale wrists disappearing down into the paler material of the Brothers' parchment robes.

He lifted the violin to his shoulder then, and raised the bow. And he played.

Zhi yin. Jem had told her once that it meant understanding music, and also a bond that went deeper than friendship. Jem played, and he played the years of Will's life as he had seen them. He played two little boys in a training room, one showing the other how to throw knives, and he played the ritual of *parabatai*: the fire and the vows and the burning runes. He played two young men running through the streets of London in the dark, stopping to lean up against a wall and laugh together. He played the day in the library when he and Will had jested with Tessa about ducks, and he played the train to Yorkshire on which Jem had said that *parabatai* were meant to love each other as they loved their own souls. He played that love, and he played their love for Tessa, and hers for them, and he played Will saying, *In your eyes I have always found grace.* He played the too few times he had seen them since he had joined the Brotherhood—the brief meetings at the Institute; the time when Will had been bitten by a Shax demon and nearly died, and Jem had come from the Silent City and sat with him all night, risking discovery and punishment. And he played the birth of their first son, and the protection ceremony that had been carried out on the child in the Silent City. Will would have no other Silent Brother but Jem perform it. And Jem played the way he had covered his scarred face with his hands and turned away when he'd found out the child's name was James.

He played of love and loss and years of silence, words unsaid and vows unspoken, and all the spaces between his heart and theirs; and when he was done, and he'd set the violin back in its box, Will's eyes were closed, but Tessa's were full of tears. Jem set down his bow, and came toward the bed, drawing back his hood, so she could see his closed eyes and his scarred face. And he had sat down beside them on the bed, and taken Will's hand, the one that Tessa was not holding, and both Will and Tessa had heard Jem's voice in their minds.

I take your hand, brother, so that you may go in peace.

Will had opened the blue eyes that had never lost their color over all the passing years, and looked at Jem and then Tessa, and smiled, and died, with Tessa's head on his shoulder and his hand in Jem's.

It never had stopped hurting, remembering when Will had

died. After he was gone, Tessa had fled. Her children were grown, had children of their own; she told herself they did not need her and hid in the back of her mind the thought that haunted her: She could not bear to remain and watch them grow older than she was. It had been one thing to survive the death of her husband. To survive the death of her children—she could not sit by and watch it. It would happen, must happen, but she would not stay in that familiar house and wait for it. Instead she had taken her own path, a new path, one which would lead her back to her family now and again, but after these visits she would always return to the singular life she was creating for herself.

There was something Will had asked her to do.

The road that led from Shrewsbury to Welshpool was no longer as it had been when Will had ridden across it in a mad, heedless dash to save her from Mortmain. Will had left instructions, details, descriptions of towns, of a certain spreading oak tree. She had puttered up and down the road several times in her Morris Minor before she'd found it: the tree, just as he had drawn it in the journal he had given her, his hand shaking a little but his memory clear.

The dagger was there among the roots of the trees, which had grown around the hilt. She had had to cut some of them away, and dig at the dirt and rocks with a trowel, before she could free it. Jem's blade, stained dark now with weather and the passage of time.

She had brought it to Jem that year on the bridge. It was 1937 and the Blitz had not yet come to level the buildings around Saint Paul's, to strafe the sky with fire and burn the walls of the city Tessa loved. Still, there was a shadow over the world, the hint of a coming darkness.

"They kill each other and kill each other, and we can do nothing," Tessa had said, her hands on the worn stone of the bridge parapet. She was thinking of the Great War, of the spendthrift waste of life. Not a Shadowhunter war, but out of blood and war were demons born, and it was the responsibility of the Nephilim to keep demons from wreaking even greater destruction.

We cannot save them from themselves, Jem had replied. He wore his hood up, but the wind blew it back, showing her the edge of his scarred cheek.

"There is something coming. A horror Mortmain could only have imagined. I feel it in my bones."

No one can rid the world of all evil, Tessa.

And when she drew his dagger, wrapped in silk, though still dirty and stained with earth and Will's blood, from the pocket of her coat and gave it to him, he bent his head and held it to him, hunching his shoulders over it, as if protecting a wound to his heart.

"Will wanted you to see it," she said. "I know you cannot take it with you."

Keep it for me. There may come a day.

She did not ask him what he meant, but she kept it. Kept it when she left England, the white cliffs of Dover retreating like clouds in the distance as she crossed the Channel. In Paris she found Magnus, who was living in a garret apartment and painting, an occupation for which he had no aptitude whatsoever. He let her sleep on a mattress by the window, and in the night, when she woke up screaming for Will, he came and put his arms around her, smelling of turpentine.

"The first one is always the hardest," he said.

"The first?"

"The first one you love who dies," he said. "It gets easier, after."

When the war came to Paris, they went to New York together, and Magnus reintroduced her to the city she had been born in—a busy, bright, buzzing metropolis she barely recognized, where motorcars crowded the streets like ants, and trains whizzed by on elevated platforms. She did not see Jem that year, because the Luftwaffe was strafing London with fire and he had deemed it too dangerous to meet, but in the years after—

"Tessa?"

Her heart stopped.

A great wave of lurching dizziness passed over her, and for a moment she wondered if she were going mad, if after so many years the past and present had blended within her memories until she could no longer tell the difference. For the voice she heard was not the soft, silent voice-within-her-mind of Brother Zachariah. The voice that had echoed in her head once a year for the past one hundred and thirty years.

This was a voice that drew out memories stretched thin by years of recollection, like paper unfolded and refolded too many times. A voice that brought back, like a wave, the memory of another time on this bridge, a night so long ago, everything black and silver and the river rushing away under her feet . . .

Her heart was pounding so hard, she felt as if it might break through her rib cage. Slowly she turned, away from the balustrade. And stared.

He stood on the pavement in front of her, smiling shyly, hands in the pockets of a pair of very modern jeans. He wore a blue cotton jumper pushed up to the elbows. Faint white scars decorated his forearms like lacework. She could see the shape of the rune of Quietude, which had been so black and strong against his skin, faded now to a faint imprint of silver.

"Jem?" she whispered, realizing why she had not seen him when she'd been searching the crowd for him. She had been looking for Brother Zachariah, wrapped in his parchment-white robe, moving, unseen, through the throng of Londoners. But this was not Brother Zachariah.

This was Jem.

She couldn't tear her gaze away from him. She had always thought Jem was beautiful. He was no less beautiful to her now. Once he had had silver-white hair and eyes like gray skies. This Jem had raven-black hair, curling slightly in the humid air, and dark brown eyes with glints of gold in the irises. Once his skin had been pale; now it had a flush of color to it. Where his face had been unmarked before he'd become a Silent Brother, there were two dark scars, the first runes of the Brotherhood, standing out starkly and blackly at the arch of each cheekbone.

Where the collar of his jumper dipped slightly, she could see the delicate shape of the *parabatai* rune that had once tied him to Will. That might tie them still, if one imagined souls could be tied even over the divide of death.

"Jem," she breathed again. At first glance he looked perhaps nineteen years old, or twenty, a bit older than he had been when he had become a Silent Brother. When she looked more deeply, she saw a man—the long years of pain and wisdom at the backs of his eyes; even the way he moved spoke of the care of quiet sacrifice. "You are"—her voice rose with wild hope—"this is permanent? You are not bound to the Silent Brothers anymore?"

"No," he said. There was a rapid hitch in his breath; he was looking at her as if he had no idea how she would react to his sudden appearance. "I am not."

"The cure—you found it?"

"I did not find it myself," he said slowly. "But—it was found."

"I saw Magnus in Alicante only a few months ago. We spoke of you. He never said . . ."

"He didn't know," Jem said. "It has been a hard year, a dark year, for Shadowhunters. But out of the blood and the fire, the loss and the sorrow, there have been born some great new changes." He held out his arms, self-deprecatingly, and with a little amazement in his voice, as he said: "I myself am changed."

"How—"

"I will tell you the story of it. Another story of Lightwoods and Herondales and Fairchilds. But it will take more than an hour in the telling, and you must be cold." He moved forward as if to touch her shoulder, then seemed to remember himself, and let his hand fall.

"I—" Words had deserted her. She was still feeling the shock of seeing him like this, bone-deep. Yes, she had seen him every year, here in this place, on this bridge. But it was not until this moment that she realized how much she had been seeing a Jem transmuted. But this—this was like falling into her own past, all the last century erased, and she felt dizzy and elated and terrified with it. "But—after today? Where will you go? To Idris?"

He looked, for a moment, honestly bewildered—and despite how old she knew him to be, so *young*. "I don't know," he said. "I've never had a lifetime to plan for before."

"Then . . . to another Institute?" *Don't go*, Tessa wanted to say. *Stay. Please.*

"I do not think I will go to Idris, or to an Institute anywhere," he said, after a pause so long that she felt as if her knees might give way under her if he did not speak. "I don't know how to live in the world as a Shadowhunter without Will. I don't think I even want to. I am still a *parabatai*, but my other half is gone. If I were to go to some Institute and ask them to take me in, I would never forget that. I would never feel whole."

"Then what—"

"That depends on you."

"On me?" A sort of terror gripped her. She knew what she wanted him to say, but it seemed impossible. In all the time she had seen him, since he had become a Silent Brother, he had seemed remote. Not unkind or unfeeling, but as if there were a layer of glass between him and the world. She remembered the boy she had known, who'd given his love as freely as breathing, but that was not the man she had met only once each year for more than a century. She knew how much the time between then and now had changed her. How much more must it have changed him? She did not know what he wanted from his new life or, more immediately, from her. She wanted to tell him whatever he wanted to hear, wanted to catch at him and hold him, to seize his hands and reassure herself of their shape—but she did not dare. Not without knowing what he wanted from her. It had been so many years. How could she presume he still felt as he once had?

"I—" He looked down at his slender hands, gripping the concrete of the bridge. "For a hundred and thirty years every hour of my life has been scheduled. I thought often of what

I would do if I were free, if there were ever a cure found. I thought I would bolt immediately, like a bird released from a cage. I had not imagined I would emerge and find the world so changed, so desperate. Subsumed in fire and blood. I wished to survive it, but for only one reason. I wished . . ."

"What did you wish for?"

He did not reply. Instead he reached over to touch her pearl bracelet with light fingers. "This is your thirtieth-anniversary bracelet," he said. "You still wear it."

Tessa swallowed. Her skin was prickling, her pulse racing. She realized she hadn't felt this, this particular brand of excited nervousness, in so many years that she had nearly forgotten it. "Yes."

"Since Will, have you never loved anyone else?"

"Don't you know the answer to that?"

"I don't mean the way you love your children, or the way you love your friends. Tessa, you *know* what I'm asking."

"I don't," she said. "I think I need you to tell me."

"We were once going to be married," he said. "And I have loved you all this time—a century and a half. And I know that you loved Will. I saw you together over the years. And I know that that love was so great that it must have made other loves, even the one we had when we were both so young, seem small and unimportant. You had a whole lifetime of love with him, Tessa. So many years. Children. Memories I cannot hope to—"

He broke off with a violent start.

"No," he said, and let her wrist fall. "I can't do it. I was a fool to think— Tessa, forgive me," he said, and drew away from her, plunging into the throng of people surging across the bridge.

Tessa stood for a moment in shock; it was just a moment, but it was enough time for him to vanish into the crowd. She put out a hand to steady herself. The stone of the bridge was cold under her fingers—cold, just as it had been that night when they had first come to this place, where they had first talked. He had been the first person she had ever voiced her deepest fear to: that her power made her something other, something that was not human. *You are human*, he had said. *In all the ways that matter.*

She remembered him, remembered the lovely dying boy who had taken the time to comfort a frightened girl he did not know, and had not voiced a word of his own fear. Of course he had left his fingerprints on her heart. How could it be otherwise?

She remembered the time he had offered her his mother's jade pendant, held out in his shaking hand. She remembered kisses in a carriage. She remembered walking into his room, spilled full with moonlight, and the silver boy standing in front of the window, wringing music more beautiful than desire out of the violin in his hands.

Will, he had said. *Is it you, Will?*

Will. For a moment her heart hesitated. She remembered when Will had died, her agony, the long nights alone, reaching across the bed every morning when she woke up, for years expecting to find him there, and only slowly growing accustomed to the fact that that side of the bed would always be empty. The moments when she had found something funny and turned to share the joke with him, only to be shocked anew that he was not there. The worst moments, when, sitting alone at breakfast, she had realized that she had forgotten the precise blue of his eyes or the depth of his laugh; that, like the sound of Jem's violin music, they had faded into the distance where memories are silent.

Jem was mortal now. He would grow old like Will, and like Will he would die, and she did not know if she could bear it again.

And yet.

Most people are lucky to have even one great love in their life. You have found two.

Suddenly her feet were moving, almost without her volition. She was darting into the crowd, pushing past strangers, gasping out apologies as she nearly tripped over the feet of passersby or knocked into them with her elbows. She didn't care. She was running flat out across the bridge, skidding to a halt at the very end of it, where a series of narrow stone steps led down to the water of the Thames.

She took them two at a time, almost slipping on the damp stone. At the bottom of the steps was a small cement dock, ringed around with a metal railing. The river was high and splashed up between the gaps in the metal, filling the small space with the smell of silt and river water.

Jem stood at the railing, looking out at the water. His hands were jammed tightly into his pockets, his shoulders hunched as if against a strong wind. He was staring ahead almost blindly, and with such fixed intent that he didn't seem to hear her as she came up behind him. She caught at his sleeve, swinging him around to face her.

"What," she said breathlessly. "What were you trying to ask me, Jem?"

His eyes widened. His cheeks were flushed, whether from

running or the cold air, she wasn't sure. He looked at her as if she were some bizarre plant that had sprung up on the spot, astonishing him. "Tessa—you followed me?"

"Of course I followed you. You ran off in the middle of a sentence!"

"It wasn't a very good sentence." He looked down at the ground, and then up at her again, a smile, as familiar as her own memories, tugging at the corner of his mouth. It came back to her then, a memory lost but not forgotten: Jem's smile had always been like sunlight. "I never was the one who was good with words," he said. "If I had my violin, I would be able to play you what I wanted to say."

"Just try."

"I don't—I'm not sure I can. I had six or seven speeches prepared, and I was running through all of them, I think."

His hands were stuffed deep into the pockets of his jeans. Tessa reached out and took him gently by the wrists. "Well, *I* am good with words," she said. "So let me ask you, then."

He drew his hands from his pockets and let her wrap her fingers around his wrists. They stood, Jem looking at her from under his dark hair—it had blown across his face in the wind off the river. There was still a single streak of silver in it, startling against the black.

"You asked me if I have loved anyone but Will," she said. "And the answer is yes. I have loved you. I always have, and I always will."

She heard his sharp intake of breath. There was a pulse pounding in his throat, visible under the pale skin still laced with the fading white lines of the Brotherhood's runes.

"They say you cannot love two people equally at once," she said. "And perhaps for others that is so. But you and Will—you are not like two ordinary people, two people who might have been jealous of each other, or who would have imagined my love for one of them diminished by my love of the other. You merged your souls when you were both children. I could not have loved Will so much if I had not loved you as well. And I could not love you as I do if I had not loved Will as I did."

Her fingers ringed his wrists lightly, just below the cuffs of his jumper. To touch him like this—it was so strange, and yet it made her want to touch him more. She had almost forgotten how much she missed the touch of someone she loved.

She forced herself to release her hold on him, though, and reached her hand into the collar of her shirt. Carefully she took hold of the chain around her throat and lifted it so that he could see, dangling from it, the jade pendant he had given her so long ago. The inscription on the back still gleamed as if new:

When two people are at one in their inmost hearts, they shatter even the strength of iron or bronze.

"You remember, that you left it with me?" she said. "I've never taken it off."

He closed his eyes. His lashes lay against his cheeks, long and fine. "All these years," he said, and his voice was a low whisper, and it was not the voice of the boy he had been once, but it was still a voice she loved. "All these years, you wore it? I never knew."

"It seemed that it would only have been a burden on you, when you were a Silent Brother. I feared you might think that my wearing it meant I had some sort of expectation of you. An expectation you could not fulfill."

He was silent for a long time. Tessa could hear the lap of the river, the traffic in the distance. It seemed to her she could hear the clouds move across the sky. Every nerve in her body screamed for him to speak, but she waited: waited as the expressions chased themselves across his face, and finally he spoke.

"To be a Silent Brother," he said, "it is to see everything and nothing all at once. I could see the great map of life, spread out before me. I could see the currents of the world. And human life began to seem a sort of passion play, acted at a distance. When they took the runes from me, when the mantle of the Brotherhood was removed, it was as if I had awoken from a long dream, or as if a shield of glass around me had shattered. I felt everything, all at once, rushing in upon me. All the humanity the Brotherhood's spells had taken from me. That I had so much humanity to return to me . . . That is because of you. If I had not had you, Tessa, if I had not had these yearly meetings as my anchor and my guide, I do not know if I could have come back."

There was light in his dark eyes now, and her heart soared in her chest. She had only ever loved two men in her life, and she had never thought to see either of their faces again. "But you have," she whispered. "And it is a miracle. And you remember what I once told you about miracles."

He smiled again at that. "'One does not question miracles, or complain that they are not constructed perfectly to one's liking.' I suppose that is true. I wish that I could have come back to you earlier. I wish I were the same boy I was when you loved me, once. I fear that the years have changed me into someone else."

Tessa searched his face with her eyes. In the distance she could hear the sound of traffic passing, but here, by the river's edge, she could almost imagine that she was a girl again, and the air full of fog and smoke, the rattling sound of the railway in the distance . . . "The years have changed me, too," she said. "I have been a mother and a grandmother, and I have seen those I love die, and seen others be born. You speak of the currents of the world. I have seen them too. If I were still the same girl I was when you knew me first, I would not have been able to speak my heart as freely to you as I just have. I would not be able to ask you what I am about to ask you now."

He brought his hand up and cupped her cheek. She could see the hope in his expression, slowly dawning. "And what is that?"

"Come with me," she said. "Stay with me. Be with me. See everything with me. I have traveled the world and seen so much, but there is so much more, and no one I would rather see it with than you. I would go everywhere and anywhere with you, Jem Carstairs."

His thumb slid along the arch of her cheekbone. She shivered. It had been so long since someone had looked at her like that, as if she were the world's great marvel, and she knew she was looking at him like that too. "It seems unreal," he said huskily. "I have loved you for so long. How can this be true?"

"It is one of the great truths of my life," Tessa said. "Will you come with me? For I cannot wait to share the world with you, Jem. There is so much to see."

She was not sure who reached for who first, only that a moment later she was in his arms and he was whispering "Yes, of course, yes," against her hair. He sought her mouth tentatively—she could feel his gentle tension, the weight of so many years between their last kiss and this. She reached up, curling her hand around the back of his neck, drawing him down, whispering *"Bie zhao ji." Don't worry, don't worry.* She kissed his cheek, the edge of his mouth, and finally his mouth, the pressure of his lips on hers intense and glorious, and *Oh, the beat of his heart, the taste of his mouth, the rhythm of his breath.* Her senses blurred with memory: how thin he had been once, the feeling of his shoulder blades as sharp as knives beneath the fine linen of the shirts he had once worn. Now she could feel strong, solid muscle when she held him, the thrum of life through his body where it pressed against hers, the soft cotton of his jumper gripped between her fingers.

Tessa was aware that above their small embankment people were still walking along Blackfriars Bridge, that the traffic was still passing, and that passersby were probably staring, but she didn't care; after enough years you learned what was important and what wasn't. And this was important: Jem, the speed and stutter of his heart, the grace of his gentle hands sliding to cup her face, his lips soft against hers as he traced the shape of her mouth with his. The warm solid definitive realness of him. For the first time in many long years she felt her heart open, and knew love as more than a memory.

No, the last thing she cared about was whether people were staring at the boy and girl kissing by the river, as London, its cities and towers and churches and bridges and streets, circled all about them like the memory of a dream. And if the Thames that ran beside them, sure and silver in the afternoon light, recalled a night long ago when the moon shone as brightly as a shilling on this same boy and girl, or if the stones of Blackfriars knew the tread of their feet and thought to themselves: *At last, the wheel comes full circle*, they kept their silence.

A Note on Tessa's England

As in *Clockwork Angel* and *Clockwork Prince*, the London and Wales of *Clockwork Princess* is, as much as I could make it, an admixture of the real and the unreal, the famous and the forgotten. The Lightwood family house is based upon Chiswick House, which you can still visit. As for No. 16 Cheyne Walk, where Woolsey Scott lives, it was at the time actually rented together by Algernon Charles Swinburne, Dante Gabriel Rossetti, and George Meredith. They were members of the aesthetic movement, like Woolsey. Although none of them were ever (proved to be) werewolves. The Argent Rooms are based on the scandalous Argyle Rooms.

As for Will's mad ride across the countryside from London to Wales, I am indebted to Clary Booker, who helped me map the route, found inns that Will would have stayed at on the way, and speculated on the weather. As much as possible I tried to stick to roads and inns that did exist. (The Shrewsbury-Welshpool road is now the A458.) I have been to Cadair Idris myself and climbed it, visited Dolgellau and Taly-Llyn, and seen Llyn Cau, though never jumped in to see where it would take me.

Blackfriars Bridge exists of course, then and now, and the description of it in the epilogue is as close to my experience of the bridge as I could make it. The Infernal Devices began with a daydream of Jem and Tessa on Blackfriars Bridge, and I think it is fitting that it ends there too.

Acknowledgments

Special thanks to Cindy and Margaret Pon for help with Mandarin Chinese; Clary Booker for mapping Will's journey from London to Cadair Idris; Emily-Jo Thomas for help with Will's and Cecily's Welsh; Aspasia Diafa, Patrick Oltman, and Wayne Miller for help with Latin and ancient Greek. Thank you to Moritz Wiest for scanning the whole manuscript so it could be delivered during Hurricane Sandy.

Much thanks for familial support from my mother and father, as well as Jim Hill and Kate Connor; Nao, Tim, David, and Ben; Melanie, Jonathan, and Helen Lewis; Florence and Joyce. To those who read and critiqued and pointed out anachronisms—Sarah Smith, Delia Sherman, Holly Black, Kelly Link, Ellen Kushner, Clary Booker—tons of thanks. And thanks to those whose smiling faces and snarky remarks keep me going another day: Elka Cloke, Holly Black, Robin Wasserman, Emily Houk, Maureen Johnson, Libba Bray, and Sarah Rees Brennan. My always-gratitude to my agent, Russell Galen; my editor, Karen Wojtyla; and the teams at Simon & Schuster and Walker Books for making it all happen. And lastly, my thanks to Josh, who brought me tea and cats while I worked.

Tessa, Will, and Jem's stories
continue in the Last Hours, coming in 2018.
Take a sneak peek at their adventures in

The Midnight Heir,

BY CASSANDRA CLARE

AND SARAH REES BRENNAN,

AN EXCERPT FROM

THE BANE CHRONICLES.

———➤◆◄———

It took Magnus nearly twenty minutes to notice the boy shooting out all the lights in the room, but to be fair, he had been distracted by the décor.

It had been nearly a quarter century since Magnus had been in London. He had missed the place. Certainly New York had an energy at the turn of the century that no other city could match. Magnus loved being in a carriage rattling into the dazzling lights of Longacre Square, pulling up outside the Olympia Theatre's elaborate French Renaissance facade, or rubbing elbows with a dozen different kinds of people at the hot dog festival in Greenwich Village. He enjoyed traveling on the elevated railways, squealing brakes and all, and he was much looking forward to traveling through the vast underground systems they were building below the very heart of the city. He had seen the construction of the great station at Columbus Circle just before he had left, and hoped to return to find it finished at last.

But London was London, wearing its history in layers, with every age contained in the new age. Magnus had history here too. Magnus had loved people here, and hated them. There had been one woman whom he had both loved and hated, and he had fled London to escape that memory. He sometimes wondered if he had been wrong to leave, if he should have endured the bad memories for the sake of the good, and suffered, and stayed.

Magnus slouched down in the tufted velvet chair—shabby at the arms, worn by decades of sleeves rubbing away the fabric—and gazed around the room. There was a gentility to English places that America, in all her brash youthfulness, could not match. Glimmering chandeliers dripped from the ceiling—cut glass, of course, not crystal, but it shed a pretty light—and electric sconces lined the walls. Magnus still found electricity rather thrilling, though it was duller than witchlight.

Groups of gentlemen sat at tables, playing rounds of faro and piquet. Ladies who were no better than they should be, whose dresses were too tight and too bright and too all the things Magnus liked most, lounged on velvet-covered benches along the walls. Gentlemen who had done well at the tables approached them, flushed with victory and pound notes; those whom Lady Luck had not smiled on drew on their coats at the door and slunk off silently into the night, bereft of money and companionship.

It was all very dramatic, which Magnus enjoyed. He had not yet grown tired of the pageantry of ordinary life and ordinary people, despite the passage of time and the fact that people were all very much the same in the end.

A loud explosion caused him to look up. There was a boy standing in the middle of the room, a cocked silver pistol in his hand. He was surrounded by broken glass, having just shot off one arm of the chandelier.

Magnus was overwhelmed with the feeling the French called déjà vu, the feeling that *I have been here before*. He had, of course, been in London before, twenty-five years past.

This boy's face was a face to recall the past. This *was* a face from the past, one of the most beautiful faces Magnus could ever recall seeing. It was a face so finely cut that it cast the shabbiness of this place into stark relief—a beauty that burned so fiercely that it put the glare of the electric lights to shame. The boy's skin was so white and clear that it seemed to have a light shining behind it. The lines of his cheekbones, his jaw, and his throat—exposed by a linen shirt open at the collar—were so clean and perfect that he almost would have looked like a statue were it not for the much disheveled and slightly curling hair falling into his face, as black as midnight against his lucent pallor.

The years drew Magnus back again, the fog and gaslight of a London more than twenty years lost rising to claim Magnus. He found his lips shaping a name: Will. Will Herondale.

Magnus stepped forward instinctively, the movement feeling as if it were not of his own volition.

The boy's eyes went to him, and a shock passed through Magnus. They were not Will's eyes, the eyes Magnus remembered being as *blue as a night sky in Hell*, eyes Magnus had seen both despairing and tender.

This boy had shining golden eyes, like a crystal glass filled brimful with crisp white wine and held up to catch the light of a blazing sun. If his skin was luminous, his eyes were radiant. Magnus could not imagine these eyes as tender. The boy was very, very lovely, but his was a beauty like that Helen of Troy might have had once, disaster written in every line. The light of his beauty made Magnus think of cities burning.

Fog and gaslight receded into memory. His momentary lapse into foolish nostalgia was over. This was not Will. That broken, beautiful boy would be a man now, and this boy was a stranger.

Still, Magnus did not think that such a great resemblance could be a coincidence. He made his way toward the boy with little effort, as the other denizens of the gaming hell seemed, perhaps understandably, reluctant to approach him. The boy was standing alone as though the broken glass all around him were a shining sea and he were an island.

"Not precisely a Shadowhunter weapon," Magnus murmured. "Is it?"

Those golden eyes narrowed into bright slits, and the long-fingered hand not holding the pistol went to the boy's sleeve, where Magnus presumed his nearest blade was concealed. His hands were not quite steady.

"Peace," Magnus added. "I mean you no harm. I am a warlock the Whitelaws of New York will vouch for as being quite—well, mostly—harmless."

There was a long pause that felt somewhat dangerous. The boy's eyes were like stars, shining but giving no clue to his feelings. Magnus was generally good at reading people, but he found it difficult to predict what this boy might do.

Magnus was truly surprised by what the boy said next.

"I know who you are." His voice was not like his face; it had gentleness to it.

Magnus managed to hide his surprise and raised his eyebrows in silent inquiry. He had not lived three hundred years without learning not to rise to every bait offered.

"You are Magnus Bane."

Magnus hesitated, then inclined his head. "And you are?"

"I," the boy announced, "am James Herondale."

"You know," Magnus murmured, "I rather thought you might be called something like that. I am delighted to hear that I am famous."

"You're my father's warlock friend. He would always speak of you to my sister and me whenever other Shadowhunters spoke slightingly of Downworlders in our presence. He would say he knew a warlock who was a better friend, and more worth trusting, than many a Nephilim warrior."

The boy's lips curled as he said it, and he spoke mockingly but with more contempt than amusement behind the mockery, as if his father had been a fool to tell him this, and James himself was a fool to repeat it.

Magnus found himself in no mood for cynicism.

They had parted well, he and Will, but he knew Shadowhunters. The Nephilim were swift to judge and condemn a Downworlder for ill deeds, acting as if every sin were graven in stone for all time, proving that Magnus's people were evil by nature. Shadowhunters' conviction of their own angelic virtue and righteousness made it easy for them to let a warlock's good deeds slip their minds, as if they were written in water.

He had not expected to see or hear of Will Herondale on this journey, but if Magnus had thought of it, he would have been unsurprised to be all but forgotten, a petty player in a boy's tragedy. Being remembered, and remembered so kindly, touched him more than he would have thought possible.

The boy's star-shining, burning-city eyes traveled across Magnus's face and saw too much.

"I would not set any great store by it. My father trusts a great many people," James Herondale said, and laughed. It was quite clear suddenly that he was extremely drunk. Not that Magnus had imagined he was firing at chandeliers while stone-cold sober. "Trust. It is like placing a blade in someone's hand and setting the very point against your own heart."

"I have not asked you to trust me," Magnus pointed out mildly. "We have just met."

"Oh, I'll trust you," the boy told him carelessly. "It hardly matters. We are all betrayed sooner or later—all betrayed, or traitors."

"I see that a flair for the dramatic runs in the blood," Magnus said under his breath. It was a different kind of dramatics, though. Will had made an exhibition of vice in private, to drive away those nearest and dearest to him. James was making a public spectacle.

Perhaps he loved vice for vice's own sake.

"What?" James asked.

"Nothing," said Magnus. "I was merely wondering what the chandelier had done to offend you."

James looked up at the ruined chandelier, and down at the shards of glass at his feet, as if he were noticing them only now.

"I was bet," he said, "twenty pounds that I would not shoot out all the lights of the chandelier."

"And who bet you?" said Magnus, not divulging a hint of what he thought—that anyone who bet a drunk seventeen-year-old boy that he could wave around a deadly weapon with impunity ought to be in gaol.

"That fellow there," James announced, pointing.

Magnus looked in the general direction James was gesturing toward, and spied a familiar face at the faro table.

"The green one?" Magnus inquired. Coaxing drunken Shadowhunters into making fools of themselves was a favorite occupation among the Downworlders, and this performance had been a tremendous success. Ragnor Fell, the High Warlock of London, shrugged, and Magnus sighed inwardly. Perhaps gaol would be a bit extreme, though Magnus still felt his emerald friend could use taking down a peg or two.

"Is he *really* green?" James asked, not seeming to care overmuch. "I thought that was the absinthe."

Then James Herondale, son of William Herondale and Theresa Gray, the two Shadowhunters who had been the closest of their kind to friends that Magnus had ever known—though Tessa had not been quite a Shadowhunter, or not entirely—turned his back on Magnus, set his sights on a woman serving drinks to a table surrounded by werewolves, and shot her down. She collapsed on the floor with a cry, and all the gamblers sprang from their tables, cards flying and drinks spilling.

James laughed, and the laugh was clear and bright, and it was then that Magnus began to be truly alarmed. Will's voice would have shaken, betraying that his cruelty had been part of his playacting, but his son's laugh was that of someone genuinely delighted by the chaos erupting all around him.

Magnus's hand shot out and grasped the boy's wrist, the hum and light of magic crackling along his fingers like a promise. "That's enough."

"Be easy," James said, still laughing. "I am a very good shot, and Peg the tavern maid is famous for her wooden leg. I think that is why they call her Peg. Her real name, I believe, is Ermentrude."

"And I suppose Ragnor Fell bet you twenty pounds that you couldn't shoot her without managing to draw blood? How very clever of you both."

James drew his hand back from Magnus's, shaking his head. His black locks fell around a face so like his father's that it prompted an indrawn breath from Magnus. "My father told me you acted as a sort of protector to him, but I do not need your protection, warlock."

"I rather disagree with that."

"I have taken a great many bets tonight," James Herondale informed him. "I must perform all the terrible deeds I have promised. For am I not a man of my word? I want to preserve my honor. And I want another drink!"

"What an excellent idea," Magnus said. "I have heard alcohol only improves a man's aim. The night is young. Imagine how many barmaids you can shoot before dawn."

"A warlock as dull as a scholar," said James, narrowing his amber eyes. "Who would have thought such a thing existed?"

"Magnus has not always been so dull," said Ragnor, appearing at James's shoulder with a glass of wine in hand. He gave it to the boy, who took it and downed it in a distressingly practiced manner. "There was a time, in Peru, with a boat full of pirates—"

James wiped his mouth on his sleeve and set down his glass. "I should love to sit and listen to old men reminiscing about their lives, but I have a pressing appointment to do something that is actually interesting. Another time, chaps."

He turned upon his heel and left. Magnus made to follow him.

"Let the Nephilim control their brat, if they can," Ragnor said, always happy to see chaos but not be involved in it. "Come have a drink with me."

"Another night," Magnus promised.

"Still such a soft touch, Magnus," Ragnor called after him. "Nothing you like better than a lost soul or a bad idea."

Magnus wanted to argue with that, but it was difficult when he was already forsaking warmth and the promise of a drink and a few rounds of cards, and running out into the cold after a deranged Shadowhunter.

Said deranged Shadowhunter turned on him, as if the narrow cobbled street were a cage and he some wild, hungry animal held there too long.

"I wouldn't follow me," James warned. "I am in no mood for company. Especially the company of a prim magical chaperone who does not know how to enjoy himself."

"I know perfectly well how to enjoy myself," remarked Magnus, amused, and he made a small gesture so that for an instant all the iron streetlamps lining the street rained down varicolored sparks of light. For an instant he thought he saw a light that was softer and less like burning in James Herondale's golden eyes, the beginnings of a childlike smile of delight.

The next moment, it was quenched. James's eyes were as bright as the jewels in a dragon's hoard, and no more alive or joyful. He shook his head, black locks flying in the night air, where the magic lights were fading.

"But you do not wish to enjoy yourself, do you, James Herondale?" Magnus asked. "Not really. You want to go to the devil."

"Perhaps I think I will enjoy going to the devil," said James Herondale, and his eyes burned like the fires of Hell, enticing, and promising unimaginable suffering. "Though I see no need to take anyone else with me."

No sooner had he spoken than he vanished, to all appearances softly and silently stolen away by the night air, with no one but the winking stars, the glaring streetlamps, and Magnus as witnesses.

Magnus knew magic when he saw it. He spun, and at the same moment heard the click of a decided footstep against a cobblestone. He turned to face a policeman walking his beat, truncheon swinging at his side, and a look of suspicion on his stolid face as he surveyed Magnus.

It was not Magnus the man had to watch out for.

Magnus saw the buttons on the man's uniform cease their gleaming, even though he was under a streetlamp. Magnus was able to discern a shadow falling where there was nothing to cast it, a surge of dark within the greater darkness of the night.

The policeman gave a shout of surprise as his helmet was whisked away by unseen hands. He stumbled forward, hands fumbling blindly in the air to retrieve what was long gone.

Magnus gave him a consoling smile. "Cheer up," he said. "You can find far more flattering headgear at any shop in Bond Street."

The man fainted. Magnus considered pausing to help him, but there was being a soft touch, and then there was being ridiculous enough to not pursue a most enticing mystery. A Shadowhunter who could turn into a shadow? Magnus turned and bolted after the bobbing policeman's helmet, held aloft only by a taunting darkness.

They ran down street after street, Magnus and the darkness,

until the Thames barred their path. Magnus heard the sound of its rushing swiftness rather than saw it, the dark waters at one with the night.

What he did see was white fingers suddenly clenched on the brim of the policeman's helmet, the turn of James Herondale's head, darkness replaced with the tilt of his slowly appearing grin. Magnus saw a shadow coalescing once more into flesh.

So the boy had inherited something from his mother as well as his father, then. Tessa's father had been a fallen angel, one of the kings of demons. The boy's lambent golden eyes seemed to Magnus like his own eyes suddenly, a token of infernal blood.

James saw Magnus looking, and winked before he hurled the helmet up into the air. It flew for a moment like a strange bird, spinning gently around in the air, then hit the water. The darkness was disrupted by a silver splash.

"A Shadowhunter who knows magic tricks," Magnus observed. "How novel."

A Shadowhunter who attacked the mundanes it was his mandate to protect—how delighted the Clave would be by that.

"We are but dust and shadows, as the saying goes," said James. "Of course, the saying does not add, 'Some of us also turn into shadows occasionally, when the mood takes us.' I suppose nobody predicted that I would come to pass. It's true that I have been told I am somewhat unpredictable."

"May I ask who bet you that you could steal a policeman's helmet, and why?"

"Foolish question. Never ask about the last bet, Bane," James advised him, and reached casually to his belt, where his gun was slung, and then he drew it in one fluid, easy motion. "You should be worrying about the next one."

"There isn't any chance," Magnus asked, without much hope, "that you are rather a nice fellow who believes he is cursed and must make himself seem unlovable to spare those around him from a terrible fate? Because I have heard that happens sometimes."

James seemed amused by the question. He smiled, and as he smiled, his waving black locks blended with the night, and the glow of his skin and his eyes grew as distant as the light of the stars until they became so pale, they diffused. He was nothing but a shadow among shadows again. He was an infuriating Cheshire cat of a boy, nothing left of him but the impression of his smile.

"My father was cursed," James said from the darkness. "Whereas I? I'm damned."

The London Institute was exactly as Magnus remembered it, tall and white and imposing, its tower cutting a white line against the dark sky. Shadowhunter Institutes were built as monuments to withstand the ravages of demons and time. When the doors opened, Magnus beheld again the massive stone entryway and the two flights of stairs.

A woman with wildly curling red hair, whom Magnus was sure he should remember but didn't, answered the door, her face creased with sleep and crossness. "What d'you want, warlock?" she demanded.

Magnus shifted the burden in his arms. The boy was tall, and Magnus had had a long night besides. Annoyance made his tone rather sharp as he answered:

"I want you to go tell Will Herondale that I have brought his whelp home."

The woman's eyes widened. She gave an impressed sort of whistle and vanished abruptly. A handful of moments later Magnus saw a white figure come softly down one of the staircases.

Tessa was like the Institute: hardly changed at all. She had the same smooth youthful face that she had worn twenty-five years before. Magnus thought she must have stopped aging no more than three or four years after he had last seen her. Her hair was in a long brown plait, hanging over one shoulder, and she was holding a witchlight in one hand and had a small sphere of light shining in her palm in the other.

"Been taking magic lessons, have we, Tessa?" Magnus asked.

"Magnus!" Tessa exclaimed, and her grave face lit with a welcoming smile that sent a pang of sweetness through Magnus. "But they said— Oh, no. Oh, where did you find Jamie?"

She reached the bottom of the steps, went over to Magnus, and cradled the boy's damp head in her hand in an almost absentminded gesture of affection. In that gesture Magnus saw how she had changed, saw the ingrained habit of motherhood, love for someone she had created and whom she cherished.

No other warlock would ever have a child of their own blood. Only Tessa could have that experience.

Magnus turned his head away from Tessa at the sound of a new footfall on the stairs.

The memory of Will the boy was so fresh that it was something of a shock to see Will himself now, older, broader of shoulder, but still with the same tousled black hair and laughing blue eyes. He looked just as handsome as he had ever been—more so perhaps, since he seemed so much happier. Magnus saw more marks of laughter than of time on his face, and found himself smiling. It was true what Will had said, he realized. They were friends.

Recognition crossed Will's face, and with it pleasure, but almost instantly he saw the burden Magnus carried, and worry erased all else.

"Magnus," he said. "What on earth happened to James?"

"What happened?" Magnus asked musingly. "Well, let me see. He stole a bicycle and rode it, not using his hands at any point, through Trafalgar Square. He attempted to climb Nelson's Column and fight with Nelson. Then I lost him for a brief period of time, and by the time I caught up with him, he had wandered into Hyde Park, waded into the Serpentine, spread his arms wide, and was shouting, 'Ducks, embrace me as your king!'"

"Dear God," said Will. "He must have been vilely drunk. Tessa, I can bear it no longer. He is taking awful risks with his life and rejecting all the principles I hold most dear. If he continues making an exhibition of himself throughout London, he will be called to Idris and kept there away from the mundanes. Does he not realize that?"

Magnus shrugged. "He also made inappropriate amorous advances to a startled grandmotherly sort selling flowers, an Irish wolfhound, an innocent hat stand in a dwelling he broke into, and myself. I will add that I do not believe his admiration of my person, dazzling though I am, to be sincere. He told me I was a beautiful, sparkling lady. Then he abruptly collapsed, naturally in the path of an oncoming train from Dover, and I decided it was well past time to take him home and place him in the bosom of his family. If you had rather I put him in an orphanage, I fully understand."

Will was shaking his head, shadows in his blue eyes now. "Bridget," he shouted, and Magnus thought, *Oh, yes, that was the maid's name.* "Call for the Silent Brothers," Will finished.

"You mean call for Jem," Tessa said, dropping her voice, and she and Will shared a look—what Magnus could describe only as a *married* look, the look of two people who understood each other completely and yet found each other adorable all the same.

It was quite sickening.

He cleared his throat. "Still a Silent Brother, then, is he?"

Will gave Magnus a withering look. "It does tend to be a permanent state. Here, give me my son."

Magnus let Will take James from his arms, which were left lighter if more damp, and Magnus followed Will's and Tessa's lead up the stairs. Inside the Institute it was clear they had been redecorating. Charlotte's dark drawing room now held several comfortable-looking sofas, and the walls were covered in light damask. Tall shelves were lined with books, volumes with the gilt rubbed off their spines and, Magnus was sure, the pages much thumbed. It appeared both Tessa and Will remained great readers.

Will deposited James onto one of the sofas. Tessa rushed to find a blanket as Magnus turned toward the door, only to find his hand caught in Will's grasp.

"It was very good of you to bring Jamie home," Will said. "But you were always so good to me and mine. I was little more than a boy then, and not as grateful or as gracious as I should have been."

"You were well enough, Will," said Magnus. "And I see you have grown to be better. Also, you are not bald, and neither have you grown fat. All that dashing about and fighting evil you people do is at least useful for keeping a trim figure in middle age."

Will laughed. "It's very good to see you, too." He hesitated. "About Jamie . . ."

Magnus tensed. He had not wanted to distress Will and Tessa too much. He had not told them that James had fallen when he was in the Serpentine, and made very little effort to rescue himself from drowning. He had not seemed to want to be taken from the cold depths of the water: had fought Magnus as he dragged him out, then laid his pale cheek against the dank earth of the riverbank and hid his face in his arms.

For a moment Magnus had thought he was crying, but as he stooped down to check on the boy, he found he was barely conscious. With his cruel golden eyes closed, he once again reminded Magnus of the lost boy Will had been. Magnus touched his damp hair gently and said "James," in as kind a voice as he could.

The boy's pale hands were splayed against the dark earth. The glimmer of the Herondale ring shone against his skin, and the edge of something metallic shone under his sleeve as well. His eyes were shut, the black lashes ink-dark crescents against the lines of his cheekbones. Sparkling drops of water were caught in the curling ends of those lashes, which made him look unhappy in a way he did not when awake.

"*Grace*," James had whispered in his sleep, and was silent.

Magnus had not been angry: he had found himself wishing for a benevolent grace many times himself. He bent and gathered the boy up in his arms. His head lolled against Magnus's shoulder. In sleep James had looked peaceful and innocent, and wholly human.

"This just isn't like him," Will was saying now as Tessa drew a blanket up over the boy, tucking him in firmly.

Magnus raised an eyebrow. "He's *your* son."

"What are you trying to imply?" Will demanded, and for a moment Magnus saw his eyes flash, and saw the boy with messy black hair and glaring blue eyes standing in his drawing room, furious at the whole world and at no part of it more than himself.

"It isn't like him," Tessa agreed. "He's always been so quiet, so studious. Lucie was the impetuous one, but they are both kind, good-hearted children. At parties Jamie could most often be found curled up in a corner with his Latin, or laughing at a private joke with his *parabatai*. He always kept Matthew out of trouble as well as himself. He was the only one who could make that indolent boy attend to his studies," she remarked, with a slight smile that betokened she was fond of her son's *parabatai*, no matter what his faults. "Now he is out at all hours, doing the most disgraceful things, and he will not listen to reason. He will not listen to anybody. I understand what you mean about Will, but Will was lonely and wretched in the days when he behaved badly. James has been wrapped in love all his life."

"Betrayed!" Will muttered. "Cruelly maligned by my friend and now by my own cherished wife, scorned, my name blackened—"

"I see you are still fond of histrionics, Will," said Magnus. "As well as still handsome."

They had grown up. Neither of them looked startled at all. Tessa raised her eyebrows, and Magnus saw something of her son in her then. They both had the same expressive, arched brows, giving their faces a look of both inquiry and amusement, though in James's face the amusement was bitter.

"Do stop flirting with my husband," said Tessa.

"I shall not," Magnus declared, "but I will pause briefly so that I may catch up on your news. I have not heard from you since you sent word the baby had arrived and both he and his lovely mother were thriving."

Will looked surprised. "But we sent you several letters in care of the Morgensterns, who were going to visit the Whitelaws at the New York Institute. It was you who proved to be a shocking correspondent."

"Ah," said Magnus. He himself was not even slightly surprised. This was typical behavior from Shadowhunters. "The Morgensterns must have forgotten to deliver them. How careless."

Tessa, he saw, did not look too surprised either. She was both warlock and Shadowhunter, and yet not quite either. The Shadowhunters believed that Shadowhunter blood trumped all else, but Magnus could well believe that many of the Nephilim might be unkind to a woman who could do magic and whom the years did not touch.

He doubted any of them dared be unkind in front of Will, though.

"We will be more careful about whom we entrust with our letters in future," Tessa said decisively. "We have been out of touch for far too long. How fortunate that you are here in London, both for us and for Jamie. What brings you here, business or pleasure?"

"I wish it were the business of pleasure," Magnus told her. "But no, it is very dull. A Shadowhunter I believe you know sent for me—Tatiana Blackthorn? The lady used to be a Lightwood, did she not?" Magnus turned to Will. "And your sister Cecily married her brother. Gilbert. Gaston. I have a shocking memory for Lightwoods."

"I begged Cecily not to throw herself away on a Lightworm," Will muttered.

"Will!" said Tessa. "Cecily and Gabriel are very happy together."

Will threw himself dramatically into an armchair, touching his son's wrist as he passed by, with a light, careful caress that spoke volumes.

"At least you must admit, Tess, that Tatiana is as mad as a mouse trapped in a teapot. She refuses to speak to any of us, and that includes her brothers, because she says we had a hand in her father's death. Actually, she says we pitilessly slew him. Everybody tries to point out that at the time of the pitiless slaying her father was a giant worm who had eaten her husband and followed up his meal with a palate-cleansing servant sorbet, but she insists on lurking about the manor house and sulking with all the curtains drawn."

"She has lost a great deal. She lost her child," Tessa said. "And she did speak to us that once, in Idris." She stroked back her son's hair, her face troubled. Will looked to James and fell silent.

"Mrs. Blackthorn has come from Idris to her family manor in England specifically so I might visit her, and she sent me a message through the usual Downworlder channels promising me a princely sum if I would come and cast a few spells to increase the attractions of her young ward," Magnus said, attempting to strike a lighter note. "I gather she wishes to marry her off."

Tatiana would not be the first Shadowhunter to seek a

warlock's spells to make her life easier and more pleasant. She was, however, the Shadowhunter offering the best price.

"Did she?" Will asked. "It's not as if the girl looks like a toad in a bonnet."

Tessa laughed and stifled the laugh against her hand, and Will grinned, looking pleased with himself, as he always had when he'd managed to amuse Tessa.

"I suppose I should not be casting aspersions on anybody else's children, since my son is all about in his wits. He shoots things, you know."

"I did know that he shoots things," Magnus said tactfully. "Yes."

Will sighed. "The Angel grant me patience so I do not strangle him, and wisdom so I can talk some sense into his great fat head."

"I do wonder where he gets it from," said Magnus pointedly.

"It is not the same," said Tessa. "When Will was Jamie's age, he tried to drive everyone he loved away. Jamie is as loving as ever to us, to Lucie, to Matthew, his *parabatai*. It is himself he wishes to destroy."

"And yet there is no reason for it," Will said, striking the arm of his chair with his clenched fist. "I know my son, and he would not behave this way unless he felt he had no other choice. Unless he was trying to achieve a goal, or punish himself in some way, because he felt he had done some wrong—"

You called for me? I am here.

Magnus looked up to see Brother Zachariah standing in the doorway. He was a slender outline, the hood of his robe down, baring his face. The Silent Brothers rarely bared their faces, knowing how most Shadowhunters reacted to the scars and disfigurement of their skin. It was a sign of trust that Jem showed himself to Will and Tessa in this way.

Jem was still Jem—like Tessa, he had not aged. The Silent Brothers were not immortal but aged incredibly slowly. The powerful runes that gave them knowledge and allowed them to speak with their minds also slowed their bodies' aging, turning the Brothers to living statues. Jem's hands were pale and slender under the cuffs of his robe, still musician's hands after all this time. His face seemed carved out of marble, his eyes shuttered crescents, the dark runes of the Brothers standing out on his high cheekbones. His hair waved around his temples, darkness shot with silver.

A great sadness welled up in Magnus at the sight of him. It was human to age and die, and Jem stood outside that humanity now, outside the light that burned so brightly and so briefly. It was cold outside that light and fire. No one had greater cause to know that cold than Magnus did.

On seeing Magnus, Jem inclined his head. *Magnus Bane. I did not know you would be here.*

"I—" Magnus began, but Will was already on his feet, striding across the room to Jem. He had lit up at the sight of him, and Magnus could feel Jem's attention move from himself to Will, and catch there. Those two boys had been so different, yet at times they had seemed so wholly one that it was strange for Magnus to see Will changed as all humans changed, while Jem was set apart, to see that both had gone somewhere the other could not follow. He imagined it must be even stranger for them.

And yet. There was still about them what had always reminded Magnus of an old legend he'd heard of the red thread of fate: that an invisible scarlet thread bound certain people, and however tangled it became, it could not and would not break.

The Silent Brothers moved the way one imagined a statue would move if it could. Jem had moved the same way coming in, but as Will neared him, Jem took a step toward his former *parabatai*, and the step was swift, eager, and human, as if being close to the people whom he loved made him feel made of flesh and racing blood once more.

"You're here," said Will, and implicit in the words was the sense that Will's contentment was complete. Now Jem was there, all was right with the world.

"I knew you would come," said Tessa, rising from her son's side to go after her husband, toward Jem. Magnus saw Brother Zachariah's face glow at the sound of her voice, runes and pallor no longer mattering. He was a boy again for an instant, his life just beginning, his heart full of hope and love.

How they loved each another, these three, how they had suffered for each another, and yet how much joy they clearly took from simply being in the same room. Magnus had loved before, many times, but he did not ever recall feeling the peace that radiated out from these three only from being in the others' presence. He had craved peace sometimes, like a man wandering for centuries in the desert never seeing water and having to live with the want of it.

Tessa, Will, and their lost Jem stood together in a tight knot. Magnus knew that for a few moments nothing existed in the world but the three of them.

He looked at the sofa where James Herondale lay, and saw that he was awake, his gold eyes like watchful flames teaching the candles to burn brightly. James was the young one, the boy with his whole life ahead of him, but there was no hope or joy in his face. Tessa, Will, and Jem looked natural being together, but even in this room with those who loved him better than life, James looked utterly alone. There was something desperate and desolate about his face. He tried to lean up on one elbow, and collapsed back against the cushions of the sofa, his black head tipped back as if it were too heavy for him to bear. A Herondale ring glittered on his finger, a silver bracelet on his wrist.

Tessa, Will, and Jem were murmuring together, Will's hand on Jem's arm. Magnus had never seen anyone touch a Silent Brother like that, in simple friendship. It made him ache inside, and he saw that hollow ache reflected on the face of the boy on the sofa.

Obeying an impetuous impulse, Magnus crossed the room and knelt down by the couch, close to Will's son, who looked at him with tired golden eyes. "You see them," James said. "The way they all love one another. I used to think everyone loved that way. The way it is in fairy tales. I used to think that love was giving and generous and good."

"And now?" Magnus asked.

The boy turned his face away. Magnus found himself facing the back of James's head, seeing his mop of black hair so like his father's, and the edge of his *parabatai* rune just under his collar. It must be on his back, Magnus thought, above the blade of his shoulder, where an angel's wing would be.

"James," said Magnus in a low, hurried voice. "Once your father had a terrible secret that he thought he could not tell to a soul in the world, and he told me. I can see that there is something gnawing at you, something you are keeping hidden. If there is anything you want to tell me, now or at any time, you have my word that I will keep your secrets, and that I will help you if I can."

James shifted to look at Magnus. In his face Magnus thought he caught a glimpse of softening, as if the boy were releasing his relentless grip on whatever was tormenting him. "I am not like my father," he said. "Do not mistake my despair for nobility in disguise, for it is not that. I suffer for myself, not for anyone else."

"But *why* do you suffer?" Magnus said in frustration. "Your mother was correct when she said you have been loved all your life. If you would just let me help you—"

The boy's expression shut like a door. He turned his face away from Magnus again, and his eyes closed, the light falling on the fringe of his eyelashes.

"I gave my word I would never tell," he said. "And there is not a living soul on this earth who can help me."

"James," Magnus said, honestly surprised by the despair in the boy's tone, and the alarm in Magnus's voice caught the attention of the others in the room. Tessa and Will looked away from Jem and to their son, the boy who bore Jem's name, and as one they all moved over to where he lay, Will and Tessa hand in hand.

Brother Zachariah bent over the back of the sofa and touched James's hair tenderly with those musician's fingers.

"Hello, Uncle Brother Zachariah," James said without opening his eyes. "I would say that I'm sorry to bother you, but I'm sure this is the most excitement you've had all year. Not so lively in the City of Bones, now is it?"

"James!" Will snapped. "Don't talk to Jem like that."

As if I am not used to badly behaved Herondales, Brother Zachariah said, in the way Jem had always tried to make peace between Will and the world.

"I suppose the difference is that Father always cared what you thought about him," said James. "And I don't. But don't take it personally, Uncle Jem. I do not care what anybody thinks."

And yet he made a habit of making an exhibition of himself, as Will had put it, and Magnus had no doubt it was deliberate. He must care what someone thought. He must be doing all this for a purpose. *But what purpose could it be?* Magnus wondered.

"James, this is so unlike you," Tessa said worriedly. "You have always cared. Always been kind. What is troubling you?"

"Perhaps nothing is troubling me. Perhaps I have simply realized I was rather boring before. Don't you think I was boring? All that studying, and the Latin." He shuddered. "Horrible."

There is nothing boring about caring, or about an open, loving heart, said Jem.

"So say all of you," replied James. "And it is easy to see why, the three of you, falling over yourself to love one another—each more than the other. And it *is* kind of you to trouble yourselves about me." His breath caught a little, and then he smiled, but it was a smile of great sadness. "I wish I did not trouble you so."

Tessa and Will exchanged looks of despair. The room was thick with worry and parental concerns. Magnus was beginning to feel bowed under by the weight of humanity.

"Well," he announced. "As educational and occasionally damp as this evening has been, I do not wish to intrude on a family reunion, and I really do not wish to experience any family drama, as I find with Shadowhunters that it tends to be extensive. I must be on my way."

"But you could stay here," Tessa offered. "Be our guest. We would be delighted to have you."

"A warlock in the hallowed chambers of a Shadowhunter Institute?" Magnus shuddered. "Only think."

Tessa gave him a sharp look. "Magnus—"

"Besides, I have an appointment," Magnus said. "One I should not be late for."

Will looked up with a frown. "At this time of night?"

"I have a peculiar occupation, and keep peculiar hours," said Magnus. "I seem to recall you coming to me for assistance quite a few times at odd hours of the night." He inclined his head. "Will. Tessa. Jem. Good evening."

Tessa moved to his side. "I will show you out."

"Good-bye, whoever you are," said James sleepily, closing his eyes. "I cannot recall your name."

"Don't mind him," Tessa said in a low voice as she moved with Magnus toward the exit. She paused in the doorway for a moment, looking back at her son and the two men who stood with him. Will and Jem were shoulder to shoulder, and from across the room it was impossible to miss Jem's slighter frame, the fact that he had not aged, as Will had. Though, there was in Will's voice all the eagerness of a boy when he said, in answer to a question Magnus did not hear, "Why, yes, of course you can play it before you go. It is in the music room as always, kept ever the same for you."

"His violin?" Magnus murmured. "I did not think the Silent Brothers cared for music."

Tessa sighed softly and moved out into the corridor, Magnus beside her. "Will does not see a Silent Brother when he looks at James," she said. "He sees only Jem."

"Is it ever difficult?" he asked.

"Is what difficult?"

"Sharing your husband's heart so entirely with someone else," he said.

"If it were different, it would not be Will's heart," Tessa said. "He knows he shares my heart with Jem as well. I would have it no other way—and he would have it no other way with me."

So much a part of one another that there was no way to be untangled, even now, and no wish to be so. Magnus wanted to ask if Tessa was ever afraid of what would happen to her when Will was gone, when their bond was finally severed, but he did not. It would with luck be a long time until Tessa's first death, a long time before she entirely realized the burden of being immortal and yet loving that which was not.

"Very beautiful," Magnus said instead. "Well, I wish you all the best with your little hellion."

"We shall see you again before you leave London, of course," said Tessa in that tone of hers she had had even as a girl, that brooked no contradiction.

"Indeed," Magnus said. He hesitated. "And, Tessa, if you ever need me—and I hope if you do, it will be many long, happy years from now—send me a message, and I will be with you at once."

They both knew what he meant.

"I will," said Tessa, and she gave him her hand. Hers was small and soft, but her grip was surprisingly strong.

"Believe me, dear lady," Magnus told her with an assumption of lightness. He released her hand and bowed with a flourish. "Call me and I come!"

As Magnus turned to walk away from the church, he heard

the sound of violin music carried to him on the cloudy London air, and remembered another night, a night of ghosts and snow and Christmas music, and Will standing on the steps of the Institute, watching Magnus as he went. Now it was Tessa who stood at the door with her hand lifted in farewell until Magnus was at the gate with its ominous lettered message: WE ARE DUST AND SHADOWS. He looked back and saw her slight pale figure at the Institute threshold and thought again, *Yes, perhaps I was wrong to leave London.*

It was not the first time Magnus had made his way from London to Chiswick to visit Lightwood House. Benedict Lightwood's home had often been thrown open to Downworlders who'd been amenable to his idea of a good time.

It had been a grand manor once, the stone brilliant white and adorned with Greek statuary and too many pillars to count. The Lightwoods were proud and ostentatious people, and their home, in all its neoclassical glory, had reflected that.

Magnus knew what had become of all that pride. The patriarch, Benedict Lightwood, had contracted a disease from consorting with demons and had transformed into a murderous monster that his own sons had been forced to slay, with the assistance of a host of other Shadowhunters. Their manor had been taken away by the Clave as punishment, their monies confiscated, and their family had become a laughingstock, a byword for sin and a betrayal of all that the Shadowhunters held dear.

Magnus had little time for the Shadowhunters' overweening arrogance, and usually enjoyed seeing them taken down a peg, but even he had rarely seen a family fall so far so terribly fast. Gabriel and Gideon, Benedict's two sons, had managed to claw their way back to respectability through good behavior and the graces of the Consul, Charlotte Branwell. Their sister, however, was another matter entirely.

How she had managed to get Lightwood House back into her clutches, Magnus did not know. *As mad as a mouse trapped in a teapot,* Will had said of her, and knowing of the family's disgraced state, Magnus hardly expected the grandeur of Benedict's time. Doubtless the place would be shabby now, dusty with time, only a few servants left to keep it up and in order—

The carriage Magnus had hired came to a stop. "The place looks abandoned," opined the driver, casting a doubtful eye over at the iron gates, which looked rusted shut and bound with vines.

"Or haunted," Magnus suggested brightly.

"Well, I can't get in. Them gates won't open," said the driver gruffly. "You'll have to get out and walk, if you're that determined."

Magnus was. His curiosity was alight now, and he approached the gates like a cat, ready to scale them if need be.

A tweak of magic, a bit of an opening spell, and the gates burst wide with a shower of rusted metal flakes, onto a long, dark overgrown drive that led up to a ghostly manor house in the distance, glimmering like a tombstone under the full moon.

Magnus closed the gates and went forward, listening to the sound of night birds in the trees overhead, the rustle of leaves in the night wind. A forest of blackened tangles loomed all about him, the remains of the famous Lightwood gardens. Those gardens had been lovely once. Magnus distantly recalled overhearing Benedict Lightwood drunkenly saying that they had been his dead wife's joy.

Now the high hedges of the Italian garden had formed a maze, a twisted one from which there was clearly no escape. They had killed the monster Benedict Lightwood had become in these gardens, Magnus remembered hearing, and the black ichor had seeped from the monster's veins into the earth in a dark unstoppable flood.

Magnus felt a scratch against one hand and looked down to see a rosebush that had survived but gone wild. It took him a moment to identify the plant, for though the shape of the blooms was familiar, the color was not. The roses were as black as the blood of the dead serpent.

He plucked one. The flower crumbled in his palm as if it were made of ash, as if it had already been dead.

Magnus passed on toward the house.

The corruption that had claimed the roses had not spared the manor. What had once been a smooth white facade was now gray with years, streaked with the black of dirt and the green of rot. The shining pillars were twined about with dying vines, and the balconies, which Magnus remembered as like the hollows of alabaster goblets, were now filled with the dark snarls of thorns and the debris of years.

The door knocker had been an image of a shining golden lion with a ring held in its mouth. Now the ring lay rotted on the steps, and the gray lion's mouth hung open and empty in a hungry snarl. Magnus knocked briskly on the door. He heard the sound echo through the inside of the house as if all were the heavy silence of a tomb therein and ever would be, as if any noise was a disturbance.

The conviction that everyone in this house must be dead had gained such a hold on Magnus that it was a shock when the woman who had summoned him here opened the door.

It was, of course, rather odd for a lady to be opening her own front door, but from the look of the place, Magnus assumed the entire staff of servants had been given the decade off.

Magnus had a dim recollection of seeing Tatiana Lightwood at one of her father's parties: a glimpse of a perfectly ordinary girl with wide green eyes, behind a hastily closing door.

Even after seeing the house and the grounds, he was not prepared for Tatiana Blackthorn.

Her eyes were still very green. Her stern mouth was bracketed with lines of bitter disappointment and grave pain. She looked like a woman in her sixties, not her forties. She was wearing a gown of a fashion decades past—it hung from her wasted shoulders and fluttered around her body like a shroud. The fabric bore dark brown stains, but in patches it was a faded pastel bordering on white, while other spots remained what Magnus thought must have been its original fuchsia.

She should have looked ridiculous. She was wearing a silly bright pink dress for a younger woman, someone who was almost a girl, in love with her husband and going on a visit to her papa.

She did not look ridiculous. Her stern face forbade pity. She, like the house, was awe-inspiring in her ruin.

"Bane," Tatiana said, and held the door open wide enough that Magnus could pass through. She said no word of welcome.

She shut the door behind Magnus, the sound as final as the closing of a tomb. Magnus paused in the hall, waiting for the woman behind him, and as he waited, he heard another footstep above their heads, a sign there was someone else alive in the house.

Down the wide curving staircase toward them came a girl. Magnus had always found mortals to be beautiful, and had seen many mortals whom anybody would have described as beautiful.

This was extraordinary beauty, beauty unlike the beauty of most mortals.

In the stained and filthy ruin the house had become, she shone like a pearl. Her hair was the color of a pearl too, palest ivory with a sheen of gold on it, and her skin was the luminous pink and white of a seashell. Her lashes were thick and dark, veiling eyes of deep unearthly gray.

Magnus drew in a breath. Tatiana heard him and looked over, smiling a triumphant smile. "She's glorious, isn't she? My ward. My Grace."

Grace.

The realization struck Magnus like a blow. Of course James Herondale had not been calling out for something as inchoate and distant as a benediction, the soul's yearning for divine mercy and understanding. His desperation had been centered on something far more flesh-and-blood than that.

But why is it a secret? Why can no one help him? Magnus struggled to keep his face a blank as the girl moved toward him and offered her hand.

"How do you do," she murmured.

Magnus stared down at her. Her face was a porcelain cup, upturned; her eyes held promises. The combination of beauty, innocence, and the promise of sin was staggering. "Magnus Bane," she said, in a breathy, soft voice. Magnus couldn't help staring at her. Everything about her was so perfectly constructed to appeal. She was beautiful, yes, but it was more than that. She seemed shy, yet all her attention was focused on Magnus, as if he were the most fascinating thing she had ever seen. There was no man who did not want to see himself reflected like that in a beautiful girl's eyes. And if the neckline of her dress was a shade low, it did not seem scandalous, for her gray eyes were full of an innocence that said that she did not know of desire, not yet, but there was a lushness to the curve of her lip, a dark light in her eyes that said that under the right hands she would be a pupil who yielded the most exquisite result. . . .

Magnus took a step back from her as if she were a poisonous snake. She did not look hurt, or angry, or even startled. She turned a look on Tatiana, a sort of curious inquiry. "Mama?" she said. "What is wrong?"

Tatiana curled her lip. "This one is not like others," she said. "I mean, he likes girls well enough, and boys as well, I hear, but his taste does not run to Shadowhunters. And he is not mortal. He has been alive a long time. One cannot expect him to have the normal—reactions."

Magnus could well imagine what the normal reactions would be—the reactions of a boy like James Herondale, sheltered and taught that love was gentle, love was kind, that one should love with all one's heart and give away all one's soul. Magnus could imagine the normal reactions to this girl, a girl whose every gesture, every expression, every line, cried, *Love her, love her, love her.*

But Magnus was not that boy. He reminded himself of his manners, and bowed.

"Charmed," he said. "Or whatever effect would please you best, I'm sure."

Grace regarded him with cool interest. Her reactions were muted, Magnus thought, or rather, carefully gauged. She seemed a creature made to attract everyone and express nothing real, though it would take a master observer, like Magnus, to know it.

She reminded Magnus suddenly not of any mortal but of the vampire Camille, who had been his latest and most regrettable real love.

Magnus had spent years imagining there was fire behind Camille's ice, that there were hopes and dreams and love waiting for him. What he had loved in Camille had been nothing but illusion. Magnus had acted like a child, fancying there were shapes and stories to be made of the clouds in the sky.

He turned away from the sight of Grace in her trim white-and-blue dress, like a vision of Heaven in the gray hell of this house, and looked to Tatiana. Her eyes were narrowed with contempt.

"Come, warlock," she said. "I believe we have business to discuss."

Magnus followed Tatiana and Grace up the stairs and down a long corridor that was almost pitch black. Magnus heard the crack and crunch of broken glass beneath his feet, and in the dim, hardly-there light he saw something scuttling away from his approach. He hoped it was something as harmless as a rat, but something about its movements suggested a shape far more grotesque.

"Do not try to open any doors or drawers while you are here, Bane." Tatiana's voice floated back to him. "My father left behind many guardians to protect what is ours."

She opened the door, and Magnus beheld the room within.

There were an upturned desk and heavy curtains sagging in the windows like bodies from a gibbet, and on the wooden floor were splinters and streaks of blood, the marks of a long-ago struggle nobody had cleaned up.

There were many picture frames hanging askew or with the glass broken. A great many of them seemed to contain nautical adventures—Magnus had been put off the sea by his ill-fated attempt to live a piratical life for a day—but even the pictures that were whole were clouded with gray. The painted ships appeared to be sinking in seas of dust.

There was only one portrait that was whole and clean. It was an oil painting, with no glass covering it, but there was not a speck of dust on its surface. It was the only clean thing, besides Grace, in the entire house.

The portrait was of a boy, about seventeen years old. He was sitting in a chair, his head resting against the back as if he did not have the strength to support it on his own. He was terribly thin and as white as salt. His eyes were a deep, still green, like a woodland pool hidden under the overhanging leaves of a tree, never exposed to sun or wind. He had dark hair falling, as fine-spun and straight as silk, across his brow, and his long fingers were curled over the arms of the chair, almost clinging to it, and the desperate clutch of those hands told a silent story of pain.

Magnus had seen portraits like this before, the last images of the lost. He could tell even across the years how much effort it had cost the boy to sit for that portrait, for the comfort of loved ones who would live after he was gone.

His pallid face had the distant look of one who had already taken too many steps along the path to death for him to be recalled. Magnus thought of James Herondale, burning up with too much light, too much love, too much, too much— while the boy in the portrait was as lovely as a dying poet, with the fragile beauty of a candle about to gutter out.

On the ragged wallpaper that might once have been green and that had mutated to a grayish-green color, like a sea flooded with waste, were words written in the same dark brown as the stains on Tatiana's dress. Magnus had to admit to himself what that color was: blood that had been spilled years since and yet never washed clean.

The wallpaper was hanging off the walls in tatters. Magnus could make out only a word here and there on the remaining pieces: PITY, REGRET, INFERNAL.

The last sentence in the series was still legible. It read, MAY GOD HAVE MERCY ON OUR SOULS. Beneath this, written not in blood but cut through the wallpaper into the wall by what Magnus suspected was a different hand, were the words, GOD HAS NO MERCY AND NOR WILL I.

Tatiana sank into an armchair, its upholstery worn and stained by the years, and Grace knelt at her adoptive mother's side on the grimy floor. She knelt daintily, delicately, her skirts billowing around her like the petals of a flower. Magnus supposed that it must have been a habit with her to come to rest in filth, and rise from it to all outward appearance radiantly pure.

"To business, then, madam," said Magnus, and he added silently to himself, *To leaving this house as soon as possible.* "Tell me exactly why you have need of my fabulous and unsurpassed powers, and what you would have me do."

"You can already see, I trust," said Tatiana, "that my Grace is in no need of spells to enhance her natural charms."

Magnus looked at Grace, who was gazing at her hands linked in her lap. Perhaps she was already using spells. Perhaps she was simply beautiful. Magic or nature, they were much the same thing to Magnus.

"I'm sure she is already an enchantress in her own right."

Grace said nothing, only glanced up at him from under her lashes. It was a demurely devastating look.

"I want something else from you, warlock. I want you," Tatiana said, slowly and distinctly, "to go out into the world and kill me five Shadowhunters. I will tell you how it is to be done, and I will pay you most handsomely."

Magnus was so astonished, he honestly believed he must have heard her incorrectly. "Shadowhunters?" he repeated. "Kill?"

"Is my request so very strange? I have no love for the Shadowhunters."

"But, my dear madam, you *are* a Shadowhunter."

Tatiana Blackthorn folded her hands in her lap. "I am no such thing."

Magnus stared at her for a long moment. "Ah," he said. "I beg your pardon. Uh, would it be terribly uncivil of me to inquire what you do believe yourself to be? Do you think that you are a lamp shade?"

"I do not find your levity amusing."

Magnus's tone was hushed as he said, "I beg your pardon again. Do you believe yourself to be a pianoforte?"

"Hold your tongue, warlock, and do not talk of matters about which you know *nothing*." Tatiana's hands were clenched suddenly, curled as tight as claws in the skirt of her once-bright dress. The note of real agony in her voice was enough to silence Magnus, but she continued. "A Shadowhunter is a warrior. A Shadowhunter is born and trained to be a hand of God upon this earth, wiping it free of evil. That is what our legends say. That is what my father taught me, but my father taught me other things too. He decreed that I would not be trained as a Shadowhunter. He told me that was not my place, that my place in life was to be the dutiful daughter of a warrior, and in time the helpmeet of a noble warrior and the mother of warriors who would carry on the glory of the Shadowhunters for another generation."

Tatiana made a sweeping gesture to the words on the walls, the stains on the floor.

"Such glory," she said, and laughed bitterly. "My father and my family were disgraced, and my husband was torn apart in front of my eyes—torn apart. I had one child, my beautiful boy, my Jesse, but he could not be trained to be a warrior. He was always so weak, so sickly. I begged them not to put the runes on him—I was certain that would kill him—but the Shadowhunters held me back and held him down as they burned the Marks into his flesh. He screamed and screamed. We all thought he would die then, but he did not. He held on for me, for his mama, but their cruelty damned him. Each year he grew sicker and weaker until it was too late. He was sixteen when they told me he could not live."

Her hands moved restlessly as she spoke, from her gesture at the walls to plucking at her gown dyed with old, old blood. She touched her arms as if they still hurt where she had been held back by the Shadowhunters, and she toyed with a large ornate locket that hung around her neck. She opened and closed it, the tarnished metal gleaming between her fingers, and Magnus thought he saw a glimpse of a ghastly portrait. Her son again?

He looked toward the picture on the wall, the pale young face, and calculated how old a child of Rupert Blackthorn's must have been when the man had died twenty-five years before. If Jesse Blackthorn had died when he was sixteen then the boy must have been dead for nine years, but perhaps a mother's mourning never ended.

"I am aware that you have suffered greatly, Mrs. Blackthorn," said Magnus, as gently as he was able. "But instead of some plot of vengeance through the senseless slaughter of Shadowhunters, consider that there are many Shadowhunters who desire nothing more than to help you, and to ease your pain."

"Indeed? Of whom do you speak? William Herondale"— and in Tatiana's mouth hatred dripped from every syllable of Will's name—"sneered at me because all I did was scream as my beloved died, but tell me, what else could I have done? What else had I ever been taught to do?" Tatiana's eyes were huge and poison-green, eyes with enough pain in them to eat away at a world and devour a soul. "Can you tell me, warlock? Could William Herondale tell me? Can anyone tell me what I should have done, when I did everything I was ever asked to do? My husband is dead, my father is dead, my brothers are lost, my home was stolen, and the Nephilim had no power to save my son. I was everything I was ever asked to be, and as my reward my life was burned to ash. Do not speak to me of easing my pain. My pain is all that I have left. Do not speak to me of being a Shadowhunter. I am not one of them. I refuse to be."

"Very well, madam. You have made your anti-Shadowhunter position amply clear," said Magnus. "What I do not know is why you think I will help you get what you want."

Magnus was many things, but he had never been a fool. The death of a few Shadowhunters was not an aim in itself. If that were all she wanted, she would not have needed to go to Magnus.

The only reason she could have to go to a warlock was if she wanted to use those deaths, to alchemize Shadowhunter lives into magic for a spell. It would be the darkest of dark spells, and the fact that Tatiana knew of it told Magnus this was not the first time she had turned to dark magic.

What Tatiana Blackthorn, whose pain had eaten away at her like a wolf inside her breast, wanted from dark magic, Magnus did not know. He did not want to know what she had done with power in the past, and he certainly did not want her to have power that could be cataclysmic now.

Tatiana frowned a little puzzled frown that made her look like Benedict Lightwood's spoiled and cosseted daughter again.

"For money, of course."

"You imagine I would kill five people, and leave untold power in your hands," said Magnus, "for money?"

Tatiana waved a hand. "Oh, don't try to drive the price up by aping your betters and pretending that you have any morals or tender feelings, demon spawn. Name a higher sum and be done with it. The hours of the night are precious to me, and I wish to waste no further time on one such as you."

It was the casualness with which she spoke that was so chilling. Mad though Tatiana might have been, here she was not raving or bitter. She was simply working from the facts as Shadowhunters knew them: that a Downworlder must be so entirely corrupt that she did not even dream he had a heart.

Of course, of course, the vast majority of the Shadowhunters thought of him as something less than human, and as far below the children of the Angel as apes were below men. He might sometimes be useful, but he was a creature to be despised, used but then discarded, his touch avoided because it was unclean.

He had been very useful to Will Herondale, after all. Will had not come to him searching for a friend but a convenient source of magic. Even the best Shadowhunters were not so different from the rest.

"Let me say to you what I said once, in an entirely different context, to Catherine the Great," Magnus declared. "My dear lady, you cannot afford me, and also, please leave that horse alone. Good night."

He made a bow and then made his way, with some speed, out of the room. As the door shut with a snap, he heard Tatiana's voice snapping to match it: "Go after him!"

He was not surprised to hear soft footsteps pattering after him down the stairs. Magnus turned from the front door and met Grace's eyes.

Her footfalls were as light as a child's, but she did not look like child. In that porcelain-pure face her eyes were gray hollows, deep alluring lakes with sirens in their depths. She met Magnus's eyes with a level gaze, and Magnus was reminded once again of Camille.

It was remarkable that a girl who looked no more than sixteen could rival a centuries-old vampire for self-possession. She had not had time to freeze past caring. *There must*, Magnus thought, *be something behind all this ice*.

"You will not return upstairs, I see," Grace said. "You want no part of Mama's plan."

It was not a question, and she did not sound shocked or curious. It did not seem unthinkable to her, then, that Magnus might have scruples. Perhaps the girl had qualms of conscience herself, but she was shut up here in this dark house with a madwoman, nothing but bitterness poured into her ears from dusk to daybreak. Little wonder if she was different from other girls.

Magnus felt regret suddenly for the way he had shuddered back from Grace. She was not much more than a child, after all, and nobody knew better than he what it was like to be judged and shunned. He reached out to touch her arm. "Do you have somewhere else to go?" Magnus asked her.

"Somewhere else?" said Grace. "We reside mainly in Idris."

"What I mean is, would she let you leave? Do you need help?"

Grace moved with such speed that it was as if she were a bolt of lightning wrapped in muslin, the long gleaming blade flying from her skirts to her hand. She held the glittering point against Magnus's chest, over his heart.

Here was a Shadowhunter, Magnus thought. Tatiana had learned something from the mistakes of her father. She'd had the girl trained.

"I am no prisoner here."

"No?" Magnus asked. "Then what are you?"

Grace's awful, awe-inspiring eyes narrowed. They were glittering like the steel, and were, Magnus was sure, no less deadly. "I am my mother's blade."

Shadowhunters often died young, and left children behind to be raised by others. That was nothing unusual. It was natural that such a ward, taken into a Shadowhunter's home, would think of and speak to their guardian as a parent. Magnus had thought nothing of it. Yet now it occurred to him that a child might be so grateful to be taken in that her loyalty would be fierce, that a girl raised by Tatiana Blackthorn might not wish for rescue. She might wish for nothing more than the fulfillment of her mother's dark plans.

"Are you threatening me?" Magnus said softly.

"If you do not intend to help us," she said, "then leave this house. Dawn is coming."

"I am not a vampire," Magnus said. "I shall not disappear with the light."

"You will if I kill you before the sun comes up," said Grace. "Who would miss one warlock?"

And she smiled, a wild smile that reminded him again of Camille. That potent blend of beauty and cruelty. He had fallen victim to it himself. He could only imagine again, with growing horror, what the effect would have been on James Herondale, a gentle boy who had been reared to believe that love, too, was gentle. James had given his heart to this girl, Magnus thought, and Magnus knew well enough from Edmund and Will what it meant when a Herondale gave his heart away. It was not a gift that could be returned.

Tessa, Will, and Jem had raised James in love, and had surrounded him with love and the goodness it could produce. But they had given him no armor against the evil. They had wrapped his heart in silks and velvet, and then he had given it to Grace Blackthorn, and she had spun for it a cage of razor wire and broken glass, burned it to bits, and blown away the remains, another layer of ashes in this place of beautiful horrors.

Magnus waved a hand behind his back, then stepped away from Grace's blade, away through the magically open door.

"You will tell no one of what my mother asked of you tonight," said Grace. "Or I will ensure your destruction."

"I believe you think you could," Magnus breathed. She was terrible and brilliant, like the light shining off the edge of a razor. "Oh, and by the way? I suspect that if James Herondale had known I was coming here, he would have sent his regards."

Grace lowered her sword, nothing more. Its point rested gently on the ground. Her hand did not shake, and her lashes screened her eyes. "What do I care for James Herondale?" she asked.

"I thought you might. After all, a blade does not get to choose where it is pointed."

Grace looked up. Her eyes were still, deep pools, entirely unruffled.

"A blade does not care," she told him.

Magnus turned and made his way past tangles of black roses and undergrowth down toward the rusted gates. He looked back at the manor only once, saw the wreck of what had been grand and gracious, and saw a curtain fluttering in a window high above, and the suggestion of a face. He wondered who was watching him go.

He could warn Downworlders to steer clear of Tatiana and her endeavors. No matter what the price offered, no Downworlder would fail to listen to a warning against one of the Nephilim. Tatiana would raise no dark magic.

Magnus could do that much, but he did not see a way to help James Herondale. Grace and Tatiana might have cast a spell on him, Magnus supposed. He would not put it past either of them, but he could not see why they would. What possible role could James Herondale have to play in whatever dark plot they were hatching? More likely the boy had simply fallen prey to her charms. Love was love; there was no spell to cure a broken heart that did not also destroy that heart's capacity for love forever.

And there was no reason for Magnus to tell Will and Tessa what he had learned. James's feelings for Grace were his secret to keep. Magnus had told the boy he would never betray his secrets; he had sworn it. He had never betrayed Will's confidence, and he would not betray James's now. What good would it do Will and Tessa, to know the name of their son's pain and still have no remedy for it?

He thought once more of Camille, and how it had hurt him to learn the truth about her, how he had struggled like a man crawling over knives not to know it, and finally, with even greater pain, had been forced to accept it.

Magnus did not take such suffering lightly, but even mortals did not die of broken hearts. No matter how cruel Grace had been, he told himself, James would heal. Even though he was a Herondale.

He opened the gates with his hands, thorns scratching his flesh, and he remembered again his first sight of Grace and the feeling he'd had of being faced with a predator. She was very different from Tessa, who had always steadied and anchored Will, softened his eyes into humor and his lips to gentleness.

It would be ironic, Magnus thought, terribly and cruelly ironic, for one Herondale to be saved by love, and another Herondale damned by it.

He tried to shake off both the memory of Tessa and Will and the echo of Tatiana's condemning words. He had promised Tessa that he would return, but now he found all he wanted to do was escape. He did not want to care what Shadowhunters thought of him. He did not want to care what would become of them or their children.

He had offered help to three Shadowhunters this night. One of them had replied that he was beyond help, one had asked him to commit murder, and one had pointed a blade at him.

His relationship of mutual distant tolerance with the Whitelaws of the New York Institute seemed suddenly alluring. He was part of Downworld New York, and would have it no other way. He was glad he had left London. He discovered in himself a pang for New York and its brighter lights, and fewer broken hearts.

"Where to?" asked the driver.

Magnus thought of the ship from Southampton to New York, of standing on the deck of the boat, letting the sea air wash him clean of the musty air of London. He said, "I believe I am going home."

See where the adventures begin in

City of Bones,

BOOK ONE OF THE MORTAL INSTRUMENTS.

PANDEMONIUM

"You've got to be kidding me," the bouncer said, folding his arms across his massive chest. He stared down at the boy in the red zip-up jacket and shook his shaved head. "You can't bring that thing in here."

The fifty or so teenagers in line outside the Pandemonium Club leaned forward to eavesdrop. It was a long wait to get into the all-ages club, especially on a Sunday, and not much generally happened in line. The bouncers were fierce and would come down instantly on anyone who looked like they were going to start trouble. Fifteen-year-old Clary Fray, standing in line with her best friend, Simon, leaned forward along with everyone else, hoping for some excitement.

"Aw, come on." The kid hoisted the thing up over his head. It looked like a wooden beam, pointed at one end. "It's part of my costume."

The bouncer raised an eyebrow. "Which is what?"

The boy grinned. He was normal-enough-looking, Clary thought, for Pandemonium. He had electric blue dyed hair that stuck up around his head like the tentacles of a startled octopus, but no elaborate facial tattoos or big metal bars through his ears or lips. "I'm a vampire hunter." He pushed down on the wooden thing. It bent as easily as a blade of grass bending sideways. "It's fake. Foam rubber. See?"

The boy's wide eyes were way too bright a green, Clary noticed: the color of antifreeze, spring grass. Colored contact lenses, probably. The bouncer shrugged, abruptly bored. "Whatever. Go on in."

The boy slid past him, quick as an eel. Clary liked the lilt to his shoulders, the way he tossed his hair as he went. There was a word for him that her mother would have used—*insouciant*.

"You thought he was cute," said Simon, sounding resigned. "Didn't you?"

Clary dug her elbow into his ribs, but didn't answer.

Inside, the club was full of dry-ice smoke. Colored lights played over the dance floor, turning it into a multicolored fairyland of blues and acid greens, hot pinks and golds.

The boy in the red jacket stroked the long razor-sharp blade in his hands, an idle smile playing over his lips. It had been so easy—a little bit of a glamour on the blade, to make it look harmless. Another glamour on his eyes, and the moment the bouncer had looked straight at him, he was in. Of course, he could probably have gotten by without all that trouble, but it was part of the fun—fooling the mundies, doing it all out in the open right in front of them, getting off on the blank looks on their sheeplike faces.

Not that the humans didn't have their uses. The boy's green eyes scanned the dance floor, where slender limbs clad in scraps of silk and black leather appeared and disappeared inside the revolving columns of smoke as the mundies danced. Girls tossed their long hair, boys swung their leather-clad hips, and bare skin glittered with sweat. Vitality just *poured* off them, waves of energy that filled him with a drunken dizziness. His lip curled. They didn't know how lucky they were. They didn't know what it was like to eke out life in a dead world, where the sun hung limp in the sky like a burned cinder. Their lives burned as brightly as candle flames—and were as easy to snuff out.

His hand tightened on the blade he carried, and he had begun to step out onto the dance floor when a girl broke away from the mass of dancers and began walking toward him. He stared at her. She was beautiful, for a human—long hair nearly the precise color of black ink, charcoaled eyes. Floor-length white gown, the kind women used to wear when this world was younger. Lace sleeves belled out around her slim arms. Around her neck was a thick silver chain, on which hung a dark red pendant the size of a baby's fist. He only had to narrow his eyes to know that it was real—real and precious. His mouth started to water as she neared him. Vital energy pulsed from her like blood from an open wound. She smiled, passing him, beckoning with her eyes. He turned to follow her, tasting the phantom sizzle of her death on his lips.

It was always easy. He could already feel the power of her evaporating life coursing through his veins like fire. Humans were so stupid. They had something so precious, and they barely safeguarded it at all. They threw away their lives for money, for packets of powder, for a stranger's charming smile. The girl was a pale ghost retreating through the colored smoke. She reached the wall and turned, bunching her skirt up in her hands, lifting it as she grinned at him. Under the skirt, she was wearing thigh-high boots.

He sauntered up to her, his skin prickling with her nearness. Up close she wasn't so perfect: He could see the mascara smudged under her eyes, the sweat sticking her hair to her neck. He could smell her mortality, the sweet rot of corruption. *Got you*, he thought.

A cool smile curled her lips. She moved to the side, and he could see that she was leaning against a closed door. NO ADMITTANCE—STORAGE was scrawled across it in red paint. She reached behind her for the knob, turned it, slid inside. He caught a glimpse of stacked boxes, tangled wiring. A storage room. He glanced behind him—no one was looking. So much the better if she wanted privacy.

He slipped into the room after her, unaware that he was being followed.

"So," Simon said, "pretty good music, eh?"

Clary didn't reply. They were dancing, or what passed for it—a lot of swaying back and forth with occasional lunges toward the floor as if one of them had dropped a contact lens—in a space between a group of teenage boys in metallic corsets, and a young Asian couple who were making out passionately, their colored hair extensions tangled together like vines. A boy with a lip piercing and a teddy bear backpack was handing out free tablets of herbal ecstasy, his parachute pants flapping in the breeze from the wind machine. Clary wasn't paying much attention to their immediate surroundings—her eyes were on the blue-haired boy who'd talked his way into the club. He was prowling through the crowd as if he were looking for something. There was something about the way he moved that reminded her of something . . .

"I, for one," Simon went on, "am enjoying myself immensely."

This seemed unlikely. Simon, as always, stuck out at the club like a sore thumb, in jeans and an old T-shirt that said MADE IN BROOKLYN across the front. His freshly scrubbed hair was dark brown instead of green or pink, and his glasses perched crookedly on the end of his nose. He looked less as if he were contemplating the powers of darkness and more as if he were on his way to chess club.

"Mmm-hmm." Clary knew perfectly well that he came to Pandemonium with her only because she liked it, that he thought it was boring. She wasn't even sure why it was that she liked it—the clothes, the music made it like a dream, someone else's life, not her boring real life at all. But she was always too shy to talk to anyone but Simon.

The blue-haired boy was making his way off the dance floor. He looked a little lost, as if he hadn't found whom he was looking for. Clary wondered what would happen if she went up and introduced herself, offered to show him around. Maybe he'd just stare at her. Or maybe he was shy too. Maybe he'd be grateful and pleased, and try not to show it, the way boys did—but she'd know. Maybe—

The blue-haired boy straightened up suddenly, snapping to attention, like a hunting dog on point. Clary followed the line of his gaze, and saw the girl in the white dress.

Oh, well, Clary thought, trying not to feel like a deflated party balloon. *I guess that's that.* The girl was gorgeous, the kind of girl Clary would have liked to draw—tall and ribbon-slim, with a long spill of black hair. Even at this distance Clary could see the red pendant around her throat. It pulsed under the lights of the dance floor like a separate, disembodied heart.

"I feel," Simon went on, "that this evening DJ Bat is doing a singularly exceptional job. Don't you agree?"

Clary rolled her eyes and didn't answer; Simon hated trance music. Her attention was on the girl in the white dress. Through the darkness, smoke, and artificial fog, her pale dress shone out like a beacon. No wonder the blue-haired boy was following her as if he were under a spell, too distracted to notice anything else around him—even the two dark shapes hard on his heels, weaving after him through the crowd.

Clary slowed her dancing and stared. She could just make out that the shapes were boys, tall and wearing black clothes. She couldn't have said how she knew that they were following the other boy, but she did. She could see it in the way they paced him, their careful watchfulness, the slinking grace of their movements. A small flower of apprehension began to open inside her chest.

"Meanwhile," Simon added, "I wanted to tell you that lately I've been cross-dressing. Also, I'm sleeping with your mom. I thought you should know."

The girl had reached the wall, and was opening a door marked NO ADMITTANCE. She beckoned the blue-haired boy after her, and they slipped through the door. It wasn't anything Clary hadn't seen before, a couple sneaking off to the dark corners of the club to make out—but that made it even weirder that they were being followed.

She raised herself up on tiptoe, trying to see over the crowd. The two guys had stopped at the door and seemed to be conferring with each other. One of them was blond, the other dark-haired. The blond one reached into his jacket and drew out something long and sharp that flashed under the strobing lights. A knife. "Simon!" Clary shouted, and seized his arm.

"What?" Simon looked alarmed. "I'm not really sleeping with your mom, you know. I was just trying to get your attention. Not that your mom isn't a very attractive woman, for her age."

"Do you see those guys?" She pointed wildly, almost hitting a curvy black girl who was dancing nearby. The girl shot her an evil look. "Sorry—sorry!" Clary turned back to Simon. "Do you see those two guys over there? By that door?"

Simon squinted, then shrugged. "I don't see anything."

"There are two of them. They were following the guy with the blue hair—"

"The one you thought was cute?"

"Yes, but that's not the point. The blond one pulled a knife."

"Are you *sure*?" Simon stared harder, shaking his head. "I still don't see anyone."

"I'm sure."

Suddenly all business, Simon squared his shoulders. "I'll get one of the security guards. You stay here." He strode away, pushing through the crowd.

Clary turned just in time to see the blond boy slip through the NO ADMITTANCE door, his friend right on his heels. She looked around; Simon was still trying to shove his way across the dance floor, but he wasn't making much progress. Even if she yelled now, no one would hear her, and by the time Simon got back, something terrible might *already* have happened. Biting hard on her lower lip, Clary started to wriggle through the crowd.

"What's your name?"

She turned and smiled. What faint light there was in the storage room spilled down through high barred windows smeared with dirt. Piles of electrical cables, along with broken bits of mirrored disco balls and discarded paint cans, littered the floor.

"Isabelle."

"That's a nice name." He walked toward her, stepping carefully among the wires in case any of them were live. In the faint light she looked half-transparent, bleached of color, wrapped in white like an angel. It would be a pleasure to make her fall. . . . "I haven't seen you here before."

"You're asking me if I come here often?" She giggled, covering her mouth with her hand. There was some sort of bracelet around her wrist, just under the cuff of her dress—then, as he neared her, he saw that it wasn't a bracelet at all but a pattern inked into her skin, a matrix of swirling lines.

He froze. "You—"

He didn't finish. She moved with lightning swiftness, striking out at him with her open hand, a blow to his chest that would have sent him down gasping if he'd been a human being. He staggered back, and now there was something in her hand, a coiling whip that glinted gold as she brought it down, curling around his ankles, jerking him off his feet. He hit the ground, writhing, the hated metal biting deep into his skin. She laughed, standing over him, and dizzily he thought that he should have *known*. No human girl would wear a dress like the one Isabelle wore. She'd worn it to cover her skin—all of her skin.

Discover Emma and Julian's story in

Lady Midnight,

THE FIRST BOOK IN CASSANDRA CLARE'S
NEW SERIES, THE DARK ARTIFICES.

———◆———

Emma took her witchlight out of her pocket and lit it—and almost screamed out loud. Jules's shirt was soaked with blood and worse, the healing runes she'd drawn had vanished from his skin. They weren't working.

"Jules," she said. "I have to call the Silent Brothers. They can help you. I *have* to."

His eyes screwed shut with pain. "You can't," he said. "You know we can't call the Silent Brothers. They report directly to the Clave."

"So we'll lie to them. Say it was a routine demon patrol. I'm calling," she said, and reached for her phone.

"No!" Julian said, forcefully enough to stop her. "Silent Brothers know when you're lying! They can see inside your head, Emma. They'll find out about the investigation. About Mark—"

"You're not going to bleed to death in the backseat of a car for Mark!"

"No," he said, looking at her. His eyes were eerily blue-green, the only bright color in the dark interior of the car. "You're going to fix me."

Emma could feel it when Jules was hurt, like a splinter lodged under her skin. The physical pain didn't bother her; it was the terror, the only terror worse than her fear of the ocean. The fear of Jules being hurt, of him dying. She would give up anything, sustain any wound, to prevent those things from happening.

"Okay," she said. Her voice sounded dry and thin to her own ears. "Okay." She took a deep breath. "Hang on."

She unzipped her jacket, threw it aside. Shoved the console between the seats aside, put her witchlight on the floorboard. Then she reached for Jules. The next few seconds were a blur of Jules's blood on her hands and his harsh breathing as she pulled him partly upright, wedging him against the back door. He didn't make a sound as she moved him, but she could see him biting his lip, the blood on his mouth and chin, and she felt as if her bones were popping inside her skin.

"Your gear," she said through gritted teeth. "I have to cut it off."

He nodded, letting his head fall back. She drew a dagger from her belt, but the gear was too tough for the blade. She said a silent prayer and reached back for Cortana.

Cortana went through the gear like a knife through melted butter. It fell away in pieces and Emma drew them free, then sliced down the front of his T-shirt and pulled it apart as if she were opening a jacket.

Emma had seen blood before, often, but this felt different. It was Julian's, and there seemed to be a lot of it. It was smeared up and down his chest and rib cage; she could see where the arrow had gone in and where the skin had torn where he'd yanked it out.

"Why did you pull the arrow out?" she demanded, pulling her sweater over her head. She had a tank top on under it. She patted his chest and side with the sweater, absorbing as much of the blood as she could.

Jules's breath was coming in hard pants. "Because when someone—shoots you with an arrow—" he gasped, "your immediate response is not—'Thanks for the arrow, I think I'll keep it for a while.'"

"Good to know your sense of humor is intact."

"Is it still bleeding?" Julian demanded. His eyes were shut.

She dabbed at the cut with her sweater. The blood had slowed, but the cut looked puffy and swollen. The rest of him, though—it had been a while since she'd seen him with his shirt off. There was more muscle than she remembered. Lean muscle pulled tight over his ribs, his stomach flat and lightly ridged. Cameron was much more muscular, but Julian's spare lines were as elegant as a greyhound's. "You're too skinny," she said. "Too much coffee, not enough pancakes."

"I hope they put that on my tombstone." He gasped as she shifted forward, and she realized abruptly that she was squarely in Julian's lap, her knees around his hips. It was a bizarrely intimate position.

"I—am I hurting you?" she asked.

He swallowed visibly. "It's fine. Try with the *iratze* again."

"Fine," she said. "Grab the panic bar."

"The what?" He opened his eyes and peered at her.

"The plastic handle! Up there, above the window!" She pointed. "It's for holding on to when the car is going around curves."

"Are you sure? I always thought it was for hanging things on. Like dry cleaning."

"Julian, *now is not the time to be pedantic*. Grab the bar or I swear—"

"All right!" He reached up, grabbed hold of it, and winced. "I'm ready."

She nodded and set Cortana aside, reaching for her stele. Maybe her previous *iratzes* had been too fast, too sloppy. She'd always focused on the physical aspects of Shadowhunting, not the more mental and artistic ones: seeing through glamours, drawing runes.

She set the tip of it to the skin of his shoulder and drew, carefully and slowly. She had to brace herself with her left hand against his shoulder. She tried to press as lightly as she could, but she could feel him tense under her fingers. The skin on his shoulder was smooth and hot under her touch, and she wanted to get closer to him, to put her hand over the wound on his side and heal it with the sheer force of her will. To touch her lips to the lines of pain beside his eyes and—

Stop. She had finished the *iratze*. She sat back, her hand clamped around the stele. Julian sat up a little straighter, the ragged remnants of his shirt hanging off his shoulders. He took a deep breath, glancing down at himself—and the *iratze* faded back into his skin, like black ice melting, spreading, being absorbed by the sea.

He looked up at Emma. She could see her own reflection in his eyes: she looked wrecked, panicked, with blood on her neck and her white tank top. "It hurts less," he said in a low voice.

The wound on his side pulsed again; blood slid down the side of his rib cage, staining his leather belt and the waistband of his jeans. She put her hands on his bare skin, panic rising up inside her. His skin felt hot, too hot. Fever hot.

"I have to call," she whispered. "I don't care if the whole world comes down around us, Jules, the most important thing is that you *live*."

"Please," he said, desperation clear in his voice. "Whatever is happening, we'll fix it, because we're *parabatai*. We're forever. I said that to you once, do you remember?"

She nodded warily, hand on the phone.

"And the strength of a rune your *parabatai* gives you is special. Emma, you can do it. You can heal me. We're *parabatai* and that means the things we can do together are . . . extraordinary."

There was blood on her jeans now, blood on her hands and her tank top, and he was still bleeding, the wound still open, an incongruous tear in the smooth skin all around it.

"Try," Jules said in a dry whisper. "For me, try?"

His voice went up on the question and in it she heard the voice of the boy he had been once, and she remembered him smaller, skinnier, younger, back pressed against one of the marble columns in the Hall of Accords in Alicante as his father advanced on him with his blade unsheathed.

And she remembered what Julian had done, then. Done to protect her, to protect all of them, because he always would do everything to protect them.

She took her hand off the phone and gripped the stele, so tightly she felt it dig into her damp palm. "Look at me, Jules," she said in a low voice, and he met her eyes with his. She placed the stele against his skin, and for a moment she held still, just breathing, breathing and remembering.

Julian. A presence in her life for as long as she could remember, splashing water at each other in the ocean, digging in the sand together, him putting his hand over hers and them marveling at the difference in the shape and length of their fingers. Julian singing, terribly and off-key, while he drove, his fingers in her hair carefully freeing a trapped leaf, his hands catching her in the training room when she fell, and fell, and fell. The first time after their *parabatai* ceremony when she'd smashed her hand into a wall in rage at not being able to get a sword maneuver right, and he'd come up to her, taken her still-shaking body in his arms and said, "Emma, Emma, don't hurt yourself. When you do, I feel it, too."

Something in her chest seemed to split and crack; she marveled that it wasn't audible. Energy raced along her veins, and the stele jerked in her hand before it seemed to move on its own, tracing the graceful outline of a healing rune across Julian's chest. She heard him gasp, his eyes flying open. His hand slid down her back and he pressed her against him, his teeth gritted.

"Don't *stop*," he said.

Emma couldn't have stopped if she'd wanted to. The stele seemed to be moving of its own accord; she was blinded with memories, a kaleidoscope of them, all of them Julian. Sun in her eyes and Julian asleep on the beach in an old T-shirt and her not wanting to wake him, but he'd woken anyway when the sun went down and looked for her immediately, not smiling till his eyes found her and he knew she was there. Falling asleep talking and waking up with their hands interlocked; they'd been children in the dark together once but now they were something else, something intimate and powerful, something Emma felt she was touching only the very edge of as she finished the rune and the stele fell from her nerveless fingers.

"Oh," she said softly. The rune seemed lit from within by a soft glow.

CASSANDRA CLARE'S

#1 *New York Times* Bestselling Series

THE MORTAL INSTRUMENTS
THE INFERNAL DEVICES
THE DARK ARTIFICES

A thousand years ago, the Angel Raziel mixed his blood with the blood of men and created the race of the Nephilim. Human-angel hybrids, they walk among us, unseen but ever present, our invisible protectors.

They call themselves Shadowhunters.

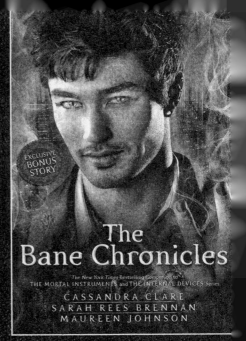

Go deeper into the world of the Shadowhunters with
THE SHADOWHUNTER'S CODEX
the essential guide to becoming one of the Nephilim

PRINT AND EBOOK EDITIONS AVAILABLE

Explore the legends and legacy of Magnus Bane in
THE BANE CHRONICLES
What happens when Magnus meets Marie Antoinette
And what *really* happened in Peru?
Find out the answers in this illustrated short-story
collection featuring everyone's favorite warlock.

PRINT AND EBOOK EDITIONS AVAILABLE

From Margaret K. McElderry Books | TEEN.SimonandSchuster.com

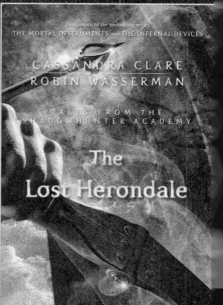

CONTINUE THE ADVENTURES OF SIMON LEWIS,

one of the stars of Cassandra Clare's internationally bestselling Mortal Instruments series, in Tales from the Shadowhunter Academy. Characters from The Mortal Instruments and The Infernal Devices will make appearances, as will characters from the upcoming Dark Artifices and Last Hours series. Once a mundane, then a vampire, Simon prepares to enter the next phase of his life: Shadowhunter.

EBOOK EDITIONS AVAILABLE

Learn more at shadowhunters.com and cassandraclare.com.

DISCOVER THE SHADOWHUNTER UNIVERSE:

The Infernal Devices | The Last Hours
The Mortal Instruments | The Dark Artifices
The Shadowhunter's Codex | The Bane Chronicles

From Margaret K. McElderry Books | TEEN.SimonandSchuster.com